Crisis on the Upsydaisy

We wouldn't fall into the Sun—not quite. McNulty's calculations showed that we could just swing past, but we'd come a lot too close for comfort, surviving only in the ship's refrigerated compartment.

Kli Yang, the Martian, pointed out the catch in this scheme. "We cannot control the ship while squatting in the ice-box like three and a half dozen strawberry sundaes. There will have to be a pilot in the bow. One individual can hold her on course—until he gets fried. So somebody has to be the fryee."

He gave his tentacle tip a sinuous wiggle "And since it cannot be denied that we Martians are far less susceptible to the extremes of heat, I suggest—"

"Nuts!" snapped McNulty.

"All right. Who else is entitled to become a crisp?"

"Me," said Jay Score. It was queer the way he voiced it. Just as if he were a candidate so obvious that only the stone-blind couldn't see him . . .

THE BEST OF
Eric Frank Russell

Introduction by
ALAN DEAN FOSTER

A Del Rey Book

BALLANTINE BOOKS • **NEW YORK**

ACKNOWLEDGMENTS

"Mana," copyright 1937 by Street & Smith Publications, Inc., for *Astounding Stories*, December 1937.

"Jay Score," copyright 1941 by Street & Smith Publications, Inc., for *Astounding Science Fiction*, May 1941.

"Homo Saps," copyright 1941 by Street & Smith Publications, Inc., for *Astounding Science Fiction*, December 1941.

"Metamorphosite," copyright 1946 by Street & Smith Publications, Inc., for *Astounding Science Fiction*, December 1946.

"Hobbyist," copyright 1947 by Street & Smith Publications, Inc., for *Astounding Science Fiction*, September 1947.

"Late Night Final," copyright 1948 by Street & Smith Publications, Inc., for *Astounding Science Fiction*, December 1948.

"Dear Devil," copyright 1950 by Clark Publishing Company, for *Other Worlds*, May 1950.

"Fast Falls the Eventide," copyright 1952 by Street & Smith Publications, Inc., for *Astounding Science Fiction*, May 1952.

"I Am Nothing," copyright 1952 by Street & Smith Publications, Inc., for *Astounding Science Fiction*, July 1952.

"Weak Spot," copyright 1954 by Street & Smith Publications, Inc., for *Astounding Science Fiction*, May 1954.

"Allamagoosa," copyright © 1955 by Street & Smith Publications, Inc., for *Astounding Science Fiction*, May 1955.

"Into Your Tent I'll Creep," copyright © 1957 by Street & Smith Publications, Inc., for *Astounding Science Fiction*, September 1957.

"Study in Still Life," copyright © 1959 by Street & Smith Publications, Inc., for *Astounding Science Fiction*, January 1959.

Contents

The Symbiote of Hooton

ONCE UPON A time a brash young fan of science fiction named Foster, Alan D., was engaged in rapt conversation with a brash, legendary editor of science fiction named Campbell, John W. The year was 1968, and the setting was a restaurant table at the World Science-Fiction Convention in Oakland, California. Foster was twenty-two and had done little. Campbell was fifty-eight and had done much.

Said Foster to Campbell after thirty minutes of impassioned rhetoric concerning the war in Vietnam, "You know, my all-time favorite science fiction writer is Eric Frank Russell."

Said Campbell to Foster in reply, with a sage nod and gentle smile, "Mine too. I wish to hell I could get him writing again."

You are about to begin a collection of stories written by a man capable of working the above effect on two disparate personalities quite different in background, political viewpoint, and many other aspects including a thirty-six-year gap in age. I am now somewhat older and have achieved a bit more than little. Many things have changed for me. One has not.

Eric Frank Russell is still my favorite writer of science fiction. Why?

He was the only one of the many miners of the imagination, of that peculiar dimension we label science fiction, who could make me both laugh and cry. He displayed more simple common sense in a short story than most writers did in a full novel. He possessed an empathy for mankind unmatched by any other sf writer I've known.

He wrote stories about ecology before it existed as a pop term.

He exhibited racial understanding in a time when it was unpopular. Consider a character named Sam Hignett, who says in "Jay Score" (1941): "I'm the ship's doctor. I couldn't have saved this man if Jay hadn't brought him in when he did." Hignett is the ship's doctor/surgeon, who happens to be black. His position in the story is as far from that of domestic servant as his dialogue is from the typical 1940s black clown-talk.

Russell was born in 1905 at Sandhurst, Surrey, England, where his father was an instructor at the military academy. Russell's fiction is a reaction to rather than a reflection of a military family upbringing. A military family moves around a lot. Apparently the Russells were no exception, spending time in various countries at different bases.

Included was a long sojourn in Egypt and the Sudan. Undoubtedly the quadrupedal characters of "Homo Saps" are based upon acquaintances Russell made during his stay in that desert region, as is the vivid landscape of Mars in the same story.

As much of his fiction rebels against the military way of doing things, so too is it an apparent reaction against the college curriculum he studied: chemistry, physics, building and steel construction, quantity surveying, mechanical drafting, metallurgy, and crystallography.

Such a background would ordinarily be expected to result in sf of the hard-science variety of which Hal Clement is the most noted practitioner. At the very least, we could be ready for hard-science stories mixed with romanticism in the style of Poul Anderson or Larry Niven, to name two.

That is not what we find, however.

In Russell's stories the science is minimal, the romanticism muted where present. We are confronted by a writer whose prime interests are psychology and sociology, not quantum mechanics. Adventure is the sometime vehicle used to explore the depths of human emotion instead of the physical cosmos. It was the universe within that most intrigued Russell.

There are those who dispute Russell's humanism. Their arguments are based primarily on a series of what I like to call humanity-über-alles tales, wherein a single man overwhelms an entire horde of befuddled aliens. But in stories like "Design for Great-day," "Now Inhale," "Brute Farce," "Diabologic," and the classic "Plus X," he is showing not the superiority of mankind so much as the stultifying effects of bureaucracy and big government on his unlucky aliens. Demonstrating the efficacy of imagination and confidence when confronted by guns and red tape was Russell's favorite ploy.

Her heroes battle not with knives, bullets, or lasers but with humor and sarcasm. His doomsday weapon was pure satire, the logical ultimate weapon for a disenchanted scion of the military establishment. You'll find no massed armadas of victorious space fleets in his stories, no worlds of dominant tower-cities or all-seeing computer minds. What you will come upon instead are people, some human, some not, coping with a universe awash in obfuscation and Big-brother governments. To combat these he utilizes not weapons of war but empathy, tolerance, patience, and compassion. Instead of a cudgel to the skull he strikes a feather to the ribs.

In "Dear Devil," a Martian poet is the only one who believes in helping the people of a devastated Earth. The resuscitation he accomplishes is more spiritual than material, and disaster is overcome without massive injections of money, advice, or interfering bureaucrats. Here's a lesson many members of modern government agencies would do well to learn. They could understand Russell's point, but I doubt they are capable of implementing it.

"I Am Nothing" is a Russell war story. It is only marginally science fiction, a sharp indication of his ability to tell a tale without sf gingerbread or setting. "Nothing" is a parable of all war stories, a rare case of a writer defining an obscenity with compassion instead of fury.

Rarely are people defeated in these tales. At the end of a Russell story the reader feels no sense of superiority or desire to gloat. Enemies are reformed, not crushed. When not beaten by laughter—or a favorite Russellian weapon, "diabologic"—opponents are often left chastened but better for the experience, as in "Design for Great-day" or "Plus X."

The unity of nature, of life, and the equality that exists among all our neighbors on this planet is a theme that recurs frequently in Russell's stories. He expands this concept to take in aliens and machines, to embrace the entire universe in a wonderful extended family where all life coexists in an atmosphere of mutual respect and understanding. There are very few inimical alien stories in the Russell oeuvre. Where they occur, as in "Spiro" (I Spy), they are alien-appearing indeed. In "Mana" for instance, the bugs are treated as children to be taught, not as unthinking enemies to be wantonly obliterated. "Dear Devil" has no aliens; its Martians are really idealized humans.

"Fast Falls the Eventide" is as close as Russell ever came to spelling out his philosophy of the universal family, a philosophy he (to my knowledge) never consciously expressed as such. "Jay Score" presents an interspecies crew so realistic that I wouldn't be one whit surprised if Kli Yang or Sug Farn walked in at any moment and challenged me to a game of chess. I wouldn't accept, of course, having no chance of winning. I don't possess Jay Score's peculiar talents.

For those still tempted to view Russell as favoring the supremacy of humankind, consider some of the other tales in this volume. In "Homo Saps" we come out looking a poor runner-up to the camel. In a very different story, "Into Your Tent I'll Creep," the true rulers of mankind, and perhaps the cosmos, are shown to be dogs, rather different from the dogs portrayed in Clifford Simak's *City*. And in "Hobbyist," the truth as presented to a single human is tinged with indifference if not outright contempt for mankind's pretensions of superiority. In addition, this is one of Russell's few stories to comment at all on the matter of religion.

When Russell does choose to unveil his version of *Homo superior*, he turns out not to be Nietzsche's heaven-storming superman or the wielder of superscience so often portrayed even in modern science fiction. John Muir is closer to Russell's idea of a better human than is Kimball Kinnison. Such humans are visible in "Design for Great-day" and in "Metamorphosite," both of which show the strong influence of Russell's friend Olaf Stapledon, particularly of the latter author's novel *Odd John*.

When Russell is not showing us how sensible folk ought to comport themselves, he's busy demolishing our pretensions. His favorite target is the smothering bureaucracy spawned by twentieth-century government. Nor are alien governments exempt from his attack, an assumption by Russell that another space-going race is apt to act just as idiotically as ours. Maybe you can keep from splitting your sides as you read "Allamagoosa." I defy you to do so with "Study in Still Life."

If the stories in this collection intrigue you, hunt up some of Russell's novels, such as *Next of Kin (The Space Willies), Wasp, Three to Conquer, Sentinels of Space*, the justly famed *Sinister Barrier*, or some of the other stories I've mentioned. You won't be disappointed.

In this volume you'll find the Eric Frank Russell who could write:

The children of this world were bugs.
And birds.
And bipeds.
Moth, magpie and man, all were related. All had the same mother . . .

You'll also find the Russell who writes tersely: "Bonhoeffer was a real woman's man; big, handsome, muscular, stupid."

Why did Russell effectively cease writing for the last eighteen years of his life? Campbell believed it was some traumatic occurrence in his personal life. As for Russell's comments on the matter, here is what he wrote to me in a letter dated October 19, 1972.

"I can't write without being enthusiastic and I can't get enthusiastic about an old-hat plot. Ninety-nine percent of today's sf yarns are decidedly old-hat. Campbell once told me he'd been offered only one new idea in four years, that being slow glass. Hence, today's sf yarns get cheers mainly from the young who haven't read the oldies and think their plots and angles shine with pristine newness. Meanwhile, ancient geezers like me bang their heads against the wall and pray for nuggets that just ain't. Oh well, someday my muse may wake . . ."

The Russellian prose is present there, but the spirit is not. Russell neglects to recall that he repeated basic themes and approaches in his own work many times, with considerable success. Perhaps Campbell was right and the malady struck at something deeper than Russell chose to reveal to me.

Technological innovation (whether asteroid-mining or slow glass) was never his forte. He expanded upon human psychology, not physics. What eventually soured him, I cannot guess; but whatever it was could not stifle the writing ability so evident in his letters long after he'd ceased concocting "yarns," as he and Campbell liked to call them. We are poorer for his decision to stop writing, since the late fifties saw him at the peak of his wit and abilities.

In one biographical sketch Russell is reported to have claimed as an ambition "to entertain so many readers so well that some may have a momentary regret when they bury (me)."

He is gone now, this conjurer of sly laughter and profound hopes, of biting satire and naked emotion. I feel a regret at his death, but I doubt it will be momentary. I expect that after finishing this collection you may feel likewise . . .

Alan Dean Foster
Big Bear Lake, California
March 1978

Mana

LAZY WATERS LAPPED and gurgled across the silver sands. An orange sun crawled high in the heavens, poured its rays through this atmosphere, and etched the higher portion of the beach with a delicate dado of shadow palms.

Omega, the last man on earth, stood naked in the coolness beneath a feathered frond.

He sighed, turned, and strode lithely into a paradise of plants.

Six thousand years, the long, extended years of the final era, had passed over Omega's head. But he was not old as beasts and plants grow old. His age was purely mental, and represented the measure of his satiation.

His body remained young, would always be young. Thousands had died within the sixty centuries of his memory, but he could recall none who had succumbed with physical decay. Men had expired with intellectual satisfaction, the exhausting of curiosity, the desire for mental rest—even as some of the esoteric ones of primeval days had willed their passing because they had lost the urge to live.

Omega was the last, solely because he was not yet satisfied. There was one thing still to be done—if it could be done.

He had lived through and tasted every experience

within reach of mankind. He had even exercised his monofecundity and produced a child. But his son refused further issue, lived fast, learned fast and soon was satisfied.

Thus the flesh of his flesh, with the companions of his past, had slipped away like figments of a summer's dream. Men of the latter day knew the difference between what there was to learn and what it was possible to learn. Even human ingenuity could not encompass the entire cosmos. So each had quaffed his little cup and crept away to sleep. He, Omega, the unsatisfied one, lived on, determined to do that which had been declared impossible.

His feet sped swiftly up a wooded slope; he mounted the crest and saw the towers and minarets of Ultima gleaming through a golden haze that lay along the valley. Exercise had tired his muscles; he called upon will power molded by a million years of evolution; his body rose into the air, floated over the treetops and across the valley. He landed lightly upon a marble battlement.

Calf muscles ached their protest against his fondness for walking. Omega rubbed them into submission, sat and rested awhile, then stepped off the battlement and floated to the silent boulevard beneath.

Eerily, like the central figure of an allegorical picture, his form drifted across the dusty, unmarked highway, his feet swinging restfully twenty inches above the surface.

No other forms were levitated, and none walked through the peaceful avenues of that once-mighty city. Silent spires spiked to the azure vault above. Idle battlement reproduced the skyline of ancient Tintagel. Flying buttresses arched boldly to walls that knew no secrets to conceal.

Omega moved toward a dull metal door set in the opposite wall.

The door opened. Omega floated through it, along a corridor and into his laboratory. His feet felt the cold kiss of stone; he stepped to a glass-topped case and peered into it with eyes that shone as brightly as eyes that found the world still new.

"*Mana*," he murmured. His voice sighed softly, like the wind that quivers in the reeds along the water's marge. "*Mana*." He often talked to himself. The habit was his only concession to loneliness. He pressed a stud that caused a dull, warm glow to spread through the interior of the case.

"Nothing, they said, could perpetuate mankind forever," he proclaimed. "Nothing.

"Nothing that man could make, or produce, or build, or give, could endure as long as Nature endures. The valleys shall be raised, and the hills shall be made low. All that humanity has made, all that humanity can leave, shall crumble into the dust; and the empire that once was, and soon is not, shall be given over to the birds of the air, the beasts of the field, the trees, the shrubs, and the creeping growths."

His fingers rapped on the case; he noted resulting movements below the glass.

"Patience," he told himself. "The thousandth failure may but precede the first success."

Eagerly he strode to a complicated chair that stood with tilted back against a maze of instruments. Suspended above the seat by simple counterweights was a great metal hood.

"It must be photons," declared Omega, standing before the chair. "A thousand experiments have shown that either cosmic rays or photons perform the function of carriers of *mana*. And I still maintain that it cannot be cosmic rays. If it were, there could be no *mana* upon the ozone-wrapped Perdel, in Alpha Centauri."

Seating himself in the chair, he continued to reason.

"Therefore, by simple elimination, it must be photons. And upon this planet only we bipeds were really susceptible to their natural intensity, other life being less affected. But if I can increase the strength, passing an abnormal load along a beam of photons, a positive reaction should be hereditary. It would, I think, be handed from generation to generation, and—"

His lips snapped shut; he raised an arm and pulled down the hood until it covered his head completely. A contact on the armrest closed beneath his firm fingers, and the apparatus woke to life.

There was no noise, nothing to indicate action save a swift turn and steady trembling of needles within three dials, and a mighty, angling leap of a concentrated beam of cold light.

Omega sat limply, the machine behind him driving a double cone of psychowaves through the back of his head. The cones narrowed through his brain, emerged from his eyes, passed through lenses set in the front of the hood, and entered the wave trap that gleamed mirrorlike at the base of the light transmission tube. In effect, the trap was the focal point of Omega's mind.

The beam of cold light was a thin column of intense brilliance as it poured up the tube, angled across to the case, and again angled into the interior. The glow from the case was vanquished by the new and mightier illumination.

For fifteen minutes the last man sat half concealed beneath the metal sheath. Then his damp fingers opened the contact; his hand raised the hood and exposed a face strained with fatigue.

He crossed to the case, stared through its glass top.

"Mechanistic behaviorism may serve as a crutch— but never as a ladder," he told the unheedful subjects of his experiment.

A small heap of rotten wood lay in one corner of the case. In the center, between two highways swarming with pedestrians, stood a midget box mounted upon microscopic wheels. Near it rested a Lilliputian bow with a bundle of tiny arrows.

Raising the lid of the case, Omega inserted a hand, and moved the little cart with a touch of slender fingers. Delicately, he shot an arrow from the miniature bow, and saw ants scuttle in all directions. Patiently, he rubbed two shreds of wood into flame, and let them burn at a safe distance from the rest of the heap.

"I feel one degree more stupid after each attempt. The light must be transporting it somewhere."

He watched the agitated ants as he stood and mused awhile. Then he sighed, closed the lid, and floated from the room.

Timeless day and immeasurable night upon a world that rolled in sluggish mourning for glories long departed. Omega stood upon a battlement and turned his face to the fiery ring that split the midnight sky from horizon to horizon. Incredibly ancient scrawlings upon records long since perished had described the beauty of the satellite from which this ring was born. Omega doubted whether the serene loveliness of the Moon had exceeded the glory of the remnants.

The light of the lees of Luna served to reveal the triumph upon the face of the last man, and the case of ants clasped firmly in his arms. With a frown for his sensation of mental weakness, but a contrasting smile upon his lips, he stepped off the battlement and glided like a phantom above the leafy cohorts that pressed eagerly upon the marble outskirts of Ultima. His figure floated onward, far above the treetops where wooden arms were raised in worship of the ring.

Over a tiny glade he ceased his forward progress, wavered in the slight, cool breeze, descended slowly, and felt his feet sink into a dewy cushion of earth. He placed the case upon the grass, opened its lid, tilted it, and watched the ants depart.

Satisfaction shone upon his features while he studied a group of insects laboriously urging out the midget cart. They pushed, and pulled, twisted its wheels this way and that, and finally trundled it into the secret paths of the grassy jungle. He watched it disappear with its load of splinters of rotten wood, the bow and arrows resting on top. He stretched his form, and raised a glowing face to the heavens.

"When the first hairy biped rode the waters on a log, that was *mana*," he proclaimed. "When fire was found, and made, and used, that was *mana*. Whenever men struggled one step higher up the ladder of life, it was *mana*." He swung an arm in a sweep embracing the entire cosmos. "Even as it was given to us by those whom we could never know, I give it to those who can never know men. I give it as our everlasting monument."

His nerves grew taut as he summoned his weakened will. He floated upward, faster, faster, toward the elegiac ring. He was bound for space, where eternal sleep came easily and was undisturbed. There were no regrets within his soul, and he uttered no farewell. He cast one glance downward at aimless billows surging on a printless shore. His eyes passed thence to the woodland glade, caught the first flicker of a tiny fire, and he was satisfied.

Omega, the last man, had presented the ants with fire, the wheel and the bow. But, best of all, he had given them what both the first man and the last had called *mana—intelligence*.

Jay Score

THERE ARE VERY good reasons for everything they do. To the uninitiated some of their little tricks and some of their regulations seem mighty peculiar—but rocketing through the cosmos isn't quite like paddling a bathtub across a farm pond, no, sir!

For instance, this stunt of using mixed crews is pretty sensible when you look into it. On the outward runs toward Mars, the Asteroids or beyond, they have white Terrestrials to tend the engines because they're the ones who perfected modren propulsion units, know most about them and can nurse them like nobody else. All ships' surgeons are black Terrestrials because for some reason none can explain no Negro gets gravity-bends or space nausea. Every outside repair gang is composed of Martians, who use very little air, are tiptop metal workers and fairly immune to cosmic-ray burn.

As for the inward trips to Venus, they mix them similarly except that the emergency pilot is always a big clunker like Jay Score. There's a motive behind that; he's the one who provided it. I'm never likely to forget him. He sort of sticks in the mind, for keeps. What a character!

Destiny placed me at the top of the gangway the first time he appeared. Our ship was the *Upskadaska City*, a brand new freighter with limited passenger accommodation, registered in the Venusian spaceport from which she took her name. Needless to say she was known among hardened spacement as the *Upsydaisy*.

We were lying in the Colorado Rocket Basin, north of Denver, with a fair load aboard, mostly watch-making machinery, agricultural equipment, aeronautical jigs and tools for Upskadaska, as well as a case of radium needles for the Venusian Cancer Research Institute. There were eight passengers, all emigrating agriculturalists planning on making hay thirty million miles nearer the Sun. We had ramped the vessel and were waiting for the blow-brothers-blow siren, due in forty minutes, when Jay Score arrived.

He was six feet nine, weighed at least three hundred pounds yet toted this bulk with the easy grace of a ballet dancer. A big guy like that, moving like that, was something worth watching. He came up the duralumin gangway with all the nonchalance of a tripper boarding the bus for Jackson's Creek. From his hamlike right fist dangled a rawhide case not quite big enough to contain his bed and maybe a wardrobe or two.

Reaching the top, he paused while he took in the crossed swords on my cap, said, "Morning, Sarge. I'm the new emergency pilot. I have to report to Captain McNulty."

I knew we were due for another pilot now that Jew Durkin had been promoted to the snooty Martial scent-bottle *Prometheus*. So this was his successor. He was a Terrestrial all right, but neither black nor white. His expressionless but capable face looked as if covered with old, well-seasoned leather. His eyes held fires resembling phosphorescence. There was an air about him that marked him an exceptional individual the like of which I'd never met before.

"Welcome, Tiny," I offered, getting a crick in the neck as I stared up at him. I did not offer my hand because I wanted it for use later on. "Open your satchel and leave it in the sterilizing chamber. You'll find the skipper in the bow."

"Thanks," he responded without the glimmer of a

smile. He stepped into the airlock, hauling the rawhide haybarn with him.

"We blast in forty minutes," I warned.

Didn't see anything more of Jay Score until we were two hundred thousand out, with Earth a greenish moon at the end of our vapor-trail. Then I heard him in the passage asking someone where he could find the sergeant-at-arms. He was directed through my door.

"Sarge," he said, handing over his official requisition, "I've come to collect the trimmings." Then he leaned on the barrier, the whole framework creaked and the top tube sagged in the middle.

"Hey!" I shouted.

"Sorry!" He unleaned. The barrier stood much better when he kept his mass to himself.

Stamping his requisition, I went into the armory, dug out his needle-ray projector and a box of capsules for same. The biggest Venusian mud-skis I could find were about eleven sizes too small and a yard too short for him, but they'd have to do. I gave him a can of thin, multipurpose oil, a jar of graphite, a Lepanto power-pack for his microwave radiophone and, finally, a bunch of nutweed pellicules marked: "Compliments of the Bridal Planet Aromatic Herb Corporation."

Shoving back the spicy lumps, he said, "You can have 'em—they give me the staggers." The rest of the stuff he forced into his side-pack without so much as twitching an eyebrow. Long time since I'd seen anyone so poker-faced.

All the same, the way he eyed the spacesuits seemed strangely wistful. There were thirty bifurcated ones for the Terrestrials, all hanging on the wall like sloughed skins. Also there were six head-and-shoulder helmets for the Martians, since they needed no more than three pounds of air. There wasn't a suit for him. I couldn't have fitted him with one if my life had depended upon it. It'd have been like trying to can an elephant.

Well, he lumbered out lightly, if you get what I mean. The casual, loose-limbed way he transported his ton-nage made me think I'd like to be some place else if ever he got on the rampage. Not that I thought him likely to run amok; he was amiable enough though sphinxlike. But I was fascinated by his air of calm assurance and by his motion, which was fast, silent and eerie. Maybe the latter was due to his habit of wearing an inch of sponge-rubber under his big dogs.

I kept an interested eye on Jay Score while the *Upsy-daisy* made good time on her crawl through the void. Yes, I was more than curious about him because his type was a new one on me despite that I've met plenty in my time. He remained uncommunicative but kind of quietly cordial. His work was smoothly efficient and in every way satisfactory. McNulty took a great fancy to him, though he'd never been one to greet a newcomer with love and kisses.

Three days out, Jay made a major hit with the Martians. As everyone knows, those goggle-eyed, ten-tentacled, half-breathing kibitzers have stuck harder than glue to the Solar System Chess Championship for more than two centuries. Nobody outside of Mars will ever pry them loose. They are nuts about the game and many's the time I've seen a bunch of them go through all the colors of the spectrum in sheer excitement when at last somebody has moved a pawn after thirty minutes of profound cogitation.

One rest-time Jay spent his entire eight hours under three pounds pressure in the starboard airlock. Through the lock's phones came long silences punctuated by wild and shrill twitterings as if he and the Martians were turning the place into a madhouse. At the end of the time we found our tentacled outside-crew exhausted. It turned out that Jay had consented to play Kli Yang and had forced him to a stalemate. Kli had been sixth runner-up in the last Solar melee, had been beaten only ten times—each time by a brother Martian, of course.

The red-planet gang had a finger on him after that, or I should say a tentacle-tip. Every rest-time they waylaid him and dragged him into the airlock. When we were eleven days out he played the six of them simultaneously, lost two games, stalemated three, won one. They thought he was a veritable whizzbang—for a mere Terrestrial. Knowing their peculiar abilities in this respect, I thought so, too. So did McNulty. He went so far as to enter the sporting data in the log.

You may remember the stunt that the audiopress of 2270 boosted as "McNulty's Miracle Move"? It's practically a legend of the spaceways. Afterward, when we'd got safely home, McNulty disclaimed the credit and put it where it rightfully belonged. The audiopress had a good excuse, as usual. They said he was the captain, wasn't he? And his name made the headline alliterative, didn't it? Seems that there must be a sect of audiojournalists who have to be alliterative to gain salvation.

What precipitated that crazy stunt and whitened my hair was a chunk of cosmic flotsam. Said object took the form of a gob of meteoric nickel-iron ambling along at the characteristic speed of *pssst!* Its orbit lay on the planetary plane and it approached at right angles to our sunward course.

It gave us the business. I'd never have believed anything so small could have made such a slam. To the present day I can hear the dreadful whistle of air as it made a mad break for freedom through that jagged hole.

We lost quite a bit of political juice before the autodoors sealed the damaged section. Pressure already had dropped to nine pounds when the compensators held it and slowly began to build it up again. The fall didn't worry the Martians; to them nine pounds was like inhaling pig-wash.

There was one engineer in that sealed section. Another escaped the closing doors by the skin of his left ear. But the first, we thought, had drawn his fateful number and eventually would be floated out like so many spacemen who've come to the end of their duty.

The guy who got clear was leaning against a bulwark, white-faced from the narrowness of his squeak. Jay Score came pounding along. His jaw was working, his eyes were like lamps, but his voice was cool and easy.

He said, "Get out. Seal this room. I'll try make a snatch. Open up and let me out fast when I knock."

With that he shoved us from the room, which we sealed by closing its autodoor. We couldn't see what the big hunk was doing but the telltale showed he'd released and opened the door to the damaged section. Couple of seconds later the light went out, showing the door had been closed again. Then came a hard, urgent knock. We opened. Jay plunged through hell-for-leather with the engineer's limp body cuddled in his huge arms. He bore it as if it were no bigger and heavier than a kitten and the way he took it down the passage threatened to carry him clear through the end of the ship.

Meanwhile we found we were in a first-class mess. The rockets weren't functioning any more. The venturi tubes were okay and the combustion chambers undamaged. The injectors worked without a hitch—providing that they were pumped by hand. We had lost none of our precious fuel and the shell was intact save for that one jagged hole. What made us useless was the wrecking of our coordinated feeding and firing controls. They had been located where the big bullet went through and now they were so much scrap.

This was more than serious. General opinion called it certain death though nobody said so openly. I'm pretty certain that McNulty shared the morbid notion even if his official report did under-describe it as "an embarrassing predicament." That is just like McNulty. It's a wonder he didn't define our feelings by recording that we were somewhat nonplussed.

Anyway, the Martial squad poured out, some honest work being required of them for the first time in six trips. Pressure had crawled back to fourteen pounds and they had to come into it to be fitted with their head-and-shoulder contraptions.

Kli Yang sniffed offensively, waved a disgusted tentacle and chirruped, "I could swim!" He eased up when we got his dingbat fixed and exhausted it to his customary three pounds. That is the Martian idea of sarcasm: whenever the atmosphere is thicker than they like they make sinuous backstrokes and declaim, "I could swim!"

To give them their due, they were good. A Martian can cling to polished ice and work continuously for twelve hours on a ration of oxygen that wouldn't satisfy a Terrestrial for more than ninety minutes. I watched them beat it through the airlock, eyes goggling through inverted fishbowls, their tentacles clutching power lines, sealing plates and quasi-arc welders. Blue lights made little auroras outside the ports as they began to cut, shape and close up that ragged hole.

All the time we continued to bullet sunward. But for this accursed misfortune we'd have swung a curve into the orbit of Venus in four hours' time. Then we'd have let her catch us up while we decelerated to a safe landing.

But when that peewee planetoid picked on us we were still heading for the biggest and brightest furnace hereabouts. That was the way we continued to go, our original velocity being steadily increased by the pull of our fiery destination.

I wanted to be cremated— but not yet!

Up in the bow navigation-room Jay Score remained in constant conference with Captain McNulty and the two astro-computator operators. Outside, the Martians continued to crawl around, fizzing and spitting with flashes of ghastly blue light. The engineers, of course, weren't waiting for them to finish their job. Four in spacesuits entered the wrecked section and started the task of creating order out of chaos.

I envied all those busy guys and so did many others. There's a lot of consolation in being able to do something even in an apparently hopeless situation. There's a lot of misery in being compelled to play with one's fingers while others are active.

Two Martians came back through the lock, grabbed some more sealing-plates and crawled out again. One of them thought it might be a bright idea to take his pocket chess set as well, but I didn't let him. There are times and places for that sort of thing and knight to king's fourth on the skin of a busted boat isn't one of them. Then I went along to see Sam Hignett, our Negro surgeon.

Sam had managed to drag the engineer back from the rim of the grave. He'd done it with oxygen, adrenalin and heart-massage. Only his long, dexterous fingers could have achieved it. It was a feat of surgery that has been brought off before, but not often.

Seemed that Sam didn't know what had happened and didn't much care, either. He was like that when he had a patient on his hands. Deftly he closed the chest incision with silver clips, painted the pinched flesh with iodized plastic, cooled the stuff to immediate hardness with a spray of ether.

"Sam," I told him. "You're a marvel."

"Jay gave me a fair chance," he said. "He got him here in time."

"Why put the blame on him?" I joked, unfunnily.

"Sergeant," he answered, very serious, "I'm the ship's doctor. I do the best I can. I couldn't have saved this man if Jay hadn't brought him when he did."

"All right, all right," I agreed. "Have it your own way."

A good fellow, Sam. But he was like all doctors—you know, ethical. I left him with his feebly breathing patient.

McNulty came strutting along the catwalk as I went back. He checked the fuel tanks. He was doing it personally, and that meant something. He looked worried, and that meant a devil of a lot. It meant that I need not bother to write my last will and testament because it would never be read by anything living.

His portly form disappeared into the bow navigation-room and I heard him say, "Jay, I guess you—" before the closing door cut off his voice.

He appeared to have a lot of faith in Jay Score. Well, that individual certainly looked capable enough. The skipper and the new emergency pilot continued to act like cronies even while heading for the final frizzle.

One of the emigrating agriculturalists came out of his cabin and caught me before I regained the armory. Studying me wide-eyed, he said, "Sergeant, there's a half-moon showing through my port."

He continued to pop them at me while I popped mine at him. Venus showing half her pan meant that we were now crossing her orbit. He knew it too—I could tell by the way he bugged them.

"Well," he persisted, with ill-concealed nervousness, "how long is this mishap likely to delay us?"

"No knowing." I scratched my head, trying to look stupid and confident at one and the same time. "Captain McNulty will do his utmost. Put your trust in him—Poppa knows best."

"You don't think we are . . . er . . . in any danger?"

"Oh, not at all."

"You're a liar," he said.

"I resent having to admit it," said I.

That unhorsed him. He returned to his cabin, dissatisfied, apprehensive. In short time he'd see Venus in three-quarter phase and would tell the others. Then the fat would be in the fire.

Our fat in the solar fire.

The last vestiges of hope had drained away just about the time when a terrific roar and violent trembling told that the long-dead rockets were back in action. The noise didn't last more than a few seconds. They shut off quickly, the brief burst serving to show that repairs were effective and satisfactory.

The noise brought out the agriculturalist at full gallop. He knew the worst by now and so did the others. It had been impossible to conceal the truth for the three days since he'd seen Venus as a half-moon. She was far behind us now. We were cutting the orbit of Mercury. But still the passengers clung to desperate hope that someone would perform an unheard-of miracle.

Charging into the armory, he yipped, "The rockets are working again. Does that mean?"

"Nothing," I gave back, seeing no point in building false hopes.

"But can't we turn round and go back?" He mopped perspiration trickling down his jowls. Maybe a little of it was forced out by fear, but most of it was due to the unpleasant fact that interior conditions had become anything but arctic.

"Sir," I said, feeling my shirt sticking to my back, "we've got more pull than any bunch of spacemen ever enjoyed before. And we're moving so goddam fast that there's nothing left to do but hold a lily."

"My ranch," he growled, bitterly. "I've been allotted five thousand acres of the best Venusian tobacco-growing territory, not to mention a range of uplands for beef."

"Sorry, but I think you'll be lucky ever to see it."

Crrrump! went the rockets again. The burst bent me backward and made him bow forward like he had a bad bellyache. Up in the bow, McNulty or Jay Score or someone was blowing them whenever he felt the whim. I couldn't see any sense in it.

"What's that for?" demanded the complainant, regaining the perpendicular.

"Boys will be boys," I said.

Snorting his disgust, he went to his cabin. A typical Terrestrial emigrant, big, healthy and tough, he was slow to crack and temporarily too peeved to be really worried in any genuinely soul-shaking way.

Half an hour later the general call sounded on buzzers all over the boat. It was a ground signal, never used in space. It meant that the entire crew and all other occupants of the vessel were summoned to the central cabin. Imagine guys being called from their posts in full flight!

Something unique in the history of space navigation must have been behind that call, probably a compose-yourselves-for-the-inevitable-end speech by McNulty.

Expecting the skipper to preside over the last rites, I wasn't surprised to find him standing on the tiny dais as we assembled. A faint scowl lay over his plump features but it changed to a ghost of a smile when the Martians mooched in and one of them did some imitation shark-dodging.

Erect beside McNulty, expressionless as usual, Jay Score looked at that swimming Martian as if he were a pane of glass. Then his strangely lit orbs shifted their aim as if they'd seen nothing more boring. The swim-joke was getting stale, anyway.

"Men and vedras," began McNulty—the latter being the Martian word for "adults" and, by implication, another piece of Martian sarcasm—"I have no need to enlarge upon the awkwardness of our position." That man certainly could pick his words—awkward! "Already we are nearer the Sun than any vessel has been in the whole history of cosmic navigation."

"Comic navigation," murmured Kli Yang, with tactless wit.

"We'll need your humor to entertain us later," observed Jay Score in a voice so flat that Kli Yang subsided.

"We are moving toward the luminary," went on McNulty, his scowl reappearing, "faster than any ship moved before. Bluntly, there is not more than one chance in ten thousand of us getting out of this alive." He favored Kli Yang with a challenging stare but that tentacled individual was now subdued. "However, there *is* that one chance—and we are going to take it."

We gaped at him, wondering what the devil he meant. Every one of us knew our terrific velocity made it impossible to describe a U-turn and get back without touching the Sun. Neither could we fight our way in the reverse direction with all that mighty drag upon us. There was nothing to do but go onward, onward, until the final searing blast scattered our disrupted molecules.

"What we intend is to try a cometary," continued McNulty. "Jay and myself and the astro-computators think it's remotely possible that we might achieve it and pull through."

That was plain enough. The stunt was a purely theoretical one frequently debated by mathematicians and astro-navigators but never tried out in grim reality. The idea is to build up all the velocity that can be got and at the same time to angle into the path of an elongated, elliptical orbit resembling that of a comet. In theory, the vessel might then skim close to the Sun so supremely fast that it would swing pendulumlike far out to the opposite side of the orbit whence it came. A sweet trick—but could we make it?

"Calculations show our present condition fair enough to permit a small chance of success," said McNulty. "We have power enough and fuel enough to build up the necessary velocity with the aid of the Sun-pull, to strike the necessary angle and to maintain it for the necessary time. The only point about which we have serious doubts is that of whether we can survive at our nearest to the Sun." He wiped perspiration, unconsciously emphasizing the shape of things to come. "I won't mince words, men. It's going to be a choice sample of hell!"

"We'll see it through, Skipper," said someone. A low murmur of support sounded through the cabin.

Kli Yang stood up, simultaneously waggled four jointless arms for attention, and twittered, "It is an idea. It is excellent. I, Kli Yang, endorse it on behalf of my fellow vedras. We shall cram ourselves into the refrigerator and suffer the Terrestrial stink while the Sun goes past."

Ignoring that crack about human odor, McNulty nodded and said, "Everybody will be packed into the cold room and endure it as best they can."

"Exactly," said Kli. "Quite," he added with bland disregard of superfluity. Wiggling a tentacle-tip at McNulty, he carried on, "But we cannot control the ship while squatting in the icebox like three and a half dozen strawberry sundaes. There will have to be a pilot in the bow. One individual can hold her on course—until he gets fried. So somebody has to be the fryee."

He gave the tip another sinuous wiggle, being under the delusion that it was fascinating his listeners into complete attention. "And since it cannot be denied that we Martians are far less susceptible to extremes of heat, I suggest that—"

"Nuts!" snapped McNulty. His gruffness deceived nobody. The Martians were nuisances—but grand guys.

"All right." Kli's chirrup rose to a shrill, protesting yelp. "Who else is entitled to become a crisp?"

"Me," said Jay Score. It was queer the way he voiced it. Just as if he were a candidate so obvious that only the stone-blind couldn't see him.

He was right, at that! Jay was the very one for the job. If anyone could take what was going to come through the fore observations ports it was Jay Score. He was big and tough, built for just such a task as this. He had a lot of stuff that none of us had got and, after all, he was a fully qualified emergency pilot. And most definitely this was an emergency, the greatest ever.

But it was funny the way I felt about him. I could imagine him up in front, all alone, nobody there, our lives depending on how much hell he could take, while the tremendous Sun extended its searing fingers—

"You!" ejaculated Kli Yang, breaking my train of thought. His goggle eyes bulged irefully at the big, laconic figure on the dais. "You would! I am ready to mate in four moves, as you are miserably aware, and promptly you scheme to lock yourself away."

"Six moves," contradicted Jay, airily. "You cannot do it in less than six."

"Four!" Kli Yang fairly howled. "And right at this point you—"

It was too much for the listening McNulty. He looked as if on the verge of a stroke. His purple face turned to the semaphoring Kli.

"To hell with your blasted chess!" he roared. "Return to your stations, all of you. Make ready for maximum boost. I will sound the general call immediately it becomes necessary to take cover and then you will all go to the cold room." He stared around, the purple gradually fading as his blood pressure went down. "That is, everyone except Jay."

More like old times with the rockets going full belt. They thundered smoothly and steadily. Inside the vessel the atmosphere became hotter and hotter until moisture trickled continually down our backs and a steaminess lay over the gloss of the walls. What it was like in the bow navigation-room I didn't know and didn't care to discover. The Martians were not inconvenienced yet; for once their whacky composition was much to be envied.

I did not keep check on the time but I'd had two spells of duty with one intervening sleep period before the buzzers gave the general call. By then things had become bad. I was no longer sweating: I was slowly melting into my boots.

Sam, of course, endured it most easily of all the Terrestrials and had persisted long enough to drag his patient completely out of original danger. That engineer was lucky, if it's luck to be saved for a bonfire. We put him in the cold room right away, with Sam in attendance.

The rest of us followed when the buzzer went. Our sanctuary was more than a mere refrigerator; it was the strongest and coolest section of the vessel, a heavily armored, triple-shielded compartment holding the instrument lockers, two sick bays and a large lounge for the benefit of space-nauseated passengers. It held all of us comfortably.

All but the Martians. It held them, but not comfortably. They are never comfortable at fourteen pounds pressure, which they regard as not only thick but also smelly—something like breathing molasses impregnated with aged goat.

Under our very eyes Kli Yang produced a bottle of *hooloo* scent, handed it to his half-parent Kli Morg. The latter took it, stared at us distastefully, then sniffed the bottle in an ostentatious manner that was positively insulting. But nobody said anything.

All were present excepting McNulty and Jay Score. The skipper appeared two hours later. Things must have been raw up front, for he looked terrible. His haggard face was beaded and glossy, his once-plump cheeks sunken and blistered. His usually spruce, well-fitting uniform hung upon him sloppily. It needed only one glance to tell that he'd had a darned good roasting, as much as he could stand.

Walking unsteadily, he crossed the floor, went into the first-aid cubby, stripped himself with slow, painful movements. Sam rubbed him with tannic jelly. We could hear the tormented skipper grunting hoarsely as Sam put plenty of pep into the job.

The heat was now on us with a vengeance. It pervaded the walls, the floor, the air and created a multitude of fierce stinging sensations in every muscle of my body. Several of the engineers took off their boots and jerkins. In short time the passengers followed suit, discarding most of their outer clothing. My agriculturalist sat a miserable figure in tropical silks, moody over what might have been.

Emerging from the cubby, McNulty flopped onto a bunk and said, "If we're all okay in four hours' time, we're through the worst part."

At that moment the rockets faltered. We knew at once what was wrong. A fuel tank had emptied and a relay had failed to cut in. An engineer should have been standing by to switch the conduits. In the heat and excitement, someone had blundered.

The fact barely had time to register before Kli Yang was out through the door. He'd been lolling nearest to it and was gone while we were trying to collect our overheated wits. Twenty seconds later the rockets renewed their steady thrum.

An intercom bell clanged right in my ear. Switching its mike, I croaked a throaty, "Well?" and heard Jay's voice coming back at me from the bow.

"Who did it?"

"Kli Yang," I told him. "He's still outside."

"Probably gone for their domes," guessed Jay. "Tell him I said thanks."

"What's it like around where you live?" I asked.

"Fierce. It isn't so good . . . for vision." Silence a moment, then, "Guess I can stick it . . . somehow.

Strap down or hold on ready for the next time I sound the . . . bell."

"Why?" I half yelled, half rasped.

"Going to rotate her. Try . . . distribute . . . the heat."

A faint squeak told that he'd switched off. I told the others to strap down. The Martians didn't have to bother about that because they owned enough saucer-sized suckers to weld them to a sunfishing meteor.

Kli came back, showed Jay's guess to be correct; he was dragging the squad's head-and-shoulder pieces. The load was as much as he could pull now that temperature had climbed to the point where even he began to wilt.

The Martian moochers gladly donned their gadgets, sealing the seams and evacuating them down to three pounds pressure. It made them considerably happier. Remembering that we Terrestrials use spacesuits to keep air inside, it seemed queer to watch those guys using theirs to keep it outside.

They had just finished making themselves comfortable and had laid out a chessboard in readiness for a minor journey when the bell sounded again. We braced ourselves. The Martians clamped down their suckers.

Slowly and steadily the *Upsydaisy* began to turn upon her longitudinal axis. The chessboard and pieces tried to stay put, failed, crawled along the floor, up the wall and across the ceiling. Solar pull was making them stick to the sunward side.

I saw Kli Morg's strained, heat-ridden features glooming at a black bishop while it skittered around, and I suppose that inside his goldfish bowl were resounding some potent samples of Martian invective.

"Three hours and a half," gasped McNulty.

That four hours estimate could only mean two hours of approach to the absolute deadline and two hours of retreat from it. So the moment when we had two hours to go would be the moment when we were at our nearest to the solar furnace, the moment of greatest peril.

I wasn't aware of that critical time, since I passed out twenty minutes before it arrived. No use enlarging upon the horror of that time. I think I went slightly nuts. I was a hog in an oven, being roasted alive. It's the only time I've ever thought of the Sun as a great big shining bastard that ought to be extinguished for keeps. Soon afterward I became incapable of any thought at all.

I recovered consciousness and painfully moved in my straps ninety minutes after passing the midway point. My dazed mind had difficulty in realizing that we had now only half an hour to go to reach theoretical safety.

What had happened in the interim was left to my imagination and I didn't care to try to picture it just then. The Sun blazing with a ferocity multi-million times greater than that of a tiger's eye, and a hundred thousand times as hungry for our blood and bones. The flaming corona licking out toward this shipload of half-dead entities, imprisoned in a steel bottle.

And up in front of the vessel, behind its totally inadequate quartz observation-ports, Jay Score sitting alone, facing the mounting inferno, staring, staring, staring—

Getting to my feet, I teetered uncertainly, went down like a bundle of rags. The ship wasn't rotating any longer and we appeared to be bulleting along in normal fashion. What dropped me was sheer weakness. I felt lousy.

The Martians already had recovered. I knew they'd be the first. One of them lugged me upright and held me steady while I regained a percentage of my former control. I noticed that another had sprawled right across the unconscious McNulty and three of the passengers. Yes, he'd shielded them from some of the heat and they were the next ones to come to life.

Struggling to the intercom, I switched it but got no response from the front. For three full minutes I hung by it dazedly before I tried again. Nothing doing. Jay wouldn't or couldn't answer.

I was stubborn about it, made several more attempts with no better result. The effort cost me a dizzy spell and down I flopped once more. The heat was still terrific. I felt more dehydrated than a mummy dug out of sand a million years old.

Kli Yang opened the door, crept out with dragging,

painstricken motion. His air-helmet was secure on his shoulders. Five minutes later he came back, spoke through the helmet's diaphragm.

"Couldn't get near the bow navigation-room. At the midway catwalk the autodoors are closed, the atmosphere sealed off and it's like being inside a furnace." He stared around, met my gaze, answered the question in my eyes. "There's no air in the bow."

No air meant the observation-ports had gone *phut*. Nothing else could have emptied the navigation-room. Well, we carried spares for that job and could make good the damage once we got into the clear. Meanwhile here we were roaring along, maybe on correct course and maybe not, with an empty, airless navigation-room and with an intercom system that gave nothing but ghastly silence.

Sitting around, we picked up strength. The last to come out of his coma was the sick engineer. Sam brought him through again. It was about then that McNulty wiped sweat, showed sudden excitement.

"Four hours, men," he said, with grim satisfaction. "We've done it!"

We raised a hollow cheer. By Jupiter, the superheated atmosphere seemed to grow ten degrees cooler with the news. Strange how relief from tension can breed strength; in one minute we had conquered former weakness and were ready to go. But it was yet another four hours before a quartet of spacesuited engineers penetrated the forward hell and bore their burden from the airless navigation room.

They carried him into Sam's cubbyhole, a long, heavy, silent figure with face burned black.

Stupidly I hung around him saying, "Jay, Jay, how're you making out?"

He must have heard, for he moved the fingers of his right hand and emitted a chesty, grinding noise. Two of the engineers went to his cabin, brought back his huge rawhide case. They shut the door, staying in with Sam and leaving me and the Martians fidgeting outside. Kli

Yang wandered up and down the passage as if he didn't know what to do with his tentacles.

Sam came out after more than an hour. We jumped him on the spot.

"How's Jay?"

"Blind as a statue." He shook his woolly head. "And his voice isn't there any more. He's taken an awful beating."

"So that's why he didn't answer the intercom." I looked him straight in the eyes. "Can you . . . can you do anything for him, Sam?"

"I only wish I could." His sepia face showed his feelings. "You know how much I'd like to put him right. But I can't." He made a gesture of futility. "He is completely beyond my modest skill. Nobody less than Johannsen can help him. Maybe when we get back to Earth—" His voice petered out and he went back inside.

Kli Yang said, miserably, "I am saddened."

A scene I'll never forget to my dying day was that evening we spent as guests of the Astro Club in New York. That club was then—as it is today—the most exclusive group of human beings ever gathered together. To qualify for membership one had to perform in dire emergency a feat of astro-navigation tantamount to a miracle. There were nine members in those days and there are only twelve now.

Mace Waldron, the famous pilot who saved that Martian liner in 2263, was the chairman. Classy in his soup and fish, he stood at the top of the table with Jay Score sitting at his side. At the opposite end of the table was McNulty, a broad smirk of satisfaction upon his plump pan. Beside the skipper was old, white-haired Knud Johannsen, the genius who designed the J-series and a scientific figure known to every spaceman.

Along the sides, manifestly self-conscious, sat the entire crew of the *Upsydaisy*, including the Martians, plus three of our passengers who'd postponed their trips for this occasion. There were also a couple of audio-journalists with scanners and mikes.

"Gentlemen and vedras," said Mace Waldron, "this is an event without precedent in the history of humanity, an event never thought of, never imagined by this club. Because of that I feel it doubly an honor and a privilege to propose that Jay Score, Emergency Pilot, be accepted as a fully qualified and worthy member of the Astro Club."

"Seconded!" shouted three members simultaneously.

"Thank you, gentlemen." He cocked an inquiring eyebrow. Eight hands went up in unison. "Carried," he said. "Unanimously." Glancing down at the taciturn and unmoved Jay Score, he launched into a eulogy. It went on and on and on, full of praise and superlatives, while Jay squatted beside him with a listless air.

Down at the other end I saw McNulty's gratified smirk grow stronger and stronger. Next to him, old Knud was gazing at Jay with a fatherly fondness that verged on the fatuous. The crew likewise gave full attention to the blank-faced subject of the talk, and the scanners were fixed upon him too.

I returned my attention to where all the others were looking, and the victim sat there, his restored eyes bright and glittering, but his face completely immobile despite the talk, the publicity, the beam of paternal pride from Johannsen.

But after ten minutes of this I saw J.20 begin to fidget with obvious embarrassment.

Don't let anyone tell you that a robot can't have feelings!

Homo Saps

MAJESTICALLY THE LONG caravan emerged from the thick belt of blue-green Martian *doltha* weed and paraded into the Saloma Desert. Forty-four camels stalked along with the swaying gait and high-faluting expressions of their kind. All were loaded. Beneath the burdens their deliberate, unhurried feet dug deeply into the long waves of fine, pinkish sand.

The forty-fifth animal, which was in the lead, was not a camel. It was daintier, more shapely, had a beige-colored coat and only one hump. A racing dromedary. But its expression was fully as supercilious as that worn by the others.

Sugden had the dromedary, Mitchell was on the following camel, and Ale Fa'oum formed the rearguard of one. The forty-two burdened beasts in between had modest loads and immodest odors. Ali, at the back, got the benefit of the last. It didn't matter. He was used to it. He'd miss it if it wasn't there.

Twisting in his seat, Sugden tilted his head toward the sinking sun, and said, "They'll put on the brakes pretty soon, I guess."

Mitchell nodded lugubriously. He'd sworn camels across Arabia, cursed them through the Northern Territory of Australia, and had oathed them three times around Mars. His patience was no better than on the day he'd started. Within his bosom burned a theory that

27

if there had never been camels there would have been no such thing as Oriental fatalism.

Abruptly the dromedary stopped, went down forelegs first, back legs next, and settled with a sickening heave. It didn't bother to look behind. There wasn't any need, anyway. The rest of the cavalcade followed suit, front legs first, hind legs next, the same heave. A box with loose fastenings parted from its indifferent bearer and flopped into the sand.

Ali, now compelled to dismount, did so. He found the fodder, distributed it along the resting line. Ignoring the white men, the animals ate slowly and with maddening deliberation, their disinterested eyes studying the far horizon. Ali started grooming them as they ate. He'd groomed them in Port Tewfik thirty years ago. He was still doing it. They still let him get on with it, their expressions lordly.

Lighting a cigarette, Sugden gave it a savage suck, and said, "And they talk about mules!"

Slowly the dromedary turned its head, gave him a contemptuous look. Then it resumed its contemplation of distance. It chewed monotonously and methodically, its bottom lip pursed in silent scorn.

"Same distance, same time," voiced Mitchell sourly. Thumping the heel of his jackboot, he killed a Martian twelve-legged sand spider. "Never more, never less. They clock on and clock off and they work no overtime."

"They've got us where they want us." Sugden blew a twin funnel of smoke from itching nostrils, stared distastefully at what had been the spider. "They're the only things that can cover these deserts apart from the Martians themselves. If we had tractors, we'd use tractors if there was any gasoline on this planet."

"Some day, when I'm bloated with riches," Mitchell pursued, "I'm going to be eccentric. I'm going to get them to build me a superhyperultra rocketship. One that'll carry some real tonnage."

"Then what?" inquired Sugden.

"Then start from where I left off here—only with elephants."

"Ha-ha!" laughed Sugden, with artificial violence.

The dromedary turned its head again. It made a squelching sound with its slowly moving mouth. The noise was repeated all the way along the line until the mount of Ali emitted the final salivary smack. Ali proceeded furiously with his grooming.

Mitchell snorted and said, complainingly, "You'd think the whole darned lot had loose dental plates." He started to open up the thermic meal pack. "And they stink."

"And I don't like their faces," added Sugden.

"Me neither. Give me a cigarette, will you?" Mitchell lit it, let it hang from his bottom lip. "To think the Martians kowtow to them and treat us like dirt. Funny the way they've acted like that since the first camel was imported."

"Yeah, I'd like to get to the root of it sometime."

"Try talking to a Martian. Might as well talk to a gatepost, and—yeouw, this thermic's red-hot!" Mitchell coddled his fingers. "Sixty years and never a word out of them. They ought to be able to talk, but won't." He heaved the meal pack onto its telescopic legs, slid out its trays. "Hi, Ali, come and give us a hand."

"No, sah. Finish these first. One hour."

"See?" Removing his solar topee, Mitchell flung it on the sand. "The stinkers first, us last."

The igloo-shaped lumps of Jenkinsville showed on the horizon at sunset next day. Nobody knew the Martian name of the place, but its first discoverer had been one Hiram Jenkins, originally of Key West, Florida. So from then on it was Jenkinsville. The place was precisely fourteen miles away. Nevertheless, the dromedary squatted and the rest did likewise.

Sugden dismounted with the usual scowl, raked out the usual battered cigarette, heard Mitchell air the usual curse. It couldn't have been a curse of much potency since the curve on the grief chart remained constant, with never a dip.

The same box fell into the sand again, making the same dismal thump. Phlegmatically, Ali got on with the feeding and grooming rigmarole. In superior silence the forty-five animals rested and masticated and gazed at nearby Jenkinsville much as Sugden had gazed at the squashed spider.

"I've a persistent notion," said Sugden, his sand-chafed eyes on the energetic Mr. Fa'oum, "that he sneaks up at midnight and worships them. First time I catch him I'll prove he can't salaam without presenting his rump for suitable retaliation."

"Humph!" Mitchell wrestled with the meal pack, burned his fingers as he'd done a thousand times before, let out his thousandth *yeouw!* "Hi, Ali!"

"One hour," said Ali, firmly.

"I'm clinging to life," announced Mitchell, speaking to the general outlines of Jenkinsville, "so's I can outlive the lot. One by one, as they die on me, I'm going to skin 'em. I'll make foot mats of their stinking pelts. I'll get married, wipe my feet coming in and going out and every time the cuckoo clock puts the bean on me."

The sixth camel from the front rumbled its insides. Slowly the rumble moved from stomach to gullet, ended in an emphatic burp. Taking its blank eyes off Jenkinsville, the dromedary looked backward with open approval. Mitchell enjoyed a furious kick at the thermic, denting its side.

"Now, now!" said Sugden.

Mitchell gave him a look of sudden death, twitched a tray from the thermic. He did it wholeheartedly. The tray shot clean out of the container, tilted against his ineffectual grasp, poured a mess of hot beans in tomato sauce over his jackboots. Ali paused and watched as he brought a bundle of night coats to the complacent camels. Sugden stared at Mitchell. So did Ali. Also the camels.

Looking first at Sugden, then at his boots, Mitchell said, "Notice that?"

"Yes, I've noticed it," admitted Sugden, gravely.

"Funny, isn't it?"

"Not at all. I think it unfortunate."

"Well," said Mitchell, stabbing a finger at the observing line, "*they* think it's funny."

"Oh, forget it. All animals are curious."

"Curious? Hah!" Lugging off his boots, Mitchell hefted them, swung them around, gauged their weight and handiness. All the time his eyes were on the dromedary. In the end, he changed his mind, cleaned his boots in the sand, then put them on. "They're seeing the world at our expense—and they all look at me when I do this to myself."

"Aw, let's eat," soothed Sugden. "We're hungry, and hunger makes one short-tempered. We'll feel better afterward. Besides, we'll be in Jenkinsville early in the morning."

"Sure, we will. We'll be in Jenkinsville first thing in the morning. We'll offer our junk for all the mallow seeds we can get; and if we don't dispose of the lot—as we probably won't—we'll start another one hundred-mile hike to Dead Plains to shoot the balance." Mitchell glowered at the cosmos. "If, by some miracle unique in the records of Martian trading, we do switch all we've got, we'll start back on our one hundred fifty miles of purgatory to Lemport, accompanied by forty-four camels, forty-four double-humped skunks."

"And one dromedary," Sugden reminded, delicately.

"An one one-humped skunk," agreed Mitchell. He glared across the sands to where the said skunk was enjoying its own divestive processes with true Arabian aplomb.

"If you're not going to eat," announced Sugden, "I am!" He slid another tray from the thermic, stabbed himself a couple of steaming pinnawursts. He was very partial to minced livers of the plump and succulent pinna birds.

As the food went cold in the Martian evening, Mitchell joined in. The pair ate ruminatively, in unconscious imitation of the camels.

Three hours beyond the flaming dawn the caravan slouched into the marketplace in Jenkinsville and unloaded with many animal grunts and much Terrestrial profanity. Martians came crowding in, more or less ignored the white men, took a little more notice of Ali

Fa'oum, but paid most attention to the camels. For a long time they looked at the camels and the camels looked at them, each side examining the other with the aloofish interest of ghosts discovering fairies.

Mitchell and Sugden let them get on with it. They knew that in due time, when they thought fit, the natives would turn to business. Meanwhile, the interim could be used for making all the necessary preparations, setting up the stalls, displaying the stocks, getting the books and scales ready. Each Martian had his hoard of mallow seeds, some small bags, some big bags, some with two or three.

The seeds were what the traders were after. From this product of the Martian desert mallow could be distilled—a genuine cure for Terrestrial cancer. This disease would have been wiped out long ago if only the temperamental mallow were cultivatable—which it wasn't. It grew wherever it took the fancy and nowhere else. It didn't fancy anywhere on Earth. Hence, its short, glossy-leafed bushes had to be searched for, and Martians did the searching.

In ones and twos, and in complete silence, the Martians drifted from the camels to the stalls. They were large-eyed beings, with big chests and flop ears, but otherwise human in shape. Though literally dumb, they were fairly intelligent. Terrestrial surgeons opined that the Martian voice box once had functioned, but now was petrified by centuries of disuse. Maybe they were right. Mitchell and Sugden didn't know or very much care. The traders high pressured their clients in deft sign language, sometimes helped out by writing and sketches.

An old Martian got his bag weighed, was credited with one hundred eighty dollars in gold, solid, heavy, international spondulics. Mitchell showed him a roll of batik-patterned broadcloth and a half-plate glossy photograph of Superba de la Fontaine attired in a sarong of the same material. He didn't mention that the fair Superba was originally Prunella Teitelbaum of Terre Haute. All the same, the old chap liked neither. He pulled a face at Mitchell, indicated that both were trash.

"They're getting finicky," complained Mitchell, addressing the God of Commerce. Irefully, he swung a roll of Harris tweed along the rough-wood counter, fingered it, smelled it, held it up for his customer to enjoy the heathery odor of the fabric. The customer approved, indicated that he'd take three arm spans of same. Mitchell sliced off the required length, rolled it dexterously, tossed it over.

Way down in the Communal Hall beyond the serried rows of red granite igloos a band of tribal beaters started playing on a choir of gongs. The instruments ranged all the way from a tiny, tinkling silver hand disk up to an enormous copper cylinder twenty feet in diameter. Every note was powerful and pure but the tune was blatant torture.

Scowling, Mitchell said to the old fellow, "Now how about a watch? So long as you've got the time, you'll never have to ask a policeman. Here's the very one, a magnificent, fifty-jeweled, ten-day chronometer, rectified for Mars, checked by the Deimos Observatory, and guaranteed by Mitchell & Sugden."

He tried to put it all into signs, sweating as he did it. The Martian sniffed, rejected the timepiece, chose five cheap alarm clocks. Moreover, he went right through the stock of several dozens in order to pick himself five with differing notes. Then he selected a gold bangle set with turquoises, a midget radio, an aluminum coffee percolator and a small silver pepper pot into which he solemnly emptied the inevitable packet of Martian snuff.

"That leaves you two bucks seventy," said Mitchell. The old fellow took his balance in cigarettes and canned coffee, toddled back to pay his respects to the camels. There was still a gang busy soul-mingling with the animals. "Damn the stinkers!" Mitchell heaved a huge bag of seeds onto the scales. The needle swung around. "Seven hundred smackers," he breathed. He scrawled the amount in big figures with a blue pencil, held it out to the new customer.

This one was a young Martian, taller than the average. He nodded, produced a five-year-old catalogue, opened it, pointed to illustrations, conveyed by many signs that he wanted the cash put to his credit until he had enough to get an automobile.

"No use," said Mitchell. "No gasoline. No go. No soap!" He made snakes of his arms in his efforts to explain the miserable and absolute impotence of an automobile sans juice. The Martian watched gravely, started to argue with many further references to the catalogue. Mitchell called in Sugden to help.

After ten minutes, Sugden said: "I get it. He wants a heap with a producer-gas plant. He thinks he can run it on local deadwood."

"For Pete's sake!" groaned Mitchell. "Now they're going Broadway on us! How in the name of the seven devils can we get one here?"

"In pieces," Sugden suggested. "We'll try, anyway. Why not? It may start a cult. We might end up with a million jujubes apiece. We might both be Martian producer-gas automobile tycoons, and be ambushed by blondes like they say in magazines. It'll cost this guy an unholy sum, but it's his sum. Attend to the customer, Jimson, and see that he's satisfied."

With doubtful gloom, Mitchell made out a credit slip for seven hundred, handed it across. Then he took a deep breath, looked around, noticed camels and Martians regarding each other with the same philosophical interest. Some of the animals were munching choice tidbits offered them by the natives.

More bags, more weighings, more arguments all through the rest of the day. As usual, the clients didn't want a good proportion of the Mitchell-Sugden stock, and again as usual, some of them wanted things not in stock and difficult to obtain.

On the previous trip one Martian had taken a hundred phonograph records and had ordered some minor electrical apparatus. Now he turned up, claiming his apparatus, didn't want another disk, put in an urgent order for a couple of radio transmitter tubes of special design. After half an hour's semaphoring, he had to

draw the tubes before Mitchell understood what was
wanted. There was no law against supplying such stuff,
so he booked the order.

"Oh, Jiminy," he said, wearily, "why can't you guys
talk like civilized people?"

The Martian was faintly surprised by this comment.
He considered it solemnly, his big, grave eyes wandering from the liverish Mitchell to the camels and back
again. The dromedary nodded, smirked, and let the
juice of an overripe *wushkin* drool from its bottom lip.
The Martian signed Mitchell an invitation to follow
him.

It was on the verge of dusk and time for ceasing operations anyway. Leaving his exhausted partner to close
the post, Mitchell trailed the Martian. Fifteen years before he had trailed one to an illegal still and had
crawled back gloriously blotto. It might happen again.

They passed the camels, now being groomed by the
officious Ali Fa'oum, wandered through the town to a
large igloo halfway between the marketplace and the
northern outskirts. A mile to the south the gongs of
Communal Hall were sounding a raucous evensong.
The big tremblor caused dithers in the digestive system.

Inside the igloo was a room filled with a jumble of
apparatus, some incomplete, some discarded but not
thrown out. The sight did not surprise Mitchell, since it
was well known that the Martians had scientific abilities
along their own peculiar lines. His only emotion was a
feeling of disappointment. No still.

Connecting up a thing looking like a homemade radio receiver with a tiny loudspeaker, the Martian drew
from its innards a length of thin cable terminating in a
small, silvery object which he promptly swallowed. With
the cable hanging out of his mouth, his big eyes staring
solemnly at Mitchell, he fiddled with dials. Suddenly,
an inhuman, metallic voice oozed from the loudspeaker.

"Spich! This artificial spich! Just made him. Very
hard—cannot do much!"

"Ah," said Mitchell, faintly impressed.

"So you get me tubes. Do better then—see?"

"Sure," agreed Mitchell. Then the overwhelming thought struck him that he was the first Terrestrial to hold vocal conversation with a Martian. Front-page news! He was no pressman, but he was trader enough to feel that there ought to be a thousand frogskins in this interview if he handled it right. What would a journalist do? Oh, yes, ask questions. "Why can't you guys speak properly?" he asked, with unjournalistic awkwardness.

"Properly?" squawked the loudspeaker. The Martian was astonished. "We do talk properly. Ten thousand years ago we ceased this noise-talk of low-life forms and talked here"—he touched his forehead—"so!"

"You mean you converse telepathically?"

"Of course—same as camels."

"What?" yelled Mitchell.

"Sure! They are high form of life."

"Like hell they are," bawled Mitchell, his face purpling.

"Hah!" The Martian was amused. "I prove it. They talk here." Again he touched his forehead. "And not here, like you." He touched his throat. "They toil in moderation, eat reasonable, rest adequately, wear no clothes, pay no taxes, suffer no ills, have no worries, enjoy much contemplation and are happy."

"But they darned well work," shouted Mitchell. He smacked his chest. "And for me."

"As all must, high and low alike. You also work for them. Who works the hardest? You see—*glug-glug!*" The loudspeaker gulped into silence. Hurriedly, the Martian made adjustments to the set and presently the speaker came to fresh but weaker life. "Battery nearly gone. So sorry!"

"Camels, a high form of life!" jeered Mitchell. "Ha-ha! I'll believe it when I've got a lemon-colored beard nine feet long."

"Does the delectable pinna know the superiority of our bellies? How can *you* measure the mental stature of a camel where there is no common basis? You cannot talk inside the head; you have never known at any time what a camel is thinking." The loudspeaker's fading crackle coincided with the Martian's patronizing chuckle. Mitchell disliked both noises.

"So long as it knows what I'm thinking, that's all that matters."

"Which is entirely your own point of view." Again the Martian registered his amusement. "There are others, you know, but all the same—*crackle, crackle, pop!*" The apparatus finally gave up the ghost and none of its operator's adjustments could bring it back to life. He took out the artificial larynx through which he had been talking, signed that the interview was over.

Mitchell returned to the camp in decidedly unsweet humor. Sugden met him, and said, "We shifted sixty percent. That means another hike starting tomorrow morning. A long one, too."

"Aaargh!" said Mitchell. He began to load the thermics. Sugden gave him a look, holed down in his sleeping bag and left him to work it off.

Jenkinsville was buried in slumber and Sugden was snoring loudly by the time he finished. He kept muttering to himself, "Homo saps, huh? Don't make me laugh!" all the while he worked. Then he got the last thermic sealed up, killed a spider he found scuttling around in an empty can, had a last look over the camp.

The camels were a row of blanketed, gurgling shapes in the general darkness, with the nursemaidish Ali Fa'oum a lesser shape somewhere near them.

Looking at them, Mitchell declaimed, "If I thought for one moment that you misshapen gobs of stink-meat knew what I was saying, I'd tell you something that'd take the supercilious expression off your faces for all time!"

With that blood-pressure reliever, he started back to his own sleeping bag, got nearly there, suddenly turned and raced toward the camels. His kick brought Ali into immediate wakefulness, and his bellow could be heard all over the camp.

"Which one of them made that noise?"

"No can tell," protested Ali, sleepily. "Forty-four of

them an' dromedary. How tell who makes noise? Only Allah know!"

Sugden's voice came through the night, saying, "Mitch, for heaven's sake!"

"Oh, all right." Mitchell returned, found his torch. "Telepathic bunk!" he muttered. "We'll see!" By the light of his torch he cut a playing card into forty-five pieces, numbered them with a pencil, shuffled them in the dark, shut his eyes and picked one. *Number twelve.*

Waking again, Sugden stuck his head out and said, suspiciously, "What're you doing now?"

"Crocheting for my bottom drawer," said Mitchell. Ignoring the other, he examined his gun by the light of the torch, found it fully loaded with ten powerful dynoshells. Smiling happily, he murmured, "Number twelve!" and lay down to sleep.

Ali shook him into wakefulness with the first flush of dawn. Sugden was already up, fully dressed and looking serious.

"One of the camels has scrammed," he announced. "Number twelve."

"Eh!" Mitchell shot up like a jack-in-the-box.

Sugden said, "And I don't like that funny look you put on when I told you. It was my camel, not one of yours. Have you pinned an abracadabra on it?"

"Me? What, me?" Mitchell tried to look innocent. "Oh, no!"

"Because if you have, you'd better unhex it mighty quick."

"Oh, we'll find it," comforted Mitchell. He got dressed, stowed away his gun, made the mental reservation that he'd do nothing about number twelve, nothing at all. He made the thought as powerful as he could.

The missing animal was waiting for them beside the trail one hour out from Jenkinsville. It took its position in the string as of old habit. Nobody said anything. It was a long time since Mitchell had been so quiet.

After a while Sugden's dromedary turned its neck and made a horrible face at Mitchell, riding right behind. He still said nothing. Deliberately, the caravan swayed on.

Metamorphosite

THEY LET HIM pause halfway along the gangway so that his eyes could absorb the imposing scene. He stood in the middle of the high metal track, his left hand firmly grasping a side rail, and gazed into the four-hundred-foot chasm beneath. Then he studied the immense space vessels lying in adjacent berths, his stare tracing their gangways to their respective elevator towers behind, which stood a great cluster of buildings whence the spaceport control column soared to the clouds. The height at which he stood, and the enormous dimensions of his surroundings, made him a little, doll-like figure, a man dwarfed by the mightiest works of man.

Watching him closely, his guards noted that he did not seem especially impressed. His eyes appeared to discard sheer dimensions while they sought the true meaning behind it all. His face was quite impassive as he looked around, but all his glances were swift, intelligent and assured. He comprehended things with that quick confidence which denotes an agile mind. One feature was prominent in the mystery enveloping him; it was evident that he was no dope.

Lieutenant Roka pushed past the two rearmost guards, leaned on the rail beside the silent watcher, and explained, "This is Madistine Spaceport. There are twenty others like it upon this planet. There are from two to twenty more on every one of four thousand other planets, and a few of them considerably bigger. The Empire is the greatest thing ever known or ever likely to be known. Now you see what you're up against."

" 'Numbers and size,' " quoth the other. He smiled faintly and shrugged. "What of them?"

"You'll learn what!" Roka promised. He, too, smiled, his teeth showing white and clean. "An organization can grow so tremendous that it's far, far bigger than the men who maintain it. From then on, its continued growth and development are well-nigh inevitable. It's an irresistible force with no immovable object big enough to stop it. It's a juggernaut. Its destiny, or whatever you care to call it."

"Bigness," murmured the other. "How you love bigness." He leaned over the railing, peered into the chasm. "In all probability down there is an enemy you've not conquered yet."

"Such as what?" demanded Roka.

"A cancer bug." The other's eyes swung up, gazed amusedly into the lieutenant's. "Eh?" He shrugged again. "Alas, for brief mortality!"

"Move on," snapped Roka to the leading guard.

The procession shuffled on, two guards, then the prisoner, then Roka, then two more guards. Reaching the tower at the end of the track, the sextet took an elevator to ground level, found a jet car waiting for them, a long, black sedan with the Silver Comet of the Empire embossed on its sides. Two men uniformed in myrtle green occupied its front seats while a third stood by the open door at rear.

"Lieutenant Roka with the specimen and appropriate documents," said Roka. He indicated the prisoner with a brief gesture, then handed the third man a leather dispatch case. After that, he felt in one pocket, extracted a printed pad, added, "Sign here, please."

The official signed, returned the pad, tossed the dispatch case into the back of the car.

"All right," he said to the prisoner. "Get in."

Still impassive, the other got into the car, relaxed on

the rear seat. Roka bent through the doorway, offered a hand.

"Well, sorry to see the last of you. We were just getting to know each other, weren't we? Don't get any funny ideas, will you? You're here under duress, but remember that you're also somewhat of an ambassador—that'll give you the right angle on things. Best of luck!"

"Thanks." The prisoner shook the proffered hand, shifted over as the green-uniformed official clambered in beside him. The door slammed, the jets roared, the car shot smoothly off. The prisoner smiled faintly as he caught Roka's final wave.

"Nice guy, Roka," offered the official.

"Quite."

"Specimen," the official chuckled. "Always they call 'em specimens. Whether of human shape or not, any seemingly high or presumably intelligent form of life imported from any newly discovered planet is, in bureaucratic jargon, a specimen. So that's what you are, whether you like it or whether you don't. Mustn't let it worry you, though. Nearly every worthwhile specimen has grabbed himself a high official post when his planet has become part of the Empire."

"Nothing worries me," assured the specimen easily.

"No?"

"No."

The official became self-conscious. He picked the dispatch case off the floor, jiggled it aimlessly around, judged its weight, then flopped it on his lap. The two in front maintained grim silence and scowled steadily through the windshield as the car swung along a broad avenue.

At good speed they swooped over a humpback crossing, overtook a couple of highly colored, streamlined cars, swung left at the end of the avenue. This brought them up against a huge pair of metal gates set in a great stone wall. The place would have looked like a jail to the newcomer if he'd known what jails look like—which he didn't.

The gates heaved themselves open, revealing a broad drive which ran between well-tended lawns to the main entrance of a long, low building with a clock tower at its center. The entrance, another metal job heavy enough to withstand a howitzer, lay directly beneath the tower. The black sedan curved sideways before it, stopped with a faint hiss of air brakes.

"This is it." The official at the back of the car opened a door, heaved himself out, dragging the case after him. His prisoner followed, shut the door, and the sedan swooped away.

"You see," said the man in green uniform. He gestured toward the lawns and the distant wall. "There's the wall, the gate, and a space from here to there in which you'd be immediately seen by the patrols. Beyond that wall are a thousand other hazards of which you know nothing. I'm telling you this because here's where you'll have your home until matters get settled. I would advise you not to let your impatience overcome your judgment, as others have done. It's no use running away when you've nowhere to run."

"Thanks," acknowledged the other. "I won't run until I've good reason and think I know where I'm going."

The official gave him a sharp look. A rather ordinary fellow, he decided, a little under Empire average in height, slender, dark, thirtyish and moderately good-looking. But possessed of the cockiness of youth. Under examination he'd probably prove boastful and misleading. He sighed his misgiving. A pity that they hadn't snatched somebody a good deal older.

"Harumph!" he said apropos of nothing.

He approached the door, the other following. The door opened of its own accord, the pair entered a big hall, were met by another official in myrtle green.

"A specimen from a new world," said the escort, "for immediate examination."

The second official stared curiously at the newcomer, sniffed in disdain, said, "O.K.—you know where to take him."

Their destination proved to be a large examination room at one end of a marble corridor. Here, the official handed over the dispatch case to a man in white, departed without further comment. There were seven men and one woman in the room, all garbed in white.

They studied the specimen calculatingly, then the woman asked, "You have learned our language?"

"Yes."

"Very well, then, you may undress. Remove all your clothes."

"Not likely!" said the victim in a level voice.

The woman didn't change expression. She bent over an official form lying on her desk, wrote in a neat hand in the proper section: "Sex convention normal." Then she went out.

When the door had shut behind her, the clothes came off. The seven got to work on the prisoner, completing the form as they went along. They did the job quietly, methodically, as an obvious matter of old-established routine. Height: four point two lineal units. Weight: seventy-seven migrads. Hair: type-S, with front peaked. No wisdom teeth. All fingers double-jointed. Every piece of data was accepted as if it were perfectly normal, and jotted down on the official form. Evidently they were accustomed to dealing with entities differing from whatever was regarded as the Empire norm.

They X-rayed his cranium, throat, chest and abdomen from front, back and both sides and dutifully recorded that something that wasn't an appendix was located where his appendix ought to be. Down went the details, every one of them. Membraned epiglottis. Optical astigmatism: left eye point seven, right eye point four. Lapped glands in throat in lieu of tonsils. Crenated ear lobes. Cerebral serrations complex and deep.

"Satisfied?" he asked when apparently they'd finished with him.

"You can put on your clothes."

The head man of the seven studied the almost-completed form thoughtfully. He watched the subject dressing himself, noted the careful, deliberate manner in which the garments were resumed one by one. He called three of his assistants, conferred with them in low tones.

Finally he wrote at the bottom of the form: "Not necessarily a more advanced type, but definitely a variation. Possibly dangerous. Should be watched." Unlocking the dispatch case, he shoved the form in on top of the other papers it contained, locked the case, gave it to an assistant. "Take him along to the next stage."

Stage two was another room almost as large as its predecessor and made to look larger by virtue of comparative emptiness. Its sole furnishings consisted of an enormous carpet with pile so heavy it had to be waded through, also a large desk of glossy plastic and two pneumatic chairs. The walls were of translucite and the ceiling emitted a frosty glow.

In the chair behind the desk reposed a swarthy, saturnine individual with lean features and a hooked nose. His dress was dapper and a jeweled ring ornamented his left index finger. His black eyes gazed speculatively as the prisoner was marched the full length of the carpet and seated in the second chair. He accepted the leather case, unlocked it, spent a long time submitting its contents to careful examination.

In the end, he said, "So it took them eight months to get you here even at supra-spatial speed. *Tut tut,* how we grow! Life won't be long enough if this goes on. They've brought you a devil of a distance, eh? And they taught you our language on the way. Did you have much difficulty in learning it?"

"None," said the prisoner.

"You have a natural aptitude for languages, I suppose?"

"I wouldn't know."

The dark man leaned forward, a sudden gleam in his eyes. A faint smell of morocco leather exuded from him. His speech was smooth.

"Your answer implies that there is only one language employed on your home world."

"Does it?" The prisoner stared blankly at his questioner.

The other sat back again, thought for a moment, then went on, "It is easy to discern that you are not in the humor to be cooperative. I don't know why. You've been treated with every courtesy and consideration, or should have been. Have you any complaint to make on that score?"

"No," said the prisoner bluntly.

"Why not?" The dark man made no attempt to conceal his surprise. "This is the point where almost invariably I am treated to an impassioned tirade about kidnapping. But you don't complain?"

"What good would it do me?"

"No good whatever," assured the other.

"See?" The prisoner settled himself more comfortably in his chair. His smile was grim.

For a while, the dark man contemplated the jewel in his ring, twisting it this way and that to catch the lights from its facets. Eventually he wrote upon the form the one word: "Fatalistic," after which he murmured, "Well, we'll see how far we can get, anyway." He picked up a paper. "Your name is Harold Harold-Myra?"

"That's correct."

"Mine's Helman, by the way. Remember it, because you may need me sometime. Now this Harold-Myra—is that your family name?"

"It is the compound of my father's and mother's names."

"Hm-m-m! I suppose that that's the usual practice on your world?"

"Yes."

"What if you marry a girl named Betty?"

"My name would still be Harold-Myra," the prisoner informed. "Hers would still be the compound of her own parents' names. But our children would be called Harold-Betty."

"I see. Now according to this report, you were removed from a satellite after two of our ships had landed on its parent planet and failed to take off again."

"I was certainly removed from a satellite. I know nothing about your ships."

"Do you know why they failed to take off?"

"How could I? I wasn't there!"

Helman frowned, chewed his lower lip, then rasped, "It is I who am supposed to be putting the questions."

"Go ahead then," said Harold Harold-Myra.

"Your unspoken thought being, 'And a lot of good it may do you,'" put in Helman shrewdly. He frowned again, added the word: "Stubborn" to the form before him. "It seems to me," he went on, "that both of us are behaving rather childishly. Mutual antagonism profits no one. Why can't we adopt the right attitude toward each other? Let's be frank, eh?" He smiled, revealing bright dentures. "I'll put my cards on the table and you put yours."

"Let's see yours."

Helman's smile vanished as quickly as it had appeared. He looked momentarily pained. "Distrustful" went down on the form. He spoke, choosing his words carefully.

"I take it that you learned a lot about the Empire during your trip here. You know that it is a mighty organization of various forms of intelligent life, most of them, as it happens, strongly resembling yours and mine, and all of them owing allegiance to the particular solar system in which you're now located. You have been told, or should have been told, that the Empire sprang from here, that throughout many, many centuries it has spread over four thousand worlds, and that it's still spreading."

"I've heard all of that," admitted the other.

"Good! Then you'll be able to understand that you're no more than a temporary victim of our further growth, but, in many ways, a lucky man."

"I fail to perceive the luck."

"You will, you will," soothed Helman. "All in good time." Mechanically, his smile had returned, and he was making an attempt at joviality. "Now I can assure you that an organization so old and so widespread as ours is not without a modicum of wisdom. Our science has given us incredible powers, including the power to blow whole worlds apart and desiccate them utterly, but that doesn't make us disregard caution. After a wealth of experience covering a multitude of planets we've learned that we're still not too great to be brought low. Indeed, for all our mighty power, we can err in manner disastrous to us all. So we step carefully."

"Sounds as if someone once put a scare into you," commented Harold Harold-Myra.

Helman hesitated, then said, "As a matter of fact, someone did. I'll tell you about it. Many decades ago we made a first landing on a new planet. The ship failed to take off. Our exploratory vessels always travel in threes, so a second vessel went down to the aid of its fellow. That didn't take off either. But the third ship, waiting in space, got a despairing message warning that the world held highly intelligent life of an elusive and parasitic type."

"And they confiscated the bodies you'd so kindly provided," suggested Harold.

"You know all about this life form?" Helman asked. His fingers slid toward an invisible spot on the surface of his desk.

"It's the first I've heard of them," replied the other. "Confiscation was logical."

"I suppose so," Helman admitted with some reluctance. He went on, his keen eyes on his listener. "They didn't get the chance to take over everyone. A few men realized their peril in the nick of time, locked themselves in one vessel away from the parasites and away from their stricken fellows. There weren't enough of them to take off, so they beamed a warning. The third ship saw the menace at once; if action wasn't taken swiftly it meant that we'd handed the keys of the cosmos to unknown powers. They destroyed both ships with one atomic bomb. Later, a task ship arrived, took the stern action we deemed necessary, and dropped a planet wrecker. The world dissolved into flashing gases. It was an exceedingly narrow squeak. The Empire, for all its wealth, ingenuity and might, could not stand if no citizen knew the real nature of his neighbor."

"A sticky situation," admitted Harold Harold-Myra. "I see now where I come in—I am a sample."

"Precisely." Helman was jovial again. "All we wish to discover is whether your world is a safe one."

"Safe for what?"

"For straightforward contact."

"Contact for what?" Harold persisted.

"Dear me! I'd have thought a person of your intelligence would see the mutual advantages to be gained from a meeting of different cultures."

"I can see the advantages all right. I can also see the consequences."

"To what do you refer?" Helman's amiability began to evaporate.

"Embodiment in your Empire."

"*Tut,*" said Helman impatiently. "Your world would join us only of its own free will. In the second place, what's wrong with being part of the Empire? In the third, how d'you know that your opinions coincide with those of your fellows? They may think differently. They may prove eager to come in."

"It looks like it seeing that you've got two ships stuck there."

"Ah, then you admit that they're forcibly detained?"

"I admit nothing. For all I know, your crews may be sitting there congratulating themselves on getting away from the Empire—while my people are taking steps to throw them out."

Helman's lean face went a shade darker. His long, slender hands clenched and unclenched while his disciplined mind exerted itself to suppress the retort which his emotion strove to voice.

Then he said, "Citizens of the Empire don't run away from it. Those who do run don't get very far."

"A denial and an affirmative," commented Harold amusedly. "All in one breath. You can't have it both ways. Either they run or they don't."

"You know perfectly well what I meant." Helman, speaking slowly and evenly, wasn't going to let this specimen bait him. "The desire to flee is as remote as the uselessness of it is complete."

"The former being due to the latter?"

"Not at all!" said Helman sharply.

"You damn your ramshackle Empire with every remark you make," Harold informed. "I reckon I know it better than you do."

"And how do you presume to know our Empire?" inquired Helman. His brows arched in sarcastic interrogation. "On what basis do you consider yourself competent to judge it?"

"On the basis of history," Harold told him. "Your people are sufficiently like us to be like us and if you can't understand that remark, well, I can't help it. On my world we're old, incredibly old, and we've learned a lot from a past which is long and lurid. We've had empires by the dozens, though none as great as yours. They all went the same way—down the sinkhole. They all vanished for the same fundamental and inevitable reasons. Empires come and empires go, but little men go on forever."

"Thanks," said Helman quickly. He wrote on the form: "Anarchistic," then, after further thought, added: "Somewhat of a crackpot."

Harold Harold-Myra smiled slowly and a little sadly. The writing was not within line of his vision, but he knew what had been written as surely as if he'd written it himself. To the people of his ancient planet it was not necessary to look at things in order to see them.

Pushing the form to one side, Helman said, "The position is that every time we make a landing we take the tremendous risk of presenting our secrets of space conquest to people of unknown abilities and doubtful ambitions. It's a chance that has to be taken. You understand that?" He noted the other's curt nod, then went on, "As matters stand at present, your world holds two of our best vessels. Your people, for all we can tell, may be able to gain a perfect understanding of them, copy them in large numbers, even improve on them. Your people may take to the cosmos, spreading ideas that don't coincide with ours. Therefore, in theory, the choice is war or peace. Actually, the choice for your people will be a simple one: cooperation or desiccation. I hate to tell you this, but your hostile manner forces me to do so."

"Uncommunicative might be a better word than hostile," suggested Harold Harold-Myra.

"Those who're not with us are against us," retorted Helman. "We're not being dictatorial; merely realistic. Upon what sort of information we can get out of you depends the action we take regarding your world. You are, you must understand, the representative of your kind. We are quite willing to accept that your people resemble you to within reasonable degree, and from our analysis of you we'll decide whether—"

"We get canonized or vaporized," put in Harold.

"If you like." Helman refused to be disturbed. He'd now acquired the sang-froid of one conscious of mastery. "It is for you to decide the fate of your planet. It's an enormous responsibility to place on one man's shoulders, but there it is, and you've got to bear it. And remember, we've other methods of extracting from you the information we require. Now, for the last time, are you willing to subject yourself to my cross-examination, or are you not?"

"The answer is," said Harold carefully, "not!"

"Very well then." Helman accepted it phlegmatically. He pressed the spot on his desk. "You compel me to turn from friendly interrogation to forcible analysis. I regret it, but it is your own choice." Two attendants entered, and he said to them, "Take him to stage three."

The escorting pair left him in this third and smaller room and he had plenty of time to look around before the three men engaged therein condescended to notice him. They were all in white, this trio, but more alert and less automatic than the white-garbed personnel of the medical examination room. Two of them were young, tall, muscular, and hard of countenance. The third was short, thickset, middle-aged and had a neatly clipped beard.

Briskly they were switching on a huge array of apparatus covering one wall of the room. The setup was a mass of plastic panels, dials, meters, buttons, switches, sockets with corded plugs, and multi-connection pieces. From inside or close behind this affair came a low, steady hum. Before it, centrally positioned, was a chair.

Satisfied that all was in readiness, the bearded man said to Harold, "O.K., be seated." He signed to his two assistants, who stepped forward as if eager to cope with a refusal.

Harold smiled, waved a negligent hand, sat himself in the chair. Working swiftly, the three attached cushioned metal bands to his ankles, calves, thighs, chest, neck and head. Flexible metal tubes ran from the bands to the middle of the apparatus while, in addition, the one about his head was connected to a thin, multicore cable.

They adjusted the controls to give certain readings on particular meters, after which the bearded one fixed glasses on his nose, picked up a paper, stared at it myopically. He spoke to the subject in the chair.

"I am about to ask you a series of questions. They will be so phrased that the answers may be given as simple negatives or affirmatives. You can please yourself whether or not you reply vocally—it is a matter of total indifference to me."

He glanced at Harold and his eyes, distorted into hugeness behind thick-lensed glasses, were cold and blank. His finger pressed a button; across the room a camera whirred into action, began to record the readings on the various meters.

Disregarding everything else, and keeping his attention wholly on the man in the chair, the bearded one said, "You were discovered on a satellite—yes or no?"

Harold grinned reminiscently, did not reply.

"Therefore your people know how to traverse space?"

No reply.

"In fact they can go further than to a mere satellite. They can reach neighboring planets—yes or no?"

No reply.

"Already they have explored neighboring planets?"

No reply.

"The truth is that they can do even better than that—they have reached other solar systems?"

He smiled once more, enigmatically.

"Your world is a world by itself?"

Silence.

"It is one of an association of worlds?"

Silence.

"It is the outpost world of another Empire?"

Silence.

"But that Empire is smaller than ours?"

No response.

"Greater than ours?"

"Heavens, I've been led to believe that yours is the greatest ever," said Harold sardonically.

"Be quiet!" One of the young ones standing at his side gave him an irate thrust on the shoulder.

"Or what?"

"Or we'll slap your ears off!"

The bearded man, who had paused expressionlessly through this brief interlude, carried on nonchalantly.

"Your kind are the highest form of life on your planet? There is no other intelligent life thereon? You knew of no other intelligent life anywhere previous to encountering emissaries of the Empire?"

The questioner was in no way disturbed by his victim's complete lack of response, and his bearing made that fact clear. Occasionally peering at the papers in his hand, but mostly favoring his listener with a cold, owlish stare, he plowed steadily on. The questions reached one hundred, two hundred, then Harold lost count of them. Some were substitutes or alternatives for others, some made cross reference with others asked before or to be asked later, some were obvious traps. All were cogent and pointed. All met stubborn silence.

They finished at length, and the bearded one put away his papers with the grumbling comment, "It's going to take us all night to rationalize this lot!" He gave Harold a reproving stare. "You might just as well have talked in the first place. It would have saved us a lot of bother and gained you a lot of credit."

"Would it?" Harold was incredulous.

"Take him away," snapped the bearded man.

One of the young men looked questioningly at the oldster, who understood the unspoken query and responded, "No, not there. Not yet, anyway. It mightn't be necessary. Let's see what we've got first." He took off his glasses, scratched his beard. "Put him in his apartment. Give him something to eat." He cackled gratingly. "Let the condemned man eat a hearty meal."

The apartment proved to be compact, well-appointed, comfortable. Three rooms: bathroom, bedroom, sitting room, the last with a filled bookcase, a large electric radiator, sunken heating panels for extra warmth, and a magniscreen television set.

Harold sprawled at ease in a soft, enveloping chair, watched a short-haired, burly man wheel in a generous meal. Hungry as he was, his attention didn't turn to the food. He kept it fixed on the burly man, who, unconscious of the persistent scrutiny, methodically put out the meat, bread, fruit, cakes and coffee.

As the other finished his task, Harold said casually, "What are those lizardlike things that wear black uniforms with silver braid?"

"Dranes." Short-hair turned around, gazed dully at the prisoner. His face was heavy, muscular, his eyes small, his forehead low. "We calls 'em Dranes."

"Yes, but what are they?"

"Oh, just another life form, I guess. From some other planet—maybe from one called Drane. I dunno. I used to know, but I've forgotten."

"You don't like them, eh?" suggested Harold.

"Who does?" He frowned with the unusual strain of thought, his small eyes shrinking still smaller. "I like to have ideas of my own, see? I don't care for any lizards reading my mind and telling the world what I'd sooner keep to myself, see? A man wants privacy—especially sometimes."

"So they're telepaths!" It was Harold's turn to frown. "Hm-m-m!" He mused anxiously. The other began to shove his empty meal trolley toward the door, and Harold went on hurriedly, "Any of them hereabouts?"

"No, it's too late in the evening. And there ain't a lot of them on this planet, thank Pete! Only a few here. They do some sort of official work, I dunno what. A couple of them got important jobs right in this dump, but they'll be home now. Good riddance, I says!" He scowled to show his intense dislike of the mysterious Dranes. "A guy can think what he likes while they're away." He pushed his trolley outside, followed it and closed the door. The lock clicked quietly, ominously.

Harold got on with his meal while he waited for angry men to come for him. Beardface and his two assistants had indicated that nothing more would be done with him before morning, but this last episode would speed things up considerably. He hastened his eating, vaguely surprised that he was getting it finished without interruption. They were less quick on the uptake than he'd anticipated. He employed the time usefully in working out a plan of campaign.

The apartment made his problem tough. He'd already given it a thorough scrutiny, noted that its decorated walls and doors were all of heavy metal. The windows were of armorglass molded in one piece over metal frames with sturdy, closely set bars. It was more than an apartment; it was a vault.

There was a very tiny lens cunningly concealed in the wall high up in one corner. It would have escaped discovery by anyone with lesser powers of observation. He'd found another mounted on the stem of the hour hand of the clock. It looked like a jewel. He knew it to be a scanner of some kind, and suspected that there were others yet to be found. Where there were scanners there would also be microphones, midget jobs hard to dig out when you don't want to make a search too obvious. Oh, yes, they'd know all about his little conversation with Short-hair—and they'd be along.

They were. The lock clicked open just as he ended his meal. Helman came in, followed by a huge fellow in uniform. The latter closed the door, leaned his broad back against it, pursed his lips in a silent whistle while he studied the room with obvious boredom. Helman went to a chair, sat in it, crossed his legs, looked intently at the prisoner. A vein pulsed in his forehead and the effect of it was menacing.

He said, "I've been on the televox to Roka. He swears that he's never mentioned the Dranes in your presence. He's positive that they've never been mentioned or described in your hearing by anyone on the ship. Nothing was said about them by the guards who brought you here. You've seen none in this building. So how d'you know about them?"

"Mystifying, isn't it?" commented Harold pleasantly.

"There is only one way in which you could have found out about the Dranes," Helman went on. "When the examiners finished with you in stage three an assistant pondered the notion of passing you along to stage four, but the idea was dropped for the time being. Stage four is operated by the Dranes."

"Really?" said Harold. He affected polite surprise.

"The Dranes were never mentioned," persisted Helman, his hard eyes fixed on his listener, "but they were thought of. You read those thoughts. You are a telepath!"

"And you're surprised by the obvious?"

"It wasn't obvious because it wasn't expected," Helman retorted. "On four thousand worlds there are only eleven truly telepathic life forms and not one of them human in shape. You're the first humanoid possessing that power we've discovered to date."

"Nevertheless," persisted Harold, "it should have been obvious. My refusal to cooperate—or my stubbornness, as you insist on calling it—had good reason. I perceived all the thoughts behind your questions. I didn't like them. I still don't like them."

"Then you'll like even less the ones I'm thinking now," snapped Helman.

"I don't," Harold agreed. "You've sent out a call for the Dranes, ordered them to come fast, and you think they'll be here pretty soon. You expect them to suck me dry. You've great confidence in their powers even though you can't conceive the full extent of mine." He stood up, smiled as Helman uncrossed his legs with a look of sudden alarm. He stared into Helman's black eyes, and his own were sparkling queerly. "I think," he said, "that this is a good time for us to go trundle our hoops—don't you?"

"Yes," Helman murmured. Clumsily he got to his feet, stood there with an air of troubled preoccupation. "Yes, sure!"

The guard at the door straightened up, his big hands held close to his sides. He looked inquiringly at the vacant Helman. When Helman failed to respond, he shifted his gaze to the prisoner, kept the gaze fixed while slowly the alertness faded from his own optics.

Then, although he'd not been spoken to, he said hoarsely, "O.K., we'll get along. We'll get a move on." He opened the door.

The three filed out, the guard leading, Helman in the rear. They moved rapidly along the corridors, passing other uniformed individuals without challenge or comment until they reached the main hall. Here, the man in myrtle green, whose little office held the lever controlling the automatic doors, sat at his desk and felt disposed to be officious.

"You can't take him out until you've signed him out, stating where he's being taken, and on whose authority," he enunciated flatly.

"On my authority," said Helman. He voiced the words in stilted tones as if he were a ventriloquist's dummy, but the officious one failed to notice it.

"Oh, all right," he growled. He shoved a large, heavy tome to one end of his desk. "Sign there. Name in column one, destination in column two, time of return in column three." He looked at the huge guard who was watching dumbly, emitted a resigned sigh, inquired, "I suppose you need a car?"

"Yes," said Helman mechanically.

The official pressed a button; a sonorous gong clanged somewhere outside the building. Then he pulled his tiny lever; the great doors swung open. The trio strolled out with deceptive casualness, waited a moment while the doors closed behind them. It was fairly dark now, but not completely so, for a powdering of stars lay across the sky, and a steady glow of light emanated from the surrounding city.

Presently a jet car swept around one end of the building, stopped before them. The three got in. Harold sat at the back between Helman and the big guard, both of whom were strangely silent, ruminative. The driver turned around, showed them a face with raised eyebrows.

"Downtown," uttered Helman curtly.

The driver nodded, faced front. The car rolled toward the gates in the distant wall, reached them, but they remained closed. Two men in green emerged from the shadow of the wall, focused light beams on the vehicle's occupants.

One said, "Inquisitor Helman, one specimen—I guess it's O.K." He waved his light beam toward the gates, which parted slowly and ponderously. Emitting a roar from its jets, the car swept through.

They dropped Harold Harold-Myra in the midsouthern section of the city, where buildings grew tallest and crowds swarmed thickest. Helman and the guard got out of the car, talked with him while the driver waited out of earshot.

"You will both go home," Harold ordered, "remembering nothing of this and behaving normally. Your forgetfulness will persist until sunrise. Until you see the sun you will be quite unable to recall anything which has occurred since you entered my room. Do you understand?"

"We understand."

Obediently they got back into the car. They were a pair of automatons. He stood on the sidewalk, watched their machine merge into the swirl of traffic and disappear. The sky was quite dark now, but the street was colorful with lights that shifted and flickered and sent eccentric shadows skittering across the pavement.

For a few minutes he stood quietly regarding the

shadows and musing. He was alone—alone against a world. It didn't bother him particularly. His situation was no different from that of his own people, who formed a solitary world on the edge of a great Empire. He'd one advantage which so far stood him in good stead: he knew his own powers. His opponents were ignorant in that respect. On the other hand, he suffered the disadvantage of being equally ignorant, for although he'd learned much about the people of the Empire, he still did not know the full extent of their powers. And theirs were likely to be worthy of respect. Alliance of varied life forms with varied talents could make a formidable combination. The battle was to be one of Homo superior versus Homo sapiens plus the Dranes plus other things of unknown abilities—with the odds much in favor of the combine.

Now that he was footloose and fancy-free he could appreciate that guard's argument that there's no point in being free unless one knows where to nurse one's freedom. The guard, though, had implied something and overlooked something else. He'd implied that there were places in which freedom could be preserved, and he'd forgotten that escapees have a flair for discovering unadvertised sanctuaries. If his own kind were half as wise and a quarter as crafty as they ought to be, thought Harold, the tracing of such a sanctuary should not be difficult.

He shrugged, turned to go, found himself confronted by a tall, thin fellow in black uniform with silver buttons and silver braid. The newcomer's features were gaunt and tough, and they changed color from gold to blood-red as the light from a nearby electric sign flickered over it.

Harold could hear the other's mind murmuring, *"Queer outlandish clothes this fellow's wearing. Evidently a recent importee—maybe a specimen on the lam,"* even as the thinker's mouth opened and he said audibly, "Let me see your identity card!"

"Why?" asked Harold, stalling for time. Curse the clothes—he'd not had time to do anything about them yet.

"It's the regulation," the other returned irritably. "You should know that every citizen must produce his card when called upon to do so by the police." His eyes narrowed, his mind spoke silently but discernibly. *"Ah, he hesitates. It must be that he doesn't possess a card. This looks bad."* He took a step forward.

Harold's eyes flamed with an odd glow. "You don't really want to see my card?" he said gently. "Do you?"

The policeman had a momentary struggle with himself before he answered, "No . . . no . . . of course not!"

"It was just your mistake?"

"Just my mistake!" admitted the other slowly. His mind was now completely muddled. A random thought, *"He's dangerous!"* fled wildly through the cerebral maze, pursued, outshouted and finally silenced by other, violently imposed thoughts saying, *"Silly mistake. Of course he's got a card. I interfere too much."*

With shocking suddenness, another thought broke in, registering clearly and succinctly despite the telepathic hubbub of a hundred surrounding minds. *"By the Blue Sun, did you catch that, Gaeta? A fragment of hypnotic projection! Something about a card. Turn the car around!"*

A cold sweat beaded on Harold's spine; he closed his mind like a trap, sent his sharp gaze along the road. There was too great a flood of cars and too many swiftly changing lights to enable him to pick out any one vehicle turning in the distance. But he'd know that car if it came charging down upon him. Its driver might be of human shape, but its passengers would be lizard-like.

Machines whirled past him four, five and sometimes six abreast. The eerie voice, which had faded, suddenly came back, waxed strong, faded away again.

It said, *"I might be wrong, of course. But I'm sure the amplitude was sufficient for hypnosis. No, it's gone now—I can't pick it up at all. All these people make too much of a jumble on the neural band."*

Another thought, a new one, answered impatiently,

"Oh, let it pass, you're not on duty now. If we don't—"
It waned to indiscernibility.

Then the policeman's mind came back, saying, *"Well, why am I standing here like a dummy? Why was I picking on this guy? It must've been for something! I didn't stop him for the fun of it—unless I'm scatty!"*

Harold said quickly and sharply, "You didn't stop me. I stopped you. Intelligence Service—remember?"

"Eh?" The cop opened his mouth, closed it, looked confused.

"Wait a moment," added Harold, a strong note of authority in his voice. He strained his perception anxiously. A river of surrounding thoughts flowed through his mind, but none with the power and clarity of the invisible Gaeta and his alert companion. Could they, too, close their minds? There wasn't any way of telling!

He gave it up, returned his attention to the cop, and said, "Intelligence Service. I showed you my official warrant. Good heavens, man, have you forgotten it already?"

"No." The man in black was disconcerted by this unexpected aggressiveness. The reference to a nonexistent Intelligence Service warrant made his confusion worse confounded. "No," he protested, "I haven't forgotten." Then, in weak effort to make some sort of a comeback: "But you started to say something, and I'm waiting to hear the rest."

Harold smiled, took him by the arm. "Look, I'm authorized to call upon you for assistance whenever needed. You know that, don't you?"

"Yes, sure, but—"

"What I want you to do is very simple. It's necessary that I change attire with a certain suspected individual and that he be kept out of circulation overnight. I'll point him out to you when he comes along. You're to tell him that you're taking him in for interrogation. You'll then conduct us somewhere where we can change clothes, preferably your own apartment if you've got one. I'll give you further instructions when we get there."

"All right," agreed the cop. He blinked as he tried to rationalize his mind. Thoughts gyrated bafflingly in his cranium. *"Not for you to reason why. Do your duty and ask no questions. Let higher-ups take the responsibility. This guy's got all the authority in the world—and he knows what he's doing."* There was something not quite right about those thoughts. They seemed to condense inward instead of expanding outward, as thoughts ought to do. But they were powerful enough, sensible enough, and he wasn't able to give birth to any contrary ideas. "All right," he repeated.

Studying the passers-by, Harold picked a man of his own height and build. Of all the apparel streaming past, this fellow's looked made to fit him to a nicety. He nudged the cop.

"That's the man."

The officer strode majestically forward, stopped the victim, said, "Police! I'm taking you in for interrogation."

"Me?" The man was dumbfounded. "I've done nothing!"

"Then what've you got to worry about?"

"Nothing," hastily assured the other. He scowled with annoyance. "I guess I'll have to go. But it's a waste of time and a nuisance."

"So you think the Empire's business is a nuisance?" inquired Harold, joining the cop.

The victim favored him with a look of intense dislike, and complained, "Go on, try making a case against me. Having it stick will be something else!"

"We'll see!"

Cutting down a side street, the trio hit a broad avenue at its farther end. No cars here; it was solely for pedestrians. The road was divided into six moving strips, three traveling in each direction, slowest on the outsides, fastest in the middle. Small groups of people, some chatting volubly, some plunged in boredom, glided swiftly along the road and shrank in the distance.

A steady rumbling sound came from beneath the rubbery surface of the road.

The three skipped onto an outer slow strip, thence to the medium fast strip, finally to the central rapid strip. The road bore them ten blocks before they left it. Harold could see it rolling on for at least ten blocks more.

The cop's apartment proved to be a modernistic, three-roomed bachelor flat on the second floor of a tall, graystone building. Here, the captive started to renew his protests, looked at Harold, found his opinions changing even as he formed them. He waxed cooperative, though in a manner more stupefied than willing. Emptying the contents of his pockets on a table, he exchanged clothes.

Now dressed in formal, less outlandish manner, Harold said to the police officer, "Take off your jacket and make yourself at home. No need to be formal on this job. We may be here some time yet. Get us a drink while I tell this fellow what's afoot." He waited until the cop had vanished into an adjoining room, then his eyes flamed at the vaguely disgruntled victim. "Sleep!" he commanded, "sleep!"

The man stirred in futile opposition, closed his eyes, let his head hang forward. His whole body slumped wearily in its chair. Raking rapidly through the personal possessions on the table, Harold found the fellow's identity card. Although he'd never seen such a document before, he wasted no time examining it, neither did he keep it. With quick dexterity, he dug the cop's wallet out of his discarded jacket, extracted the police identity card, substituted the other, replaced the wallet. The police card he put in his own pocket. Way back on the home planet it was an ancient adage that double moves are more confusing that single ones.

He was barely in time. The cop returned with a bottle of pink, oily liquid, sat down, looked dully at the sleeper, said, "Huh?" and transferred his lackluster stare to Harold. Then he blinked several times, each time more slowly than before, as if striving to keep his eyes open against an irresistible urge to keep them shut. He failed. Imitating his captive, he hung his head—and began to snore.

"Sleep," murmured Harold, "sleep on toward the dawn. Then you may awake. But not before!"

Leaning forward, he lifted a small, highly polished instrument from its leather case beneath the policeman's armpit. A weapon of some sort. Pointing it toward the window, he pressed the stud set in its butt. There was a sharp, hard crack, but no recoil. A perfect disk of glassite vanished from the center of the window. Cold air came in through the gap, bringing with it a smell like that of roasted resin. Giving the weapon a grim look, he shoved it back into its holster, dusted his fingers distastefully.

"So," he murmured, "discipline may be enforced by death. Verily, I'm back in the dark ages!"

Ignoring the sleepers, he made swift search of the room. The more he knew about the Empire's ordinary, everyday citizens the better it'd be for him. Knowledge—the right knowledge—was a powerful arm in its own right. His people understood the value of intangibles.

Finished, he was about to leave when a tiny bell whirred somewhere within the wall. He traced the sound as emanating from behind a panel, debated the matter before investigating further. Potential danger lurked here; but nothing ventured, nothing gained. He slid the panel aside, found himself facing a tiny loudspeaker, a microphone, a lens, and a small circular screen.

The screen was alive and vivid with color, and a stern, heavily jowled face posed in sharp focus within its frame. The caller raked the room with one quick, comprehending glance, switched his attention to Harold.

"So the missing Guarda *is* indisposed," he growled. "He slumbers before a bottle. He awaits three charges: absent from duty, improperly dressed, and drunk! We'll deal with this at once." He thinned his lips. "What is your name and the number of your identity card, citizen?"

"Find out," suggested Harold. He slammed the panel before the tiny scanner could make a permanent record of his features—if he had not done so already.

That was an unfortunate episode: it cut down his self-donated hours of grace to a few minutes. They'd be on their way already, and he'd have to move out fast.

He was out of the apartment and the building in a trice. A passing car stopped of its own accord and took him downtown. Its driver was blissfully unaware of the helplessness of his own helpfulness.

Here, the city seemed brighter than ever mostly because the deeper darkness of the sky enhanced the multitude of lights. A few stars still shone, and a string of colored balls drifted high against the backdrop, where some unidentifiable vessel drove into space.

He merged with the crowds still thronging the sidewalks. There was safety in numbers. It's hard to pick one guy out of the mob, especially when he's dressed like the mob, behaves like the mob. For some time he moved around with the human swarm though his movements were not as aimless. He was listening to thoughts, seeking either of two thought-forms, one no more than slightly helpful, the other important. He found the former, not the latter.

A fat man wandered past him and broadcast the pleasurable notion of food shared in large company. He turned and followed the fat man, tracking him along three streets and another moving avenue. The fat man entered a huge restaurant with Harold at his heels. They took an unoccupied table together.

Plenty of active thoughts here. In fact the trouble was that there were far too many. They made a constant roar right across the telepathic band; it was difficult to separate one from another, still more difficult to determine who was emanating which. Nevertheless, he persisted in his effort to sort out individual broadcasts, taking his food slowly to justify remaining there as long as possible. Long after the fat man had left he was still seated there, listening, listening. There were many thoughts he found interesting, some revealing, some making near approach to the notions he sought, but none quite on the mark, not one.

In the end, he gave it up, took his check from the waiter. It was readily apparent what the waiter had on his mind, namely, this crazy stuff called money. Roka had told him a lot about money, even showing him samples of the junk. He remembered that Roka had been dumbfounded by his ignorance concerning a common medium of exchange. With amusing superiority, the worthy lieutenant had assumed that Harold's people had yet to discover what they'd long since forgotten.

There had been some of this money—he didn't know just how much—in the pockets of this suit, but he'd left it all with the suit's hapless donor. There wasn't any point in snatching someone else's tokens. Besides, having managed without it all his life, he wasn't going to become a slave to it now.

He paid the waiter with nothing, putting it into the fellow's hand with the lordly air of one dispensing a sizable sum. The waiter gratefully accepted nothing, put nothing into his pocket, initialed the check, bowed obsequiously. Then he rubbed his forehead, looked vague and confused, but said nothing. Harold went out.

It was on the sidewalk that Harold made the contact he was seeking, though not in the manner he'd expected. He was looking for a mutinous thinker who might lead him to the underworld of mutinous thinkers. Instead, he found a friend.

The fellow was twenty yards away and walking toward him with a peculiarly loose-jointed gait. He was humanoid in all respects but one—his skin was reptilian. It was a smooth but scaly skin of silvery gray in which shone an underlying sheen of metallic blue. The pupils of his eyes were a very light gray, alert, intelligent.

Those eyes looked straight into Harold's as they came abreast, a flood of amity poured invisibly from them as he smiled and said in an undertone, "Come with me." He walked straight on, without a pause. He didn't look back to see whether Harold followed.

Harold didn't wait to consider the matter. This was a time for quick decision. Swiveling on one heel, he trailed along behind the speaker. And as he trod warily after the other, his mind was active with thoughts, and his thinking was done within a mental shell through which nothing could probe.

Evidently the scaly man was an outsider, a product of some other world. His queer skin was proof of that. There were other factors, too. He hadn't read Harold's mind—Harold was positive of that—yet in some strange, inexplicable way he'd recognized a kinship between them and had acknowledged it without hesitation. Moreover, he was strolling along with his mind wide open, but Harold was totally unable to analyze his thoughts. Those thoughts, in all probability, were straightforward and logical enough, but they oscillated in and out of the extreme edge of the neural band. Picking them up was like trying to get frequency modulation on a receiver designed for amplitude modulation. Those thought-forms might be normal, but their wave-forms were weird.

Still not looking back, the subject of his speculations turned into an apartment building took a levitator to the tenth floor. Here he unlocked a door, gazed around for the first time, smiled again at his follower, motioned him inside.

Harold went in. The other closed the door after him. There were two similar entities in the apartment. One sat on the edge of a table idly swinging his legs; the other lounged on a settee and was absorbed in a magazine.

"Oh, Melor, there's a—" began the one on the settee. He glanced up, saw the visitor, grinned in friendly fashion. Then his expression changed to one of surprise, and he said, "By the everlasting light, its *you!* Where did you find him, Melor?"

This one's mind was fully as baffling and Harold

found himself unable to get anything out of it. The same applied to the being perched upon the table: his thoughts wavered in and out of the borderline of detection.

"I found him on the street," replied the one called Melor, "and I invited him along. He has a most attractive smell." He sat down, invited Harold to do likewise. Looking at the one on the settee, he went on, "What did you mean by, 'Oh, it's *you*'? D'you know him?"

"No." The other switched on a teleset at his side. "They broadcast a call for him a few minutes ago. He's wanted—badly." He moved a second switch. "Here's the recording. Watch!"

The set's big screen lit up. A sour-faced man in flamboyant uniform appeared on the screen, spoke with official ponderousness.

"All citizens are warned to keep watch for and, if possible, apprehend an escaped specimen recently brought from the Frontier. Name: Harold Harold-Myra. Description——" He went on at great length, giving everything in minute detail, then finished, "His attire is noticeably unconventional and he has not yet been provided with an identity card. Citizens should bear in mind that he may possess attributes not familiar to Empire races and that he is wanted alive. In case of necessity, call Police Emergency on Stud Four. Here is his likeness."

The screen went blank, lit up again, showed Harold's features in full color. He recognized part of his former prison in the background. Those midget scanners had done their job!

"Tush!" scoffed the being on the settee. He switched off, turned to Harold. "Well, you're in good hands. That's something. We wouldn't give anyone in authority a magni-belt to hold up his pants. My name's Tor. The one industriously doing nothing on the table is Vern. The one who brought you here is Melor. Our other names don't matter much. As maybe you've guessed, we aren't of this lousy, over-organized world. We're from

Linga, a planet which is a devil of a long way off, too far away for my liking. The more I think of it, the farther it seems."

"It's no farther than my own world," said Harold. He leaned forward. "Look, can you read my mind?"

"Not a possibility of it," Tor answered. "You're like the local breed in that respect—you think pulsatingly and much too far down for us. Can you read ours?"

"I can't. You wobble in and out of my limit." He frowned. "What beats me is what made Melor pick me out if he can't read my thoughts."

"I smelled you," Melor put in.

"Huh?"

"That's not strictly correct, but it's the best way I can explain it. Most of the Empire's peoples have some peculiar faculty they call a sense of smell. We don't possess it. They talk about bad odors and sweet ones, which is gibberish to us. But we can sense affinities and oppositions, we can sort of 'smell' friends and enemies, instantly, infallibly. Don't ask me how we do it, for how can I tell you?"

"I see the difficulty," agreed Harold.

"On our world," Melor continued, "most life forms have this sense which seems peculiar to Linga. We've no tame animals and no wild ones—they're tame if you like them, wild if you don't. None would be driven by curiosity to make close approach to a hunter, none would flee timidly from someone anxious to pet them. Instinctively they know which is friend and which is enemy. They know it as certainly as you know black from white or night from day."

Tor put in, "Which is an additional reason why we're not very popular. Skin trouble's the basic one, d'you understand? So among an appalling mixture of hostile smells we welcome an occasional friendly one—as yours is."

"Do the Dranes smell friendly?"

Tor pulled a face. "They stink!" he said with much emphasis. Gazing ruminatively at the blank television screen, he went on, "Well, the powers-that-be are after your earthly body, and I'm afraid we can't offer you much encouragement though we're willing to give you all the help we can. Something like twenty specimens have escaped in the last ten or twelve years. All of them broke loose by suddenly displaying long-concealed and quite unexpected powers which caught their captors by surprise. But none stayed free. One by one they were roped in, some sooner than others. You can't use your strength without revealing what you've got, and once the authorities know what you've got they take steps to cope with it. Sooner or later the fugitive makes a try for his home planet—and finds the trappers waiting."

"They're going to have a long, long wait," Harold told him, "for I'm not contemplating a return to my home world. Leastways, not yet. What's the use of coming all the way here just to go all the way back again?"

"We took it that you hadn't much choice about the coming," said Tor.

"Nor had I. Circumstances made it necessary for me to come. Circumstances make it necessary for me to stay awhile."

The three were mildly surprised by this phlegmatic attitude.

"I'm more of a nuisance here," Harold pointed out. "This is the Empire's key planet. Whoever bosses this world bosses the Empire. It may be one man, it may be a small clique, but on this planet is the mind or minds which make the Empire tick. I'd like to retune that tick."

"You've *some* hopes!" opined Tor gloomily. "The Big Noise is Burkinshaw Three, the Lord of Terror. You've got to have forty-two permits, signed and countersigned, plus an armed escort, to get within sight of him. He's exclusive!"

"That's tough, but the situation is tougher." He relaxed in his chair and thought awhile. "There's a Lord of Terror on every planet, isn't there. It's a cockeyed title for the bosses of imperial freedom!"

"Terror means greatness, superior wisdom, intellect of godlike quality," explained Tor.

"Oh, does it? My mistake! We use the same-

sounding word on my planet, and there it means fear."
Suddenly a strange expression came into his face. He
ejaculated, "Burkinshaw! Burkinshaw! Ye gods!"

"What's the matter?" Melor inquired.

"Nothing much. It's only that evidence is piling up on
top of a theory. It should help. Yes, it ought to help a
lot." Getting up, he paced the room restlessly. "Is there
an underground independence movement on Linga?" he
asked.

Tor grinned with relish, and said, "I'd not be far
from the truth if I guessed that there's such a movement
on every planet excepting this one. Imperially speaking,
we're all in the same adolescent condition: not quite
ripe for self-government. We'll all get independence tomorrow, but not today." He heaved a resigned sigh.
"Linga's been getting it tomorrow for the last seven
hundred years."

"As I thought," Harold commented. "The same old
setup. The same old stresses, strains and inherent weak-
nesses. The same blindness and procrastination. We've
known it all before—it's an old, old tale to us."

"What is?" persisted the curious Melor.

"History," Harold told him.

Melor looked puzzled.

"There's an ancient saying," Harold continued, "to
the effect that the bigger they come the harder they fall.
The more ponderous and top-heavy a structure the ri-
per it is for toppling." He rubbed his chin, studied his
listeners with a peculiarly elfish gaze. "So the problem
is whether we can shove hard enough to make it teeter."

"Never!" exclaimed Tor. "Nor a thousand either. It's
been tried times without number. The triers got buried—whenever there was enough to bury."

"Which means that they tried in the wrong
way, and/or at the wrong time. It's up to us to push in
the right way at the right time."

"How can you tell the right time?"

"I can't. I can choose only the time which, when everything's taken into account, seems the most favor-
able—and then hope that it's the right time. It'll be just
my hard luck if I'm wrong." He reflected a moment,

then went on, "The best time ought to be nine days hence. If you can help me to keep under cover that long, I'll promise not to involve you in anything risky in the meanwhile. Can you keep me nine days?"

"Sure we can." Tor regarded him levelly. "But what do we get out of it other than the prospect of premature burial?"

"Nothing except the satisfaction of having had a finger in the pie."

"Is that all?" Tor asked.

"That's all," declared Harold positively. "You Lingans must fight your way as we're fighting ours. If ever my people help you, it will be for the sake of mutual benefit or our own satisfaction. It won't be by way of reward."

"That suits me." Tor said flatly. "I like good, plain talk, with no frills. We're tired of worthless promises. Count us with you to the base of the scaffold, but not up the steps—we'd like to indulge second thoughts before we mount those!"

"Thanks a lot," acknowledged Harold gratefully. "Now here are some ideas I've got which—"

He stopped as the television set emitted a loud chime. Tor reached over, switched on the apparatus. Its screen came to life, depicting the same uniformed sourpuss as before.

The official rumbled, "Urgent call! Citizens are warned that the escaped specimen Harold Harold-Myra, for whom a call was broadcast half an hour ago, is now known to be a telepath, a mesman, a seer and a recorder. It is possible that he may also possess telekinetic powers of unknown extent. Facts recently brought to light suggest that he's a decoy and therefore doubly dangerous. Study his likeness; he must be brought in as soon as possible."

The screen blanked, lit up again, showed Harold's face for a full minute. Then the telecast cut off.

"What does he mean, a seer and a recorder?" inquired Harold, mystified.

"A seer is one who makes moves in anticipation of

two, three, four or more of his opponent's moves. A chessmaster is a seer."

"Heavens, do they play chess here, too?"

"Chess is popular all over the Empire. What of it?"

"Never mind," said Harold. "We'll stick the fact on top of the pile. Go on."

"A recorder," explained Tor, "is someone with a photographic memory. He doesn't write anything down. He remembers it all, accurately, in full detail."

"Humph! I don't think there's anything extraordinary about that."

"We Lingans can't do it. In fact, we know of only four life forms that can." Respect crept into Tor's snake-skinned face. "And do you really have telekinetic power as well?"

"No. It's a false conclusion to which they've jumped. They appear to think I'm a poltergeist or something— goodness only knows why." He mused a moment. "Maybe it's because of that analysis in stage three. I can control my heartbeats, my blood pressure, my thoughts, and I made their analytical apparatus go haywire. They can get out of it nothing but contradictory nonsense. Evidently they suspect that I sabotaged its innards by some form of remote control."

"Oh!" Tor was openly disappointed.

Before any of them could venture further remark, the television set called for attention and Sourpuss appeared for the third time.

"All nonnative citizens will observe a curfew tonight from midnight until one hour after dawn," he droned. "During this period the police may call at certain apartments. Any nonnative citizens found absent from their apartments and unable to give satisfactory reason therefor, or any nonnative citizens who obstruct the police in the execution of their duty, will be dealt with in accordance with pan-planetary law." He paused, stared out of the screen. He looked bellicose. "The fugitive, Harold Harold-Myra, is in possession of identity card number AMB 307-40781, entered in the name of Robertus Bron. That is all."

"Bron," echoed Harold. "Bron . . . Burkinshaw . . . chessmasters. Dear me!"

The three Lingans were apprehensive, and Melor ventured, "You can see their moves. One: they're satisfied that by now you've found a hiding place. Two: they know you're hiding with outsiders and not with natives. Since there aren't more than sixty thousand outsiders on this planet, sharing one third that number of apartments, it's not impossible to pounce on the lot at one go." His forehead wrinkled with thought. "It's no use you fleeing elsewhere because this curfew is planet-wide. It covers everywhere. I reckon your easiest way out would be to hypnotize a native and stay in his apartment overnight. If, as they say, you're a mesman, it should be easy."

"Except for one thing."

"What is that?"

"It's what they expect me to do. In fact, it's what they're trying to make me do."

"Even so," persisted Melor, "what's to stop you?"

"The routine. A master race always has a routine. It's drilled into them; it's part of their education. Having been warned that a badly wanted specimen is on the loose and about to bolt, they will take the officially prescribed precautions." He grinned at them reassuringly, but they didn't derive much comfort from it. "I can only guess what that routine will be, but I reckon it'll include some method of advertising my presence in a native's apartment even though its occupant is helpless. Scanners coupled to the Police Emergency system and switched in by the opening of a door, or something like that. When I take risks, I pick my own. It's asking for trouble to let the opposition pick 'em for you."

"Maybe you're right," agreed Melor. "We do know that local people have certain facilities denied to outsiders."

"Now if a couple of cops come along to give this place a look over, and I take control of their minds and send them away convinced that I'm just another Lingan, the powers-that-be will have been fooled, won't they?"

"I hadn't thought of that," put in Tor. He was disgusted with his own lack of imagination. "It was so obvious that I didn't see it."

"So obvious," Harold pointed out, "that the authorities know that's just what would occur should they find me here."

"Then why the curfew and the search?"

"Bluff!" defined Harold. "They hope to make me move or, failing that, put scare into those harboring me. They're banging on the walls hoping the rat will run. I won't run! With your kind permission, I'll sit tight."

"You're welcome to stay," Tor assured. "We can find you a spare bed, and if you—"

"Thanks!" Harold interrupted, "but I don't need one. I don't sleep."

"You don't!" They were dumbfounded.

"Never slept a wink in my life. It's a habit we've abandoned." He walked around the room, studying its fittings. "Impatience is the curse of plotters. Nothing bores me more than waiting for time to ripen. I've simply got to wait nine days. Are you really willing to put up with me that long or, if not, can you find me some place else?"

"Stay here," said Tor. "You repay us with your company. We can talk to each other of homes beyond reach. We can talk about the freedom of subject peoples and of things it is not wise to discuss outside. It is sweet to dream dreams. It is good to play with notions of what one might do if only one could find a way to do it."

"You're a little pessimistic," gibed Harold.

On the fourth day his idleness became too much to bear. He went out, strolled along the streets of the city. Two more irate broadcasts had advertised his extended liberty, but the last of them had been three days before. Since then, silence.

His trust reposed in the inability of the public to remember that morning's broadcast, let alone the details of the twentieth one before it, and his confidence was not misplaced. People wandered past him with vacant expressions and preoccupied minds. In most cases, their eyes looked at him without seeing him. In a few cases, his features registered, but no significance registered with them. The farther he walked, the safer he felt.

Downtown he found a smart, modernistic store well stocked with scientific instruments. This simplified matters. He'd been trying to solve the problem of how to get Melor to shop for him without using this silly stuff called money. The Lingan's respect for it equaled his own contempt for it, therefore he couldn't ask his hosts to spend their own on his behalf. Instinct rather than deliberate reasoning had made him recognize this simple ethic of a moneyed world.

Boldly entering the store, he examined its stock. Here were some things he wanted, others capable of ready adaptation to what he desired. Different cultures evolved differing modes of manufacture. Conventional jobs would need alteration to become conventional according to his other-worldly notions, but the simplest tools would enable him to deal with these. Making a list of his requirements, he prowled around until it was complete, handed it to a salesman.

The latter, a shrewd individual, looked the list over, said sharply, "This stuff is for microwave radiation."

"I know it," said Harold blandly.

"It is not for sale to the public except on production of an official permit," he went on. Then, stiffly, "Have you such a permit? May I see your identity card?"

Harold showed him the card.

"Ah!" mouthed the salesman, his manner changing, "the police!" His laugh was apologetic and forced. "Well, you didn't catch me disregarding regulations!"

"I'm not trying to catch you. I've come to get some necessary equipment. Pack it up and let me have it. I'm on urgent business and in a hurry."

"Certainly, certainly." Bustling to and fro, anxious to placate, the salesman collected the equipment, packaged it. Then he made careful note of the name and number on Harold's identity card. "We charge this to the Police Department, as usual?"

"No," Harold contradicted. "Charge it to the Analysis Division of the Immigration Department, Stage Three."

He had a satisfied smile as he went out. When the Bearded One got the bill he could stick it in his analyzer and watch the meters whirl. Which reminded him now that he came to think of it—there didn't seem to be an overmuch sense of humor on this world.

Safely back in the Lingans' apartment, he unloaded his loot, got started on it. His hosts were out. He kept the door locked, concentrated on his task and progressed with speed and dexterity which would have astounded his former captors. When he'd been at work an hour the set in the corner chimed urgently, but he ignored it and was still engrossed in his task when the Lingans came in some time later.

Carefully closing and fastening the door, Melor said, "Well, they've got worried about you again."

"Have they?"

"Didn't you catch the recent broadcast?"

"I was too busy," explained Harold.

"They've discovered that you've got a police card and not the card they first announced. They broadcast a correction and a further warning. The announcer was somewhat annoyed."

"So'd I be," said Harold, "if I were Sourpuss."

Melor's eyes, which had been staring absently at the litter of stuff on which Harold was working, suddenly realized what they saw.

"Hey, where did you get all that?" he asked, with alarm. "Have you been outdoors?"

"Sure! I had to get this junk somehow or other and I couldn't think of how to get it any other way. I couldn't wish it into existence. We've not progressed quite *that* far—yet!" He glanced at the uneasy Lingan. "Take it easy. There's nothing to worry about. I was out for less than a couple of hours, and I might have been born and bred in this city for all the notice anyone took of me."

"Maybe so." Melor flopped into a chair, massaged his scaly chin. Ripples of underlying blueness ran through it as his skin moved. "But if you do it too often you'll meet a cop, or a spaceman, or a Drane. Cops are too inquisitive. Spacemen recognize outsiders and rarely forget a face. Dranes know too much and can divine too much. It's risky." He looked again at the litter of apparatus. "What're you making, anyway?"

"A simple contactor."

"What's that for?"

"Making contact with someone else." Harold wangled an electric iron into the heart of the mess, deftly inserted a condenser smaller than a button, linked it into the circuit with two dabs of solder. "If two people, uncertain of each other's whereabouts, are seeking each other within the limits of the same horizon, they can trace each other with contactors."

"I see," said Melor, not seeing at all. "Why not make mental contact?"

"Because the telepathic range is far too short. Thoughts fade swiftly within distance, especially when blanketed by obstacles."

The three were still watching him curiously when he finished the job shortly before midnight. Now he had a small transmitter-receiver fitted with three antennae, one being a short, vertical rod, the second a tiny silver loop rotatable through its horizontal plane, the third a short silver tube, slightly curved, also rotatable horizontally.

"Now to tune it up," he told them.

Connecting the setup to the power supply, he let it warm through before he started tuning it with a glassite screwdriver. It was a tricky job. The oscillatory circuit had to be steered a delicate margin past peak so that it would swing dead on to resonance when hand-capacity was removed. And, strangely enough, hand-capacity was greater on this planet. The correct margin had to be discovered by trial and error, by delicate adjustment and readjustment.

He manipulated the tuning with fingers as firm and sensitive as any surgeon's. His jawbone ached. Tuning the set onward, he took his hand away. The circuit swung short. He tried again and again. Eventually he stood away from the apparatus, rubbed his aching jaw, in which dull pain was throbbing, switched off the power.

"That'll do," he remarked.

"Aren't you going to use it now?" Melor inquired.

"I can't. Nobody's looking for me yet."

"Oh!" The trio were more puzzled than ever. They gave it up and went to bed.

Putting away his apparatus, Harold dug a book on ancient history out of the Lingans' small but excellent library, setting himself down to the fourth successive night of self-education. There was dynamite in these books for those who had eyes to see. No Lord of Terror had seen them in the light in which he saw them!

The ninth day dawned in manner no different from any other. The sun came up and the Empire's boss city stirred to officially conducted life.

When Melor appeared, Harold said to him, "I believe this is your free day. Have you any plans for it?"

"Nothing important. Why?"

"The fun starts today, or ought to start if my calculations are correct. I could do with your help."

"In what way?"

"You're going to be mighty useful if I come up against someone who can control his thoughts or shield them entirely. Hatred or animosity aren't thoughts— they're emotions of which antagonistic thoughts are born. You Lingans respond to such emotions. You can go on reading the heart long after the mind is closed to me."

"I get the point but not the purpose," confessed Melor.

"Look," said Harold patiently, "when I say the fun starts I don't mean that there's going to be wholesale violence. We've found better ways. It's possible, for instance, to talk oneself into anything or out of anything provided one says the right things to the right person at the right time. The waving blade hasn't half the potency of the wagging tongue. And the tongue isn't messy." He smiled grimly. "My people have had more than their fill of messy methods. We don't bother with them these days. We're grown up."

"So?" prompted Melor.

"So I need you to tell me how I'm doing if, mayhap, I'm working on someone with a closed mind."

"That's easy. I could tell you when hatred, fear or friendliness intensifies or lessens by one degree."

"Just what I need," enthused Harold. "My form of life has its shortcomings as well as its talents, and we don't let ourselves forget it. Last time some of us forgot it, the forgetters thought themselves a collective form of God. The delusion bred death!"

His tongue gently explored a back tooth as his gaze went to the transmitter-receiver waiting at one side of the room.

Nothing happened until midday. The two kept company through the morning, the fugitive expectant and alert, his host uneasy and silently speculative. At noon the television set chimed and Melor switched it on.

Helman came on the screen. He stared straight at the watching pair in manner suggesting that he saw them as clearly as they saw him. His dark features were surly.

"This is a personal broadcast for the benefit of the specimen known as Harold Harold-Myra," Helman enunciated, "or to any citizen illegally maintaining contact with him. Be it known, Harold Harold-Myra, that a summary of all the available data on your world type has been laid before the Council of Action, which Council, after due consideration thereof, has decided that it is to the essential interest of the Empire that your life form be exterminated with the minimum of delay. By midday tomorrow an order will be sent to appropriate war vessels requiring them to vaporize your native planet—unless, in the meantime, you have surrendered yourself and provided new evidence which may persuade the Council of Action to reconsider its decision."

Helman stopped, licked his lips. His air was that of one still nursing a severe reprimand.

He went on, "This notification will be rebroadcast in one hour's time. Watchers in touch with the fugitive are advised to bring it to his attention as this will be the last warning." His surliness increased as he finished, "In the event of his prompt surrender, the Council of Action will extend gracious pardon to those who have been harboring this specimen."

The screen blanked.

"Mate in one move," said Melor glumly. "We told you that it was a waste of time to sit and plot. They get 'em all, one way or another."

"It's check—and your move."

"All right then—what's your move?"

"I don't know yet. We've still got to wait. If you sit by the chimney long enough, Santa Claus comes down."

"In the name of the Blue Sun, who is Santa Claus?" asked Melor peevishly.

"The man with a million lollies."

"Lollies?"

"Things you lick."

"Oh, cosmos!" said Melor. "What madman wants to own a million things to lick? Is this anything to do with your sermon about wagging tongues? If so, *we're* licked!"

"Forget it," Harold advised. "I talk in riddles to pass the time."

A pain suddenly pulsed in his jawbone. It brought an exclamation from him which stirred the nervous Melor. Putting two fingers into his mouth, Harold unscrewed the crown of a back molar, took it out, put it on the table. A tiny splinter of crystal glittered within the base of the crown. The crystal was fluorescent. Melor gaped at it fascinatedly.

Swiftly powering the transmitter-receiver, Harold let it warm up. A faint, high-pitched whistle crept into its little phone. He swung the loop slowly while the whistle strengthened, then weakened, finally faded out. Slightly offsetting the loop to bring back the signal, he pressed a stud. The note grew stronger.

"That side," he murmured, indicating the face of the loop nearest to the watching Melor.

Returning the loop to fade-out position, he switched

in the transmitter, swung its curved tube antenna until it paralleled the direction faced by the receiver's loop. Again he offset the loop, and the signal returned. He waited expectantly. In a little while, the signal broke into three short pips, then resumed its steady note. He flipped his transmitter switch three times.

For half an hour the two sat and waited while the whistle maintained itself and gave triple pips at regular intervals. Then, suddenly, it soared up in power and gave one pip.

Carefully, Harold repeated all the rigmarole with the antenna, this time obtaining a different direction. Three pips came as his reward, and again he switched his transmitter in acknowledgment. Another long wait. Then, slowly, weakly and distantly, a voice crept into his mind.

"A blue car. A blue car."

Going to the window, he looked down into the street. From his height of ten floors he had a clear view extending several blocks in both directions. He found a score of automobiles on the street, half a dozen of them blue.

"Stop, step out, get in again," he thought. He repeated the mental impulse, driving it outward with maximum intensity.

A car stopped, a human shape got out, looked around, stepped back into the vehicle. It was a blue car.

Harold crossed the room, disconnected the contactor, and returned to the window. Looking downward, he thought powerfully.

"I believe I've got you. Drive on slowly . . . slowly . . . here you are . . . stop there! The building immediately on your right. Ten floors up."

He continued to keep watch as the car pulled in by the opposite sidewalk. Two men emerged from it, crossed the road with casual nonchalance, disappeared beneath him. No other cars halted, nobody followed the men into the building.

A voice reached him strongly, *"Are we dragging any-thing?"*

"Not that I can see."

"Good!"

Melor said plaintively, "I know that you're communicating with someone. Santa Claus, I presume? How you can read each other's toothache is a mystery to me."

"Our throbs are no worse than your wobbles."

"You bounce around," said Melor, "and, according to you, we dither. Some day we'll come across some other life form which spins around in circles, like a mental dervish. Or even an entity capable of logical reasoning without thought at all; a sort of Bohr-thinker who skips straight from premise to conclusion without covering the intervening distance." His eyes found the crystal still on the table, noted that it had ceased to glow. "Better plant your key-frequency back in your face before somebody sets it in a ring."

Harold smiled, took up the crystal, screwed it back into place. Opening the door, he looked out just as the pair from the car arrived on the landing. He beckoned them in, locked the door behind them, introduced them to the Lingan.

"This is Melor, a friend from Linga. Melor, meet George Richard-Eve and Burt Ken-Claudette."

Melor looked askance at the newcomers' neat space uniforms and the silver comet insignia glittering on their epaulettes. He commented, "Well, they smell as good as they look bad. You'll produce a pally Drane next!"

"Not likely!" Harold assured.

Burt sat down, said to Harold, "You know the locals by now. Are they crafty enough to have drawn a bead on that transmission and if so, how long d'you think they'll give us? If time's short, we can beat it in the car and delay matters a little."

"They know how I got the stuff, where I got it, and its purpose, and they're not too dopey to listen out," Harold replied. "As I guess, I give them half an hour."

"That'll do."

Melor put in, "Talk mentally if it suits you better. I don't mind."

"You're in this," Harold told him, "so we'll talk vocally. You're entitled to listen." He turned to Burt. "What's cooking?"

"There's fun and games on four out of the five. The fifth proved useless for our purpose: it held nothing but a few time-serving bureaucrats on high pay. But four should do, I reckon."

"Go on."

"All the appointed ones have gone beyond and the first of them ought to have reached their destinations by now. It's six days to the nearest system, so they've a good margin." He smoothed his dark hair, looked reminiscent. *"Nemo* is due to pop off any moment now. That was a tough job! We took forty people off it, but had to scour the place from end to end to find the last pair of them. We got 'em, though. They've been dumped in safety."

"Good!"

"This has been an education," Burt went on. "Better than going to the zoo. There's an underground message system on number three, for instance, which has to be seen to be believed. By 'underground' they mean ten thousand feet up! How d'you think they do it?"

"I've no idea," said Harold.

"With birds! Among the minority life forms there is one which is beaked and feathered. They talk with birds. They chirrup and squawk at them, and every bird understands what's said."

"Orniths," informed Melor. "They came originally from Gronat, the Empire's eight hundredth conquest. They're scattered around and there are a few of them here, maybe a dozen or so. When you've had time to tour the Empire you'll find it contains even stranger forms. And the humanoids don't even dislike them all."

"It would seem that the humanoids don't even like each other much," Burt commented. "To most of them, a brother from a neighboring planet is a foreigner."

"Still in the schoolkid stage," said Harold. "Rah-rah and all that."

Burt nodded and continued, "As you know, we've had to move too fast in too little time to put over anything really drastic, but what's been done ought to be enough to show what could be done—which is all that matters." A faraway look came into his eyes. "When we triumphantly cast our bread upon the waters we little thought it'd come back—all wet."

"So you've found confirmation of that?"

"Plenty," Burt replied. "Have you?"

"Any amount of it." Harold went to the bookshelf, selected a heavy tome titled *The Imperial Elect*. He skimmed through its pages, found an illustration, showed it to Burt. "Look!"

"*Phew!*" said Burt.

"The Budding Cross," breathed George, looking over Burt's shoulder. "And the Circle of Infinity!"

"That shelf is crammed with stuff," Harold told them as he replaced the book, "I've been going through it like a man in a strange dream." He came back, sat down. "Anything more to report?"

"Not much. Jon has stayed on number three. He had a stroke of luck and got at the Lord, a fat personage named Amilcare. Temporarily, His Eminence doesn't know which shoe is on which foot."

Harold opened his mouth to comment, closed it without saying anything. His mental perception perked up, listened intently. Burt and George listened likewise. Melor began to fidget. For the first time, Harold noticed that a fringe of fine hairs lay along the rims of the Lingan's ears, and that these hairs were now fully extended and quivering.

"There's a stink of hostility," complained Melor uneasily. In his lithe, loose-jointed gait, he went to the window.

A hubbub lay across the ether, a confused mixture of thoughts from which it was impossible to extract more than odd, disjointed phrases.

"Line 'em across that end . . . rumble, rumble . . . yes, take the ground floor . . . rumble, buzz, buzz . . . work upward . . . rumble . . . ten of you . . . look out for . . . rumble . . . they may be . . ."

"I expect visitors," remarked George, easily. He joined Melor at the window.

The others followed, and the four looked down at the street. It was a hive of activity. A dozen cars were drawn across one end, blocking it completely. Another dozen jockeyed for position to block the opposite end. Cars plugged the three side streets in between. Something invisible droned steadily overhead; it sounded like a squadron of helicopters. More than two hundred black-uniformed men were scattered along the sidewalk in little groups.

"Their bearings must have been rough." Burt pulled a face at the cohort below. "It got them this section of the street but not the building. I'd be ashamed of such a sloppy job."

"It's good enough," Harold answered. He filtered the telepathic surge once again. It was entirely human, involuntary and nonreceptive. "We could go down and save them some bother, but I'm a bit curious about those butterfly minds down there. Surely they'd have brought something potent along with them."

"Test it," suggested Burt.

Dropping their mental shields, the three let their thoughts flow forth bearing a perfect picture of their location. Instantly the hubbub was overwhelmed by an alien mind which imposed itself upon the ether. It was clear, sharp, penetrating, and of remarkable strength.

"They're in that building there! Ten floors high! Three of them and a Lingan. They contemplate no resistance!"

"A Drane!" said Harold.

It was impossible to locate the creature amid the mass of men and automobiles beneath, nor could he sense its general direction, for, having said all it considered essential, it had closed its mind and its powerful impulse was gone.

"Judging by the throb, there was a Drane down there," offered Melor belatedly. "Did you hear it? I couldn't understand what it said."

"It got us fixed. It identified your erratic thought-flow and said that a Lingan was with us."

"And what are we going to do about it? Do we stand like sheep and wait to be taken away?"

"Yes," Harold informed.

Melor's face registered approaching martyrdom, but he offered no further remark.

There wasn't an immediate response to the Drane's revelation. For reasons unknown to the watchers, a short time-lag intervened. It ended when a car roared along the street with a silver-spangled official bawling orders from its side window. As one man, the uniformed clusters made a determined rush for the front entrance of the building.

It was Melor who opened the door and admitted a police captain and six men. All seven wore the strained expressions of people called upon to deal with things unimaginable, and all seven were armed. Little blasters, similar to the one Harold had found so objectionable, were ready in their hands.

The captain, a big, burly man, but pale of face, entered the room with his blaster held forward, and gabbled hastily through his prepared speech.

"Listen to me, you four, before you try any tricks. We've reversed the controls on these guns. They stay safe while they're gripped but go off immediately our hands loosen—and hypnosis causes involuntary relaxation of the muscles which you can't prevent!" He swallowed hard. "Any clever stunts will do no more than turn this place into a shambles. In addition, there are more men outside, more on every floor, more in the street. You can't cope with the lot!"

Smiling amiably, Harold said, "You tempt us to persuade you to toss those toys out of the window, and your pants after them. But we want to talk to the Council of Action and have no time for amusement. Let's go."

The captain didn't know whether to scowl or look relieved. Cautiously he stood to one side, his gun held level, as the four filed out through the door. The escorts were equally leery. They surrounded the quartet, but not too closely, bearing themselves with the air of men compelled to nurse vipers to their bosoms.

As they marched along the landing toward the levitators Burt nudged the nearest guard and demanded, "What's your name?"

The fellow, a lanky, beetle-browed individual, was startled and apprehensive as he answered, "Walt Bron."

"Tut!" said Burt.

The guard didn't like that *"tut."* His brows came down, his small eyes held a stupefied expression as his mind said to itself, *"Why should he want my name? Why pick on me? I ain't done him any harm. What's he up to now?"*

Burt smiled broadly and his own mind reached out to George's and Harold's, saying, *"Something has got them worried, though the higher-ups aren't likely to have told them much."*

"Yes—it looks as if there's irritation in influential circles and the cops got bawled out in consequence. Evidently news is coming through." Pause. *"Did you feel any probe?"*

"No."

"Neither did we. That Drane must have gone." Pause. *"Pity we can't talk with Melor this way. He's walking behind like a fatalist pacing to certain death."* Pause. *"Got plenty of guts, the way he's taken us on trust."*

"Yes—but we'll look after him!"

They reached the levitators. The entire landing was now solid with armed police and a number of them were pressing eagerly into the deserted apartment, intent on thorough search.

Herded into a levitator, the captured quartet and their escort of seven crammed it to capacity. The glassite doors slid shut. The burly captain pressed a button and the levitator soared smoothly upward while its occupants watched the rising indicator with offhand interest. They stopped at the twenty-seventh floor.

The captain didn't permit the doors to open. He stood with his attention fixed upon the indicator while slowly his beefy face changed color. Suddenly, he rammed his big thumb on the ground-level button and the levitator shot downward.

Harold: *"Who did that?"*

Burt: *"Me. I couldn't resist it."* Then, vocally, and loudly, "I didn't notice any guns go off. Did you?"

The other captives grinned. The captain glared at the up-flying shaft but said nothing. The escort's uneasiness registered more openly on their faces.

A veritable guard of honor had lined up between the front entrance and the waiting car. About sixty guns were held in readiness on either side—in flat disregard of the fact that one had only to start something and let the fire of one rank bring down half the opposite rank, thus providing plentiful company in death.

The four got into the car, and its driver, a thin-featured, pessimistic individual, looked even less happy for their arrival. He had a cop for company in front. The car blew its jets and started off with half a dozen cars leading and a full dozen following. It was a cavalcade worthy of the year's best burial, and its pace was suitably funereal as it wended its way through a succession of side streets to the outskirts of the city. A thousand feet above them a helicopter and two gyros drifted along, carefully following every bend and turn on their route.

The destination proved to be an immense, needlelike skyscraper, tall, slender, graceful. It soared majestically from spacious, well-tended grounds around which stood a high wall surmounted by the spidery wiring of a photoelectric telltale system. As they swept through the great gateway, the prisoners caught a glimpse of the telltale marker-board in the granite lodge and a group of heavily armed guards lounging behind the gates.

"The palace of the Council," Melor informed. "This is where they make worlds and break them—or so they claim."

"Be quiet!" snapped the cop in front. Then, in a high, squeaky voice, he added, "There are fairies at the bottom of my garden!"

"Indeed?" said Burt, affecting polite surprise.

The cop's sour face whitened. His grip tightened on his blaster, forgetting in his emotion that a stronger hold was supposed to be ineffective.

"Let him alone, Burt!" thought Harold.

"I don't like him," Burt came back. *"His ears stick out."*

"How he smells of fury!" criticized Melor, openly.

Conversation ended as the procession halted in front of the skyscraper's ornate entrance. The quartet climbed out, paraded through another wary guard of honor, entered the building. Here, more black-uniformed men conducted them two levels below ground, ushered them into an apartment which, ominously, had a beryllium-steel grille in lieu of a door. The last man out turned a monster key in the grille and departed.

Before the inmates had time thoroughly to examine their new prison, an attendant appeared, thrust packaged foods through the bars of the grille, and told them, "I haven't got the key and don't know who has. Neither can I find out. If you want anything, call for me, but don't think you can make me open up. I couldn't do it even if I wanted—which I don't!"

"Dear me," said Burt, "that's unkind of you." Going to the grille, he swung it open, looked out at the astounded attendant and continued, "Tell the Council that we are very comfortable and appreciate their forethought. We shall be pleased to call upon them shortly."

The attendant's scattered wits came together. He took to his heels as if the breath of death was on his neck.

"How did you do that?" demanded Melor, his eyes wide. He ambled loose-jointedly to the grille, looked at its lock, swung it to and fro on its hinges.

"The gentleman with the key locked it, then unlocked it, and wandered away satisfied that duty had been done," Burt released a sigh. "Life is full of delusions." Opening a packet, he examined its contents. "Calorbix!" he said disgustedly, and tossed the package on a table.

"Here they come," George announced.

A horde arrived. They locked the grille, put two heavy chains around its end post, padlocked those. The four watched in amused silence. A pompous little man, with much silver braid strewn over his chest, then tried the grille, shaking it furiously. Satisfied, he scowled at the four, went away, the horde following.

Burt mooched restlessly around the room. "There are scanners watching us, microphones listening to us and, for all I know, some cockeyed gadget tasting us. I'm fed up with this. Let's go see the Council."

"Yes, it's about time we did," George agreed.

"The sooner the better," added Harold.

Melor offered no comment. The conversation of his friends, he decided, oft was confusing and seemingly illogical. They had a habit of going off at the queerest slants. So he contented himself with staring at the grille, through which nothing but some liquid form of life could pass, while he wondered whether Tor and Vern had yet been dragged into the net. He hoped not. It was better to execute one Lingan than three.

A minute later the man with the keys came back accompanied by two guards and a tall, gray-haired official clad in myrtle green. The badge of the Silver Comet glittered on the latter's shoulder straps. His keen gaze rested on the warden as that worthy surlily unlocked the padlocks, withdrew the chains, freed the grille.

Then he said to the four, "Most remarkable!" He waited for a response, but none came, so he carried on. "This warder hasn't the least notion of what he's doing. As the Council expected, you influenced him to return and unlock the gate. We kept him under observation. It has been an interesting demonstration of what hypnosis can achieve." His smile was amiable. "But you didn't expect him to return accompanied, eh?"

"What does it matter?" Harold answered. "Your brain advertises that the Council is ready to deal with us."

"I waste my breath talking." The official made a gesture of futility. "All right. Come with me."

The Council looked small. Its strength a mere eight, all but two of them human. They sat at a long table, the six humans in the middle, a nonhuman at each end. The thing on the extreme right had a head like a purple globe, smooth, shining, hairless, possessing no features except a pair of retractable eyes. Below was a cloaked shapelessness suggesting no shoulders and no arms. It was as repulsive as the sample on the left was beautiful. The one on the left had a flat, circular, golden face surrounded by golden petals, large and glossy. The head was supported by a short, fibrous green neck from the knot of which depended long, delicate arms terminating in five tentacles. Two black-knobbed stamens jutted from the face, and a wide, mobile mouth was visible beneath them. It was lovely, like a flower.

Between this table and the staring captives hung a barrier of wire. Harold, Burt and George could *see* that it was loaded, and their perceptions examined it gingerly. They diagnosed its purpose simultaneously; it bore an alternating current imposed upon a pulsing potential. Two hundred cycles per second, with a minimum pressure of four thousand volts rising to peak points of seven thousand every tenth cycle.

"Hypnocast jammer!" reported Burt. He was puzzled. "But that doesn't blank neural sprays. They're different bands. Can you hear what they're thinking?"

"Not a thing," answered Harold. "Neither could I get your thoughts while you were speaking."

"I've lost contact, too," put in George. "Something which isn't that screen is droning out a bass beat note that makes a mess of the telepathic band."

Sniffing with distaste, Melor said, "This is where I come in. I know what's the matter. There's a Drane in the room. He's doing it."

"Are you sure of that?"

"I can sense him." He pointed at the flowerlike being on the left. "Furthermore, Dranes can't speak. They've no vocal cords. The Florans function as their interpreters—that's why this one's here."

One of the humans on the Council, a bull-headed, heavily jowled man, leaned forward, fixed glittering eyes on the four. His voice was harsh.

"The Lingan is right. Since we are not assembled to be entertained by your alien antics, nor to listen to your lies, but solely for the purpose of weighing fresh truths with justice and with wisdom, we find it necessary to employ a Drane."

So saying, he made a dramatic gesture. The Floran reached a tentacled hand down behind the table, lifted the hidden Drane, placed it on the polished surface.

Mental visualization, Harold realized had proved correct with regard to shape and appearance but had misled him in the matter of size. He'd taken it for granted that a Drane possessed bulk comparable with his own. But this creature was no larger than his fist. Its very smallness shocked him.

It was lizardlike, but not so completely as first appeared, and now that he could see it closely, its tiny but perfect uniform looked absurd. While they regarded it, the thing sat there and stared at them with eyes like pinpoints of flaming crimson, and as it stared the strange beat note disappeared, a psychic flood poured through the screen and lapped around their minds.

But already the three shields were up, while the fourth—the Lingan—felt the force only as an acute throb. The pressure went up and up; it was amazing that such a midget brain could emit so mighty a mental flow of power. It felt and probed and thrust and stabbed, its violence increasing without abate.

Perspiration beaded the features of the trio as they gazed fixedly at the same spot on the Drane's jacket while maintaining their shields against its invisible assault. Melor sat down, cradled his head in his arms, began to rock slowly from side to side. The Council watched impassively. The Drane's optics were jewels of fire.

"Keep it up," whispered Harold. "It's almost on the boil."

Like the lizards it resembled, the Drane's pose was fixed, unmoving. It had remained as motionless as a carved ornament since it had reached the table, and its baleful eyes had never blinked. Still its psychic output went up.

Then, suddenly, it pawed at its jacket, snatched the paw away. A thin wisp of smoke crawled out of the cloth. The next instant, the creature had fled from the table, the mental pressure collapsing as its source disappeared. Its sharp, peaky voice came into their minds as the thing snaked through a tiny door, fled along the outer passage. The voice faded with distance.

"Burning . . . burning . . . burning!"

The Council member who had spoken originally now sat staring through the screen at the prisoners. His hand was on the table, and his fingers rapped its surface nervously. The other members maintained blank expressions. He turned his head, looked at the Floran.

"What happened?"

"The Drane said he was burning," enunciated the mouth in the flowerlike head. Its tones were weak, but precise. "His mind was very agitated. The peril destroyed his ability to concentrate, and he had to flee lest worse befall."

"Pyrotics!" said the Council member incredulously. "There are legends of such." His attention returned to the captives. "So you're pyrotics—fire-raisers!"

"Some of your people can do it—but don't know it themselves," Harold told him. "They've caused most of any seemingly inexplicable fires you've experienced." He made a gesture of impatience. "Now that we've got rid of that Drane how about giving way to what's on your mind? We can read what is written there, and we know the next move: you're to call Burkinshaw, Helman and Roka, after which the parley will start."

Frowning, but making no retort, the Council member pressed a red button on his desk. His attitude was one of expectancy.

In short time, Helman and Roka entered the room, took seats at the table. The former's bearing was surly and disgruntled. The latter grinned sheepishly at the quartet, even nodded amiably to Harold.

One minute after them, Burkinshaw Three, the Supreme Lord, came in and took the center seat. His awesome name and imposing title fitted him like somebody else's glove, for he was a small, thin man, round-shouldered, narrow-chested, with a pale, lined face. His balding head had wisps of gray hair at the sides, and his eyes peered myopically through rimless pince-nez. His whole appearance was that of a mild and perpetually preoccupied professor—but his mind was cold, cold.

That mind was now wide open to the three. It was a punctilious mind, clear and sharp in form, operating deliberately and calculatingly through the mixed output of the other humans at the Council table.

Arranging some papers before him, and keeping his gaze fixed upon the top sheets, Burkinshaw spoke in measured, unhurried tones, saying, "I don't doubt that you can read my mind and are reading it now, but in justice to the Lingan, who cannot do so, and for the benefit of my fellows, who are not telepathic either, I must use ordinary speech." He adjusted the pince-nez, turned over a sheet of paper and continued.

"We, of the Imperial Council of Action, have decided that the safety of the Empire demands that we obliterate the planet known to us as KX-724 together with any adjacent planets, satellites or asteroids harboring its dominant life form. We are now met to consider this life form's final plea for preservation, and it is the duty of each of us to listen carefully to what new evidence may be offered, weighing it not with favor or with prejudice, but with justice."

Having thus spoken, the Supreme Lord removed his pince-nez, polished each lens, clipped them carefully on his nose, stared owlishly over their tops at the prisoners. His eyes were a very pale blue, looked weak, but were not weak.

"Have you chosen your spokesman?"

Their minds conferred swiftly, then Harold said, "I shall speak."

"Very well then." Burkinshaw relaxed in his seat. "Before you commence it is necessary to warn you that our grave decision concerning the fate of your people is neither frivolous nor heartless. In fact, it was reached with the greatest reluctance. We were driven to it by the weight of evidence and, I regret to say, additional data which we've recently gained is of a nature calculated to support our judgment. Bluntly, your kind of life is a menace to our kind. The responsibility now rests with you to prove otherwise—to our satisfaction."

"And if I can't?" queried Harold.

"We shall destroy you utterly."

"If you can," said Harold.

The assembled minds reacted promptly. He could hear them, aggressive and fuming. The purple thing exuded no thoughts but did give out a queer suggestion of imbecilic amusement. The Floran's attitude was one of mild surprise mixed with interest.

Burkinshaw wasn't fazed. "If we can," he agreed blandly, while his brain held little doubt that they could. "Proceed in your own way," he invited. "You have about fourteen hours in which to convince us that our decision was wrong, or impracticable."

"You've tempted us into giving minor demonstrations of our powers," Harold began. "The Drane was planted here for a similar purpose; you used him as a yardstick with which to measure our mental abilities. From your viewpoint, I guess, the results have strengthened your case and weakened ours. Only the yardstick wasn't long enough."

Burkinshaw refused to rise to the bait. Placing his fingertips together as if about to pray, he stared absently at the ceiling, said nothing. His mind was well disciplined, for it registered no more than the comment, *"A negative point."*

"Let it pass," Harold went on, "while I talk about coincidences. On my world, a coincidence is a purely fortuitous lining-up of circumstances and either is isolated or recurs haphazardly. But when a seeming coincidence repeats itself often enough, it ceases to be a coincidence. You know that, too—or ought to know it. For example, let's take the once-alleged coincidence of meteoric phenomena appearing simultaneously with earthquakes. It occurred so frequently that eventually one of your scientists became curious, investigated the matter, discovered solar-dynamic space-strain, the very force which since has been utilized to boost your astrovessels to supra-spatial speeds. The lesson, of course, is that one just can't dismiss coincidences as such when there are too many of them."

"A thrust—toward where?" mused the Floran.

"No point yet apparent," thought Burkinshaw.

"I don't like the way he gabbles," said Helman's mind uneasily *"He's talking to gain time. Maybe the three of them are trying to push something through that screen. They burned the Drane through it, didn't they?"* He fidgeted in his seat. *"I don't share B's faith in that screen. Curses on Roka and all the rest of the pioneering crowd—they'll be the end of us yet!"*

Smiling to himself, Harold continued, "We've found out that the game of chess is generally known all over the Empire."

"Pshaw!" burst out the harsh-voiced man seated on Burkinshaw's left. "That's no coincidence. It spread from a central source, as anyone with a modicum of intelligence should have deduced."

"Be quiet, Dykstra," reproved Burkinshaw.

"Which source?" Harold asked him.

Dykstra looked peeved as he replied, "Us! We spread it around. What of it?"

"We had it long before you contacted us," Harold told him.

Dykstra opened his mouth, glanced at Burkinshaw, closed his mouth and swallowed hard. Burkinshaw continued to survey the ceiling.

Harold pursued, "We've had it so long that we don't know how long. The same board, same pieces, same moves, same rules. If you work it out, you'll find that that involves a very large number of coincidences."

They didn't comment vocally, but he got their reactions.

Four of the Council were confused.

"Surprising, but possible," mused the Floran.

"What of it, anyway?" inquired Dykstra's mind.

"No point yet apparent," thought Burkinshaw coolly.

The purple thing's brain emitted a giggle.

"Bron," said Harold. "Walt Bron, Robertus Bron

and umpteen other Brons. Your directory of citizens is full of them. My world, likewise, is full of them, always coupled with the other parent's name, of course, and occasionally spelled Brown, but pronounced the same. We've also got Roberts and Walters." He looked at Helman. "I know four men named Hillman." He shifted his gaze to the Supreme Lord. "And among our minor musicians is one named Theodore Burkinshaw-May."

Burkinshaw removed his stare from the ceiling and concentrated on the wall. *"I see where he's going. Reserve judgment until he arrives."*

"The vessel which brought us here was named the *Fenix,* in characters resembling those of our own alphabet," Harold continued. "And in days long gone by, when we had warships, there was one named the *Phoenix.* We found your language amazingly easy to learn. Why? Because one-fifth of your vocabulary is identical with ours. Another fifth is composed of perversions of our words. The remainder consists of words which you have changed beyond all recognition or words you've acquired from the peoples you've conquered. But, basically, your language is ours. Have you had enough coincidences?"

"Nonsense!" exclaimed Dykstra loudly. "Impossible!"

Burkinshaw turned and looked at Dykstra with eyes that were reproving behind their lenses. "Nothing is impossible," he contradicted mildly. "Continue," he ordered Harold, while his thoughts ran on, *"The pleader is making the inevitable point—too late."*

"So you can see where I'm going," Harold remarked to him. "Just for one final coincidence, let me say I was stupid enough to misunderstand the imperial title. I thought they called themselves Lords of Terror. A silly mistake." His voice slowed down. "Their title is a mystic one rooted deep in your past. They call themselves Lords of Terra!"

"Dear me," said Dykstra, "isn't that nice!"

Ignoring him, Harold spoke to Roka. "You're awake by now. Last night something clicked in your mind and you found yourself remembering things you didn't know you'd forgotten. Do you remember what my people call their parent planet?"

"Terra," Roka responded promptly. "I reported it to the Supreme Lord this morning. You call yourselves Terrestrials."

Dykstra's heavy face went dark red, and accusations of blasphemy were welling within his mind when Burkinshaw beat him to it.

"This morning's revised report of Lieutenant Roka and certain survivors of his crew now lies before the Council." He indicated the papers on the table. "It has already been analyzed by the police commissioner, Inquisitor Hellman and myself. We now believe that the pleader's assertions are founded in truth and that in discovering KX.724 we have discovered our long-lost point of origin. We have found our mother planet. The *Fenix*, unknown to any of us, was homeward bound!"

Half the Council were dumbfounded. The purple creature was not; it registered that human rediscoveries were of little consequence to purple things. The Floran thought similarly. Dykstra's mind was a turmoil of confusion.

"A difference of three light-years has separated us for two thousand centuries," Harold told them quietly. "In that tremendous past we'd grown great and venturesome. We sent several convoys of colonists to the nearest system, four and a half light-years away. We never knew what happened to them, for then followed the final atomic war which reduced us to wandering tribes sunk lower than savages. We've been climbing back ever since. The path of our climb has been very different from yours, for roving particles had done strange things to us. Some of those things died out, some were rooted out, others persisted and made us what we are today."

"What are you?" inquired the member next to Roka.

"Humanity metamorphosed," Burkinshaw answered for him.

"In the awful struggle for life on new and hostile

worlds, you, too, sank," Harold continued. "But you climbed again, and once more reached for the stars. Naturally, you sought the nearest system, one and a half light-years away, for you had forgotten the location of your home, which was spoken of only in ancient legends. We were three light-years farther away than your nearest neighboring system. Logically, you picked that—and went away from us. You sank again, climbed again, went on again, and you never came back until you'd built a mighty Empire on the rim of which we waited, and changed, and changed."

Now they were all staring at him fascinatedly. Even Dykstra was silent, his mind full of the mighty argosy across the ages. Half of it was schoolbook stuff to him, but not when presented in this new light.

"Those of you who are of the Brotherhood of the Budding Cross know that this is true—that you have completed the circle and reached the Seat of Sol." He made a swift and peculiar sign. Two of his audience responded automatically.

"It's of little use," Burt's thought came over strongly. *"They're too factual."*

"Wait!"

The Council was silent a long time, and eventually the Floran said, "All this is very touching—but how touching will it be when they take over our Empire?" To which its mind added, *"And we Florans swap one master for another. I am against it. Better the devil you know than the devil you don't."*

Resting his thin arms on the table, Burkinshaw Three blinked apologetically at the Terrans and spoke smoothly. "If they knew what we know, the Empire's sentimentalists might be against your destruction. However, the fabric of our cosmic edifice cannot be sustained by anything so soft as sentiment. Moreover, the prodigal sons have no intention of presenting this fatted calf to their long-lost fathers. Your removal from the scheme of things appears to me as necessary as ever— perhaps even more necessary—and that it will be patricide makes no difference to the fact." His thin, ascetic face held an ingratiating wish to please. "I feel sure that you understand our position. Have you anything more to say?"

"No luck," whispered Melor. "The hatred has gone—to be replaced by fear."

Harold grimaced, said to the Supreme Lord, "Yes, I'd like to say that you can blast Terra out of existence, and its system along with it, but it'll do you no good."

"We are not under the delusion that it will do us any good," declared Burkinshaw. "Nor would we sanction so drastic an act for such a purpose." He removed his pince-nez, screwed up his eyes as he looked at his listeners. "The motive is more reasonable and more urgent—it is to prevent harm."

"It won't do that, either."

"Why not?"

"Because you're too late."

"I feared you'd say that." Burkinshaw leaned back in his seat, tapped his glasses on a thumbnail. *If he can't satisfy me that his claim is well based, I shall advance the hour!* Then he said, "You'll have to prove that."

"There's trouble on four out of the five other planets in this system. You've just had news of it. Nothing serious, merely some absenteeism, sabotage, demonstrations, but no violence. It's trouble all the same—and it could be worse."

"There's always trouble on one planet or another," put Helman sourly. "When you're nursing four thousand of them, you get used to unrest."

"You overlook the significance of coincidences, I fear. Normal troubles pop up here and there, haphazardly. These have come together. They've kept an appointment in time!"

"We'll deal with them," Helman snapped.

"I don't doubt it," said Harold evenly. "You'll also deal with an uproar in the next system when you get news of it soon. You'll deal with four planets simultaneously, or forty planets—simultaneously. But four hundred planets—simultaneously—and then four thousand! Somewhere is the number that'll prove too much for even the best of organizations."

"It's not possible," Helman asserted stubbornly. "Only two dozen of you Terrans got here, Roka told us that. You took over his ship, substituted two dozen Terrestrials for part of his crew, impressed false memories on his and the other's minds, causing them to suspect nothing until their true memories suddenly returned." He scowled. The pulse in his forehead was beating visibly. "Very clever of you. Very, very clever. But twenty-four aren't enough."

"We know it. Irrespective of relative powers, some numbers are needed to deal with numbers." Harold's sharp-eyed gaze went from Helman to Burkinshaw. "If you people are no more and no less human than you were two hundred thousand years ago—and I think that your expansive path *has* kept you much the same—I'd say that your bureaucrats still live in watertight compartments. So long as supposedly missing ships fail to observe the officially prescribed rigmarole for reporting, it's taken that they're still missing. And, ten to one, your Department of Commerce doesn't even know that the Navy has mislaid anything."

It was a tribute to the Supreme Lord's quick-wittedness that his mind was way ahead of his confreres', for he acted while they were still stewing it over. He switched on the televisor set in the wall on one side.

Looking at its scanner, he said sharply, "Get me the Department of Commerce, Movements Section."

The screen colored, a fat man in civilian attire appeared. An expression of intense respect covered his ample features as he identified his caller.

"Yes, your excellency?"

"The Navy has reported two vessels immobilized beyond the Frontier. They're the *Callan* and the *Mathra*. Have they been recorded recently in any movements bulletins?"

"A moment, your excellency." The fat man disappeared. After some time, he came back, a puzzled frown on his face. "Your excellency, we have those two ships recorded as obsolete war vessels functioning as freighters. Their conversion was assumed by us, since they are transporting passengers and tonnage. The *Callan* has cleared four ports in the Frontier Zone, Sector B, in the last eight days. The *Mathra* departed from the system of Hyperion after landing passengers and freight on each of its nine planets. Its destination was given as external to the Frontier Zone, Sector J."

"Inform the Navy Department," Burkinshaw ordered, and switched off. He was the least disturbed individual at the table. His manner was calm, unruffled as he spoke to Harold. "So they're busily bringing in Terrans or Terrestrials or whatever you call yourselves. The logical play is to have those two vessels blown out of existence. Can it be done?"

"I'm afraid not. It depends largely upon whether the ships getting such an order have or have not already come under our control. The trouble with warships and atom bombs and planet-wreckers is that they're useful only when they work when and where you want them to work. Otherwise, they're liabilities." He gestured to indicate Burt and George. "According to my friends, the bomb allocated to Terra is on the ship *Warcat* clearing from your third neighbor. Ask Amilcare about it."

It required some minutes to get the third planet's Lord on the screen, and then his image was cloudy with static.

"Where's the *Warcat*?" rasped Burkinshaw.

The image moved, clouded still more, then cleared slightly. "Gone," said Amilcare jovially. "I don't know where."

"On whose authority?"

"Mine," Amilcare answered. His chuckle was oily and a little crazy. "Jon wanted it so I told him to take it. I couldn't think of anything you'd find more gratifying. Don't you worry about Jon—I'm looking after him for you."

Burkinshaw cut him off. "This Jon is a Terran, I suppose?"

"A Terrestrial," Harold corrected.

"Put a call out for him," urged Dykstra irefully. "The police won't all be bereft of their senses even if Amilcare is."

"Let me handle this," Burkinshaw said. Then, to Harold, "What has he done with the *Warcat*?"

"He'll have put somebody on it to control the crew and they'll be giving you a demonstration of what a nuisance planet-wreckers can be when they drop where they shouldn't."

"So your defense is attack? The bloodshed has started? In that case, the war is on, and we're all wasting our—"

"There will be no bloodshed," Harold interrupted. "We're not so infantile as that. None's been shed so far, and none will be shed if it can be avoided. That's what we're here for—to avoid it. The fact that we'd inevitably win any knock-down and drag-out affair you care to start hasn't blinded us to the fact that losers can lose very bloodily." He waved a hand toward the televisor. "Check up with your watertight bureaucrats. Ask your astronomers whether that refueling asteroid of yours is still circling."

Burkinshaw resorted to the televisor for the third time. All eyes were on its screen as he said, "Where is *Nemo* now?"

"*Nemo*? Well, your excellency, at the present moment it is approaching alignment with the last planet *Drufa* and about twenty hours farther out."

"I'm not asking where it ought to be! I want to know whether it's actually there!"

"Pardon me, your excellency." The figure slid off the screen and was gone a long time. When it returned, its voice crept out of the speaker hushed and frightened. "Your excellency, it would seem that some strange disaster has overtaken the body. I cannot explain why we've failed to observe—"

"Is it there?" rapped Burkinshaw impatiently.

"Yes, your excellency. But it is in gaseous condition. One would almost believe that a planet-wrecker had—"

"Enough!" Without waiting to hear the rest, he switched off.

Lying back in his chair, he brooded in complete disregard of the fact that his mind was wide open to some even though not to all. He didn't care who picked up his impressions.

"We may be too late. Possibly we were already too late the day Roka came back. At long last we've fallen into the trap we've always feared, the trap we avoided when we vaporized that world of parasites. Nevertheless, we can still destroy Terra—they can't possibly have taken over every world and every ship and we can still wipe her out. But to what avail? Revenge is sweet only when it's profitable. Will it profit us? It all depends on how many of these people have sneaked into our ranks, and how many more can get in before we destroy their base."

Helman thought, *"This is it! Any fool could tell it had to come sooner or later. Every new world is a risk. We've been lucky to get through four thousand of them without getting in bad. Well, the end could have been worse. At least, these are our own kind and should favor us above all other shapes."*

Melor murmured, "Their hate has weakened, and their fear turns to personal worry. Excepting the Purple One and the Floran. The Purple One, who was amused, is now angry. The Floran, who was interested and amiable, now fears."

"That's because we're not of their shape. Racial antagonisms and color antagonisms are as nothing to the mutual distrust between different shapes. There lies the Empire's weak spot. Every shape desires mastery of its own territory. So far as we're concerned, they can have it," Harold commented.

Putting his glasses back on his nose, Burkinshaw sighed and said, "Since you intend to take over the Empire, our only remaining move is to issue a general order for the immediate destruction of Terra. No matter how many confiscated ships try to thwart my purpose, obedience by one loyal vessel will suffice." His hand reached out toward the televisor switch.

"We aren't taking over your Empire," Harold told him swiftly. "Neither do we wish to do so. We're concerned only that you don't take over our world. All we want is a pact of noninterference in each other's affairs, and the appointment of a few Lingans to act as ambassadors through whom we can maintain such contact as suits us. We want to go our own way along our own path, we've the ability to defend our right to do so, and the present situation is our way of demonstrating the fact. No more than that. If, peevishly, you destroy our world, then, vengefully, we shall disrupt your ramshackle collection of worlds, not with our own strength, but by judiciously utilizing yours! Leave us in peace and we shall leave you in peace."

"Where's our guarantee of that?" asked Burkinshaw cynically. "How do we know that a century of insidious penetration will not follow such a pact?" He stared at the four, his blue eyes shrewd and calculating to a degree not apparent before. "In dealing with us you've been able to use an advantage you possess which Florans, Lingans, Rethrans and others have not got, namely, you know us as surely as you know your own kith and kin." He bent forward. "Likewise, *we* know *you!* If you're of sound and sane mind, you'll absorb gradually what you can't gulp down in one lump. That's the way we acquired the Empire, and that's the way you'll get it!"

"We've proved to you that we can take it over," Harold agreed evenly, "and that is our protection. Your distrust is the measure of ours. You'll never know how many of us are within your Empire and you'll never find out—but obliteration of our parent world will no longer obliterate our life form. We have made our own guarantee. Get it into your head, there is no winner in this game. It's stalemate!" He watched interestedly as Burkinshaw's forefinger rested light on the switch. "You're too late, much too late. We don't want your Empire because we're in the same fix—we're too late."

Burkinshaw's eyes narrowed and he said, "I don't see why it's too late for you to do what you've been so anxious to prove you can do."

"The desire doesn't exist. We've greater desires. It's because we have wended our way through a hell of our own creation that we have changed, and our ambitions have changed with us. Why should we care about territorial conquests when we face prospects infinitely greater? Why should we gallivant in spaceships around the petty limits of a galaxy when some day we shall range unhampered through infinity? How d'you think we knew you were coming, and prepared for you, even though we were uncertain of your shape and unsure of your intentions?"

"I'm listening," observed Burkinshaw, his fingers still toying with the switch, "but all I hear is words. Despite your many differences from us, which I acknowledge, the ancient law holds good: that shape runs true to shape."

Harold glanced at Burt and George. There was swift communion between them.

Then he said, "Time has been long, and the little angle between the paths of our fathers has opened to a mighty span. Our changes have been violent and many. A world of hard radiation has molded us anew, has made us what you cannot conceive, and you see us in a guise temporarily suitable for our purpose." Without warning, his eyes glowed at the Purple One. "Even that creature, which lives on life force and has been sucking steadily at us all this time, would now be dead had he succeeded in drawing one thin beam of what he craves!"

Burkinshaw didn't bother to look at the purple thing, but commented boredly, "The Rethran was an experiment that failed. If he was of any use, he'd have got you long before now." He rubbed his gray side-hairs, kept his hand on the switch. "I grow tired of meaningless noises. You are now hinting that you are no longer of our shape. I prefer to believe the evidence of my eyes." His optics sought the miniature time-recorder set in a ring on his finger. "If I switch on, it may mean the end of us all, but you cannot hypnotize a scanner, and the scene registered in this room will be equivalent to my unspoken order—death to Terra! I suspect you of playing for time. We can ill afford further time. I give you one minute to prove that you are now as different from us as is this Floran or this Rethran or that Lingan. If you do so, we'll deal with this matter sensibly and make a pact such as you desire. If not"—he waggled the switch suggestively—"the slaughter starts. We may lose—or we may not. It's a chance we've got to take."

The three Terrestrials made no reply. Their minds were in complete accord and their response was simultaneous.

Dykstra sobbed, "Look! Oh, eternity, look!" then sank to his knees and began to gabble. The purple creature withdrew its eyes right into its head so that it could not see. Burkinshaw's hand came away from the switch; his glasses fell to the floor and lay there, shattered, unheeded. Roka and Helman and the other humans on the Council covered their faces with their hands, which slowly took on a tropical tan.

Only the Floran came upright. It arose to full height, its golden petals completely extended, its greenish arms trembling with ecstasy.

All flowers love the sun.

Hobbyist

THE SHIP ARCED out of a golden sky and landed with a whoop and a wallop that cut down a mile of lush vegetation. Another half mile of growths turned black and drooped to ashes under the final flicker of the tail rocket blasts. That arrival was spectacular, full of verve, and worthy of four columns in any man's paper. But the nearest sheet was distant by a goodly slice of a lifetime, and there was none to record what this far corner of the cosmos regarded as the pettiest of events. So the ship squatted tired and still at the foremost end of the ashy blast-track and the sky glowed down and the green world brooded solemnly all around.

Within the transpex control dome, Steve Ander sat and thought things over. It was his habit to think things over carefully. Astronauts were not the impulsive daredevils so dear to the stereopticon-loving public. They couldn't afford to be. The hazards of the profession required an infinite capacity for cautious, contemplative thought. Five minutes' consideration had prevented many a collapsed lung, many a leaky heart, many a fractured frame. Steve valued his skeleton. He wasn't conceited about it and he'd no reason to believe it in any way superior to anyone else's skeleton. But he'd had it a long time, found it quite satisfactory, and had an intense desire to keep it—intact.

Therefore, while the tail tubes cooled off with their

usual creaking contractions, he sat in the control seat, stared through the dome with eyes made unseeing by deep preoccupation, and performed a few thinks.

Firstly, he'd made a rough estimate of this world during his hectic approach. As nearly as he could judge, it was ten times the size of Terra. But his weight didn't seem abnormal. Of course, one's notions of weight tended to be somewhat wild when for some weeks one's own weight has shot far up or far down in between periods of weightlessness. The most reasonable estimate had to be based on muscular reaction. If you felt as sluggish as a Saturnian sloth, your weight was way up. If you felt as powerful as Angus McKittrick's bull, your weight was down.

Normal weight meant Terrestrial mass despite this planet's tenfold volume. That meant light plasma. And that meant lack of heavy elements. No thorium. No nickel. No nickel-thorium alloy. Ergo, no getting back. The Kingston-Kane atomic motors demanded fuel in the form of ten-gauge nickel-thorium alloy wire fed directly into the vaporizers. Denatured plutonium would do, but it didn't occur in natural form, and it had to be made. He had three yards nine and a quarter inches of nickel-thorium left on the feed-spool. Not enough. He was here for keeps.

A wonderful thing, logic. You could start from the simple premise that when you were seated your behind was no flatter than usual, and work your way to the inevitable conclusion that you were a wanderer no more. You'd become a native. Destiny had you tagged as suitable for the status of oldest inhabitant.

Steve pulled an ugly face and said, "Darn!"

The face didn't have to be pulled far. Nature had given said pan a good start. That is to say, it wasn't handsome. It was a long, lean, nut-brown face with pronounced jaw muscles, prominent cheekbones, and a thin, hooked nose. This, with his dark eyes and black hair, gave him a hawklike appearance. Friends talked to him about tepees and tomahawks whenever they wanted him to feel at home.

Well, he wasn't going to feel at home any more; not

unless this brooding jungle held intelligent life dopey enough to swap ten-gauge nickel-thorium wire for a pair of old boots. Or unless some dopey search party was intelligent enough to pick this cosmic dust mote out of a cloud of motes, and took him back. He estimated this as no less than a million-to-one chance. Like spitting at the Empire State hoping to hit a cent-sized mark on one of its walls.

Reaching for his everflo stylus and the ship's log, he opened the log, looked absently at some of the entries.

"Eighteenth day: The spatial convulsion has now flung me past rotal-range of Rigel. Am being tossed into uncharted regions.

"Twenty-fourth day: Arm of convulsion now tails back seven parsecs. Robot recorder now out of gear. Angle of throw changed seven times today.

"Twenty-ninth day: Now beyond arm of the convulsive sweep and regaining control. Speed far beyond range of the astrometer. Applying braking rockets cautiously. Fuel reserve: fourteen hundred yards.

"Thirty-seventh day: Making for planetary system now within reach."

He scowled, his jaw muscles lumped, and he wrote slowly and legibly, "Thirty-ninth day: Landed on planet unknown, primary unknown, galactic area standard reference and sector numbers unknown. No cosmic formations were recognizable when observed shortly before landing. Angles of offshoot and speed of transit not recorded, and impossible to estimate. Condition of ship: workable. Fuel reserve: three and one quarter yards."

Closing the log, he scowled again, rammed the stylus into its desk-grip, and muttered, "Now to check on the outside air and then see how the best girl's doing."

The Radson register had three simple dials. The first recorded outside pressure at thirteen point seven pounds, a reading he observed with much satisfaction. The second said that oxygen content was high. The third had a bi-colored dial, half white, half red, and its needle stood in the middle of the white.

"Breathable," he grunted, clipping down the register's lid. Crossing the tiny control room, he slid aside a

metal panel, looked into the padded compartment behind. "Coming out, Beauteous?" he asked.

"Steve loves Laura?" inquired a plaintive voice.

"You bet he does!" he responded with becoming
passion. He shoved an arm into the compartment,
brought out a large, gaudily colored macaw. "Does
Laura love Steve?"

"Hey-hey!" cackled Laura harshly. Climbing up his
arm, the bird perched on his shoulder. He could feel the
grip of its powerful claws. It regarded him with a beady
and brilliant eye, then rubbed its crimson head against
his left ear. "Hey-hey! Time flies!"

"Don't mention it," he reproved. "There's plenty to
remind me of the fact without you chipping in."

Reaching up, he scratched her poll while she
stretched and bowed with absurd delight. He was fond
of Laura. She was more than a pet. She was a bona fide
member of the crew, issued with her own rations and
drawing her own pay. Every Probe ship had a crew of
two: one man, one macaw. When he'd first heard of it,
the practice had seemed crazy—but when he got the
reasons, it made sense.

"Lonely men, probing beyond the edge of the charts,
get queer psychological troubles. They need an anchor
to Earth. A macaw provides the necessary companionship—and more! It's the space-hardiest bird we've got,
its weight is negligible, it can talk and amuse, it can
fend for itself when necessary. On land, it will often
sense dangers before you do. Any strange fruit or food
it may eat is safe for you to eat. Many a man's life has
been saved by his macaw. Look after yours, my boy,
and it'll look after you!"

Yes, they looked after each other, Terrestrials both.
It was almost a symbiosis of the spaceways. Before the
era of astronavigation nobody had thought of such an
arrangement, though it had been done before. Miners
and their canaries.

Moving over to the miniature air lock, he didn't
bother to operate the pump. It wasn't necessary with so
small a difference between internal and external pressures. Opening both doors, he let a little of his higher-

pressured air sigh out, stood on the rim of the lock, jumped down. Laura fluttered from his shoulder as he leaped, followed him with a flurry of wings, got her talons into his jacket as he staggered upright.

The pair went around the ship, silently surveying its condition. Front braking nozzles O.K., rear steering flares O.K., tail propulsion tubes O.K. All were badly scored but still usable. The skin of the vessel likewise was scored but intact. Three months' supply of food and maybe a thousand yards of wire could get her home, theoretically. But only theoretically, Steve had no delusions about the matter. The odds were still against him even if given the means to move. How do you navigate from you-don't-know-where to you-don't-know-where? Answer: you stroke a rabbit's foot and probably arrive you-don't-know-where-else.

"Well," he said, rounding the tail, "it's something in which to live. It'll save us building a shanty. Way back on Terra they want fifty thousand smackers for an all-metal, streamlined bungalow, so I guess we're mighty lucky. I'll make a garden here, and a rockery there, and build a swimming pool out back. You can wear a pretty frock and do all the cooking."

"Yawk!" said Laura derisively.

Turning, he had a look at the nearest vegetation. It was of all heights, shapes and sizes, of all shades of green with a few tending toward blueness. There was something peculiar about the stuff but he was unable to decide where the strangeness lay. It wasn't that the growths were alien and unfamiliar—one expected that on every new world—but an underlying something which they shared in common. They had a vague, shadowy air of being not quite right in some basic respect impossible to define.

A plant grew right at his feet. It was green in color, a foot high, and monocotyledonous. Looked at as a thing in itself, there was nothing wrong with it. Near to it flourished a bush of darker hue, a yard high, with green, firlike needles in lieu of leaves, and pale, waxy berries scattered over it. That, too, was innocent enough when studied apart from its neighbors. Beside it grew a similar plant, differing only in that its needles were longer and its berries a bright pink. Beyond these towered a cactus-like object dragged out of somebody's drunken dreams, and beside it stood an umbrella-frame which had taken root and produced little purple pods. Individually, they were acceptable. Collectively, they made the discerning mind search anxiously for it knew not what.

That eerie feature had Steve stumped. Whatever it was, he couldn't nail it down. There was something stranger than the mere strangeness of new forms of plant life, and that was all. He dismissed the problem with a shrug. Time enough to trouble about such matters after he'd dealt with others more urgent such as, for example, the location and purity of the nearest water supply.

A mile away lay a lake of some liquid that might be water. He'd seen it glittering in the sunlight as he'd made his descent, and he'd tried to land fairly near to it. If it wasn't water, well, it'd be just his tough luck and he'd have to look someplace else. At worst, the tiny fuel reserve would be enough to permit one circumnavigation of the planet before the ship became pinned down forever. Water he must have if he wasn't going to end up imitating the mummy of Rameses the Second.

Reaching high, he grasped the rim of the port, dexterously muscled himself upward and through it. For a minute he moved around inside the ship, then reappeared with a four-gallon freezocan which he tossed to the ground. Then he dug out his popgun, a belt of explosive shells, and let down the folding ladder from lock to surface. He'd need that ladder. He could muscle himself up through a hole seven feet high, but not with fifty pounds of can and water.

Finally, he locked both the inner and outer air lock doors, skipped down the ladder, picked up the can. From the way he'd made his landing the lake should be directly bow-on relative to the vessel, and somewhere the other side of those distant trees. Laura took a fresh grip on his shoulder as he started off. The can swung from his left hand. His right hand rested warily on the gun. He was perpendicular on this world instead of horizontal on another because, on two occasions, his hand had been ready on the gun, and because it was the most nervous hand he possessed.

The going was rough. It wasn't so much that the terrain was craggy as the fact that impeding growths got in his way. At one moment he was stepping over an ankle-high shrub, the next he was facing a burly plant struggling to become a tree. Behind the plant would be a creeper, then a natural zareba of thorns, a fuzz of fine moss, followed by a giant fern. Progress consisted of stepping over one item, ducking beneath a second, going around a third, and crawling under a fourth.

It occurred to him, belatedly, that if he'd planted the ship tail-first to the lake instead of bow-on, or if he'd let the braking rockets blow after he'd touched down, he'd have saved himself much twisting and dodging. All this obstructing stuff would have been reduced to ashes for at least half the distance to the lake—together with any venomous life it might conceal.

That last thought rang like an alarm bell within his mind just as he doubled up to pass a low-swung creeper. On Venus were creepers that coiled and constricted, swiftly, viciously. Macaws played merry hell if taken within fifty yards of them. It was a comfort to know that, this time, Laura was riding his shoulder unperturbed—but he kept the hand on the gun.

The elusive peculiarity of the planet's vegetation bothered him all the more as he progressed through it. His inability to discover and name this unnamable queerness nagged at him as he went on. A frown of self-disgust was on his lean face when he dragged himself free of a clinging bush and sat on a rock in a tiny clearing.

Dumping the can at his feet, he glowered at it and promptly caught a glimpse of something bright and shining a few feet beyond the can. He raised his gaze. It was then he saw the beetle.

The creature was the biggest of its kind ever seen by

human eyes. There were other things bigger, of course, but not of this type. Crabs, for instance. But this was no crab. The beetle ambling purposefully across the clearing was large enough to give any crab a severe inferiority complex, but it was a genuine, twenty-four-karat beetle. And a beautiful one. Like a scarab.

Except that he clung to the notion that little bugs were vicious and big ones companionable, Steve had no phobia about insects. The amiability of large ones was a theory inherited from schoolkid days when he'd been the doting owner of a three-inch stag-beetle afflicted with the name of Edgar.

So he knelt beside the creeping giant, placed his hand palm upward in its path. It investigated the hand with waving feelers, climbed onto his palm, paused there ruminatively. It shone with a sheen of brilliant metallic blue and it weighed about three pounds. He jogged it on his hand to get its weight, then put it down, let it wander on. Laura watched it go with a sharp but incurious eye.

"*Scarabaeus anderii*," Steve said with glum satisfaction. "I pin my name on him—but nobody'll ever know it!"

"Dinna fash y'rsel'!" shouted Laura in a hoarse voice imported straight from Aberdeen. "Dinna fash! Stop chunnerin', wumman! Y' gie me a pain ahint ma sporran! Dinna—"

"Shut up!" Steve jerked his shoulder, momentarily unbalancing the bird. "Why d'you pick up that barbaric dialect quicker than anything else, eh?"

"McGillicuddy," shrieked Laura with ear-splitting relish. "McGilli-Gilli-Gillicuddy! The great black—!" It ended with a word that pushed Steve's eyebrows into his hair and surprised even the bird itself. Filming its eyes with amazement, it tightened its claw-hold on his shoulder, opened the eyes, emitted a couple of raucous clucks, and joyfully repeated, "The great black—"

It didn't get the chance to complete the new and lovely word. A violent jerk of the shoulder unseated it in the nick of time and it fluttered to the ground, squawking protestingly. *Scarabaeus anderii* lumbered out from behind a bush, his blue armor glistening as if freshly polished, and stared reprovingly at Laura.

Then something fifty yards away released a snort like the trumpet of doom and took one step that shook the earth. *Scarabaeus anderii* took refuge under a projecting root. Laura made an agitated swoop for Steve's shoulder and clung there desperately. Steve's gun was out and pointing northward before the bird had found its perch. Another step. The ground quivered.

Silence for a while. Steve continued to stand like a statue. Then came a monstrous whistle more forceful than that of a locomotive blowing off steam. Something squat and wide and of tremendous length charged headlong through the half-concealing vegetation while the earth trembled beneath its weight.

Its mad onrush carried it blindly twenty yards to Steve's right, the gun swinging to cover its course, but not firing. Steve caught an extended glimpse of a slate-gray bulk with a serrated ridge on its back which, despite the thing's pace, took long to pass. It seemed several times the length of a fire ladder.

Bushes were flung roots topmost and small trees whipped aside as the creature pounded grimly onward in a straight line which carried it far past the ship and into the dim distance. It left behind a tattered swathe wide enough for a first-class road. Then the reverberations of its mighty tonnage died out, and it was gone.

Steve used his left hand to pull out a handkerchief and wipe the back of his neck. He kept the gun in his right hand. The explosive shells in that gun were somewhat wicked; any one of them could deprive a rhinoceros of a hunk of meat weighing two hundred pounds. If a man caught one, he just strewed himself over the landscape. By the looks of that slate-colored galloper, it would need half a dozen shells to feel incommoded. A seventy-five-millimeter bazooka would be more effective for kicking it in the back teeth, but Probe ship boys don't tote around such artillery. Steve finished the mopping, put the handkerchief back, picked up the can.

Laura said pensively, "I want my mother."

He scowled, made no reply, set out toward the lake. Her feathers still ruffled, Laura rode his shoulder and lapsed into surly silence.

The stuff in the lake was water, cold, faintly green and a little bitter to the taste. Coffee would camouflage the flavor. If anything, it might improve the coffee since he liked his java bitter, but the stuff would have to be tested before absorbing it in any quantity. Some poisons were cumulative. It wouldn't do to guzzle gaily while building up a death-dealing reserve of lead, for instance. Filling the freezocan, he lugged it to the ship in hundred-yard stages. The swathe helped; it made an easier path to within short distance of the ship's tail. He was perspiring freely by the time he reached the base of the ladder.

Once inside the vessel, he relocked both doors, opened the air vents, started the auxiliary lighting-set and plugged in the perocolator, using water out of his depleted reserve supply. The golden sky had dulled to orange, with violet streamers creeping upward from the horizon. Looking at it through the transpex dome, he found that the perpetual haze still effectively concealed the sinking sun. A brighter area to one side was all that indicated its position. He'd need his lights soon.

Pulling out the collapsible table, he jammed its supporting leg into place, plugged into its rim the short rod which was Laura's official seat. She claimed the perch immediately, watched him beadily as he set out her meal of water, melon seeds, sunflower seeds, pecans and unshelled oleo nuts. Her manners were anything but ladylike and she started eagerly, without waiting for him.

A deep frown lay across his brown, muscular features as he sat at the table, poured out his coffee and commenced to eat. It persisted through the meal, was still there when he lit a cigarette and stared speculatively up at the dome.

Presently, he murmured, "I've seen the biggest bug that ever was. I've seen a few other bugs. There were a couple of little ones under a creeper. One was long and brown and many-legged, like an earwig. The other was round and black, with little red dots on its wing cases. I've seen a tiny purple spider and a tinier green one of different shape, also a bug that looked like an aphid. But not an ant."

"Ant, ant," hooted Laura. She dropped a piece of oleo nut, climbed down after it. "Yawk!" she added from the floor.

"Nor a bee."

"Bee," echoed Laura, companionably. "Bee-ant. Laura loves Steve."

Still keeping his attention on the dome, he went on, "And what's cockeyed about the plants is equally cock-eyed about the bugs. I wish I could place it. Why can't I? Maybe I'm going nuts already."

"Laura loves nuts."

"I know it, you technicolored belly!" said Steve rudely.

And at that point night fell with a silent bang. The gold and orange and violet abruptly were swamped with deep, impenetrable blackness devoid of stars or any random gleam. Except for greenish glowings on the instrument panel, the control room was stygian, with Laura swearing steadily on the floor.

Putting out a hand, Steve switched on the indirect lighting. Laura got to her perch with the rescued titbit, concentrated on the job of dealing with it and let him sink back into his thoughts.

"Scarabaeus anderii and a pair of smaller bugs and a couple of spiders, all different. At the other end of the scale, that gigantosaurus. But no ant, or bee. Or rather, no ants, no bees." The switch from singular to plural stirred his back hairs queerly. In some vague way, he felt that he'd touched the heart of the mystery. "No ant—no ants," he thought. "No bee—no bees." Almost he had it—but still it evaded him.

Giving it up for the time being, he cleared the table, did a few minor chores. After that, he drew a standard sample from the freezocan, put it through its paces. The bitter flavor he identified as being due to the presence of magnesium sulphate in quantity far too small to prove embarrassing. Drinkable—that was something! Food, drink and shelter were the three essentials of survival. He'd enough of the first for six or seven weeks. The lake and the ship were his remaining guarantees of life.

Finding the log, he entered the day's report, bluntly, factually, without any embroidery. Partway through, he found himself stuck for a name for the planet. *Ander,* he decided, would cost him dear if the million-to-one chance put him back among the merciless playmates of the Probe Service. O.K. for a bug, but not for a world, *Laura* wasn't so hot, either—especially when you knew Laura. It wouldn't be seemly to name a big, gold planet after an oversized parrot. Thinking over the golden aspect of this world's sky, he hit upon the name of *Oro,* promptly made the christening authoritative by entering it in his log.

By the time he'd finished, Laura had her head buried deep under one wing. Occasionally she teetered and swung erect again. It always fascinated him to watch how her balance was maintained even in her slumbers. Studying her fondly, he remembered that unexpected addition to her vocabulary. This shifted his thoughts to a fiery-headed and fierier-tongued individual named Menzies, the sworn foe of another volcano named McGillicuddy. If ever the opportunity presented itself, he decided, the educative work of said Menzies was going to be rewarded with a bust on the snoot.

Sighing, he put away the log, wound up the forty-day chronometer, opened his folding bunk and lay down upon it. His hand switched off the lights. Ten years back, a first landing would have kept him awake all night in dithers of excitement. He'd got beyond that now. He'd done it often enough to have grown phlegmatic about it. His eyes closed in preparation for a good night's sleep, and he did sleep—for two hours.

What brought him awake within that short time he didn't know, but suddenly he found himself sitting bolt upright on the edge of the bunk, his ears and nerves stretched to their utmost, his legs quivering in a way they'd never done before. His whole body fizzed with that queer mixture of palpitation and shock which follows narrow escape from disaster.

This was something not within previous experience. Sure and certain in the intense darkness, his hand sought and found his gun. He cuddled the butt in his palm while his mind strove to recall a possible nightmare, though he knew he was not given to nightmares.

Laura moved restlessly on her perch, not truly awake, yet not asleep, and this was unusual in her.

Rejecting the dream theory, he stood up on the bunk, looked out through the dome. Blackness, the deepest, darkest, most impenetrable blackness it was possible to conceive. And silence! The outside world slumbered in the blackness and the silence as in a sable shroud.

Yet never before had he felt so wide awake in this, his normal sleeping time. Puzzled, he turned slowly round to take in the full circle of unseeable view, and at one point he halted. The surrounding darkness was not complete. In the distance beyond the ship's tail moved a tall, stately glow. How far off it might be was not possible to estimate, but the sight of it stirred his soul and caused his heart to leap.

Uncontrollable emotions were not permitted to master his disciplined mind. Narrowing his eyes, he tried to discern the nature of the glow while his mind sought the reason why the mere sight of it should make him twang like a harp. Bending down, he felt at the head of the bunk, found a leather case, extracted a pair of powerful night glasses. The glow was still moving, slowly, deliberately, from right to left. He got the glasses on it, screwed the lenses into focus, and the phenomenon leaped into closer view.

The thing was a great column of golden haze much like that of the noonday sky except that small, intense gleams of silver sparkled within it. It was a shaft of lustrous mist bearing a sprinkling of tiny stars. It was like nothing known to or recorded by any form of life lower than the gods. But was it life?

It moved, though its mode of locomotion could not be determined. Self-motivation is the prime symptom of life. It could be life, conceivably though not credibly, from the Terrestrial viewpoint. Consciously, he preferred to think it a strange and purely local feature comparable with Saharan sand-devils. Subconsciously, he knew it was life, tall and terrifying.

He kept the glasses on it while slowly it receded into the darkness, foreshortening with increasing distance and gradually fading from view. To the very last the observable field shifted and shuddered as he failed to control the quiver in his hands. And when the sparkling haze had gone, leaving only a pall over his lenses, he sat down on the bunk and shivered with eerie cold.

Laura was dodging to and fro along her perch, now thoroughly awake and agitated, but he wasn't inclined to switch on the lights and make the dome a beacon in the night. His hand went out, feeling for her in the darkness, and she clambered eagerly onto his wrist, thence to his lap. She was fussy and demonstrative, pathetically yearning for comfort and companionship. He scratched her poll and fondled her while she pressed close against his chest with funny little crooning noises. For some time he soothed her and, while doing it, fell asleep. Gradually he slumped backward on the bunk. Laura perched on his forearm, clucked tiredly, put her head under a wing.

There was no further awakening until the outer blackness disappeared and the sky again sent its golden glow pouring through the dome. Steve got up, stood on the bunk, had a good look over the surrounding terrain. It remained precisely the same as it had been the day before. Things stewed within his mind while he got his breakfast; especially the jumpiness he'd experienced in the nighttime. Laura also was subdued and quiet. Only once before had she been like that—which was when he'd traipsed through the Venusian section of the Panplanetary Zoo and had shown her a crested eagle. The eagle had stared at her with contemptuous dignity.

Though he'd all the time in his life, he now felt a peculiar urge to hasten. Getting the gun and the freezocan, he made a full dozen trips to the lake, wasting no minutes, nor stopping to study the still enigmatic plants and bugs. It was late in the afternoon by the time he'd filled the ship's fifty-gallon reservoir, and had the satisfaction of knowing that he'd got a drinkable quota to match his food supply.

There had been no sign of gigantosaurus or any other animal. Once he'd seen something flying in the far distance, birdlike or batlike. Laura had cocked a sharp eye at it but betrayed no undue interest. Right now she was more concerned with a new fruit. Steve sat in the rim of the outer lock door, his legs dangling, and watched her clambering over a small tree thirty yards away. The gun lay in his lap; he was ready to take a crack at anything which might be ready to take a crack at Laura.

The bird sampled the tree's fruit, a crop resembling blue-shelled lychee nuts. She ate one with relish, grabbed another. Steve lay back in the lock, stretched to reach a bag, then dropped to the ground and went across to the tree. He tried a nut. Its flesh was soft, juicy, sweet and citrous. He filled the bag with the fruit, slung it into the ship.

Nearby stood another tree, not quite the same, but very similar. It bore nuts like the first except that they were larger. Picking one, he offered it to Laura, who tried it, spat it out in disgust. Picking a second, he slit it, licked the flesh gingerly. As far as he could tell, it was the same. Evidently he couldn't tell far enough: Laura's diagnosis said it was not the same. The difference, too subtle for him to detect, might be sufficient to roll him up like a hoop and keep him that shape to the unpleasant end. He flung the thing away, went back to his seat in the lock, and ruminated.

That elusive, nagging feature of Oro's plants and bugs could be narrowed down to these two nuts. He felt sure of that. If he could discover why—parrotwise—one nut was a nut while the other nut was not, he'd have his finger right on the secret. The more he thought about those similar fruits the more he felt that, in sober fact, his finger was on the secret already—but he lacked the power to lift it and see what lay beneath.

Tantalizingly, his mulling over the subject landed him

the same place as before; namely, nowhere. It got his dander up, and he went back to the trees, subjected both to close examination. His sense of sight told him that they were different individuals of the same species. Laura's sense of whatchamacallit insisted that they were different species. Ergo, you can't believe the evidence of your eyes. He was aware of that fact, of course, since it was a platitude of the spaceways, but when you couldn't trust your optics it was legitimate to try to discover just why you couldn't trust 'em. And he couldn't discover even that!

It soured him so much that he returned to the ship, locked its doors, called Laura back to his shoulder and set off on a tailward exploration. The rules of first landings were simple and sensible. Go in slowly, come out quickly, and remember that all we want from you is evidence of suitability for human life. Thoroughly explore a small area rather than scout a big one—the mapping parties will do the rest. Use your ship as a base and centralize it where you can live—don't move it unnecessarily. Restrict your trips to a radius representing daylight-reach and lock yourself in after dark.

Was Oro suitable for human life? The unwritten law was that you don't jump to conclusions and say, "Of course! I'm still living, aren't I?" Cameron, who'd plonked his ship on Mithra, for instance, thought he'd found paradise until, on the seventeenth day, he'd discovered the fungold plague. He'd left like a bat out of hell and had spent three sweaty, swearing days in the Lunar Purification Plant before becoming fit for society. The authorities had vaporized his ship. Mithra had been taboo ever since. Every world a potential trap baited with scenic delight. The job of the Probe Service was to enter the traps and jounce on the springs. Another dollop of real estate for Terra—if nothing broke your neck.

Maybe Oro was loaded for bear. The thing that walked in the night, Steve mused, bore awful suggestion of nonhuman power. So did a waterspout, and whoever heard of anyone successfully wrestling with a waterspout? If this Oro-spout were sentient, so much the worse for human prospects. He'd have to get the measure of it, he decided, even if he had to chase it through the blank avenues of night. Plodding steadily away from the tail, gun in hand, he pondered so deeply that he entirely overlooked the fact that he wasn't on a pukka Probe job anyway, and that nothing else remotely human might reach Oro in a thousand years. Even spaceboys can be creatures of habit. Their job: to look for death; they were liable to go on looking long after the need had passed, in bland disregard of the certainty that if you look for a thing long enough, ultimately you find it!

The ship's chronometer had given him five hours to darkness. Two and a half hours each way; say ten miles out and ten back. The water had consumed his time. On the morrow, and henceforth, he'd increase the radius to twelve and take it easier.

Then all thoughts fled from his mind as he came to the edge of the vegetation. The stuff didn't dribble out of existence with hardy spurs and offshoots fighting for a hold in rocky ground. It stopped abruptly, in light loam, as if cut off with a machete, and from where it stopped spread a different crop. The new growths were tiny and crystalline.

He accepted the crystalline crop without surprise, knowing that novelty was the inevitable feature of any new locale. Things were ordinary only by Terrestrial standards. Outside of Terra, nothing was supernormal or abnormal except insofar as it failed to jibe with its own peculiar conditions. Besides, there were crystalline growths on Mars. The one unacceptable feature of the situation was the way in which vegetable growths ended and crystalline ones began. He stepped back to the verge and made another startled survey of the borderline. It was so straight that the sight screwed his brain around. Like a field. A cultivated field. Dead straightness of that sort couldn't be other than artificial. Little beads of moisture popped out on his back.

Squatting on the heel of his right boot, he gazed at the nearest crystals and said to Laura, "Chicken, I think these things got planted. Question is, who planted 'em?"

"McGillicuddy," suggested Laura brightly.

Putting out a finger, he flicked the crystal sprouting near the toe of his boot, a green, branchy object an inch high.

The crystal vibrated and said, *"Zing!"* in a sweet, high voice.

He flicked its neighbor, and that said, *"Zang!"* in lower tone.

He flicked a third. It emitted no note, but broke into a thousand shards.

Standing up, he scratched his head, making Laura fight for a claw-hold within the circle of his arm. One zinged and one zanged and one returned to dust. Two nuts. Zings and zangs and nuts. It was right in his grasp if only he could open his hand and look at what he'd got.

Then he lifted his puzzled and slightly ireful gaze, saw something fluttering erratically across the crystal field. It was making for the vegetation. Laura took off with a raucous cackle, her blue-and-crimson wings beating powerfully. She swooped over the object, frightening it so low that it dodged and sideslipped only a few feet above Steve's head. He saw that it was a large butterfly, frill-winged, almost as gaudy as Laura. The bird swooped again, scaring the insect but not menacing it. He called her back, set out to cross the area ahead. Crystals crunched to powder under his heavy boots as he tramped on.

Half an hour later he was toiling up a steep, crystal-coated slope when his thoughts suddenly jelled and he stopped with such abruptness that Laura spilled from his shoulder and perforce took to wing. She beat round in a circle, came back to her perch, made bitter remarks in an unknown language.

"One of this and one of that," he said. "No twos or threes or dozens. Nothing I've seen has repeated itself. There's only one gigantosaurus, only one *Scarabaeus anderii,* only one of every other danged thing. Every item is unique, original, and an individual creation in its own right. What does that suggest?"

"McGillicuddy," offered Laura.

"For Pete's sake, forget McGillicuddy."

"For Pete's sake, for Pete's sake," yelled Laura, much taken by the phrase. "The great black—"

Again he upset her in the nick of time, making her take to flight while he continued talking to himself. "It suggests constant and all-pervading mutation. Everything breeds something quite different from itself and there aren't any dominant strains." He frowned at the obvious snag in this theory. "But how the blazes does anything breed? What fertilizes which?"

"McGilli—," began Laura, then changed her mind and shut up.

"Anyway, if nothing breeds true, it'll be tough on the food problem," he went on. "What's edible on one plant may be a killer on its offspring. Today's fodder is tomorrow's poison. How's a farmer to know what he's going to get? Hey-hey, if I'm guessing right, this planet won't support a couple of hogs."

"No, sir. No hogs. Laura loves hogs."

"Be quiet," he snapped. "Now, what shouldn't support a couple of hogs demonstrably does support gigantosaurus—and any other fancy animals which may be mooching around. It seems crazy to me. On Venus or any other place full of consistent fodder, gigantosaurus would thrive, but here, according to my calculations, the big lunk has no right to be alive. He ought to be dead."

So saying, he topped the rise and found the monster in question sprawling right across the opposite slope. It *was* dead.

The way in which he determined its deadness was appropriately swift, simple and effective. Its enormous bulk lay draped across the full length of the slope and its dragon-head, the size of a lifeboat, pointed toward him. The head had two dull, lackluster eyes like dinner plates. He planted a shell smack in the right eye and a sizable hunk of noggin promptly splashed in all directions. The body did not stir.

There was a shell ready for the other eye should the

creature leap to frantic, vengeful life, but the mighty hulk remained supine.

His boots continued to desiccate crystals as he went down the slope, curved a hundred yards off his route to get around the corpse, and trudged up the farther rise. Momentarily, he wasn't much interested in the dead beast. Time was short and he could come again tomorrow, bringing a full-color stereoscopic camera with him. Gigantosaurus would go on record in style, but would have to wait.

This second rise was a good deal higher, and more trying a climb. Its crest represented the approximate limit of this day's trip, and he felt anxious to surmount it before turning back. Humanity's characteristic urge to see what lay over the hill remained as strong as on the day determined ancestors topped the Rockies. He had to have a look, firstly because elevation gave range to the vision, and secondly because of that prowler in the night—and, nearly as he could estimate, the prowler had gone down behind this rise. A column of mist, sucked down from the sky, might move around aimlessly, going nowhere, but instinct maintained that this had been no mere column of mist, and that it was going somewhere.

Where?

Out of breath, he pounded over the crest, looked down into an immense valley, and found the answer.

The crystal growths gave out on the crest, again in a perfectly straight line. Beyond them the light loam, devoid of rock, ran gently down to the valley and up the farther side. Both slopes were sparsely dotted with queer, jellylike lumps of matter which lay and quivered beneath the sky's golden glow.

From the closed end of the valley jutted a great, glistening fabrication, flat-roofed, flat-fronted, with a huge, square hole gaping in its mid-section at front. It looked like a tremendous oblong slab of polished, milk-white plastic half-buried endwise in a sandy hill. No decoration disturbed its smooth, gleaming surface. No road led to the hole in front. Somehow, it had the new-old air of

a house that struggles to look empty because it is full—
of fiends.

Steve's back hairs prickled as he studied it. One thing
was obvious—Oro bore intelligent life. One thing was
possible—the golden column represented that life. One
thing was probable—fleshly Terrestrials and hazy
Orons would have difficulty in finding a basis for
friendship and cooperation.

Whereas enmity needs no basis.

Curiosity and caution pulled him opposite ways. One
urged him down into the valley while the other drove
him back, back, while yet there was time. He consulted
his watch. Less than three hours to go, within which he
had to return to the ship, enter the log, prepare supper.
That milky creation was at least two miles away, a good
hour's journey there and back. Let it wait. Give it another day and he'd have more time for it, with the benefit of needful thought betweentimes.

Caution triumphed. He investigated the nearest jelly-
blob. It was flat, a yard in diameter, green, with bluish
streaks and many tiny bubbles hiding in its semitrans-
parency. The thing pulsated slowly. He poked it with
the toe of his boot, and it contracted, humping itself in
the middle, then sluggishly relaxed. No amoeba, he decided. A low form of life, but complicated withal. Laura
didn't like the object. She skittered off as he bent over
it, vented her anger by bashing a few crystals.

This jello dollop wasn't like its nearest neighbor, or
like any other. One of each, only one. The same rule:
one butterfly of a kind, one bug, one plant, one of these
quivering things.

A final stare at the distant mystery down in the valley, then he retraced his steps. When the ship came into
sight he speeded up like a gladsome voyager nearing
home. There were new prints near the vessel, big, three-
toed, deeply-impressed spoor which revealed that something large, heavy and two-legged had wandered past in
his absence. Evidently an animal, for nothing intelligent
would have meandered on so casually without circling
and inspecting the nearby invader from space. He dis-

missed it from his mind. There was only one thingum-
bob, he felt certain of that.

Once inside the ship, he relocked the doors, gave
Laura her feed, ate his supper. Then he dragged out the
log, made his day's entry, had a look around from the
dome. Violet streamers once more were creeping upward from the horizon. He frowned at the encompassing vegetation. What sort of stuff had bred all this in the
past? What sort of stuff would this breed in the future?
How did it progenerate, anyway?

Wholesale radical mutation presupposed modification of genes by hard radiation in persistent and considerable blasts. You shouldn't get hard radiation on light-
weight planets—unless it poured in from the sky. Here,
it didn't pour from the sky, or from any place else. In
fact, there wasn't any.

He was pretty certain of that fact because he'd a special interest in it and had checked up on it. Hard radiation betokened the presence of radioactive elements
which, in a pinch, might be usable as fuel. The ship was
equipped to detect such stuff. Among the junk was a
cosmiray counter, a radium hen, and a gold-leaf electroscope. The hen and the counter hadn't given so much as
one heartening cluck, in fact the only clucks had been
Laura's. The electroscope he'd charged on landing and
its leaves still formed an inverted V. The air was dry,
ionization negligible, and the leaves didn't look likely to
collapse for a week.

"Something's wrong with my theorizing," he complained to Laura. "My think-stuff's not doing its job."

"Not doing its job," echoed Laura faithfully. She
cracked a pecan with a grating noise that set his teeth
on edge. "I tell you it's a hoodoo ship. I won't sail. No,
not even if you pray for me. I won't, I won't, I won't.
Nope. Nix. Who's drunk? That hairy Lowlander Mc—"

"Laura!" he said sharply.

"Gillicuddy," she finished with bland defiance. Again
she rasped his teeth. "Rings bigger'n Saturn's. I saw
them myself. Who's a liar? Yawk! She's down in Gray-
way Bay, on Tethis. Boy, what a torso!"

He looked at her hard and said, "You're nuts!"

"Sure! Sure, pal! Laura loves nuts. Have one on me."

"O.K.," he accepted, holding out his hand.

Cocking her colorful pate, she pecked at his hand, gravely selected a pecan and gave it to him. He cracked it, chewed on the kernel while starting up the lighting-set. It was almost as if night were waiting for him. Blackness fell even as he switched on the lights.

With the darkness came a keen sense of unease. The dome was the trouble. It blazed like a beacon and there was no way of blacking it out except by turning off the lights. Beacons attracted things, and he'd no desire to become a center of attraction in present circumstances. That is to say, not at night.

Long experience had bred fine contempt for alien animals, no matter how whacky, but outlandish intelligences were a different proposition. So filled was he with the strange inward conviction that last night's phenomenon was something that knew its onions that it didn't occur to him to wonder whether a glowing column possessed eyes or anything equivalent to a sense of sight. If it had occurred to him, he'd have derived no comfort from it. His desire to be weighed in the balance in some eerie, extrasensory way was even less than his desire to be gaped at visually in his slumbers.

An unholy mess of thoughts and ideas was still cooking in his mind when he extinguished the lights, bunked down and went to sleep. Nothing disturbed him this time, but when he awoke with the golden dawn his chest was damp with perspiration and Laura again had sought refuge on his arm.

Digging out breakfast, his thoughts began to marshal themselves at he kept his hands busy. Pouring out a shot of hot coffee, he spoke to Laura.

"I'm durned if I'm going to go scatty trying to maintain a three-watch system single-handed, which is what I'm supposed to do if faced by powers unknown when I'm not able to beat it. Those armchair warriors at headquarters ought to get a taste of situations not precisely specified in the book of rules."

"Burp!" said Laura contemptuously.

"He who fights and runs away lives to fight another day," Steve quoted. "That's the Probe Law. It's a nice, smooth, lovely law—when you can run away. We can't!"

"Burrup!" said Laura with unnecessary emphasis.

"For a woman, your manners are downright disgusting," he told her. "Now I'm not going to spend the brief remainder of my life looking fearfully over my shoulder. The only way to get rid of powers unknown is to convert 'em into powers known and understood. As Uncle Joe told Willie when dragging him to the dentist, the longer we put it off the worse it'll feel."

"Dinna fash y'rsel'," declaimed Laura. "Burp-gollop-bop!"

Giving her a look of extreme distaste, he continued, "So we'll try tossing the bull. Such techniques disconcert bulls sometimes." Standing up, he grabbed Laura, shoved her into her traveling compartment, slid the panel shut. "We're going to blow off forthwith."

Climbing up to the control seat, he stamped on the energizer stud. The tail rockets popped a few times, broke into a subdued roar. Juggling the controls to get the preparatory feel of them, he stepped up the boost until the entire vessel trembled and the rear venturis began to glow cherry-red. Slowly the ship commenced to edge its bulk forward and, as it did so, he fed it the take-off shot. A half-mile blast kicked backward and the probe ship plummeted into the sky.

Pulling it round in a wide and shallow sweep, he thundered over the borderline of vegetation, the fields of crystals and the hills beyond. In a flash he was plunging through the valley, braking rockets blazing from the nose. This was tricky. He had to coordinate forward shoot, backward thrust and downward surge, but like most of his kind he took pride in the stunts performable with these neat little vessels. An awe-inspired audience was all he lacked to make the exhibition perfect. The vessel landed fairly and squarely on the milk-white roof of the alien edifice, slid halfway to the cliff, then stopped.

"Boy," he breathed, "am I good!" He remained in his seat, stared around through the dome, and felt that he ought to add, "And too young to die." Occasionally eying the chronometer, he waited awhile. The boat must have handed that roof a thump sufficient to wake the dead. If anyone were in, they'd soon hotfoot out to see who was heaving hundred-ton bottles at their shingles. Nobody emerged. He gave them half an hour, his hawk-like face strained, alert. Then he gave it up, said, "Ah, well," and got out of the seat.

He freed Laura. She came out with ruffled dignity, like a dowager who's paraded into the wrong room. Females were always curious critters, in his logic, and he ignored her attitude, got his gun, unlocked the doors, jumped down onto the roof. Laura followed reluctantly, came to his shoulder as if thereby conferring a great favor.

Walking past the tail to the edge of the roof, he looked down. The sheerness of the five-hundred-foot drop took him aback. Immediately below his feet, the entrance soared four hundred feet up from the ground and he was standing on the hundred-foot lintel surmounting it. The only way down was to walk to the side of the roof and reach the earthy slope in which the building was embedded, seeking a path down that.

He covered a quarter of a mile of roof to get to the slope, his eyes examining the roof's surface as he went, and failing to find one crack or joint in the uniformly smooth surface. Huge as it was, the erection appeared to have been molded all in one piece—a fact which did nothing to lessen inward misgivings. Whoever did this mighty job weren't Zulus!

From ground level the entrance loomed bigger than ever. If there had been a similar gap at the other side of the building, and a clear way through, he could have taken the ship in at one end and out at the other as easily as threading a needle.

Absence of doors didn't seem peculiar; it was difficult to imagine any sort of door huge enough to fill this opening yet sufficiently balanced to enable anyone—or anything—to pull it open or shut. With a final, cautious look around which revealed nothing moving in the valley, he stepped boldly through the entrance, blinked his eyes, found interior darkness slowly fading as visual retention lapsed and gave up remembrance of the golden glow outside.

There was a glow inside, a different one, paler, ghastlier, greenish. It exuded from the floor, the walls, the ceiling, and the total area of radiation was enough to light the place clearly, with no shadows. He sniffed as his vision adjusted itself. There was a strong smell of ozone mixed with other, unidentifiable odors.

To his right and left, rising hundreds of feet, stood great tiers of transparent cases. He went to the ones on his right and examined them. They were cubes, about a yard each way, made of something like transpex. Each contained three inches of loam from which sprouted a crystal. No two crystals were alike; some small and branchy, others large and indescribably complicated.

Dumb with thought, he went around to the back of the monster tier, found another ten yards behind it. And another behind that. And another and another. All with crystals. The number and variety of them made his head whirl. He could study only the two bottom rows of each rack, but row on row stepped themselves far above his head to within short distance of the roof. Their total number was beyond estimation.

It was the same on the left. Crystals by the thousands. Looking more closely at one especially fine example, he noticed that the front plate of its case bore a small, inobtrusive pattern of dots etched upon the outer surface. Investigation revealed that all cases were similarly marked, differing only in the number and arrangement of the dots. Undoubtedly, some sort of cosmic code used for classification purposes.

"The Oron Museum of Natural History," he guessed, in a whisper.

"You're a liar," squawked Laura violently. "I tell you it's a hoodoo—" She stopped, dumfounded, as her own voice roared through the building in deep, organlike tones, "A hoodoo— A hoodoo—"

"Holy smoke, will you keep quiet!" hissed Steve. He tried to keep watch on the exit and the interior simultaneously. But the voice rumbled away in the distance without bringing anyone to dispute their invasion.

Turning, he paced hurriedly past the first blocks of tiers to the next batteries of exhibits. Jelly blobs in this lot. Small ones, no bigger than his wristwatch, numberable in thousands. None appeared to be alive, he noted.

Sections three, four and five took him a mile into the building as nearly as he could estimate. He passed mosses, lichens and shrubs, all dead but wondrously preserved. By this time he was ready to guess at section six—plants. He was wrong. The sixth layout displayed bugs, including moths, butterflies, and strange, unfamiliar objects resembling chitinous humming-birds. There was no sample of *Scarabaeus anderii,* unless it were several hundred feet up. Or unless there was an empty box ready for it—when its day was done.

Who made the boxes? Had it prepared one for him? One for Laura? He visualized himself, petrified forever, squatting in the seventieth case of the twenty-fifth row of the tenth tier in section something-or-other, his front panel duly tagged with its appropriate dots. It was a lousy picture. It made his forehead wrinkle to think of it.

Looking for he knew not what, he plunged steadily on, advancing deeper and deeper into the heart of the building. Not a soul, not a sound, not a footprint. Only that all-pervading smell and the unvarying glow. He had a feeling that the place was visited frequently but never occupied for any worthwhile period of time. Without bothering to stop and look, he passed an enormous case containing a creature faintly resembling a bison-headed rhinoceros, then other, still larger cases holding equally larger exhibits—all carefully dot-marked.

Finally, he rounded a box so tremendous that it sprawled across the full width of the hall. It contained the grandpappy of all trees and the great-grandpappy of all serpents. Behind, for a change, reared five hundred feet high racks of metal cupboards, each cupboard with a stud set in its polished door, each ornamented with more groups of mysteriously arranged dots.

Greatly daring, he pressed the stud on the nearest cupboard and its door swung open with a juicy click. The result proved disappointing. The cupboard was filled with stacks of small, glassy sheets, each smothered with dots.

"Super filing-system," he grunted, closing the door. "Old Prof Heggarty would give his right arm to be here."

"Heggarty," said Laura, in a faltering voice. "For Pete's sake!"

He looked at her sharply. She was ruffled and fidgety, showing signs of increasing agitation.

"What's the matter, Chicken?"

She peeked at him, returned her anxious gaze the way they had come, side-stepped to and fro on his shoulder. Her neck feathers started to rise. A nervous cluck came from her beak and she cowered close to his jacket.

"Darn!" he muttered. Spinning on one heel, he raced past successive filing blocks, got into the ten yards' space between the end block and the wall. His gun was out and he kept watch on the front of the blocks while his free hand tried to soothe Laura. She snuggled up close, rubbing her head into his neck and trying to hide under the angle of his jaw.

"Quiet, Honey," he whispered. "Just you keep quiet and stay with Steve, and we'll be all right."

She kept quiet, though she'd begun to tremble. His heart speeded up in sympathy though he could see nothing, hear nothing to warrant it.

Then, while he watched and waited, and still in absolute silence, the interior brightness waxed, became less green, more golden. And suddenly he knew what it was that was coming. He *knew* what it was!

He sank on one knee to make himself as small and inconspicuous as possible. Now his heart was palpitating wildly and no coldness in his mind could freeze it down to slower, more normal beat. The silence, the awful silence of its approach was the unbearable feature. The crushing thud of a weighty foot or hoof would have been better. Colossi have no right to steal along like ghosts.

And the golden glow built up, drowning out the green radiance from floor to roof, setting the multitude of case-surfaces afire with its brilliance. It grew as strong as the golden sky, and stronger. It became all-pervading, unendurable, leaving no darkness in which to hide, no sanctuary for little things.

It flamed like the rising sun or like something drawn from the heart of a sun, and the glory of its radiance sent the cowering watcher's mind awhirl. He struggled fiercely to control his brain, to discipline it, to bind it to his fading will—and failed.

With drawn face beaded by sweat, Steve caught the merest fragmentary glimpse of the column's edge appearing from between the stacks of the center aisle. He saw a blinding strip of burnished gold in which glittered a pure white star, then a violent effervescence seemed to occur within his brain and he fell forward into a cloud of tiny bubbles.

Down, down he sank through myriad bubbles and swirls and sprays of iridescent froth and foam which shone and changed and shone anew with every conceivable color. And all the time his mind strove frantically to battle upward and drag his soul to the surface.

Deep into the nethermost reaches he went while still the bubbles whirled around in their thousands and their colors were of numberless hues. Then his progress slowed. Gradually the froth and the foam ceased to rotate upward, stopped its circling, began to swirl in the reverse direction and sink. He was rising! He rose for a lifetime, floating weightlessly, in a dreamlike trance.

The last of the bubbles drifted eerily away, leaving him in a brief hiatus of nonexistence—then he found himself sprawled full length on the floor with a dazed Laura clinging to his arm. He blinked his eyes, slowly, several times. They were strained and sore. His heart was still palpitating and his legs felt weak. There was a strange sensation in his stomach as if memory had sickened him with a shock from long, long ago.

He didn't get up from the floor right away; his body was too shaken and his mind too muddled for that. While his wits came back and his composure returned, he lay and noted that all the invading goldness had gone and that again the interior illumination was a dull, shadowless green. Then his eyes found his watch and he sat up, startled. Two hours had flown!

That fact brought him shakily to his feet. Peering around the end of the bank of filing cabinets, he saw that nothing had changed. Instinct told him that the golden visitor had gone and that once more he had this place to himself. Had it become aware of his presence? Had it made him lose consciousness or, if not, why had he lost it? Had it done anything about the ship on the roof?

Picking up his futile gun, he spun it by its stud guard and looked at it with contempt. Then he holstered it, helped Laura onto his shoulder, where she perched groggily, went around the back of the racks and still deeper into the building.

"I reckon we're O.K., Honey," he told her. "I think we're too small to be noticed. We're like mice. Who bothers to trap mice when he's got bigger and more important things in mind?" He pulled a face, not liking the mouse comparison. It wasn't flattering to either him or his kind. But it was the best he could think of at the moment. "So, like little mice, let's look for cheese. I'm not giving up just because a big hunk of something has sneaked past and put a scare into us. We don't scare off, do we, Sweetness?"

"No," said Laura unenthusiastically. Her voice was still subdued and her eyes perked apprehensively this way and that. "No scare. I won't sail, I tell you. Blow my sternpipes! Laura loves nuts!"

"Don't you call me a nut!"

"Nuts! Stick to farming—it gets you more eggs. McGillicuddy, the great—"

"Hey!" he warned.

She shut up abruptly. He put the pace on, refusing to admit that his system felt slightly jittery with nervous strain or that anything had got him bothered. But he knew that he'd no desire to be near that sparkling giant again. Once was enough, more than enough. It wasn't that he feared it, but something else, something he was quite unable to define.

Passing the last bank of cabinets, he found himself facing a machine. It was complicated and bizarre—and it was making a crystalline growth. Near it, another and different machine was manufacturing a small, horned lizard. There could be no doubt at all about the process of fabrication because both objects were half-made and both progressed slightly even as he watched. In a couple of hours' time, perhaps less, they'd be finished, and all they'd need would be . . . would be—

The hairs stiffened on the back of his neck and he commenced to run. Endless machines, all different, all making different things, plants, bugs, birds and fungoids. It was done by electroponics, atom fed to atom like brick after brick to build a house. It wasn't synthesis because that's only assembly, and this was assembly plus growth in response to unknown laws. In each of these machines, he knew, was some key or code or cipher, some weird master-control of unimaginable complexity, determining the patterns each was building—and the patterns were infinitely variable.

Here and there pieces of apparatus stood silent, inactive, their tasks complete. Here and there other monstrous layouts were in pieces, either under repair or readied for modification. He stopped by one which had finished its job. It had fashioned a delicately shaded moth which perched motionless like a jeweled statue within its fabrication jar. The creature was perfect as far as he could tell, and all it was waiting for was . . . was—

Beads of moisture popped out on his forehead. All that moth needed was the breath of life!

He forced a multitude of notions to get out of his mind. It was the only way to retain a hold on himself.

Divert your attention—take it off this and place it on that! Firmly, he fastened his attention on one tremendous, partly disassembled machine lying nearby. Its guts were exposed, revealing great field coils of dull gray wire. Bits of similar wire lay scattered around on the floor.

Picking up a short piece, he found it surprisingly heavy. He took off his wristwatch, opened its back, brought the wire near to its works. The Venusian jargoon bearing fluoresced immediately. V-jargoons invariably glowed in the presence of near radiation. This unknown metal was a possible fuel. His heart gave a jump at the mere thought of it.

Should he drag out a huge coil and lug it up to the ship? It was very heavy, and he'd need a considerable length of the stuff—if it was usable as fuel. Supposing the disappearance of the coil caused mousetraps to be set before he returned to search anew?

It pays to stop and think whenever you've got time to stop and think; that was a fundamental of Probe Service philosophy. Pocketing a sample of the wire, he sought around other disassembled machines for more. The search took him still deeper into the building and he fought harder to keep his attention concentrated solely on the task. It wasn't easy. There was that dog, for instance, standing there, statuclike, waiting, waiting. If only it had been anything but indubitably and recognizably an Earth-type dog. It was impossible to avoid seeing it. It would be equally impossible to avoid seeing other, even more familiar forms—if they were there.

He'd gained seven samples of different radioactive wires when he gave up the search. A cockatoo ended his peregrinations. The bird stood steadfastly in its jar, its blue plumage smooth and bright, its crimson crest raised, its bright eye fixed in what was not death but not yet life. Laura shrieked at it hysterically and the immense hall shrieked back at her with long-drawn roars and rumbles that reverberated into dim distances. Laura's reaction was too much; he wanted no cause for similar reaction of his own.

He sped through the building at top pace, passing the

filing cabinets and the mighty array of exhibition cases unheedingly. Up the loamy side slopes he climbed almost as rapidly as he'd gone down, and he was breathing heavily by the time he got into the ship.

His first action was to check the ship for evidence of interference. There wasn't any. Next, he checked the instruments. The electroscope's leaves were collapsed. Charging them, he watched them flip open and flop together again. The counter showed radiation aplenty. The hen clucked energetically. He'd blundered somewhat—he should have checked up when first he landed on the roof. However, no matter. What lay beneath the roof was now known; the instruments would have advised him earlier but not as informatively.

Laura had her feed while he accompanied her with a swift meal. After that, he dug out his samples of wire. No two were the same gauge and one obviously was far too thick to enter the feed holes of the Kingston-Kanes. It took him half an hour to file it down to a suitable diameter. The original piece of dull gray wire took the first test. Feeding it in, he set the controls to minimum warming-up intensity, stepped on the energizer. Nothing happened.

He scowled to himself. Someday they'd have jobs better than the sturdy but finicky Kingston-Kanes, jobs that'd eat anything eatable. Density and radioactivity weren't enough for these motors; the stuff fed to them had to be right.

Going back to the Kingston-Kanes, he pulled out the wire, found its end fused into shapelessness. Definitely a failure. Inserting the second sample, another gray wire not so dull as the first, he returned to the controls, rammed the energizer. The tail rockets promptly blasted with a low, moaning note and the thrust dial showed sixty per cent normal surge.

Some people would have got mad at that point. Steve didn't. His lean, hawklike features quirked, he felt in his pocket for the third sample, tried that. No soap. The fourth likewise was a flop. The fifth produced a peculiar and rhythmic series of blasts which shook the vessel from end to end and caused the thrust-dial needle to waggle between one hundred twenty per cent and zero. He visualized the probe patrols popping through space like outboard motors while he extracted the stuff and fed the sixth sample. The sixth roared joyously at one hundred seventy per cent. The seventh sample was another flop.

He discarded all but what was left of the sixth wire. The stuff was about twelve gauge and near enough for his purpose. It resembled deep-colored copper but was not as soft as copper nor as heavy. Hard, springy and light, like telephone wire. If there were at least a thousand yards of it below, and if he could manage to drag it up to the ship, and if the golden thing didn't come along and ball up the works, he might be able to blow free. Then he'd get to some place civilized—if he could find it. The future was based on an appalling selection of "ifs."

The easiest and most obvious way to salvage the needed treasure was to blow a hole in the roof, lower a cable through it, and wind up the wire with the aid of the ship's tiny winch. Problem: how to blow a hole without suitable explosives. Answer: drill the roof, insert unshelled pistol ammunition, say a prayer and pop the stuff off electrically. He tried it, using a hand drill. The bit promptly curled up as if gnawing on a diamond. He drew his gun, bounced a shell off the roof; the missile exploded with a sharp, hard crack and fragments of shell casing whined shrilly into the sky. Where it had struck, the roof bore a blast smudge and a couple of fine scratches.

There was nothing for it but to go down and heave on his shoulders as much loot as he could carry. And do it right away. Darkness would fall before long, and he didn't want to encounter that golden thing in the dark. It was fateful enough in broad light of day, or in the queer, green glow of the building's interior, but to have it stealing softly behind him as he struggled through the nighttime with his plunder was something of which he didn't care to think.

Locking the ship and leaving Laura inside, he returned to the building, made his way past the mile of cases and cabinets to the machine section at back. He stopped to study nothing on his way. He didn't wish to study anything. The wire was the thing, only the wire. Besides, mundane thoughts of mundane wire didn't twist one's mind around until one found it hard to concentrate.

Nevertheless, his mind was afire as he searched. Half of it was prickly with alertness, apprehensive of the golden column's sudden return; the other half burned with excitement at the possibility of release. Outwardly, his manner showed nothing of this; it was calm, assured, methodical.

Within ten minutes he'd found a great coil of the coppery metal, a huge ovoid, intricately wound, lying beside a disassembled machine. He tried to move it, could not shift it an inch. The thing was far too big, too heavy for one to handle. To get it onto the roof he'd have to cut it up and make four trips of it—and some of its inner windings were fused together. So near, so far! Freedom depended upon his ability to move a lump of metal a thousand feet vertically. He muttered some of Laura's words to himself.

Although the wire cutters were ready in his hand, he paused to think, decided to look farther before tackling this job. It was a wise decision which brought its reward, for at a point a mere hundred yards away he came across another, differently shaped coil, wheel-shaped, in good condition, easy to unreel. This again was too heavy to carry, but with a tremendous effort which made his muscles crack he got it up on its rim and proceeded to roll it along like a monster tire.

Several times he had to stop and let the coil lean against the nearest case while he rested a moment. The last such case trembled under the impact of the weighty coil and its shining, spidery occupant stirred in momentary simulation of life. His dislike of the spider shot up with its motion, he made his rest brief, bowled the coil onward.

Violet streaks again were creeping from the horizon when he rolled his loot out of the mighty exit and reached the bottom of the bank. Here, he stopped, clipped the wire with his cutters, took the free end, climbed the bank with it. The wire uncoiled without hindrance until he reached the ship, where he attached it to the winch, wound the loot in, rewound it on the feed spool.

Night fell in one ominous swoop. His hands were trembling slightly but his hawklike face was firm, phlegmatic as he carefully threaded the wire's end through the automatic injector and into the feed hole of the Kingston-Kanes. That done, he slid open Laura's door, gave her some of the fruit they'd picked off the Oron tree. She accepted it morbidly, her manner still subdued, and not inclined for speech.

"Stay inside, Honey," he soothed. "We're getting out of this and going home."

Shutting her in, he climbed into the control seat, switched on the nose beam, saw it pierce the darkness and light up the facing cliff. Then he stamped on the energizer, warmed the tubes. Their bellow was violent and comforting. At seventy per cent better thrust he'd have to be a lot more careful in all his adjustments: it wouldn't do to melt his own tail off when success was within his grasp. All the same, he felt strangely impatient, as if every minute counted, aye, every second!

But he contained himself, got the venturis heated, gave a discreet puff on his starboard steering flare, watched the cliff glide sidewise past as the ship slewed around on its belly. Another puff, then another, and he had the vessel nose-on to the front edge of the roof. There seemed to be a faint aura in the gloom ahead and he switched off his nose beam to study it better.

It was a faint yellow haze shining over the rim of the opposite slope. His back hairs quivered as he saw it. The haze strengthened, rose higher. His eyes strained into the outer pall as he watched it fascinatedly, and his hands were frozen on the controls. There was dampness on his back. Behind him, in her traveling compartment,

Laura was completely silent, not even shuffling uneasily as was her wont. He wondered if she was cowering.

With a mighty effort of will which strained him as never before, he shifted his control a couple of notches, lengthened the tail blast. Trembling in its entire fabric, the ship edged forward. Summoning all he'd got, Steve forced his reluctant hands to administer the take-off boost. With a tearing crash that thundered back from the cliffs, the little vessel leaped skyward on an arc of fire. Peering through the transpex, Steve caught a fragmentary and foreshortened glimpse of the great golden column advancing majestically over the crest; the next instant it had dropped far behind his tail and his bow was arrowing for the stars.

An immense relief flooded through his soul though he knew not what there had been to fear. But the relief was there and so great was it that he worried not at all about where he was bound or for how long. Somehow, he felt certain that if he swept in a wide, shallow curve he'd pick up a Probe beat-note sooner or later. Once he got a beat-note, from any source at all, it would lead him out of the celestial maze.

Luck remained with him, and his optimistic hunch proved correct, for while still among completely strange constellations he caught the faint throb of Hydra III on his twenty-seventh day of sweep. That throb was his cosmic lighthouse beckoning him home.

He let go a wild shriek of "Yipee!" thinking that only Laura heard him—but he was heard elsewhere.

Down on Oro, deep in the monster workshop, the golden giant paused blindly as if listening. Then it slid stealthily along the immense aisles, reached the filing system. A compartment opened, two glassy plates came out.

For a moment the plates contacted the Oron's strange, sparkling substance, became etched with an array of tiny dots. They were returned to the compartment, and the door closed. The golden glory with its imprisoned stars then glided quietly back to the machine section.

Something nearer to the gods had scribbled its notes.

Nothing lower in the scale of life could have translated them or deduced their full purport.

In simplest sense, one plate may have been inscribed, "Biped, erect, pink, homo intelligens type P.739, planted on Sol III, Condensation Arm BDB—moderately succccssful."

Similarly, the other plate may have recorded, "Flapwing, large, hook-beaked, vari-colored, periquito macao type K.8, planted on Sol III, Condensation Arm BDB—moderately successful."

But already the sparkling hobbyist had forgotten his passing notes. He was breathing his essence upon a jeweled moth.

Late Night Final

COMMANDER CRUIN WENT down the extending metal ladder, paused a rung from the bottom, placed one important foot on the new territory, and then the other. That made him the first of his kind on an unknown world.

He posed there in the sunlight, a big bull of a man meticulously attired for the occasion. Not a spot marred his faultlessly cut uniform of gray-green on which jeweled orders of merit sparkled and flashed. His jackboots glistened as they had never done since the day of launching from the home planet. The golden bells of his rank tinkled on his heelhooks as he shifted his feet slightly. In the deep shadow beneath the visor of his ornate helmet his hard eyes held a glow of self-satisfaction.

A microphone came swinging down to him from the air lock he'd just left. Taking it in a huge left hand, he looked straight ahead with the blank intentness of one who sees long visions of the past and longer visions of the future. Indeed, this was as visionary a moment as any there had been in his world's history.

"In the name of Huld and the people of Huld," he enunciated officiously, "I take this planet." Then he saluted swiftly, slickly, like an automaton.

Facing him, twenty-two long, black spaceships simultaneously thrust from their forward ports their glorypoles ringed with the red-black-gold colors of Huld. Inside the vessels twenty-two crews of seventy men apiece stood rigidly erect, saluted, broke into well-drilled song, "Oh, heavenly fatherland of Huld."

When they had finished, Commander Cruin saluted again. The crews repeated their salute. The glorypoles were drawn in. Cruin mounted the ladder, entered his flagship. All locks were closed. Along the valley the twenty-two invaders lay in military formation, spaced equidistantly, noses and tails dead in line.

On a low hill a mile to the east a fire sent up a column of thick smoke. It spat and blazed amid the remnants of what had been the twenty-third vessel—and the eighth successive loss since the fleet had set forth three years ago. Thirty then. Twenty-two now.

The price of empire.

Reaching his cabin, Commander Cruin lowered his bulk into the seat behind his desk, took off his heavy helmet, adjusted an order of merit which was hiding modestly behind its neighbor.

"Step four," he commented with satisfaction.

Second Commander Jusik nodded respectfully. He handed the other a book. Opening it, Cruin meditated aloud.

"Step one: Check planet's certain suitability for our form of life." He rubbed his big jowls. "We know it's suitable."

"Yes, sir. This is a great triumph for you."

"Thank you, Jusik." A craggy smile played momentarily on one side of Cruin's broad face. "Step two: Remain in planetary shadow at distance of not less than one diameter while scout boats survey world for evidence of superior life forms. Three: Select landing place far from largest sources of possible resistance but adjacent to a source small enough to be mastered. Four: Declare Huld's claim ceremoniously, as prescribed in manual on procedure and discipline." He worked his jowls again. "We've done all that."

The smile returned, and he glanced with satisfaction out of the small port near his chair. The port framed the smoke column on the hill. His expression changed to a scowl, and his jaw muscles lumped.

"Fully trained and completely qualified," he growled sardonically. "Yet he had to smash up. Another ship and crew lost in the very moment we reach our goal. The eighth such loss. There will be a purge in the astronautical training center when I return."

"Yes, sir," approved Jusik, dutifully. "There is no excuse for it."

"There are no excuses for anything," Cruin retorted.

"No, sir."

Snorting his contempt, Cruin looked at his book. "Step five: Make all protective preparations as detailed in defense manual." He glanced up into Jusik's lean, clearcut features. "Every captain has been issued with a defense manual. Are they carrying out its orders?"

"Yes, sir. They have started already."

"They better had! I shall arrange a demotion of the slowest." Wetting a large thumb, he flipped a page over. "Step six: If planet does hold life forms of suspected intelligence, obtain specimens." Lying back in his seat he mused a moment, then barked: "Well, for what are you waiting?"

"I beg your pardon, sir?"

"Get some examples," roared Cruin.

"Very well, sir." Without blinking, Jusik saluted, marched out.

The self-closer swung the door behind him. Cruin surveyed it with a jaundiced eye.

"Curse the training center," he rumbled. "It has deteriorated since I was there."

Putting his feet on the desk, he waggled his heels to make the bells tinkle while he waited for the examples.

Three specimens turned up of their own accord. They were seen standing wide-eyed in a row near the prow of number twenty-two, the endmost ship of the line. Captain Somir brought them along personally.

"Step six calls for specimens, sir," he explained to Commander Cruin. "I know that you require ones better than these, but I found these under our nose."

"Under your nose? You land and within short time other life forms are sightseeing around your vessel? What about your protective precautions?"

"They are not completed yet, sir. They take some time."

"What were your lookouts doing—sleeping?"

"No, sir," assured Somir desperately. "They did not think it necessary to sound a general alarm for such as these."

Reluctantly, Cruin granted the point. His gaze ran contemptuously over the trio. Three kids. One was a boy, knee-high, snubnosed, chewing at a chubby fist. The next, a skinny-legged, pigtailed girl obviously older than the boy. The third was another girl almost as tall as Somir, somewhat skinny, but with a hint of coming shapeliness hiding in her thin attire. All three were freckled, all had violently red hair.

The tall girl said to Cruin: "I'm Marva—Marva Meredith." She indicated her companions. "This is Sue and this is Sam. We live over there, in Williamsville." She smiled at him and suddenly he noticed that her eyes were a rich and startling green. "We were looking for blueberries when we saw you come down."

Cruin grunted, rested his hands on his paunch. The fact that this planet's life manifestly was of his own shape and form impressed him not at all. It had never occurred to him that it could have proved otherwise. In Huldian thought, all superior life must be humanoid and no exploration had yet provided evidence to the contrary.

"I don't understand her alien gabble and she doesn't understand Huldian," he complained to Somir. "She must be dull-witted to waste her breath thus."

"Yes, sir," agreed Somir. "Do you wish me to hand them over to the tutors?"

"No. They're not worth it." He eyed the small boy's freckles with distaste, never having seen such a phenomenon before. "They are badly spotted and may be diseased. *Pfaugh!*" He grimaced with disgust. "Did they pass through the ray-sterilizing chamber as they came in?"

"Certainly, sir. I was most careful about that."

"Be equally careful about any more you may encounter." Slowly, his authoritative stare went from the boy to the pigtailed girl and finally to the tall one. He didn't want to look at her, yet knew that he was going to. Her cool green eyes held something that made him vaguely uncomfortable. Unwillingly he met those eyes. She smiled again, with little dimples. "Kick 'em out!" he rapped at Somir.

"As you order, sir."

Nudging them, Somir gestured toward the door. The three took hold of each other's hands, filed out.

"Bye!" chirped the boy, solemnly.

"Bye!" said pigtails, shyly.

The tall girl turned in the doorway. "Good-by!"

Gazing at her uncomprehendingly, Cruin fidgeted in his chair. She dimpled at him, then the door swung to.

"Good-by." He mouthed the strange word to himself. Considering the circumstances in which it had been uttered, evidently it meant farewell. Already he had picked up one word of their language.

"Step seven: Gain communication by tutoring specimens until they are proficient in Huldian."

Teach them. Do not let them teach you—teach *them*. The slaves must learn from the masters, not the masters from the slaves.

"Good-by." He repeated it with savage self-accusation. A minor matter, but still an infringement of the book of rules. There are no excuses for anything.

Teach them.

The slaves—

Rockets rumbled and blasted deafeningly as ships maneuvered themselves into the positions laid down in the manual of defense. Several hours of careful belly-edging were required for this. In the end, the line had reshaped itself into two groups of eleven-pointed stars, noses at the center, tails outward. Ash of blast-destroyed grasses, shrubs and trees covered a wide area beyond the two menacing rings of main propulsion tubes which could incinerate anything within one mile.

This done, perspiring, dirt-coated crews lugged out their forward armaments, remounted them pointed outward in the spaces between the vessels' splayed tails. Rear armaments still aboard already were directed upward and outward. Armaments plus tubes now provided a formidable field of fire completely surrounding the double encampment. It was the Huldian master plan conceived by Huldian master planners. In other more alien estimation, it was the old covered-wagon technique, so incredibly ancient that it had been forgotten by all but the most earnest students of the past. But none of the invaders knew that.

Around the perimeter they stacked the small, fast, well-armed scouts, of which there were two per ship. Noses outward, tails inward, in readiness for quick take-off, they were paired just beyond the parent vessels, below the propulsion tubes, and out of line of the remounted batteries. There was a lot of moving around to get the scouts positioned at precisely the same distances apart and making precisely the same angles. The whole arrangement had that geometrical exactness beloved of the military mind.

Pacing the narrow catwalk running along the top surface of his flagship, Commander Cruin observed his toiling crews with satisfaction. Organization, discipline, energy, unquestioning obedience—those were the prime essentials of efficiency. On such had Huld grown great. On such would Huld grow greater.

Reaching the tail-end, he leaned on the stop-rail, gazed down upon the concentric rings of wide, stubby venturis. His own crew were checking the angles of their two scouts already positioned. Four guards, heavily armed, came marching through the ash with Jusik in the lead. They had six prisoners.

Seeing him, Jusik bawled: "Halt!" Guard and guarded stopped with a thud of boots and a rise of dust. Looking up, Jusik saluted.

"Six specimens, sir."

Cruin eyed them indifferently. Half a dozen middle-aged men in drab, sloppily fitting clothes. He would not have given a snap of the fingers for six thousand of them.

The biggest of the captives, the one second from the left, had red hair and was sucking something that gave off smoke. His shoulders were wider than Cruin's own though he didn't look half the weight. Idly, the commander wondered whether the fellow had green eyes; he couldn't tell that from where he was standing.

Calmly surveying Cruin, this prisoner took the smoke-thing from his mouth and said, tonelessly: "By hokey, a brasshat!" Then he shoved the thing back between his lips and dribbled blue vapor.

The others looked doubtful, as if either they did not comprehend or found it past belief.

"Jeepers, *no!*" said the one on the right, a gaunt individual with thin, saturnine features.

"I'm telling you," assured Redhead in the same flat voice.

"Shall I take them to the tutors, sir?" asked Jusik.

"Yes." Unleaning from the rail, Cruin carefully adjusted his white gloves. "Don't bother me with them again until they are certified as competent to talk." Answering the other's salute, he paraded back along the catwalk.

"See?" said Redhead, picking up his feet in time with the guard. He seemed to take an obscure pleasure in keeping in step with the guard. Winking at the nearest prisoner, he let a curl of aromatic smoke trickle from the side of his mouth.

Tutors Fane and Parth sought an interview the following evening. Jusik ushered them in, and Cruin looked up irritably from the report he was writing.

"Well?"

Fane said: "Sir, these prisoners suggest that we share their homes for a while and teach them to converse there."

"How did they suggest that?"

"Mostly by signs," explained Fane.

"And what made you think that so nonsensical a plan had sufficient merit to make it worthy of my attention?"

"There are aspects about which you should be consulted," Fane continued stubbornly. "The manual of procedure and discipline declares that such matters must be placed before the commanding officer whose decision is final."

"Quite right, quite right." He regarded Fane with a little more favor. "What are these matters?"

"Time is important to us, and the quicker these prisoners learn our language the better it will be. Here, their minds are occupied by their predicament. They think too much of their friends and families. In their own homes it would be different, and they could learn at great speed."

"A weak pretext," scoffed Cruin.

"That is not all. By nature they are naive and friendly. I feel that we have little to fear from them. Had they been hostile they would have attacked by now."

"Not necessarily. It is wise to be cautious. The manual of defense emphasizes that fact repeatedly. These creatures may wish first to gain the measure of us before they try to deal with us."

Fane was prompt to snatch the opportunity. "Your point, sir, is also my final one. Here, they are six pairs of eyes and six pairs of ears in the middle of us, and their absence is likely to give cause for alarm in their home town. Were they there, complacency would replace that alarm—and *we* would be the eyes and ears!"

"Well put," commented Jusik, momentarily forgetting himself.

"Be silent!" Cruin glared at him. "I do not recall any ruling in the manual pertaining to such a suggestion as this. Let me check up." Grabbing his books, he sought through them. He took a long time about it, gave up, and said: "The only pertinent rule appears to be that in circumstances not specified in the manual the decision is wholly mine, to be made in light of said circumstances providing that they do not conflict with the rul-

ings of any other manual which may be applicable to
the situation, and providing that my decision does not
effectively countermand that or those of any senior
ranking officer whose authority extends to the same
area." He took a deep breath.

"Yes, sir," said Fane.

"Quite, sir," said Parth.

Cruin frowned heavily. "How far away are these prisoners' homes?"

"One hour's walk." Fane made a persuasive gesture.
"If anything did happen to us—which I consider extremely unlikely—one scout could wipe out their little
town before they'd time to realize what had happened.
One scout, one bomb, one minute!" Dexterously, he
added, "At your order, sir."

Cruin preened himself visibly. "I see no reason why
we should not take advantage of their stupidity." His
eyes asked Jusik what he thought, but that person failed
to notice. "Since you two tutors have brought this plan
to me, I hereby approve it, and I appoint you to carry it
through." He consulted a list which he extracted from a
drawer. "Take two psychologists with you—Kalma and
Hefni."

"Very well, sir." Impassively, Fane saluted and went
out, Parth following.

Staring absently at his half-written report, Cruin fiddled with his pen for a while, glanced up at Jusik, and
spat: "At what are you smiling?"

Jusik wiped it from his face, looked solemn.

"Come on. Out with it!"

"I was thinking, sir," replied Jusik, slowly, "that
three years in a ship is a very long time."

Slamming his pen on the desk, Cruin stood up. "Has
it been any longer for others than for me?"

"For you," said Jusik, daringly but respectfully, "I
think it has been longest of all."

"Get out!" shouted Cruin.

He watched the other go, watched the self-closer
push the door, waited for its last click. He shifted his
gaze to the port, stared hard-eyed into the gathering
dusk. His heelbells were silent as he stood unmoving

and saw the invisible sun sucking its last rays from the sky.

In short time, ten figures strolled through the twilight toward the distant, tree-topped hill. Four were uniformed; six in drab, shapeless clothes. They went by conversing with many gestures, and one of them laughed. He gnawed his bottom lip as his gaze followed them until they were gone.

The price of rank.

"Step eight: Repel initial attacks in accordance with techniques detailed in manual of defense." Cruin snorted, put up one hand, tidied his orders of merit.

"There have been no attacks," said Jusik.

"I am not unaware of the fact." The commander glowered at him. "I'd have preferred an onslaught. We are ready for them. The sooner they match their strength against ours the sooner they'll learn who's boss now!" He hooked big thumbs in his silver-braided belt. "And besides, it would give the men something to do. I cannot have them everlastingly repeating their drills of procedure. We've been here nine days and nothing has happened." His attention returned to the book. "Step nine: Follow defeat of initial attacks by taking aggressive action as detailed in manual of defense." He gave another snort. "How can one follow something that has not occurred?"

"It is impossible," Jusik ventured.

"Nothing is impossible," Cruin contradicted, harshly. "Step ten: In the unlikely event that intelligent life displays indifference or amity, remain in protective formation while specimens are being tutored, meanwhile employing scout vessels to survey surrounding area to the limit of their flight-duration, using no more than one-fifth of the numbers available at any time."

"That allows us eight or nine scouts on survey," observed Jusik, thoughtfully. "What is our authorized step if they fail to return?"

"Why d'you ask that?"

"Those eight scouts I sent out on your orders forty periods ago are overdue."

Viciously, Commander Cruin thrust away his book. His broad, heavy face was dark red.

"Second Commander Jusik, it was your duty to report this fact to me the moment those vessels became overdue."

"Which I have," said Jusik, imperturbably. "They have a flight-duration of forty periods, as you know. That, sir, made them due a short time ago. They are now late."

Cruin tramped twice across the room, medals clinking, heel-bells jangling. "The answer to nonappearance is immediately to obliterate the areas in which they are held. No half-measures. A salutary lesson."

"Which areas, sir?"

Stopping in mid-stride, Cruin bawled: "*You* ought to know that. Those scouts had properly formulated route orders, didn't they? It's a simple matter to—"

He ceased as a shrill whine passed overhead, lowered to a dull moan in the distance, curved back on a rising note again.

"Number one." Jusik looked at the little timemeter on the wall. "Late, but here. Maybe the others will turn up now."

"Somebody's going to get a sharp lesson if they don't!"

"I'll see what he has to report." Saluting, Jusik hurried through the doorway.

Gazing out of his port, Cruin observed the delinquent scout belly-sliding up to the nearest formation. He chewed steadily at his bottom lip, a slow, persistent chew which showed his thoughts to be wandering around in labyrinths of their own.

Beyond the fringe of dank, dead ash were golden buttercups in the grasses, and a hum of bees, and the gentle rustle of leaves on trees. Four engine-room wranglers of ship number seventeen had found this sanctuary and sprawled flat on their backs in the shade of a big-leafed and blossom-ornamented growth. With eyes closed, their hands plucked idly at surrounding grasses while they maintained a lazy, desultory conversation through which they failed to hear the ring of Cruin's approaching bells.

Standing before them, his complexion florid, he roared: "Get up!"

Shooting to their feet, they stood stiffly shoulder to shoulder, faces expressionless, eyes level, hands at their sides.

"Your names?" He wrote them in his notebook while obediently they repeated them in precise, unemotional voices. "I'll deal with you later," he promised. "March!"

Together, they saluted, marched off with a rhythmic pounding of boots, one-two-three-hup! His angry stare followed them until they reached the shadow of their ship. Not until then did he turn and proceed. Mounting the hill, one cautious hand continually on the cold butt of his gun, he reached the crest, gazed down into the valley he'd just left. In neat, exact positioning, the two star-formations of the ships of Huld were silent and ominous.

His hard, authoritative eyes turned to the other side of the hill. There, the landscape was pastoral. A wooded slope ran down to a little river which meandered into the hazy distance, and on its farther side was a broad patchwork of cultivated fields in which three houses were visible.

Seating himself on a large rock, Cruin loosened his gun in its holster, took a wary look around, extracted a small wad of reports from his pocket and glanced over them for the twentieth time. A faint smell of herbs and resin came to his nostrils as he read.

"I circled this landing place at low altitude and recorded it photographically, taking care to include all the machines standing thereon. Two other machines which were in the air went on their way without attempting to interfere. It then occurred to me that the signals they were making from the ground might be an invitation to land, and I decided to utilize opportunism as recommended in the manual of procedure. Therefore I landed. They conducted my scout vessel to a dispersal point off the runway and made me welcome."

Something fluted liquidly in a nearby tree. Cruin looked up, his hand automatically seeking his holster. It was only a bird. Skipping parts of the report, he frowned over the concluding words.

". . . lack of common speech made it difficult for me to refuse, and after the sixth drink during my tour of the town I was suddenly afflicted with a strange paralysis in the legs and collapsed into the arms of my companions. Believing that they had poisoned me by guile, I prepared for death . . . tickled my throat while making jocular remarks . . . I was a little sick." Cruin rubbed his chin in puzzlement. "Not until they were satisfied about my recovery did they take me back to my vessel. They waved their hands at me as I took off. I apologize to my captain for overdue return and plead that it was because of factors beyond my control."

The fluter came down to Cruin's feet, piped at him plaintively. It cocked its head sideways as it examined him with bright, beady eyes.

Shifting the sheet he'd been reading, he scanned the next one. It was neatly typewritten, and signed jointly by Parth, Fane, Kalma and Hefni.

"Do not appear fully to appreciate what has occurred . . . seem to view the arrival of a Huldian fleet as just another incident. They have a remarkable self-assurance which is incomprehensible inasmuch as we can find nothing to justify such an attitude. Mastery of them should be so easy that if our homing vessel does not leave too soon it should be possible for it to bear tidings of conquest as well as of mere discovery."

"Conquest," he murmured. It had a mighty imposing sound. A word like that would send a tremendous thrill of excitement throughout the entire world of Huld.

Five before him had sent back ships telling of discovery, but none had gone so far as he, none had traveled so long and wearily, none had been rewarded with a planet so big, lush, desirable—and none had reported the subjection of their finds. One cannot conquer a rocky waste. But this—

In peculiarly accented Huldian, a voice behind him said, brightly: "Good morning!"

He came up fast, his hand sliding to his side, his face hard with authority.

She was laughing at him with her clear green eyes. "Remember me—Marva Meredith?" Her flaming hair was windblown. "You see," she went on, in slow, awkward tones. "I know a little Huldian already. Just a few words."

"Who taught you?" he asked, bluntly.

"Fane and Parth."

"It is your house to which they have gone?"

"Oh, yes. Kalma and Hefni are guesting with Bill Gleeson; Fane and Parth with us. Father brought them to us. They share the welcome room."

"Welcome room?"

"Of course." Perching herself on his rock, she drew up her slender legs, rested her chin on her knees. He noticed that the legs, like her face, were freckled. "Of course. Everyone has a welcome room, haven't they?"

Cruin said nothing.

"Haven't you a welcome room in your home?"

"Home?" His eyes strayed away from hers, sought the fluting bird. It wasn't there. Somehow, his hand had left his holster without realizing it. He was holding his hands together, each nursing the other, clinging, finding company, soothing each other.

Her gaze was on his hands as she said, softly and hesitantly, "You have got a home . . . somewhere . . . haven't you?"

"No."

Lowering her legs, she stood up. "I'm so sorry."

"*You* are sorry for *me?*" His gaze switched back to her. It held incredulity, amazement, a mite of anger. His voice was harsh. "You must be singularly stupid."

"Am I?" she asked, humbly.

"No member of my expedition has a home," he went on. "Every man was carefully selected. Every man passed through a screen, suffered the most exacting tests. Intelligence and technical competence were not enough; each had also to be young, healthy, without ties of any sort. They were chosen for ability to concentrate on the task in hand without indulging morale-lowering sentimentalities about people left behind."

"I don't understand some of your long words," she complained. "And you are speaking far too fast."

He repeated it more slowly and added emphasis, finishing, "Spaceships undertaking long absence from base cannot be handicapped by homesick crews. We picked men without homes because they can leave Huld and not care a hoot. They are pioneers!"

"'Young, healthy, without ties,'" she quoted. "That makes them strong?"

"Definitely," he asserted.

"Men especially selected for space. Strong men." Her lashes hid her eyes as she looked down at her narrow feet. "But now they are not in space. They are here, on firm ground."

"What of it," he demanded.

"Nothing." Stretching her arms wide, she took a deep breath, then dimpled at him. "Nothing at all."

"You're only a child," he reminded, scornfully. "When you grow older—"

"You'll have more sense," she finished for him, chanting it in a high, sweet voice. "You'll have more sense, you'll have more sense. When you grow older you'll have more sense, tra-la-la-la-la!"

Gnawing irritatedly at his lip, he walked past her, started down the hill toward the ships.

"Where are you going?"

"Back!" he snapped.

"Do you like it down there?" Her eyebrows arched in surprise.

Stopping ten paces away, he scowled at her. "Is it any of your business?"

"I didn't mean to be inquisitive," she apologized. "I asked because . . . because—"

"Because what?"

"I was wondering whether you would care to visit my house."

"Nonsense! Impossible!" He turned to continue downhill.

"Father suggested it. He thought you might like to

share a meal. A fresh one. A change of diet. Something to break the monotony of your supplies." The wind lifted her crimson hair and played with it as she regarded him speculatively. "He consulted Fane and Parth. They said it was an excellent idea."

"They did, did they?" His features seemed molded in iron. "Tell Fane and Parth they are to report to me at sunset." He paused, added, "Without fail!"

Resuming her seat on the rock, she watched him stride heavily down the slope toward the double star-formation. Her hands were together in her lap, much as he had held his. But hers sought nothing of each other. In complete repose, they merely rested with the ineffable patience of hands as old as time.

Seeing at a glance that he was liverish, Jusik promptly postponed certain suggestions that he had in mind.

"Summon captains Drek and Belthan," Cruin ordered. When the other had gone, he flung his helmet onto the desk, surveyed himself in a mirror. He was still smoothing the tired lines on his face when approaching footsteps sent him officiously behind his desk.

Entering, the two captains saluted, remained rigidly at attention. Cruin studied them irefully while they preserved wooden expressions.

Eventually, he said: "I found four men lounging like undisciplined hoboes outside the safety zone." He stared at Drek. "They were from your vessel." The stare shifted to Belthan. "You are today's commander of the guard. Have either of you anything to say?"

"They were off-duty and free to leave the ship," exclaimed Drek. "They had been warned not to go beyond the perimeter of ash."

"I don't know how they slipped through," said Belthan, in official monotone. "Obviously the guards were lax. The fault is mine."

"It will count against you in your promotion records," Cruin promised. "Punish these four, and the responsible guards, as laid down in the manual of procedure and discipline." He leaned across the desk to survey them more closely. "A repetition will bring cere-monial demotion!"

"Yes, sir," they chorused.

Dismissing them, he glanced at Jusik. "When tutors Fane and Parth report here, send them in to me without delay."

"As you order, sir."

Cruin dropped the glance momentarily, brought it back. "What's the matter with you?"

"Me?" Jusik became self-conscious. "Nothing, sir."

"You lie! One has to live with a person to know him. I've lived on your neck for three years. I know you too well to be deceived. You have something on your mind."

"It's the men," admitted Jusik, resignedly.

"What of them?"

"They are restless."

"Are they? Well, I can devise a cure for that! What's making them restless?"

"Several things, sir."

Cruin waited while Jusik stayed dumb, then roared: "Do I have to prompt you?"

"No, sir," Jusik protested, unwillingly. "It's many things. Inactivity. The substitution of tedious routine. The constant waiting, waiting, waiting right on top of three years' close incarceration. They wait—and nothing happens."

"What else?"

"The sight and knowledge of familiar life just beyond the ash. The realization that Fane and Parth and the others are enjoying it with your consent. The stories told by the scouts about their experiences on landing." His gaze was steady as he went on. "We've now sent out five squadrons of scouts, a total of forty vessels. Only six came back on time. All the rest were late on one plausible pretext or another. The pilots have talked, and shown the men various souvenir photographs and a few gifts. One of them is undergoing punishment for bring-ing back some bottles of paralysis-mixture. But the damage has been done. Their stories have unsettled the men."

"Anything more?"

"Begging your pardon, sir, there was also the sight of you taking a stroll to the top of the hill. They envied you even that!" He looked squarely at Cruin. "I envied you myself."

"I am the commander," said Cruin.

"Yes, sir." Jusik kept his gaze on him but added nothing more.

If the second commander expected a delayed outburst, he was disappointed. A complicated series of emotions chased each other across his superior's broad, beefy features. As he lay back in his chair, Cruin's eyes looked absently through the port while his mind juggled with Jusik's words.

Suddenly, he rasped: "I have observed more, anticipated more and given matters more thought than perhaps you realize. I can see something which you may have failed to perceive. It has caused me some anxiety. Briefly, if we don't keep pace with the march of time we're going to find ourselves in a fix."

"Indeed, sir?"

"I don't wish you to mention this to anyone else: I suspect that we are trapped in a situation bearing no resemblance to any dealt with in the manuals."

"Really, sir?" Jusik licked his lips, felt that his own outspokenness was leading into unexpected paths.

"Consider our present circumstances," Cruin went on. "We are established here and in possession of power sufficient to enslave this planet. Any one of our supply of bombs could blast a portion of this earth stretching from horizon to horizon. But they're of no use unless we apply them effectively. We can't drop them anywhere, haphazardly. If parting with them in so improvident a manner proved unconvincing to our opponents, and failed to smash the hard core of their resistance, we would find ourselves unarmed in a hostile world. No more bombs. None nearer that six long years away, three there and three back. Therefore we must apply our power where it will do the most good." He began to massage his heavy chin. "We don't know where to apply it."

"No, sir," agreed Jusik, pointlessly.

"We've got to determine which cities are the key points of their civilization, which persons are this planet's acknowledged leaders, and where they're located. When we strike, it must be at the nerve-centers. That means we're impotent until we get the necessary information. In turn, that means we've got to establish communication with the aid of tutors." He started plucking at his jaw muscles. "And that takes time!"

"Quite, sir, but—"

"But while time crawls past the men's morale evaporates. This is our twelfth day and already the crews are restless. Tomorrow they'll be more so."

"I have a solution to that, sir, if you will forgive me for offering it," said Jusik, eagerly. "On Huld everyone gets one day's rest in five. They are free to do as they like, go where they like. Now if you promulgated an order permitting the men say one day's liberty in ten, it would mean that no more than ten percent of our strength would be lost on any one day. We could stand that reduction considering our power, especially if more of the others are on protective duty."

"So at last I get what was occupying your mind. It comes out in a swift flow of words." He smiled grimly as the other flushed. "I have thought of it. I am not quite so unimaginative as you may consider me."

"I don't look upon you that way, sir," Jusik protested.

"Never mind. We'll let that pass. To return to this subject of liberty—there lies the trap! There is the very quandary with which no manual deals, the situation for which I can find no officially prescribed formula." Putting a hand on his desk, he tapped the polished surface impatiently. "If I refuse these men a little freedom, they will become increasingly restless—naturally. If I permit them the liberty they desire, they will experience contact with life more normal even though alien, and again become more restless—naturally!"

"Permit me to doubt the latter, sir. Our crews are

loyal to Huld. Blackest space forbid that it should be otherwise!"

"They were loyal. Probably they are still loyal." Cruin's face quirked as his memory brought forward the words that followed. "They are young, healthy, without ties. In space, that means one thing. Here, another." He came slowly to his feet, big, bulky and imposing. "I *know!*"

Looking at him, Jusik felt that indeed he did know. "Yes, sir," he parroted, obediently.

"Therefore the onus of what to do for the best falls squarely upon me. I must use my initiative. As second commander it is for you to see that my orders are carried out to the letter."

"I know my duty, sir." Jusik's thinly-drawn features registered growing uneasiness.

"And it is my final decision that the men must be restrained from contact with our opponents, with no exceptions other than the four technicians operating under my orders. The crews are to be permitted no liberty, no freedom to go beyond the ash. Any form of resentment on their part must be countered immediately and ruthlessly. You will instruct the captains to watch for murmurers in their respective crews and take appropriate action to silence them as soon as found." His jowls lumped, and his eyes were cold as he regarded the other. "All scout-flights are canceled as from now, and all scout vessels remain grounded. None moves without my personal instructions."

"That is going to deprive us of a lot of information," Jusik observed. "The last flight to the south reported discovery of ten cities completely deserted, and that's got some significance which we ought to—"

"I said the flights are canceled!" Cruin shouted. "If I say the scout-vessels are to be painted pale pink, they will be painted pale pink, thoroughly, completely, from end to end. I am the commander!"

"As you order, sir."

"Finally, you may instruct the captains that their vessels are to be prepared for my inspection at midday tomorrow. That will give the crews something to do."

"Very well, sir."

With a worried salute, Jusik opened the door, glanced out and said: "Here are Fane, Kalma, Parth and Hefni, sir."

"Show them in."

After Cruin had given forcible expression to his views, Fane said: "We appreciate the urgency, sir, and we are doing our best, but it is doubtful whether they will be fluent before another four weeks have passed. They are slow to learn."

"I don't want fluency," Cruin growled. "All they need are enough words to tell us the things we want to know, the things we *must* know before we can get anywhere."

"I said sufficient fluency," Fane reminded. "They communicate mostly by signs even now."

"That flame-headed girl didn't."

"She has been quick," admitted Fane. "Possibly she has an above-normal aptitude for languages. Unfortunately she knows the least in any military sense and therefore is of little use to us."

Cruin's gaze ran over him balefully. His voice became low and menacing. "You have lived with these people many days. I look upon your features and find them different. Why is that?"

"Different?" The four exchanged wondering looks.

"Your faces have lost their lines, their space-gauntness. Your cheeks have become plump, well-colored. Your eyes are no longer tired. They are bright. They hold the self-satisfied expression of a fat *skodar* wallowing in its trough. It is obvious that you have done well for yourselves." He bent forward, his mouth ugly. "Can it be that you are in no great hurry to complete your task?"

They were suitably shocked.

"We have eaten well and slept regularly," Fane said. "We feel better for it. Our physical improvement has enabled us to work so much the harder. In our view, the foe is supporting us unwittingly with his own hospitality, and since the manual of—"

"Hospitality?" Cruin cut in, sharply.

Fane went mentally off-balance as vainly he sought for a less complimentary synonym.

"I give you another week," the commander harshed. "No more. Not one day more. At this time, one week from today, you will report here with the six prisoners adequately tutored to understand my questions and answer them."

"It will be difficult, sir."

"Nothing is difficult. Nothing is impossible. There are no excuses for anything." He studied Fane from beneath forbidding brows. "You have my orders—obey them!"

"Yes, sir."

His hard stare shifted to Kalma and Hefni. "So much for the tutors; now *you*. What have you to tell me? How much have you discovered?"

Blinking nervously, Hefni said: "It is not a lot. The language trouble is—"

"May the Giant Sun burn up and perish the language trouble! How much have you learned while enjoyably larding your bellies?"

Glancing down at his uniform-belt as if suddenly and painfully conscious of its tightness, Hefni recited: "They are exceedingly strange in so far as they appear to be highly civilized in a purely domestic sense but quite primitive in all others. This Meredith family lives in a substantial, well-equipped house. They have every comfort, including a color-television receiver."

"You're dreaming! We are still seeking the secrets of plain television even on Huld. Color is unthinkable."

Kalma chipped in with: "Nevertheless, sir, they have it. We have seen it for ourselves."

"That is so," confirmed Fane.

"Shut up!" Cruin burned him with a glare. "I have finished with you. I am now dealing with these two." His attention returned to the quaking Hefni: "Carry on."

"There is something decidedly queer about them which we've not yet been able to understand. They have no medium of exchange. They barter goods for goods without any regard for the relative values of either. They work when they feel like it. If they don't feel like it, they don't work. Yet, in spite of this, they work most of the time."

"Why?" demanded Cruin, incredulously.

"We asked them. They said that one works to avoid boredom. We cannot comprehend that viewpoint." Hefni made a defeated gesture. "In many places they have small factories which, with their strange, perverted logic, they use as amusement centers. These plants operate only when people turn up to work."

"Eh?" Cruin looked baffled.

"For example, in Williamsville, a small town an hour's walk beyond the Meredith home, there is a shoe factory. It operates every day. Some days there may be only ten workers there, other days fifty or a hundred, but nobody can remember a time when the place stood idle for lack of one voluntary worker. Meredith's elder daughter, Marva, has worked there three days during our stay with them. We asked her the reason."

"What did she say?"

"For fun."

"Fun . . . fun . . . fun?" Cruin struggled with the concept. "What does that mean?"

"We don't know," Hefni confessed. "The barrier of speech—"

"Red flames lick up the barrier of speech!" Cruin bawled. "Was her attendance compulsory?"

"No, sir."

"You are certain of that?"

"We are positive. One works in a factory for no other reason than because one feels like it."

"For what reward?" topped Cruin, shrewdly.

"Anything or nothing." Hefni uttered it like one in a dream. "One day she brought back a pair of shoes for her mother. We asked if they were her reward for the work she had done. She said they were not, and that someone named George had made them and given them to her. Apparently the rest of the factory's output for that week was shipped to another town where shoes were required. This other town is going to send back a supply of leather, nobody knows how much—and nobody seems to care."

"Senseless," defined Cruin. "It is downright imbecility." He examined Hefni as if suspecting him of inventing confusing data. "It is impossible for even the most primitive of organizations to operate so haphazardly. Obviously you have seen only part of the picture; the rest has been concealed from you, or you have been too dull-witted to perceive it."

"I assure you, sir," began Hefni.

"Let it pass," Cruin cut in. "What should I care how they function economically? In the end, they'll work the way *we* want them to!" He rested his heavy jaw in one hand. "There are other matters which interest me more. For instance, our scouts have brought in reports of many cities. Some are organized but grossly underpopulated; others are completely deserted. The former have well-constructed landing places with air-machines making use of them. How is it that people so primitive have air-machines?"

"Some make shoes, some make air-machines, some play with television. They work according to their aptitudes as well as their inclinations."

"Has this Meredith got an air-machine?"

"No." The look of defeat was etched more deeply on Hefni's face. "If he wanted one he would have his desire inserted in the television supply-and-demand program."

"Then what?"

"Sooner or later, he'd get one, new or secondhand, either in exchange for something or as a gift."

"Just by asking for it?"

"Yes."

Getting up, Cruin strode to and fro across his office. The steel heelplates on his boots clanked on the metal floor in rhythm with the bells. He was ireful, impatient, dissatisfied.

"In all this madness is nothing which tells us anything of their true character or their organization." Stopping his stride, he faced Hefni. "You boasted that *you* were to be the eyes and ears." He released a loud snort. "Blind eyes and deaf ears! Not one word about their numerical strength, not one—"

"Pardon me, sir," said Hefni, quickly, "there are twenty-seven million of them."

"Ah!" Cruin registered sharp interest. "Only twenty-seven million? Why, there's a hundred times that number on Huld, which has no greater area of land surface." He mused a moment. "Greatly underpopulated. Many cities devoid of a living soul. They have air-machines and other items suggestive of a civilization greater than the one they now enjoy. They operate the remnants of an economic system. You realize what all this means?"

Hefni blinked, made no reply. Kalma looked thoughtful. Fane and Parth remained blank-faced and tight-lipped.

"It means two things," Cruin pursued. "War or disease. One or the other, or perhaps both—and on a large scale. I want information on that. I've got to learn what sort of weapons they employed in their war, how many of them remain available, and where. Or, alternatively, what disease ravished their numbers, its source, and its cure." He tapped Hefni's chest to emphasize his words. "I want to know what they've got hidden away, what they're trying to keep from your knowledge against the time when they can bring it out and use it against us. Above all, I want to know which people will issue orders for their general offensive and where they are located."

"I understand, sir," said Hefni, doubtfully.

"That's the sort of information I need from your six specimens. I want information, not invitations to meals!" His grin was ugly as he noted Hefni's wince. "If you can get it out of them before they're due here, I shall enter the fact on the credit side of your records. But if I, your commander, have to do your job by extracting it from them myself—" Ominously, he left the sentence unfinished.

Hefni opened his mouth, closed it, glanced nervously at Kalma, who stood stiff and dumb at his side.

"You may go," Cruin snapped at the four of them. "You have one week. If you fail me, I shall deem it a front-line offense and deal with it in accordance with the active-service section of the manual of procedure and discipline."

They were pale as they saluted. He watched them file out, his lips curling contemptuously. Going to the port, he gazed into the gathering darkness, saw a pale star winking in the east. Low and far it was—but not so far as Huld.

In the mid-period of the sixteenth day, Commander Cruin strode forth polished and bemedaled, directed his bell-jangling feet toward the hill. A sour-faced guard saluted him at the edge of the ash and made a slovenly job of it.

"Is that the best you can do?" He glared into the other's surly eyes. "Repeat it!"

The guard saluted a fraction more swiftly.

"You're out of practice," Cruin informed. "Probably all the crews are out of practice. We'll find a remedy for that. We'll have a period of saluting drill every day." His glare went slowly up and down the guard's face. "Are you dumb?"

"No, sir."

"Shut up!" roared Cruin. He expanded his chest. "Continue with your patrol."

The guard's optics burned with resentment as he saluted for the third time, turned with the regulation heel-click and marched along the perimeter.

Mounting the hill, Cruin sat on the stone at the top. Alternately he viewed the ships lying in the valley and the opposite scene with its trees, fields and distant houses. The metal helmet with its ornamental wings was heavy upon his head but he did not remove it. In the shadow beneath the projecting visor, his cold eyes brooded over the landscape to one side and the other.

She came eventually. He had been sitting there for one and a half periods when she came, as he had known she would—without knowing what weird instinct had made him certain of this. Certainly, he had no desire to see her—no desire at all.

Through the trees she tripped light-footed, with Sue and Sam and three other girls of her own age. The newcomers had large, dark, humorous eyes, their hair was dark, and they were leggy.

"Oh, hello!" She paused as she saw him.

"Hello!" echoed Sue, swinging her pigtails.

" 'Lo!" piped Sam, determined not to be left out.

Cruin frowned at them. There was a high gloss on his jackboots, and his helmet glittered in the sun.

"These are my friends," said Marva, in her alien-accented Huldian. "Becky, Rita and Joyce."

The three smiled at him.

"I brought them to see the ships."

Cruin said nothing.

"You don't mind them looking at the ships, do you?"

"No," he growled with reluctance.

Lankily but gracefully she seated herself on the grass. The others followed suit, with the exception of Sam, who stood with fat legs braced apart, sucking his thumb and solemnly studying Cruin's decorated jacket.

"Father was disappointed because you could not visit us."

Cruin made no reply.

"Mother was sorry, too. She's a wonderful cook. She loves a guest."

No reply.

"Would you care to come this evening?"

"No."

"Some other evening?"

"Young lady," he harshed, severely, "I do not pay visits. Nobody pays visits."

She translated this to the others. They laughed so heartily that Cruin reddened and stood up.

"What's funny about that?" he demanded.

"Nothing, nothing." Marva was embarrassed. "If I told you, I fear that you would not understand."

"I would not understand." His grim eyes became alert, calculating as they went over her three friends. "I do not think, somehow, that they were laughing at me. Therefore they were laughing at what I do not know. They were laughing at something I ought to know but which you do not wish to tell me." He bent over her, huge and muscular, while she looked up at him with her great green eyes. "And what remark of mine revealed my amusing ignorance?"

Her steady gaze remained on him while she made no answer. A faint but sweet scent exuded from her hair.

"I said that nobody pays visits," he repeated. "That was the amusing remark—nobody pays visits. And I am not a fool!" Straightening, he turned away. "So I am going to call the rolls!"

He could feel their eyes upon him as he started down the valley. They were silent except for Sam's high-pitched, childish "Bye!" which he ignored.

Without once looking back, he gained his flagship, mounted its metal ladder, made his way to the office and summoned Jusik.

"Order the captains to call their rolls at once."

"Is something wrong, sir?" inquired Jusik, anxiously.

"Call the rolls!" Cruin bellowed, whipping off his helmet. "Then we'll know whether anything is wrong." Savagely, he flung the helmet onto a wall hook, sat down, mopped his forehead.

Jusik was gone for most of a period. In the end he returned, set-faced, grave.

"I regret to report that eighteen men are absent, sir."

"They laughed," said Cruin, bitterly. "They laughed—because they *knew!*" His knuckles were white as his hands gripped the arms of his chair.

"I beg your pardon, sir?" Jusik's eyebrows lifted.

"How long have they been absent?"

"Eleven of them were on duty this morning."

"That means the other seven have been missing since yesterday?"

"I'm afraid so, sir."

"But no one saw fit to inform me of this fact?"

Jusi fidgeted. "No, sir."

"Have you discovered anything else of which I have not been informed?"

The other fidgeted again, looked pained.

"Out with it, man!"

"It is not the absentees' first offense," Jusik said with difficulty. "Nor their second. Perhaps not their sixth."

"How long has this been going on?" Cruin waited a while, then bawled: "Come on! You are capable of speech!"

"About ten days, sir."

"How many captains were aware of this and failed to report it?"

"Nine, sir. Four of them await your bidding outside."

"And what of the other five?"

"They . . . they—" Jusik licked his lips.

Cruin arose, his expression dangerous. "You cannot conceal the truth by delaying it."

"They are among the absentees, sir."

"I see!" Cruin stamped to the door, stood by it. "We can take it for granted that others have absented themselves without permission, but were fortunate enough to be here when the rolls were called. That is their good luck. The real total of the disobedient cannot be discovered. They have sneaked away like nocturnal animals, and in the same manner they sneak back. All are guilty of desertion in the face of the enemy. There is one penalty for that."

"Surely, sir, considering the circ—"

"Considering nothing!" Cruin's voice shot up to an enraged shout. "Death! The penalty is death!" Striding to the table, he hammered the books lying upon it. "Summary execution as laid down in the manual of procedure and discipline. Desertion, mutinous conduct, defiance of a superior officer, conspiracy to thwart regulations and defy my orders—all punishable by death!" His voice lowered as swiftly as it had gone up. "Besides, my dear Jusik, if we fail through disintegration attributable to our own deliberate disregard of the manuals, what will be the penalty payable by *us*? What will it be, eh?"

"Death," admitted Jusik. He looked at Cruin. "On Huld, anyway."

"We are on Huld! *This* is Huld! I have claimed this planet in the name of Huld and therefore it is part of it."

"A mere claim, sir, if I may say—"

"Jusik, are *you* with these consipirators in opposing my authority?" Cruin's eyes glinted. His hand lay over his gun.

"Oh, no, sir!" The second commander's features mirrored the emotions conflicting within him. "But permit me to point out, sir, that we are a brotherly band who've been cooped together a long, long time and already have suffered losses getting here as we shall do getting back. One can hardly expect the men to—"

"I expect obedience!" Cruin's hand remained on the gun. "I expect iron discipline and immediate, willing, unquestionable obedience. With those, we conquer. Without them, we fail." He gestured to the door. "Are those captains properly prepared for examination as directed in the manuals?"

"Yes, sir. They are disarmed and under guard."

"Parade them in." Leaning on the edge of his desk, Cruin prepared to pass judgment on his fellows. The minute he waited for them was long, long as any minute he had ever known.

> *There had been scent in her hair.*
> *And her eyes were cool and green.*
> *Iron discipline must be maintained.*
> *The price of power.*

The manual provided an escape. Facing the four captains, he found himself taking advantage of the legal loophole to substitute demotion for the more drastic and final penalty.

Tramping the room before them while they stood in a row, pale-faced and rigid, their tunics unbuttoned, their ceremonial belts missing, the guards impassive on either side of them, he rampaged and swore and sprinkled them with verbal vitriol while his right fist hammered steadily into the palm of his left hand.

"But since you were present at the roll call, and therefore are not technically guilty of desertion, and since you surrendered yourself to my judgment immediately you were called upon to do so, I hereby sentence you to be demoted to the basic rank, the circumstances attending this sentence to be entered in your records." He dismissed them with a curt flourish of his white-gloved hand. "That is all."

They filed out silently.

He looked at Jusik. "Inform the respective lieutenant captains that they are promoted to full captains and now must enter recommendations for their vacated positions. These must be received by me before nightfall."

"As you order, sir."

"Also warn them to prepare to attend a commanding officer's court which will deal with the lower-ranking absentees as and when they reappear. Inform Captain Somir that he is appointed commander of the firing squad which will carry out the decisions of the court immediately they are pronounced."

"Yes, sir." Gaunt and hollow-eyed, Jusik turned with a click of heels and departed.

When the closer had shut the door, Cruin sat at his desk, placed his elbows on its surface, held his face in his hands. If the deserters did not return, they could not be punished. No power, no authority could vent its wrath upon an absent body. The law was impotent if its subjects lacked the essential feature of being present. All the laws of Huld could not put memories of lost men before a firing squad.

It was imperative that he make an example of the offenders. Their sly, furtive trips into the enemy's camp, he suspected, had been repeated often enough to have become a habit. Doubtless by now they were settled wherever they were visiting, sharing homes—welcome rooms—sharing food, company, laughter. Doubtless they had started to regain weight, to lose the space lines on their cheeks and foreheads, and the light in their eyes had begun to burn anew; and they had talked with signs and pictures, played games, tried to suck smoke things, and strolled with girls through the fields and the glades.

A pulse was beating steadily in the thickness of his neck as he stared through the port and waited for some sign that the tripled ring of guards had caught the first on his way in. Down, down, deep down inside him at a depth too great for him to admit that it was there, lay the disloyal hope that none would return.

One deserter would mean the slow, shuffling tread of the squad, the hoarse calls of "Aim!" and "Fire!" and the stepping forward of Somir, gun in hand, to administer the mercy shot.

Damn the manuals.

At the end of the first period after nightfall Jusik burst into the office, saluted, breathed heavily. The glare of the ceiling illumination deepened the lines on his thin features, magnified the bristles on his unshaven chin.

"Sir, I have to report that the men are getting out of control."

"What d'you mean?" Cruin's heavy brows came down as he stared fiercely at the other.

"They know of the recent demotions, of course. They know also that a court will assemble to deal with the absentees." He took another long-drawn breath. "And they also know the penalty these absentees must face."

"So?"

"So more of them have deserted—they've gone to warn the others not to return."

"Ah!" Cruin smiled lopsidedly. "The guards let them walk out, eh? Just like that?"

"Ten of the guards went with them," said Jusik.

"Ten?" Coming up fast, Cruin moved near to the other, studied him searchingly. "How many went altogether?"

"Ninety-seven."

Grabbing his helmet, Cruin slammed it on, pulled the metal chin strap over his jaw muscles. "More than one complete crew." He examined his gun, shoved it back, strapped on a second one. "At that rate they'll all be gone by morning." He eyed Jusik. "Don't you think so?"

"That's what I'm afraid of, sir."

Cruin patted his shoulder. "The answer, Jusik, is an easy one—we take off immediately."

"Take off?"

"Most certainly. The whole fleet. We'll strike a balanced orbit where it will be impossible for any man to leave. I will then give the situation more thought. Probably we'll make a new landing in some locality where none will be tempted to sneak away because there'll be nowhere to go. A scout can pick up Fane and his party in due course."

"I doubt whether they'll obey orders for departure, sir."

"We'll see, we'll see." He smiled again, hard and craggy. "As you would know if you'd studied the manuals properly, it is not difficult to smash incipient mutiny. All one has to do is remove the ringleaders. No mob is composed of men, as such. It is made up of a few ringleaders and a horde of stupid followers." He patted his guns. "You can always tell a ringleader—invariably he is the first to open his mouth!"

"Yes, sir," mouthed Jusik, with misgivings.

"Sound the call for general assembly."

The flagship's siren wailed dismally in the night. Lights flashed from ship to ship, and startled birds woke up and squawked in the trees beyond the ash.

Slowly, deliberately, impressively, Cruin came down the ladder, faced the audience whose features were a mass of white blobs in the glare of the ships' beams. The captains and lieutenant captains ranged themselves behind him and to either side. Each carried an extra gun.

"After three years of devoted service to Huld," he enunciated pompously, "some men have failed me. It seems that we have weaklings among us, weaklings unable to stand the strain of a few extra days before our triumph. Careless of their duty, they disobey orders, fraternize with the enemy, consort with our opponents' females, and try to snatch a few creature comforts at the expense of the many." His hard, accusing eyes went over them. "In due time they will be punished with the utmost severity."

They stared back at him expressionlessly. He could shoot the ears off a running man at twenty-five yards, and he was waiting for his target to name itself. So were those at his side.

None spoke.

"Among you may be others equally guilty but not discovered. They need not congratulate themselves, for they are about to be deprived of further opportunities to exercise their disloyalty." His stare kept flickering over them while his hand remained ready at his side. "We are going to trim the ships and take off, seeking a balanced orbit. That means lost sleep and plenty of hard work for which you have your treacherous comrades to thank." He paused a moment, finished with: "Has anyone anything to say?"

One man holding a thousand.

Silence.

"Prepare for departure," he snapped, and turned his back upon them.

Captain Somir, now facing him, yelped: "Look out, commander!" and whipped up his gun to fire over Cruin's shoulder.

Cruin made to turn, conscious of a roar behind him, his guns coming out as he twisted around. He heard no crack from Somir's weapon, saw no more of his men as their roar cut off abruptly. There seemed to be an intolerable weight upon his skull, the grass came up to meet him, he let go his guns and put out his hands to save himself. Then the hazily dancing lights faded from his eyesight and all was black.

Deep in his sleep he heard vaguely and uneasily a prolonged stamping of feet, many dull, elusive sounds as of people shouting far, far away. This went on for a considerable time, and ended with a series of violent reports that shook the ground beneath his body.

Someone splashed water over his face.

Sitting up, he held his throbbing head, saw pale fingers of dawn feeling through the sky to one side. Blinking his aching eyes to clear them, he perceived Jusik, Somir and eight others. All were smothered in dirt, their faces bruised, their uniforms torn and bedraggled.

"They rushed us the moment you turned away from them," explained Jusik, morbidly. "A hundred of them in the front. They rushed us in one united frenzy, and the rest followed. There were too many for us." He regarded his superior with red-rimmed optics. "You have been flat all night."

Unsteadily, Cruin got to his feet, teetered to and fro. "How many were killed?"

"None. We fired over their heads. After that—it was too late."

"Over their heads?" Squaring his massive shoulders, Cruin felt a sharp pain in the middle of his back, ignored it. "What are guns for if not to kill?"

"It isn't easy," said Jusik, with the faintest touch of defiance. "Not when they're one's own comrades."

"Do you agree?" The commander's glare challenged the others.

They nodded miserably, and Somir said: "There was little time, sir, and if one hesitates, as we did, it becomes—"

"There are no excuses for anything. You had your orders; it was for you to obey them." His hot gaze burned one, then the other. "You are incompetent for your rank. You are both demoted!" His jaw came forward, ugly, aggressive, as he roared: "Get out of my sight!"

They mooched away. Savagely, he climbed the ladder, entered his ship, explored it from end to end. There was not a soul on board. His lips were tight as he reached the tail, found the cause of the earth-rocking detonations. The fuel tanks had been exploded, wrecking the engines and reducing the whole vessel to a useless mass of metal.

Leaving, he inspected the rest of his fleet. Every ship was the same, empty and wrecked beyond the possibility of repair. At least the mutineers had been thorough and logical in their sabotage. Until a report-vessel arrived, the home world of Huld had no means of knowing where the expedition had landed. Despite even a systematic and wide-scale search it might well be a thousand years before Huldians found this particular planet again. Effectively the rebels had marooned themselves for the rest of their natural lives and placed themselves beyond reach of Huldian retribution.

Tasting to the full the bitterness of defeat, he squatted on the bottom rung of the twenty-second vessel's ladder, surveyed the double star-formations that represented his ruined armada. Futilely, their guns pointed over the surrounding terrain. Twelve of the scouts, he noted, had gone. The others had been rendered as useless as their parent vessels.

Raising his gaze to the hill, he perceived silhouettes against the dawn where Jusik, Somir and the others were walking over the crest, walking away from him, making for the farther valley he had viewed so often. Four children joined them at the top, romped beside them as they proceeded. Slowly the whole group sank from sight under the rising sun.

Returning to the flagship, Cruin packed a patrol sack with personal possessions, strapped it on his shoulders. Without a final glance at the remains of his once-mighty command he set forth away from the sun, in the direction opposite to that taken by the last of his men.

His jackboots were dull, dirty. His orders of merit hung lopsidedly and had a gap where one had been torn off in the fracas. The bell was missing from his right boot; he endured the pad-*ding,* pad-*ding* of its fellow for twenty steps before he unscrewed it and slung it away.

The sack on his back was heavy, but not so heavy as the immense burden upon his mind. Grimly, stubbornly he plodded on, away from the ships, far, far into the morning mists—facing the new world alone.

Three and a half years had bitten deep into the ships of Huld. Still they lay in the valley, arranged with mathematical precision, noses in, tails out, as only authority could place them. But the rust had eaten a quarter of the way through the thickness of their tough shells, and their metal ladders were rotten and treacherous. The field mice and the voles had found refuge beneath them; the birds and spiders had sought sanctuary within them. A lush growth had sprung from encompassing ash, hiding the perimeter for all time.

The man who came by them in the midafternoon rested his pack and studied them silently, from a distance. He was big, burly, with a skin the color of old leather. His deep gray eyes were calm, thoughtful as they observed the thick ivy climbing over the flagship's tail.

Having looked at them for a musing half-hour, he hoisted his pack and went on, up the hill, over the crest and into the farther valley. Moving easily in his plain, loose-fitting clothes, his pace was deliberate, methodical.

Presently he struck a road, followed it to a stone-built cottage in the garden of which a lithe, dark-haired woman was cutting flowers. Leaning on the gate, he spoke to her. His speech was fluent but strangely accented. His tones were gruff but pleasant.

"Good afternoon."

She stood up, her arms full of gaudy blooms, looked at him with rich, black eyes. "Good afternoon." Her full lips parted with pleasure. "Are you touring? Would you care to guest with us? I am sure that Jusik—my husband—would be delighted to have you. Our welcome room has not been occupied for—"

"I am sorry," he chipped in. "I am seeking the Merediths. Could you direct me?"

"The next house up the lane." Deftly, she caught a falling bloom, held it to her breast. "If their welcome room has a guest, please remember us."

"I will remember," he promised. Eying her approvingly, his broad, muscular face lit up with a smile. "Thank you so much."

Shouldering his pack, he marched on, conscious of her eyes following him. He reached the gate of the next place, a long, rambling picturesque house fronted by a flowering garden. A boy was playing by the gate.

Glancing up as the other stopped near him, the boy said: "Are you touring, sir?"

"Sir?" echoed the man. *"Sir?"* His face quirked. "Yes, sonny, I am touring. I'm looking for the Merediths."

"Why, I'm Sam Meredith!" The boy's face flushed with sudden excitement. "You wish to guest with us?"

"If I may."

"Yow-ee!" He fled frantically along the garden path, shrieking at the top of his voice, "Mom, Pop, Marva, Sue—we've got a guest!"

A tall, red-headed man came to the door, pipe in mouth. Coolly, calmly, he surveyed the visitor.

After a little while, the man removed the pipe and said: "I'm Jake Meredith. Please come in." Standing aside, he let the other enter, then called, "Mary, Mary, can you get a meal for a guest?"

"Right away," assured a cheerful voice from the back.

"Come with me." Meredith led the other to the veranda, found him an easychair. "Might as well rest while you're waiting. Mary takes time. She isn't satisfied until the legs of the table are near to collapse—and woe betide you if you leave anything."

"It is good of you." Seating himself, the visitor drew a long breath, gazed over the pastoral scene before him.

Taking another chair, Meredith applied a light to his pipe. "Have you seen the mail ship?"

"Yes, it arrived early yesterday. I was lucky enough to view it as it passed overhead."

"You certainly were lucky, considering that it comes only once in four years. I've seen it only twice, myself. It came right over this house. An imposing sight."

"Very!" endorsed the visitor, with unusual emphasis. "It looked to me about five miles long, a tremendous creation. Its mass must be many times greater than that of all those alien ships in the valley."

"Many times," agreed Meredith.

The other leaned forward, watching his host. "I often wonder whether those aliens attributed smallness of numbers to war or disease, not thinking of large-scale emigration, nor realizing what it means."

"I doubt whether they cared very much, seeing that they burned their boats and settled among us." He pointed with the stem of his pipe. "One of them lives in that cottage down there. Jusik's his name. Nice fellow. He married a local girl eventually. They are very happy."

"I'm sure they are."

They were quiet a long time, then Meredith spoke absently, as if thinking aloud. "They brought with them weapons of considerable might, not knowing that we have a weapon truly invincible." Waving one hand, he indicated the world at large. "It took us thousands of years to learn about the sheer invincibility of an idea. That's what we've got—a way of life, an idea. Nothing can blast that to shreds. Nothing can defeat an idea— except a better one." He put the pipe back in his mouth. "So far, we have failed to find a better one.

"They came at the wrong time," Meredith went on. "Ten thousand years too late." He glanced sideways at his listener. "Our history covers a long, long day. It was so lurid that it came out in a new edition every minute. But this one's the late night final."

"You philosophize, eh?"

Meredith smiled. "I often sit here to enjoy my silences. I sit here and think. Invariably I end up with the same conclusion."

"What may that be?"

"That if I, personally, were in complete possession of all the visible stars and their multitude of planets I would still be subject to one fundamental limitation"— bending, he tapped his pipe on his heel—"in this respect—that no man can eat more than his belly can hold." He stood up, tall, wide-chested. "Here comes my daughter, Marva. Would you like her to show you your room?"

Standing inside the welcome room, the visitor surveyed it appreciatively. The comfortable bed, the bright furnishings.

"Like it?" Marva asked.

"Yes, indeed." Facing her, his gray eyes examined her. She was tall, red-haired, green-eyed, and her figure was ripe with the beauty of young womanhood. Pulling slowly at his jaw muscles, he asked: "Do you think that I resemble Cruin?"

"Cruin?" Her finely curved brows crinkled in puzzlement.

"The commander of that alien expedition."

"Oh, him!" Her eyes laughed, and the dimples came into her cheeks. "How absurd! You don't look the least bit like him. He was old and severe. You are *young*—and far more handsome."

"It is kind of you to say so," he murmured. His hands moved aimlessly around in obvious embarrassment. He fidgeted a little under her frank, self-possessed gaze. Finally, he went to his pack, opened it. "It is conventional for the guest to bring his hosts a present." A tinge of pride crept into his voice. "So I have brought one. I made it myself. It took me a long time to learn . . . a long time . . . with these clumsy hands. About three years."

Marva looked at it, raced through the doorway, leaned over the balustrade and called excitedly down the stairs. "Pop, Mom, our guest has a wonderful present for us. A clock. A clock with a little metal bird that calls the time."

Beneath her, feet bustled along the passage and Mary's voice came up saying: "May I see it? Please let me see it." Eagerly, she mounted the stairs.

As he waited for them within the welcome room, his shoulders squared, body erect as if on parade, the clock whirred in Cruin's hands and its little bird solemnly fluted twice.

The hour of triumph.

Dear Devil

THE FIRST MARTIAN vessel descended upon Earth with the slow, stately fall of a landing balloon. It did resemble a large balloon in that it was spherical and had a strange buoyancy out of keeping with its metallic construction. Beyond this superficial appearance all similarity to anything Terrestrial ceased.

There were no rockets, no flaming venturis, no external projections other than several solaradiant distorting grids that served to boost the ship in any desired direction through the cosmic field. There were no observation-ports. All viewing was done through a transparent plastic band running right around the fat belly of the sphere. The bluish, nightmarish crew were assembled behind that band and surveying the new world with great, multifaceted eyes.

Together they gazed in complete silence as they examined this world called Terra. Even if they had been capable of speech they'd have said nothing just then. But none among them had a talkative faculty in any sonic sense and in this quiet moment none needed it.

The scene outside was one of untrammeled desolation. Scraggy blue-green grass clung to tired ground all the way to a horizon scarred by ragged mountains. Dismal bushes struggled for life here and there, some with the pathetic air of striving to become trees as once their ancestors had been. To the right a long, straight scar through the grass betrayed the sterile lumpiness of rocks at odd places. Too rugged and too narrow ever to have been a road, it suggested no more than the desiccated remnants of a long-gone wall. And over all this depressing wasteland there loomed a ghastly sky.

Captain Skhiva eyed his crew, spoke to them with his sign-talking tentacle. The alternative was contact-telepathy, which required physical touch.

"It is obvious that we are out of luck. We could have done no worse had we landed on the empty satellite. However, our instruments show that it is safe to go forth. Anyone who wishes to explore a little while may do so."

One of them gesticulated back at him. "Captain, don't you wish to be the first to step upon this world?"

"It is of no consequence. If anyone deems it an honor he is welcome to it." He pulled the lever opening both air-lock doors. Pressure went up a little as thicker, heavier air crowded in. "Beware of over-exertion," he warned as they went out.

Poet Fander touched him, tentacles tip to tip as he sent his thoughts racing through their nerve-ends. "Captain, this confirms all that we'd suspected during our approach. A stricken planet far gone in its death throes. What do you suppose caused it?"

"I haven't the remotest idea. Naturally I would much like to know. If it has been smitten by some kind of cosmic catastrophe, what are the chances of the same thing happening to Mars?" His troubled mind sent its throb of worry up Fander's contacting tentacle. "A pity that this planet had not been farther away from the Sun instead of closer in; we might then have observed the preceding phenomena and learned exactly what occurred. It is so difficult properly to study this planet against the Sun's persistent glare."

"That applies still more to the next world, the misty one," observed Poet Fander.

"I know it. And I am beginning to fear what we may find there. If it proves to be equally dead it will be a great misfortune for us, possibly a disaster. We shall be completely stalled until we can make the big jump outward."

"Which won't be in our lifetimes."

"I doubt it," agreed Captain Skhiva. "We might move fast and effectively with the help of friends. Alone, we shall be slow, perhaps too slow." He turned to watch his crew writhing in various directions across the grim landscape. "They find it good to be on firm ground. But what is a world without life and beauty? In a short time they will grow tired of it."

Fander said thoughtfully, "Nevertheless I would like to see more of this place. May I take out the lifeboat?"

"You are a songbird, not a pilot," reproved Skhiva. "Your function is to maintain morale by entertaining us, not to roam around in a lifeboat."

"But I know how to use it. Every one of us was trained to handle it. Let me take it that I may see more."

"Haven't we seen enough even before we landed? What else is there to see? Cracked and distorted roads about to dissolve into nothingness. Ages-old cities torn and broken, crumbling into dust. Shattered mountains and charred forests and craters little smaller than those upon the Moon. No sign of any superior lifeform still surviving. Only the miserable grass, the dreary shrubs and various animals, two- or four-legged, that flee at our approach. Why do you wish to see more?"

"There is music even in death," said Fander.

"Even so, it remains repulsive." Skhiva gave a little shiver. "All right. Take the lifeboat. Who am I to question the weird workings of a non-technical mind?"

"Thank you, Captain."

"It is nothing. See that you are back by dusk." With that he broke contact, went into the nearest lock, curled himself snakishly upon its outer rim and brooded, still without bothering to touch the new world. So much attempted, so much done—for so poor a reward.

He was coddling his gloom when the lifeboat floated from its hangar and soared skyward. Expressionlessly his multi-faceted eyes watched the energized grids change angle as the boat swung into a curve and drifted away like a little bubble. Skhiva was sensitive to futility.

The crew returned well before the fall of darkness. A few hours were enough. Just grass and shrubs and child-trees straining to grow up. Two of the crew had discovered a mile away a sterile oblong that once might have been the site of a dwelling. They brought back a small piece of the foundation, a lump of perished concrete that Skhiva put aside for later analysis.

Another had found a small, brown, six-legged insect, but his super-sensitive nerve-ends had heard its cry of fear as he picked it up, so hastily he had put it down and let it go free. Little animals had been hopping clumsily in the distance but all had dived down holes in the ground before any curious Martian could get near. All the crew were agreed upon one thing: the majestic silence and solemnity of an unknown people's passing was unendurable.

Fander beat the sinking of the Sun by half a time-unit. His bubble soared under a big, black cloud, sank to ship-level and came in. A moment later the rain started. It roared down in a frenzied torrent while they stood watching behind the transparent band and marveled at so much water.

After a while Captain Skhiva told them, "We must accept what we find. Here we have drawn a blank. The cause of this world's condition is a mystery to be solved by others with more time and better equipment. It is for us to abandon this graveyard and try the misty planet. We'll take off early in the morning."

None offered comment, but Fander followed him to his cabin, made contact with a tentacle-touch.

"One could live here, Captain."

"I am not so sure of that." Skhiva coiled on his couch, let his tentacles hang in the various limb-rests. The blue sheen of his rubbery hide was reflected by the metal wall. "In some places are rocks emitting alpha-sparks. They are dangerous."

"Of course, Captain. But I can sense them and avoid them."

"*You?*" Skhiva stared up at him.

"Yes, Captain. I wish to be left here."

"What?—in this place of appalling gloom?"

"It has an all-pervading air of ugliness and despair," admitted Poet Fander. "All destruction is ugly. But by accident I have found a touch of beauty. It heartens me. The very contrast makes it shine like a gem in the dark. I would like to seek its source."

"To what beauty do you refer?" Skhiva demanded.

Fander tried to explain the alien in non-alien terms. It was impossible.

"Draw it for me," ordered Skhiva.

Obediently Fander drew it, gave him the pictures. "There—that is it."

Gazing at it for a long time, Skhiva handed it back, spoke along the other's nerves. "We are individuals with all the rights of individuals. As an individual I don't think that picture worth the tail-tip of a domestic *arlan*. I will admit that it is not ugly, even that it is pleasing in an outlandish sort of way."

"But, Captain—"

"As an individual," Skhiva went on, "you have an equal right to your opinions, strange though they may be. So if you really wish to stay I cannot refuse you. It would be wrong of me to thwart you. I am entitled only to think you a little crazy." He regarded Fander speculatively. "When do you hope to be picked up?"

"This year, next year, sometime, never."

"It might well be never," Skhiva warned. "Are you prepared to face that grim prospect?"

"One must always be prepared to face the consequences of his own actions," Fander pointed out.

"True." Skhiva was reluctant to surrender. "But have you given this matter serious thought?"

"I am a non-technical component. I am not guided by thought."

"Then by what?"

"By my desires, emotions, instincts. By my inward feelings."

Skhiva said fervently, "The twin moons preserve us!"

"Captain, sing me a song of home and play me the tinkling harp."

"Don't be silly. I have not the ability."

"Captain, if it required no more than careful thought you would be able to do it?"

"Without a doubt," agreed Skhiva, seeing the trap but unable to avoid it.

"There you are!" said Fander pointedly.

"I give up. I cannot argue with someone who casts aside the accepted rules of logic and invents rules of his own. You are governed by notions that defeat me."

"It is not a matter of logic or illogic," Fander told him. "It is merely a matter of viewpoint. You see angles typical of yourself. I see angles typical of myself."

"For example?"

"You won't pin me down that way. I can find plenty of examples. For instance, do you remember the formula for determining the phase of a series-tuned circuit?"

"Most certainly."

"I felt sure you would. You are a technician. You have registered it in your mind for all time as a matter of technical utility." He paused, eyeing his listener thoughtfully. "I know that formula, too. It was mentioned to me, casually, many years ago. It is not of the slightest use to me—yet I have never forgotten it."

"Why?"

"Because it holds the beauty of rhythm. It is a poem."

Skhiva sighed and said, "I don't see it."

"*One upon R into omega L minus one upon omega C,*" recited Fander. "A perfect hexameter." He registered amusement at the other's surprise.

After a while, Skhiva remarked, "It could be sung. One could dance to it."

"This also is a song, an alien one and perhaps a sad one, but still a song." Fander exhibited his rough sketch. "It holds beauty. Where there is beauty there once was talent—may still be the remnants of talent for all we know. Where talent abides there is also greatness. In the realms of greatness we may find powerful friends. We *need* such friends."

"You win." Skhiva made a gesture of defeat. "We shall leave you to your self-chosen fate in the morning."

"Thank you, Captain."

That same streak of stubbornness which made Skhiva a worthy commander induced him to take one final crack at Fander shortly before departure. Summoning him to his cabin, he studied the poet calculatingly.

"You are still of the same mind?"

"Yes, Captain."

"Then does it not occur to you as strange that I should be so content to abandon this planet if indeed it does still hold some dregs of greatness?"

"No."

Skhiva stiffened slightly. "Why not?"

"Captain, I think you are a little afraid because you suspect what I suspect, namely, that there was no natural disaster, that they did it themselves—to themselves."

"We have no proof of it," said Skhiva uneasily.

"No, Captain, we haven't."

"*If* this is their own handiwork what are our chances of finding allies among people so much to be feared?"

"Poor," admitted Fander. "But that, being the product of cold thought, means little to me. I am animated by warm hopes."

"There you go again, blatantly disregarding reason in favor of an idle dream. Hoping, hoping, hoping—to achieve the impossible."

Fander gave back, "The difficult can be done at once; the impossible takes a little longer."

"Your thoughts make my orderly mind feel lopsided. Every remark is a flat denial of something that makes sense." Skhiva transmitted the sensation of a lugubrious chuckle. "Oh well, we live and learn." He came forward, moving closer to the other. "All your supplies are assembled outside. Nothing remains but to bid you goodbye."

They embraced in the Martian manner. Leaving the lock, Poet Fander watched the big sphere shudder and glide upward. It soared without a sound, shrinking steadily until it was a mere dot entering a cloud. A moment later it had gone.

He remained there looking at the cloud for a long, long time. Then he turned his attention to the load-sled holding his supplies. Climbing into its small, exposed front seat, he shifted the control that energized the flotation-grids, let the sled rise a few feet. The higher the climb the greater the expenditure of power. He wished to conserve power; there was no knowing how long he might need it. So at low altitude and gentle pace he let the sled glide in the general direction of the thing of beauty.

Later he found a dry cave in the hill on which his objective stood. It took him two days of careful, cautious raying to square its walls, ceiling and floor, plus half a day with a powered fan to drive out silicate dust. After that he stowed his supplies at the back, parked the sled near the front, set up a curtaining force-screen across the entrance. The hole in the hill was now home.

Slumber did not come easily that first night. He lay within the cave, a ropy, knotted thing of glowing blue with enormous, bee-like eyes, and found himself listening for harps that played sixty million miles away. His tentacle-tips twitched in involuntary search of the telepathic-contact songs that would go with the harps, and twitched in vain.

Darkness grew deep and all the world a monstrous stillness held. His hearing-organs craved from the eventide to high-moon for the homely flip-flop of sand-frogs, but there were no frogs. He wanted the familiar drone of night-beetles, but there were no beetles. Except for once when something faraway howled its heart at the Moon there was nothing, nothing.

In the morning he washed, ate, took out the sled and explored the site of what once had been a small town. There was little to satisfy his curiosity, only mounds of shapeless rubble on ragged, faintly oblong foundations. It was a graveyard of long-dead domiciles, rotting, weedy, near to complete oblivion. A view from five hundred feet up gave him only one extra piece of information; the orderliness of the town's outlines showed that its unknown inhabitants had been tidy and methodical.

But tidiness is not another form of loveliness. He returned to the top of his hill and sought solace with the thing that did hold beauty.

His explorations continued day by day, not in systematic manner as Skhiva would have performed them, but in accordance with his own mercurial whims. At times he saw many animals, singly or in groups, none resembling anything Martian. Most of them scattered at full gallop when his sled swooped over them. Some dived into ground-holes, showing a brief flash of white, absurd tails. Others, four-footed, sharp-faced long-toothed, hunted in packs and bayed at him in concert with harsh, defiant voices.

On the seventieth day, in a deep, shadowed glade to the north, he spotted a small group of new shapes slinking along in single file. He recognized them at a glance, knew them so well that his searching eyes telegraphed an immediate thrill of triumph to his mind. They were ragged, dirty and no more than half-grown, but the thing of beauty on the hill had told him what they were.

Hugging the ground low, he swept around in a wide curve that brought him to the farther end of the little valley. His sled sloped slightly into the drop as it entered the glade. He could see them better now, even the soiled pinkness of their thin legs. They were moving away from him, backs toward him, unaware of his presence. Their advance was being made with great caution, as if they were wary of a hidden foe. The utter silence of his swoop from behind gave them no warning.

The rearmost one of the stealthy file fooled him at the last moment. He was hanging over the side of the sled, tentacles outstretched in readiness to snatch the last one with the wild mop of yellow hair, when, responding to some sixth sense, the intended victim threw itself flat. Fander's grasp shot past a couple of feet short and he got a glimpse of frightened gray eyes before a dexterous side-tilt of the sled enabled him to make good his loss by grabbing the less wary next-in-line.

This one was dark-haired, a bit bigger and sturdier.

It fought madly at his holding limbs while the sled gained altitude. Then, suddenly realizing the queer nature of its bonds, it writhed around and looked him straight in the face. The result was unexpected. Its features paled, it closed its eyes and went completely limp.

It was still limp when he bore it into the cave but its heart continued to beat, its lungs to draw. Laying it carefully on the softness of his bed, he moved to the cave's entrance and waited for it to recover. Eventually it stirred, sat up, gazed confusedly at the facing wall. Its black eyes moved slowly around, taking in the surroundings. Then they saw Fander. They widened tremendously and their owner began to make high-pitched, unpleasant noises as it tried to back away through the solid wall. It screamed so much, in one rising throb after another, that Fander slithered out of the cave, right out of sight, and sat in the cold winds until the noises had died down.

A couple of hours later he made cautious reappearance to offer it food but its reaction was so swift, hysterical and heartrending that he dropped his gift and hid himself as if the fear were his own. The food remained untouched for two full days. On the third a little of it was eaten. Fander showed himself again.

Although the Martian did not go near, the boy cowered away saying, "Devil! Devil!" His eyes were red with rings of dark discoloration beneath them.

"Devil!" thought Fander, totally unable to repeat the alien word but wondering what it meant. He used his sign-talking tentacle in valiant effort to convey something reassuring. The attempt was wasted. The other watched its sinuous writhings half in fear, half in disgust, and showed complete lack of comprehension. Fander now let a major tentacle gently slither forward across the floor, hoping to make thought-contact. The boy recoiled from it as from a striking snake.

"Patience," Fander reminded himself. "The impossible takes a little longer."

Periodically he showed himself with food and drink. Nighttimes he slept fitfully outside the cave, on coarse,

damp grass beneath lowering skies—while the prisoner
who was his guest enjoyed the softness of the bed, the
warmth of the cave, the security of the force-screen.

Time came when Fander betrayed an unpoetic
shrewdness by using the other's belly to estimate the
ripeness of the moment. When on the eleventh day he
noted that his food-offerings were now being taken regularly, he had a meal of his own at the edge of the cave,
within plain sight, and observed that the other's appetite
was not spoiled. That night he slept just within the cave,
close to the force-screen and as far away from the boy
as possible. The prisoner stayed awake late, watching
him, always watching him, but gave way to slumber in
the small hours.

Another attempt at sign-talking brought results no
better than before and the boy still refused to touch his
offered tentacle-tip. All the same, he was gaining
ground slowly. His overtures still were rejected but with
less obvious revulsion. Gradually, ever so gradually, the
Martian shape was becoming familiar and almost acceptable.

The sweet savour of success was Fander's in the
middle of the sixteenth day. The boy had displayed several spells of emotional sickness during which he lay on
his front with quivering body and emitted low noises
while his eyes watered profusely. At such times the
Martian felt strangely helpless and inadequate. On this
occasion, during another attack, he took advantage of
the sufferer's lack of attention and slid near enough to
snatch away the box by the bed.

From the box he drew his tiny electro-harp, plugged
its connectors, switched it on, touched its strings with
delicate affection. Slowly he began to play, singing an
accompaniment deep inside himself. For he had no
voice with which to sing out loud and the harp had to
sing it for him.

The boy ceased his quiverings and sat up, all his attention upon the dexterous play of the tentacles and the
music they conjured forth. And when he judged that at
last his listener's mind was captured, Fander ceased
with easy, soothing strokes upon the strings, gently of-

fered him the harp. The boy registered interest and reluctance. Careful not to move nearer, not an inch
nearer, Fander tendered it at full tentacle length. The
boy had to take four steps to reach it. He took them.

That was the start. They played together, day after
day and sometimes a little into the night, while almost
imperceptibly the distance between them was reduced.
Finally they sat together side by side and the boy had
not yet learned to laugh but no longer did he show
unease. He could now extract a simple tune from the
instrument and was pleased with his own aptitude in a
solemn sort of way.

One evening as darkness grew and the things that
sometimes howled at the Moon were howling again,
Fander offered his tentacle-tip for the hundredth time.
Always the gesture had been unmistakable even if its
motive was not clear, yet always it had been rebuffed.
But now, now, five fingers curled around it in shy desire to please.

With a fervent prayer that human nerves would function just like Martian ones, Fander poured his thoughts
through swiftly, lest the warm grip be loosened too
soon.

"Do not fear me. I cannot help my shape any more
than you can help yours. I am your friend, your father,
your mother. I need you as much as you need me."

The boy let go of him, began quiet, half-stifled whim-
pering noises. Fander put a tentacle on his shoulder,
made little patting motions that he fondly imagined
were wholly Martian. For some inexplicable reason this
made matters worse. At his wits' end what to do for the
best, what action to take that might be understandable
in Terrestrial terms, he gave the problem up, surrendered to his instinct, put a long, ropy limb around the
boy and held him close until the noises ceased and
slumber came. It was then he realized that the child he
had taken was much younger than he had estimated. He
nursed him through the night.

Much practice was necessary to make conversation.
The boy had to learn to put mental drive behind his

thoughts, for it was beyond Fander's power to suck them out of him.

"What is your name?"

Fander got a picture of thin legs running rapidly.

He returned it in question form. "Speedy?"

An affirmative.

"What name do you call me?"

An unflattering montage of monsters.

"Devil?"

The picture whirled around, became confused. There was a distinct trace of embarrassment.

"Devil will do," assured Fander. He went on, "Where are your parents?"

More confusion.

"You must have had parents. Everyone has a father and mother, haven't they? Don't you remember yours?"

Muddled ghost-pictures. Grown-ups abandoning children. Grown-ups avoiding children almost as if they feared them.

"What is the first thing you remember?"

"Big man walking with me. Carried me a bit. Walked again."

"What happened to him?"

"Went away. Said he was sick. Said he might make me sick too."

"Long ago?"

Confusion. Everything back at the beginning of memory was long ago. It couldn't be anything else.

Fander changed his aim. "What of those other children—have they no parents either?"

"All got nobody."

"But *you* have somebody now, haven't you, Speedy?"

Doubtfully, "Yes."

Fander pushed it farther. "Would you rather have me—or those other children?" He let it rest a moment before he added, "Or both?"

"Both," said Speedy with no hesitation. His fingers toyed with the little electro-harp.

"Would you like to help me look for them tomorrow and bring them here? And if they are scared of me will you help them not to be afraid?"

"Sure!" said Speedy, licking his lips and sticking his chest out.

"Then," suggested Fander, "perhaps you'd like to take a walk today. You've been stuck in this cave too long. Will you come for a walk with me?"

"Yes, all right."

Side by side they went for a short walk, one trotting rapidly along, the other slithering. The child's spirits perked up considerably with this trip in the open; it was as if the sight of the sky and the feel of the grass made him realize at last that he was not exactly a prisoner.

His formerly solemn features became animated, he made frequent exclamations that Fander could not understand and once he laughed at nothing for the sheer joy of it. On two occasions he grabbed a tentacle-tip in order to tell Fander something, performing the action as if it were in every way as natural as his own speech.

They got out the load-sled in the morning. Fander took the front seat and the controls; Speedy squatted behind him with hands gripping his harness-belt. With a shallow upward glide they headed for the glade. Many small, white-tailed animals bolted down holes as they passed over.

"Good to eat," advised Speedy, touching him and speaking through the touch.

A horrible sickness raced through Fander's insides. Meat-eaters! It was not until a queer feeling of shame and apology came back at him that he knew the other had detected his revulsion. He wished he'd been swift to blanket that reaction before the boy could sense it but he could not be blamed for the effect of so bald a statement taking him so completely unaware. However, it had created another step in their mutual relationship—Speedy desired his good opinion.

Within fifteen minutes they struck it lucky. At a point half a mile south of the glade Speedy let out a shrill yell and pointed downward. A small, golden-haired figure was standing there on a slight rise and staring fascinatedly upward at the phenomenon in the sky. A second tiny shape with red but equally long hair was at the bottom of the slope and gazing in similar wonderment. As the sled tilted toward them, both came to their senses and turned to flee.

Ignoring the pulls on his belt and the yelps of excitement right behind him, Fander swooped, got first one and then the other. This left him dangerously short of limbs to control the sled and gain height. If the victims had fought he'd have had all his work cut out to make it. They did not fight. They shrieked as he snatched them and then relaxed with closed eyes.

The sled climbed, glided a mile at five hundred feet. Fander's attention was divided between his limp prizes, the controls and the horizon when suddenly a thunderous rattling sounded on the base of the sled, the entire framework shuddered, a thin strip of metal flew from its leading edge and things made whining noises toward the clouds.

"Old Graypate," bawled Speedy, forgetting to make contact. He jigged around but kept away from the sled's rim. "He's shooting at us!"

The spoken words meant nothing to the Martian and he could not spare a limb to seek contact. Grimly righting the sled, he gave it full power. Whatever damage it had suffered had not affected its efficiency; it shot forward at a pace that set the red and golden hair of the captives streaming in the wind. Perforce his landing by the cave was clumsy. The sled bumped down and lurched across forty yards of grass.

First things first. Taking the limp, unconscious pair into the cave, he made them comfortable on the bed, came out and examined the sled. There were half a dozen deep dents in its flat underside, two bright furrows angling across one rim. He made contact with Speedy.

"What were you trying to tell me?"

"Old Graypate shot at us."

The mind-pictures burst upon him vividly, with electrifying effect, a vision of a tall, white-haired, stern-faced old man with a tubular weapon propped upon his shoulder while it spat fire upward. A white-haired old man. An adult!

His grip tightened on the other's arm. "What is this oldster to you?"

"Nothing much. He lives near us in the shelters."

Picture of a long, dusty concrete burrow, badly damaged, its ceiling marked with the scars of a lighting system that had rotted away to nothing. The old man living hermitlike at one end, the children at the other. The old man was sour, taciturn, kept the children at a distance, spoke to them seldom but was swift to respond when they were menaced. He possessed weapons. Once he had killed many wild dogs that had eaten two children.

"People left us near the shelters because old Graypate was there and had guns," informed Speedy.

"But why does he keep away from you? Doesn't he like children?"

"Don't know," Speedy mused a moment, went on, "Once he told us that old people could become very sick and make young ones sick as well and then we'd all die. Maybe he's afraid of making us die."

So there was some much-feared disease around, something highly contagious to which adults were peculiarly susceptible. Without hesitation they abandoned their young at the first onslaught, hoping at least that the children would survive. Sacrifice after sacrifice that the remnants of the race might live. Heartbreak after heartbreak as elders chose death in loneliness rather than share it with their offspring.

Yet Graypate himself was depicted as very old. Was this an exaggeration of the child-mind?

"I must meet Graypate."

"He will shoot," declared Speedy positively. "He knows by now that you took me away. He saw you take the others. He will wait for you and shoot you on sight."

"We must find some way to avoid that."

"How?"

"When these two have become my friends, just as you have become my friend, I will take all three of you back to the shelters. You can then find Graypate for me and tell him that I am not as ugly as I look."

"But you don't look ugly," Speedy objected.

The picture Fander got along with that remark gave

him the weirdest sensation of pleasure. It was of a vague, shadowy and distorted body with a clear human face.

The new prisoners were female. Fander knew it without being told because they were daintier than Speedy and had the warm, sweet smell of females. That meant complications. Maybe they were mere children and maybe they had lived together in the shelters, but he was permitting none of that while they were in his charge. Fander might be outlandish by local standards but he had a certain primness, a touch of the school-marm in his makeup. Forthwith he cut another and smaller cave for himself and Speedy.

Neither of the girls saw him for four days. Keeping well out of their sight, he let Speedy take them food, talk to them, mentally prepare them for the shape of the thing to come. On the fifth day he presented himself for inspection at a distance. Despite forewarnings they went sheet-white, clung together but uttered no distressing sounds. Moving no nearer to them, he played his harp a little while, withdrew, came back in the evening and played for them again.

Encouraged by Speedy's constant and self-assured flow of propaganda, one of them grasped a tentacle-tip the day after. What came along the Martian's nerves was not a clear picture so much as an ache, a desire, a childish yearning. Backing out of the cave, Fander found some wood, spent the whole night using the sleepy Speedy as a model and fashioned the wood into a tiny, jointed semblance of a human being. He was no sculptor but he possessed a natural delicacy of touch and the poet in him ran through his limbs and expressed itself in the model. Making a thorough job of it, he clothed it in Terrestrial fashion, colored its face, fixed upon its features the pleasure-grimace that humans call a smile.

He gave her the doll the moment she awakened in the morning. She took it eagerly, hungrily, with wide, glad eyes. Hugging it to her unformed bosom, she crooned over it—and he knew that the strange emptiness within her was now filled.

Though Speedy was openly contemptuous of this obvious waste of effort, Fander set to and made a second manikin. It did not take quite as long as the first, practice having made him swifter, more dexterous. He was ablt to present it to the other child by mid-afternoon. Her acceptance was made with shy grace, she held the doll close as if it meant more than the whole of her sorry world. In her thrilled concentration upon the gift she failed to notice his nearness, his closeness, and when he offered her a tentacle-tip, she took it.

He said simply, "I love you."

Her mind was too untrained to drive a response but her great eyes warmed.

Fander sat on the grounded sled at a point one mile east of the glade and watched the three children walk hand in hand toward the hidden shelters. Speedy was the obvious leader, hurrying them onward, bossing them with the noisy assurance of one who has been around and considers himself sophisticated. In spite of this the girls paused at intervals to turn and wave at the ropy, bee-eyed thing they'd left behind. And Fander dutifully waved back, always using his signal-tentacle because it had not occurred to him that any tentacle would serve for such a purpose.

They sank from sight behind a rise of ground. He remained on the sled, his multifaceted gaze going over the near surroundings or studying the angry sky now threatening rain. The ground was a dull, dead gray-green all the way to the horizon. There was no relief from that drab color, not one shining patch of white, gold or crimson such as dotted the meadows of Mars. There was only the eternal gray-green and his own brilliant blueness.

Before long a sharp-faced, four-footed thing revealed itself in the grass, eyed him hungrily. It pointed its muzzle at the sky and howled. The sound was an eerily urgent wail that ran across the prairie and moaned into the distance. This call brought others of its kind, two, ten, twenty. Their courage increased with their numbers until there was a large band of them edging toward him with lips drawn back and teeth exposed.

Then came a sudden, undetectable flock-command that caused them to cease their belly-slinking and spring forward like one, slavering as they came. They did it with the starving, red-eyed frenzy of animals motivated by something akin to madness.

Repulsive though it was, the sight of creatures craving for meat—even strange blue meat—did not alarm Fander. He slid the altitude-control one notch, the flotation-grids radiated and the sled soared twenty feet.

So calm and easy an escape so casually performed infuriated the wild dog pack beyond all measure. Milling beneath the suspended sled, they made futile springs upward, fell back upon one another, bit and slashed each other, leaped again and again. The pandemonium they set up was a compound of snarls, yelps, barks and growls. They exuded a pungent odor of dry hair and animal sweat.

Reclining upon the sled in a maddening pose of disdain, Fander let the insane ones rave below. They raced around in tight circles, shrieking insults at him and snapping at each other. This went on for some time and ended with a spurt of ultra-rapid cracks from the direction of the glade. Eight dogs fell dead. Two flopped and struggled to crawl away. Ten yelped in agony and made off on three legs. The unharmed ones raced off to some place where they could ambush and make a meal of the escaping limpers. Fander lowered the sled.

Speedy stood atop the rise with Graypate. Restoring his weapon to the crook of his arm, the latter thoughtfully rubbed his chin and ambled forward.

Stopping five yards from the waiting Martian, the old Earthman again massaged his chin whiskers and said, "This is the darnedest thing, just the darnedest thing!"

"No use talking *at* him," advised Speedy. "You've got to touch him like I told you."

"I know, I know." Graypate betrayed the impatience of the aged. "All in good time. I'll touch him when I'm ready." He stood there awhile, staring at Fander with eyes that were very pale and very sharp. "Oh, well, here goes." He offered a hand.

Fander placed a tentacle-end in it.

"Jeepers, he's cold," commented Graypate, closing his grip. "Colder than a snake."

"He isn't a snake," Speedy contradicted fiercely.

"Ease up, ease up—I didn't say he is." Graypate seemed fond of repetitive phrases.

"He doesn't feel like one either," insisted Speedy, who had never felt a snake in his life and did not wish to.

Fander boosted a thought through. "I come from the fourth planet. Do you know what that means?"

"I ain't ignorant," retorted Graypate.

"There is no need to reply vocally. I receive your thoughts exactly as you receive mine. Your responses are much stronger than the boy's and I can understand you easily."

"Humph!" was Graypate's only response to that.

"I have been most anxious to find an adult because the children cannot tell me enough. I would like to ask some questions. Are you willing to answer them?"

"It depends," said Graypate leerily.

"Never mind. Answer them only if you wish. My sole desire is to help you."

"Is that so?" gave back Graypate, with open skepticism. "Why?"

"Because my kind need intelligent friends."

"Why?"

"Because our numbers are small, our resources poor. In visiting this world and the misty one we've come near to the limit of our technical abilities. But with assistance we could go farther, much farther. I think that if we could help you a time might come when you would help us."

Graypate pondered it cautiously, forgetting that the inward workings of his mind were wide open to the other. Chronic suspicion was the keynote of his thoughts, suspicion based on life experiences and recent history. But inward thoughts ran both ways and his own mind could not help but detect the clear sincerity in Fander's.

So he said, "Fair enough. What d'you want to know?"

"What caused all this?" asked Fander, waving a limb to indicate the world as a whole.

"War," said Graypate with dreadful matter-of-factness. "The last war we'll ever have. The entire planet went mad."

"How did it come about?"

"You've got me there." Graypate gave the problem grave consideration. "It wasn't just one thing. It was a multitude of things sort of piling themselves up."

"Such as?"

"Differences in people. Some were colored differently in their bodies, others in their ideas, and they couldn't get along together. Some bred faster than others, wanted more room to expand, a bigger share of the world's food. There wasn't any more room or any more food. The world was full and nobody could shove in anywhere except by pushing someone else out. My old man told me plenty before he died and he always maintained that if people had had the plain horse-sense to keep their numbers down there might not—"

"Your old man?" interjected Fander. "Your father? Didn't all this occur in your own lifetime?"

"It did not. I saw none of it. I am the son of the son of a survivor."

"Let's go back to the cave," put in Speedy, bored with all this silent-contact talk. "I want to show him our harp."

They took no notice and Fander went on, "Do you think there might be a lot of others still living?"

"Who knows?" Graypate was moody about it. "There isn't any way of telling how many are wandering around on the other side of the globe, maybe still killing each other, or starving to death, or dying of the sickness."

"What sickness is this?"

"I couldn't tell you what it's called." Graypate scratched his head confusedly. "My old man told me several times but I've long forgotten. Knowing the name wouldn't do me any good, see? He said his father told him that *his* father said it was part of the war, it got invented and was spread deliberately. It's still with us today so far as I know."

"What are its symptoms?"

"You go hot and dizzy. You get black swellings in the armpits. In twenty hours you're dead. Old folk seem to catch it first. The kids then get it unless you make away from them mighty fast."

"It is nothing familiar to me," said Fander, unable to recognize a cultivated variety of bubonic plague. "In any case, I'm not a medical expert." He eyed Graypate wonderingly. "But you seem to have avoided it."

"Sheer luck," opined Graypate. "Or perhaps I can't get it. There was a story going around during the war that some folk might be immune to it. Don't ask me why because I don't know. It could be that I'm one of the immune ones—but I'm not counting on it."

"So you try to keep your distance from these children?"

"Sure." He glanced at Speedy. "I shouldn't really have come along with this kid. He's got a lousy chance as it is without me increasing the odds."

"That is very considerate of you," Fander remarked, softly. "Especially seeing that you must be lonely."

Graypate bristled and his thought-flow became aggressive. "I ain't grieving for company. I can look after myself the same as I have done since my old man went away to die. I'm standing on my own feet and so is everyone else."

"I believe that," said Fander. "You must pardon me if I say the wrong things. I'm a stranger here, you understand? I judge you by my own feelings. Now and again I get pretty lonely."

"How's that?" demanded Graypate. "You ain't telling me they dumped you and left you all on your own?"

"Yes, they did."

"*Man!*" It was a picture much resembling Speedy's concept, a vision elusive in form but firmly human in face. The oldster was reacting to what he considered a predicament rather than a free choice and the reaction came on a wave of sympathy.

Fander struck promptly and hard. "You see how I'm

fixed. The companionship of wild animals means nothing to me. I need someone intelligent enough to like my music and forget my looks, someone intelligent enough to—"

"I ain't so sure we're that smart," Graypate chipped in. He let his sharp gaze swing morbidly around the landscape. "Not when I see this graveyard and think how it must have looked in my grandfather's days."

"Every flower blooms from the dust of a hundred dead ones," answered Fander.

"Yes? What are flowers?"

It shocked the Martian. He had projected a mind-picture of a trumpet-lily, crimson and shining. Graypate's brain had juggled it around, uncertain whether it were flesh, fish or fowl.

"Vegetable growths like these." Fander plucked half a dozen blades of grass. "But shapelier, more colorful and sweet-scented." He transmitted the brilliant vision of a mile-square field of trumpet-lilies, red and glowing.

"Glory be!" said Graypate. "We've nothing like those."

"Not here," agreed Fander. "Not here." He gestured toward the horizon. "Elsewhere maybe plenty. If we got together we could be company for each other, we could learn things from each other. We could pool our ideas, our efforts, and search for flowers far away. Perhaps we'd also find more people."

"Fat lot of good that would do. Folk just won't stick together in large bunches. They hang around in nothing bigger than family groups until the plague breaks them up—then they abandon the kids. The bigger the crowd the greater the risk of someone contaminating the lot." Graypate leaned on his gun, let his thought-forms shape themselves in dull solemnity. "When a fellow is stricken he goes away and meets his end on his own. Nobody's there to console him or make it easier for him. Death is a personal contract between him and his God, with no witnesses. It's a pretty private affair these days."

"What, after all these years? Don't you think that by this time the disease may have run its course and exhausted itself?"

"Nobody knows—and nobody's gambling on it."

"I would gamble," said Fander.

"You ain't like us. You mightn't be able to catch it."

"Or I might get it worse and die more painfully."

"Maybe," admitted Graypate doubtfully. "Anyway, you're looking at it from a different angle. You've been left here on your ownsome. What have you got to lose?"

"My life," said Fander.

Graypate frowned, thought it over. "Yes, that's true. A fellow can't bet any heavier than that." He rubbed his chin whiskers as before. "All right, all right, I'll take you up on that bet. You can come into the shelters and live with us." His knuckles whitened as the grip tightened on his gun. "On this understanding; the moment you feel sick you get out fast and for keeps. If you don't, I'll shoot you and drag you away even if that makes me catch it too. The kids come first, see?"

The shelters were far roomier than the cave. There were eighteen children living in them, all skinny with their prolonged diet of roots, edible herbs and an occasional rabbit. The youngest and most sensitive of them ceased to be terrified of Fander within ten days. In surprisingly short time his slithering shape of blue ropiness had become a normal adjunct of their small, limited world.

Six of the youngsters were males older than Speedy, one of them much older but not quite adult. Fander beguiled them with his harp, teaching them to play, now and again giving them ten-minute rides on the load-sled as a special treat. He made dolls for the girls, and queer, cone-shaped little houses for the dolls, and fanbacked chairs of woven grass for the houses. None of these toys were truly Martian in design, none were Terrestrial. They represented a pathetic compromise within his imagination: the Martian notion of what Terrestrial models might have looked like had there been any in existence.

But surreptitiously, without seeming to give any less attention to the younger ones, he directed his main efforts upon Speedy and the six older boys. To his mind these were the hope of the world—and of Mars. At no time did he bother to ponder that the non-technical brain is not without its peculiar virtues or that there are times and circumstances when it is worth dropping the short view of what is practicable for the sake of the long view of what is remotely possible.

So as best he could he concentrated upon the elder seven, educating them through the dragging weeks and months, stimulating their minds, encouraging their curiosity and continually impressing upon them the idea that fear of disease can become a folk-separating dogma unless they learned to conquer it within their souls.

He taught them that death is death, a natural process to be accepted philosophically and met with dignity. There were times when he suspected that he was teaching them nothing new, that he was merely reminding them of things forgotten, for deep within their growing, expanding minds was the ancestral strain of Terrestrialism that had mulled its way to the same conclusions ten or twenty thousands of years before. Still, he was helping to remove this disease-block from their mentalities and was driving child-logic more rapidly toward complete adult outlook. In this respect he was satisfied because he could do little more.

In time they organized group concerts, humming or making singing noises to the accompaniment of the harp, now and again improvising lines to suit Fander's tunes, arguing the respective merits of chosen words until by process of elimination they had a song. As songs grew to a repertoire and singing grew more adept, more polished, Old Graypate displayed interest, came to one performance and then another until by custom he had established his own place as a sort of one-man audience and critic.

One day the eldest boy, who was named Redhead, came to Fander and clasped a tentacle-tip. "Devil, may I operate your food-machine?"

"You mean you would like me to show you how to work it?"

"No, Devil, I know how to work it." The boy gazed confidently into the other's huge bee-eyes.

"Then tell me how it is operated."

"You fill its container with the tenderest blades of grass, being careful to exclude all roots and dirt. You are equally careful not to turn a switch before the container is full and its door properly closed. You then turn the red switch and leave it on for a count of two hundred and eighty, reverse the container, turn on the green switch for a count of forty-seven. Finally you close both switches, empty the container's warm pulp into the end molds and apply the press until the biscuits are firm and dry."

"How have you discovered all this?"

"I have watched you making biscuits for us many times. This morning, while you were busy, I tried it myself." He extended a hand. It held a biscuit. Taking it from him, Fander examined it. Firm, crisp and well-shaped. He tasted it. Perfect.

Redhead became the world's first mechanic to operate and service a Martian lifeboat's emergency premasticator. Seven years later, long after the machine had ceased to function, he managed to repower it, weakly but effectively, with dust that gave forth alpha-sparks. In another two years he had improved it, speeded it up. In twelve years he had duplicated it and had all the know-how needed to turn out premasticators on a large scale.

Fander could never have equaled this performance for, as a non-technician, he had no better notion than the average Terrestrial of the principles upon which the machine worked. Neither did he know what was meant by radiant digestion or protein enrichment. He could do little more than urge Redhead along and leave the rest to whatever inherent genius the boy possessed—which was plenty.

In similar manner Speedy and two youths named Blacky and Bigears took the load-sled out of his charge. On rare occasions, as a great privilege, he had permitted them to take up the sled for one-hour trips alone. This time they were gone from dawn to dusk. Graypate mooched worriedly around, a gun under his arm and another stuck in his belt, going frequently to the top of the rise and scanning the sky in all directions. The delinquents swooped in at sunset, bringing with them a strange boy.

Fander summoned them to him. They held hands so that his touch would give him simultaneous contact with all three.

"I am troubled. The sled has only so much power. When it has all been used there will be no more."

They eyed each other aghast.

"Unfortunately I have neither the knowledge nor the ability to energize the sled once its power-reserves become exhausted. I lack the wisdom of the friends who left me here—and that is my shame." He paused, watching them dolefully, then went on, "All I do know is that its power does not leak away. If not used too much and too frequently the reserves should last for many years." Another pause before he added, "In due time you will be grown men and may need the sled far more than you do today."

Blacky said, "But, Devil, when we are men we'll be bigger and heavier. The sled will expend more power in carrying us."

"How do you know that?" asked Fander sharply.

"More weight, more power to sustain it," opined Blacky with the air of one whose logic is incontrovertible. "It doesn't need thinking out. *It's obvious.*"

Very slowly and softly, Fander said, "You'll do. May the twin moons shine upon you someday, for I know you'll do."

"Do what, Devil?"

"Build a thousand sleds like mine or better—and explore the whole world."

From then onward they confined their trips strictly to one hour, making them less often than of yore and spending a lot of time poking and prying around the power-unit's insides.

Graypate changed character with the slow, stubborn reluctance of the aged. As two years and then three rolled past he came gradually out of his shell, was less surly, more willing to hobnob with those swiftly growing up to his own height. Without fully realizing what he was doing he joined forces with Fander, gave the children what he owned of Earthly wisdom passed down from his father's father.

He taught the boys how to care for and use guns, of which he possessed as many as eleven, some maintained mostly as a source of spare parts for the others. Once in a while he took them shell-hunting, digging deep beneath rotting foundations into stale, half-filled cellars in search of ammunition not too corroded to use.

"Guns ain't no use without shells and shells don't last forever."

Neither do buried shells. They found not one.

Of his own wisdom Graypate determinedly held back but one item until the day when Speedy and Blacky and Redhead chivvied it out of him. Then, like a father facing the hangman, he told them the truth about babies. He made no comparative mention of bees because there were no bees, nor of flowers because there were no flowers. One cannot analogize the non-existent. Nevertheless he managed to explain the matter more or less to their satisfaction, after which he mopped his forehead and went to see Fander.

"These youngsters are getting far too nosey for my comfort. They've been asking me how kids come along."

"Did you tell them?"

"Sure did." He sat down, mopped his forehead again. "I don't mind giving in to the boys when I can't beat 'em off any longer—but I'm damned if I'm going to tell the girls."

Fander said, "I've been asked about this myself. I could not tell much because I was far from certain whether you breed precisely as we do. But I told them how we breed."

"The girls too?"

"Of course."

"Jeepers! How did they take it?"

"Just as if I'd told them why water is wet or why the sky is blue."

"Must've been something in the way you put it to them," opined Graypate.

"I told them it was poetry between persons."

Throughout the course of history, Martian, Venusian or Terrestrial, some years are more noteworthy than others. The sixteenth one after Fander's marooning was outstanding for its series of events, each of which was pitifully insignificant by cosmic standards but loomed enormously in this small community's life.

To start with, the older seven—now bearded men—developed Redhead's improvements to the premasticator and by a similar technique managed to repower the exhausted sled. They took triumphantly to the air for the first time in forty months. Experiments showed that the Martian load-carrier was now slower, could bear less weight but had immense range. They used it to visit the ruins of distant cities in search of metallic junk suitable for the building of more sleds. By early summer they had constructed another one, larger than the original, clumsy to the verge of dangerousness, but still a sled.

On several occasions they failed to find metal but did discover people, odd families surviving in subsurface shelters, clinging grimly to life and passed-down scraps of knowledge. Since all these new contacts were strictly human-to-human, with no weirdly tentacled shape to scare off the parties of the second part, and since many were finding fear of plague more to be endured than terrible loneliness, a lot of families willingly returned with the explorers, settled in the shelters, accepted Fander and added their surviving skills to the community's riches.

Thus local population grew to seventy adults and four hundred children. They compounded with their plague-fear by spreading through the system of shelters, digging out half-wrecked and formerly unused expanses and moving apart to form twenty or thirty lesser groups, each one of which could be isolated should contagious death appear.

Growing morale born of added strength and confidence in numbers soon resulted in four more sleds, still clumsy but less risky to use. Above ground there appeared the first rock house standing four-square and solidly under gray skies, a defiant witness that mankind still considered itself several cuts above the rats and rabbits.

The community presented the house to Blacky and Sweetvoice, who had announced their desire to associate. An adult who claimed to know the conventional routine spoke solemn words over the happy couple before many witnesses while Fander attended the groom as best Martian.

Toward summer's end Speedy returned from a solo sledtrip of many days, brought with him one old man, one boy and four girls, all of strange, outlandish countenance. They were yellowish in complexion, had black hair, black tip-tilted eyes and spoke a language that none could understand.

Until these newcomers picked up the local speech Fander had to act as interpreter, for his mind-pictures and theirs were independent of vocal sounds. The four girls were quiet, modest and very beautiful. Within three months Speedy had married one of them, whose name was a gentle clucking sound that meant Precious Jewel Ling.

After this wedding Fander sought Graypate, placed a tentacle-tip in his right hand. "There were differences between the man and the girl, distinctive features wider apart than any we know on Mars. Are these some of the differences that caused your war?"

"Don't know. I've never seen one of these yellow folk before. They must live mighty far off." He scratched his head to help his thoughts along. "I only know what my father told me and his father told him. There were too many people of too many different kinds."

"They can't be all that different if they can fall in love."

"Maybe not," agreed Graypate.

"What if most of the people still in this world assembled here, bred together and had less different children, and the children in turn bred others still less different.

Wouldn't they eventually become all much the same—just Earthpeople?"

"Maybe."

"All speaking the same language, sharing the same culture? If they spread out slowly from a central source, always in contact by sled, continually sharing the same knowledge, the same progress, would there be room for new differences to arise?"

"I don't know," said Graypate evasively. "I'm not so young as I used to be and I can't dream as far ahead as I used to do."

"Well, it doesn't matter so long as the young ones can dream it." Fander mused a moment, continued, "If you're beginning to think of yourself as a black number you've got company. Things are getting somewhat out of hand so far as I'm concerned. The on-looker sees the most of the game and perhaps that's why I'm more sensitive than you to a certain peculiar feeling."

"To what feeling?" asked Graypate, eyeing him.

"That Terra is on the move once more. There are now many people where there were few. A house has been built and more are to follow. They talk of six more. After the six, they will talk of sixty, then six hundred, then six thousand. Some are planning to dig up sunken conduits and use them to pipe water from the northward lake. Sleds are being built, premasticators will soon be built and protective force-screens likewise. Children are being taught. Less and less is being heard of the plague and so far no more have died of it. I feel a dynamic surge of energy and ambition and genius that may grow with appalling rapidity until it becomes a mighty flood. I feel that I, too, am a back number."

"Bunkum!" said Graypate. He spat on the ground. "If you dream often enough you're bound to have a bad one once in a while."

"Perhaps it is because so many tasks have been taken over and are being done far better than I did them. I have failed to seek new jobs. Were I a technician I'd have discovered a dozen by now. Unfortunately I am not a technician, I am an ignoramus." He let go a mental sigh. "I suppose this is as good a time as any to turn to one piece of work I'd like to get done. I need your help."

"What's on your mind?"

"A long, long time ago I made a poem. It was for the beautiful thing that first impelled me to stay here. I do not know exactly what its maker intended to convey, nor whether my eyes see it as he wished it to be seen, but I have made a poem to express what I feel when I look upon his creation."

"Humph!" said Graypate, not very interested.

"There is an outcrop of solid rock beneath its base which I can shave smooth and use as a plinth on which to inscribe my words. I would like to put them down twice; in the script of Mars and the script of Earth." Fander hesitated, added apologetically, "I hope none will think it presumptuous of me. But it is many years since I wrote for all to read—and my chance may never come again."

Graypate said, "I get the idea. You want me to put down your notions in our writing so that you can copy it?"

"Yes."

"Give me your stylus and pad." Taking them, Graypate squatted on a rock, lowering himself stiffly because he was feeling the weight of his years. Resting the pad on his knees, he held the writing instrument in his right hand while his left continued to clasp a tentacle-tip. "Go ahead."

He started drawing thick, laborious marks as Fander's mind-pictures came through, enlarging the letters and keeping them well separated. When he had finished he handed over the pad.

"Asymmetrical," decided Fander, gazing at the queer letters and wishing for the first time that he had taken up the study of Earth-writing. "Cannot you make this part balance with that, and this with this?"

"It's what you said."

"It is your own translation of what I said. I would like it better balanced. Do you mind if we try again?"

They tried again. They made fourteen attempts before Fander was satisfied with the perfunctory appearance of letters and words he could not understand.

Taking the paper, he found his ray-gun, went to the base-rock of the beautiful thing and sheared the whole front to a flat, smooth surface. Adjusting his beam to cut a V-shaped channel one inch deep, he inscribed his poem on the rock in long, unpunctuated lines of neat Martian curlicues.

With less confidence and much greater care he repeated the verse in Earth's awkward, angular hieroglyphics. The task was slow and tedious. Fifty people were watching him by the time he finished. They said nothing. In complete silence they looked at the poem and at the beautiful thing and were still standing there brooding solemnly when he went away.

One by one the rest of the community visited the scene next day, coming and going with the air of pilgrims attending an ancient shrine. All stood there a long time, returned without comment. Nobody praised Fander's work, nobody damned it, nobody reproached him for alienizing something wholly Earth's. The only effect —too subtle to be noteworthy—was a greater and still growing grimness and determination that boosted the already swelling Earth-dynamic.

In that respect Fander wrought better than he knew.

A plague-scare came the next year. Two sleds had brought back families from afar and within a week of their arrival the children sickened, became spotted.

Metal gongs sounded the alarm, all work ceased, the affected section was cut off and guarded while the majority made ready to flee. It was a threatening reversal of all the things for which so many had toiled so long; a destructive scattering of the tender roots of new civilization.

Fander found Graypate, Speedy and Blacky armed to the teeth, facing a drawn-faced and restless crowd.

"About a hundred folk are isolated in that cut-off section," Graypate was telling the audience. "They ain't all got it. Maybe they won't get it. If they don't, it ain't so likely you'll go down with it either. We ought to wait and see. Let's stick around awhile."

"Listen who's talking," invited a skeptical voice in the crowd. "If you weren't immune, you'd have been buried forty years ago."

"Same goes for everyone else," snapped Graypate. "I ain't much use at speechifying so I'm just saying flatly that nobody runs away before we know whether this really is the plague or whether it's something else." He took the gun from under his arm, pointed it forward, clicked its safety-catch. "Anyone fancy himself at beating a bullet?"

The heckler in the audience muscled his way to the front. He was a swarthy man of muscular build and his dark eyes looked belligerently into Graypate's. "While there's life there's hope. If we get out now we'll live to come back, when it's safe to come back—if ever. And you know it. So I'm calling your bluff, see?" Squaring his shoulders, he began to walk away.

Graypate's finger was already tightening on the trigger when he felt the touch of Fander's tentacle on his arm. He stood as if listening to something being whispered, then lowered his weapon and called after the escapee.

"I'm going into the cut-off section and the Devil is going with me. We're running into things—not away from them. I never did like running away." Several of the audience fidgeted, murmured approval. "We'll find out for ourselves exactly what's wrong. We mightn't be able to put it right but we'll have a darned good try."

The walker paused, turned around, eyed him and Fander, said, "You can't do that."

"Why not?"

"You'll catch it yourselves. A lot of use you'll be when you're dead and stinking."

"What, and me immune?" said Graypate, grinning.

"The Devil will get it," the other hedged.

Graypate was about to retort, "What do *you* care?" but altered it slightly in response to Fander's contacting thoughts. He said more softly, "Do you *care?*"

It caught the objector off-balance. He fumbled embarrassedly within his own mind, avoided looking at the Martian, said lamely, "I don't see reason for anyone to take risks."

"He'll take them because he does care," Graypate gave back. "And I'll take them because I'm too old and useless to matter."

With that he stepped down and marched stubbornly toward the isolated section, Fander slithering at his side. The one who wished to flee stayed put and stared after them. The crowd shuffled uneasily, seemed of two minds whether to accept the situation and stick around, or rush Graypate and Fander and drag them away. Speedy and Blacky made to follow the pair but were ordered off.

No adult sickened, nobody died. Children in the affected section went one after another through the same routine of liverishness, high temperature and spots until the epidemic of measles had passed away. Not until a month after the last case had been cured by something within its own constitution did Graypate and Fander emerge.

The innocuous course and eventual disappearance of this suspected plague gave the pendulum of confidence a push, swinging it farther. Morale boosted itself almost to the verge of arrogance. More sleds appeared, more mechanics serviced them, more pilots rode them. More people flowed in from far places, more oddments of past knowledge came with them.

Humanity was off to a flying start with the salvaged seeds of bygone wisdom and the urge to do. The tormented ones of Earth were not primitive savages but surviving organisms of a greatness nine-tenths destroyed yet still remembered, each contributing his mite of know-how to restore at least some of those things that had been boiled away in atomic fires.

When in due time Redhead duplicated the premasticator, there were eight thousand stone houses standing around the hill. A community hall seventy times the size of a house, with a great green dome of hand-worked copper, reared itself upon the eastern fringe. A dam held the lake to the north. A hospital was going up in the west. The nuances and energies and talents of fifty races had built this town and were still building it. Among its population were ten Polynesians and four Icelanders and one lean, dusky child who was the last of the Seminoles.

Farms spread wide. One thousand heads of Indian corn rescued from a sheltered valley in the Andes had grown to ten thousand acres of golden grain. Water buffaloes and goats had been brought from afar to serve in lieu of the horses and sheep that would never be seen again—and no man knew why one species had survived while another had not. The horses had died out while the water buffaloes lived. The canines hunted in ferocious packs; the felines had departed from existence. There had been resistance to radiation and there had been susceptibility, causing survival on the one part and extermination on the other. There were no biologists to seek and find the explanation.

All the small herbs, about half the tubers and many grain-bearing growths had clung to life in odd areas free from blast or radioactive fallouts. These were rescued and cultivated for hungry bellies—but there were no flowers for the hungry mind. Humanity carried on, making do with what was available. No more than that could be done.

Fander was out-of-date, a back-number. He had nothing left for which to live except his songs and the affection of the others. In everything but his harp and his tunes the Terrestrials were way ahead of him. He could do no more than give of his own love in return for theirs and wait for the end with the dignified patience of one whose work is done.

At the termination of the year they buried Graypate. He died in his sleep, passing with the undramatic casualness of one who ain't much use at speechifying. They put him to rest on a knoll behind the community hall and Fander played his mourning song and Precious Jewel, who was Speedy's wife, planted the grave with sweet-smelling herbs.

In the spring of the following year Fander summoned Speedy and Blacky and Redhead. He was coiled upon a couch, blue and shivering. They held hands so that his touch would speak to them simultaneously.

"I am about to undergo my *amafa*."

He had great difficulty in putting it over in understandable thought-forms, for this was something completely beyond their Earthly experience.

"It is an unavoidable change of age during which my kind must sleep undisturbed." They reacted as if this casual reference to his kind was a strange and startling revelation, a new aspect of his character never previously imagined. He continued, "I must be left alone until this hibernation has run its natural course."

"And how long will that be, Devil?" asked Speedy, showing anxiety.

"It may stretch anywhere from four of your months to a full year, or—"

"Or what?" Speedy did not wait for a reassuring reply. His agile mind was swift to sense the spice of danger lying far back in the Martian's thoughts. "Or it may never end?"

"It may never end," admitted Fander reluctantly. He shivered again, drew his tentacles close around himself. The brilliance of his blueness now was fading visibly. "The possibility is small but it is there."

Speedy's worry transmitted itself to the others. Their minds were striving to adjust themselves and accept the appalling idea that Fander might not be a fixture, permanent, established for all time.

"We Martians do not last forever," Fander pointed out with gentle reasonableness. "All are mortal, here on Earth and there on Mars. He who survives his *amafa* has many, many happy years to follow. But some do not survive. It is a trial that must be faced as everything from beginning to end must be faced."

"But—"

"On Mars our numbers are not large," Fander went on. "We breed slowly and many of us die when halfway through the normal span. By cosmic standards we are a weak and foolish people much in need of the support of the clever and the strong. *You* are clever and strong. If ever my people should visit you again, or if any still stranger people come, always remember that you are clever and strong."

"We are strong," echoed Speedy dreamily. His gaze swung around to take in the thousands of roofs, the copper dome, the thing of beauty on the hill. "We are strong."

A prolonged shudder went through the tentacled, huge-eyed creature on the couch.

"I do not wish to be left here, an idle sleeper in the midst of life, posing like a bad example to the young. I would rather rest within the little cave where first we made friends and grew to know and understand each other. Wall it up and fix a door for me. Forbid everyone to touch me or let the light of day fall upon me until such time as I emerge of my own accord." Fander stirred sluggishly, his limbs uncoiling with noticeable lack of sinuousness. "I regret I must ask you to carry me there. Please forgive me. I have left it a little late and cannot . . . cannot . . . make it by myself."

Their faces were pictures of alarm, their minds bells of sorrow. Running for poles, they made a stretcher, edged him onto it, bore him to the cave. A long procession was following by the time they reached it. As they settled him comfortably and began to wall up the entrance, the crowd watched in the same solemn silence with which they had looked upon his verse.

He was already a tightly rolled ball of dull blueness, lying with filmed eyes, when they fitted the door and locked it, leaving him to slumber and to darkness.

Next day a tiny, brown-skinned man with eight children, all hugging dolls, came to this sanctuary. While the youngsters watched wide-eyed, he fixed upon the door a two-word name in metal letters, taking great pains over his self-imposed task and making a neat job of it.

The Martian vessel came from the stratosphere with the slow, stately fall of a landing balloon. Behind the transparent band its bluish, nightmarish crew were assembled and looking with great-multifaceted eyes at the upper surface of the clouds. The scene resembled a pink-tinged snowfield beneath which the planet remained concealed.

Captain Rdina could feel this as a tense, exciting moment even though his vessel had not the honor to be the first to make such an approach. One Captain Skhiva, now long retired, had done it many years before. Nevertheless, this second venture retained its own exploratory thrill.

Someone stationed a third of the way around the vessel's belly came writhing at top pace toward him as their drop brought them nearer the pinkish clouds. The oncomer's signaling tentacle was jiggling at a seldom-used rate.

"Captain, we have just seen an artificial object swoop across the horizon."

"What was it like?"

"It resembled a gigantic load-sled."

"It couldn't have been."

"No, Captain, of course not—but that is exactly what it appeared to be."

"Where is it now?" demanded Rdina, gazing toward the side from which the other had come.

"It dived into the mists below."

"You must have been mistaken. Long-standing anticipation can encourage the strangest delusions." He stopped a moment as the observation-band became shrouded in the vapor of a cloud. Musingly he watched the gray wall of fog slide upward as his vessel continued its descent. "That old report says definitely that there is nothing but desolation and wild animals. There is no intelligent life except some fool of a minor poet whom Skhiva left behind. Twelve to one he's dead by now. The animals may have eaten him."

"Eaten him? Eaten *meat?*" exclaimed the other, thoroughly revolted.

"Anything is possible," assured Rdina, pleased with the extreme to which his imagination could be stretched. "Except a load-sled. That is a plain silly!"

At which point he had no choice but to let the subject

drop for the simple and compelling reason that the ship came out of the base of the cloud and the sled in question was floating alongside. It could be seen in complete detail and even their own instruments were responding to the powerful output of its numerous flotation-grids.

The twenty Martians aboard the sphere sat staring bee-eyed at this enormous thing, which was fully half the size of their own vessel. The forty humans on the sled stared back with equal intentness. Ship and sled continued to descend side by side while both crews studied each other with dumb fascination that persisted until simultaneously they touched ground.

It was not until he felt the slight jolt of landing that Captain Rdina recovered sufficiently to look elsewhere. He saw the great expanse of houses, the green-domed building, the thing of beauty poised upon its hill, the many hundreds of Earth-people streaming out of their town and toward his vessel.

None of these queer, bipedal life-forms, he noted, betrayed the slightest sign of revulsion or fear. They galloped to the tryst with a bumptious self-confidence that would still be evident any place the other end of the cosmos.

It shook him a little. He kept saying to himself again and again, "They're not scared—why should you be? They're not scared—why should you be?"

Suppressing his inward apprehension and ignoring the fact that many of them bore weapons, he went out personally to meet the first of them. The leading Earthman, a big, brawny, spade-bearded two-legger, grasped his tentacle-tip as if to the manner born.

There came a mind-picture of swiftly moving limbs. "My name is Speedy."

The ship emptied itself within minutes. No Martian would stay inside who was free to smell new air. Their first visit, in a slithering bunch, was to the thing of beauty. Rdina stood quietly looking at it, his crew clustered in a half-circle around him, the Earth-folk a silent audience behind.

It was a great rock statue of a female of Earth. She was broad-shouldered, full-bosomed, wide-hipped, and wore voluminous skirts that came right down to her heavy-soled shoes. The figure's pose was a story of unutterable sadness. Her back was a little bent, her head a little bowed, and her face was hidden in her hands, deep in her toil-worn hands.

Rdina tried in vain to gain some glimpse of the tired features behind those concealing fingers. He looked at her a long while before his eyes lowered to read the script beneath, ignoring the Earth-lettering and running easily over the flowing Martian curlicues. Around him the crew also were reading this familiar script.

> *Weep my country for your sons asleep,*
> *The ashes of your homes, your tottering towers;*
> *Weep my country, O my country, weep*
> *For birds that cannot sing, for vanished flowers,*
> *The end of everything,*
> *The silenced hours.*
> *Weep! my country.*

There was no signature. Rdina mulled it many minutes while the others remained passive. Then he turned to Speedy, pointed to the Martian writing.

"Who did this?"

"One of your people. He is dead."

"Ah!" said Rdina. "That songbird of Skhiva's. I have forgotten his name. I doubt whether anyone remembers it. He was only a small and unimportant poet. How did he die?"

"He ordered us to enclose him for some long and urgent sleep he must have, and—"

"The *amafa*," put in Rdina comprehendingly. "And then?"

"We did as he asked. He warned us that he might never come out." Speedy gazed at the sky, unconscious that Rdina was picking up his sorrowful thoughts. "He has been there nearly two years and has not emerged." The gaze came down, fastened squarely on Rdina. "I don't know whether you can understand exactly what I mean, but he was one of us."

"I think I understand." Rdina pondered a short time, asked, "How long is this period you call two years?"

They managed to work it out between them, translating it from Terrestrial to Martian time-terms.

"It is long," pronounced Rdina. "Much longer than the average *amafa*. But it is not unique. Occasionally, for no known reason, someone takes even longer. Besides, Earth is Earth and Mars is Mars." He called to one of his crew. "Physician Traith, we have a prolonged-*amafa* case. We may not be too late to give it attention. Get your oils and essences and come with me." When the other had returned, he ordered Speedy, "Take us to where he lies."

Reaching the door to the walled-up cave, Rdina paused to look at the names fixed upon it in neat, incomprehensible Earth-letters. They read: DEAR DEVIL.

"What do those mean?" asked Physician Traith, pointing.

"Do not disturb," guessed Rdina carelessly. Pushing open the door, he let the other enter first, closed it to keep all the rest outside.

They reappeared two hours later. By now the total population of the city had crowded outside the cave, presumably to see the Martians. Rdina wondered why the crew had not satisfied this natural curiosity—it was unlikely that this great host would be more interested in other things, such as the fate of one minor poet.

Thirty thousand eyes were upon them as they came into the sunlight and fastened the cave's door. Rdina made contact with Speedy, gave him the news.

Stretching himself in the light as if reaching toward the sun, Speedy shouted in a voice of trememdous gladness that all could hear.

"He will be out again within twenty days."

At once a mild form of madness seemed to overcome the two-leggers. They made pleasure-grimaces, piercing mouth-noises and many went so far as to beat each other upon the back.

That same night twenty Martians felt like joining Fander through sheer exhaustion. The Martian constitution is peculiarly susceptible to emotion.

POUL ANDERSON

This was their time; the eve of fulfillment, shared between all, belonging to all.

Truth it was that they could... Maltrade should talk...
and 'twas not... because of... the sky...

Fast Falls the Eventide

It was an old world, incredibly old, with a pitted
moon and a dying sun and a sky too thin to hold a summer cloud. There were trees upon it but not the trees of
yore, for these were the result of eons of gradual accommodation. They inhaled and exhaled far less than
did their distant forebears and they sucked more persist-
ently at the aged soil.

So did the herbs.

And the flowers.

But the petal-lacking, rootless children of this sphere,
the ones able to move around of their own volition,
these could not compensate by sitting in one place and
drawing from the ground. So slowly, ever so slowly they
had dispensed with what once had been a basic need.
They could manage quite well on the bare minimum of
oxygen. Or at a pinch without any at all, experiencing
no more than mild discomfort, a certain lassitude. All
could do this without exception.

The children of this world were bugs.

And birds.

And bipeds.

Moth, magpie and man, all were related. All had the
same mother: an ancient sphere rolling around a
weakly glowing orange ball that some day would flicker
and go out. Their preparation for this end had been
long and arduous, partly involuntary, partly deliberate.

This was their time: the age of fulfillment, shared between all, belonging to all.

Thus it was in no way odd that Melisande should talk to a small beetle. It sat attentively on the back of her pale, long-fingered hand, a tiny creature, black with crimson spots, clean and shiny as if subjected to hours of patient polishing. A ladybird. An amusingly toylike entity that seemed to lack a miniature handle in its side with which to wind it up.

Of course the ladybird could not understand a word of what was being said. It was not *that* intelligent. Time had run so far and the atmosphere become so thin that the insect's wings had adapted accordingly and now were twice the size of those owned by ladybirds of long ago. And with the physical alteration there had been mental alteration; its pin-sized brain was different too. By the standard of its own humble kind it had climbed several rungs up the ladder of life. Though it could not determine meanings, it knew when it was being addressed, sought human company, derived comfort from the sound of a human voice.

And so with the others.

The birds.

The latter-day bees.

All the timid things that once had run for a hiding place or sought shelter in the dark.

Those who had survived—and many species had not—were shy no more. Regardless of whether or not they could understand the mouth-noises made, they liked to be spoken to, their existence acknowledged. They could and did listen for hours, extracting strange pleasure from the intimacy of sound. Or was the pleasure strange?

Perhaps not, for there were times when the sonic relationship was reversed and men stood fascinated while, in lilting language peculiarly its own, a blackbird or nightingale poured forth its very soul.

It was the same indefinable ecstasy.

You see?

So Melisande talked as she walked and Little Redspots listened with his own insectual pleasure until finally she gently flipped her hand and laughed, "Lady-bird, ladybird, fly away home."

It raised colorful wing-cases, spread gauzy wings and fluttered from sight. Melisande paused to look at the stars. In these times they could be seen with brilliance and clarity by day as well as by night, a phenomenon that would have made her air-loving ancestors become filled with fear lest the breath of life soon depart.

No such sensation was within her as she studied the stars. There was only curiosity and speculation coming from a purely personal source. To her, the five-miles-high atmosphere, the dim sun, the sparkling stars were all normal. Often she looked at the stars, sorting them out, identifying them, asking herself the same question again and again.

"Which one?"

And the heavens answered only, "Ah, which?"

Ceasing her speculation, she tripped lightly onward along the narrow woodland path that led into the valley. Far to her left, on the verge of the horizon, something long, slender and metallic arrowed down from the sky and vanished beyond the curve of the earth. A little later a much muted thundering came to her ears.

Neither the sight nor the sound captured her attention. They were too ordinary. The ships of space came often to this ancient world, sometimes once in a month, sometimes twice in a day. Rarely were any two alike. Rarely did the people of one vessel resemble the crew of another.

They had no common language, these visitors from the glittering dark. They spoke a multitude of tongues. Some could talk only mentally, in powerfully projected thought-forms. Some were nonvocal and nontelepathic, could not speak at all, and communicated by means of dexterous finger-motions, ultra-rapid vibration of cilia or other gesticulatory devices.

Once, not so long ago, she had been briefly enter-tained by the slate-colored, armor-skinned personnel of a ship from Khva, a world unthinkable distances be-yond Andromeda. They had been completely blind and totally dumb, making superfast limb-signals at each other and registering them through sensitive esp-organs. They had talked to her without voice and admired her without eyes.

All this was what made learning so hard. At seven hundred years of age she had just finished her final examinations and gained the status of an adult. Long, long ago one might have absorbed the wisdom of an era in a mere century. In the dimmer days still farther back one might have done it in ten years. But not today. Not today.

Now in these solemn times of the final centuries the knowledge to be imbibed was in quantity far too great for swift assimilation. It was an immense pile of data created by the impact of a mighty cosmos composed of worlds without end. Each new ship added a few modest grains to the mass, and the mountain already so built was as nothing to the titanic quantities yet to come—if this world lived long enough to receive them.

If!

There was the rub. Creation was conquered and made the slave of the shapes it had brought forth. The atom and the power within the atom were tools in the hands or pseudo-hands of matter forms able to think and move. Macrocosm and microcosm were equally the playthings of those whose ships roamed endlessly through the tremendous void.

But there were none who knew how to revive an expiring sun.

It could not be done in theory, much less in fact.

It was impossible.

So here and there, at great intervals, a senile sun would flare up a while, collapse into itself, flare again like a feeble thing making its last frantic snatch at life and then become extinguished for all time. A tiny spark in the dark suddenly blown out, unnoticed and unmissed from the limitless host that still blazed on.

Almost each vanishing marked tragedy, perhaps immediate in one case and delayed in another. Some life forms could resist cold longer than others but eventually succumbed just the same. By their superior techniques some could warm themselves and their worlds until the raw-material sources of their heat were exhausted. Then they, too, became as if they had never been.

Any system whose primary reverted to an enormous cinder thereby became the property of a great, white, greedy idiot bearing the name of Supernal Frost. He would share his drear estates with none but the dead.

Melisande thought of all these things as she reached the valley. But the thoughts were not morbid; they held nothing of sadness or resentment. She was of her own kind and it was a life form old in experience and remarkably astute. It had faced the inevitable a thousand times before and had learned the futility of battering against it head-on. It knew what to do with an immovable object: one climbs over it or burrows under it or sneaks around it. One uses one's brains because they are there to be used.

Inevitability was not to be feared.

That which cannot be stayed must be avoided with skill and ingenuity.

A great marble palace sprawled across the end of the valley. Its farther side faced a long series of shrub-dotted and flower-carpeted terraces with narrow lawns and feathery fountains. Its nearer side was the back, looking upon nothing but the valley. Melisande always approached it from the rear because the path through the woods was the shortcut to home.

Mounting the steps, she experienced a thrill of excitement as she entered the huge edifice. Wide, mosaic-floored corridors with walls bearing colorful murals led her to the east wing, whence came a steady murmur of voices and occasionally the penetrating sound of a caller-trumpet.

Bright-eyed with anticipation, she went into a large hall whose seats rose in semicircular tiers to considerable height. It was a place originally designed to hold four thousand. The number of people now seated therein came to no more than two hundred—almost a score of empty seats for every one occupied. The place looked bare. The voices of the few floated hollowly around the emptiness, were echoed by the curved walls and reflected by the overhead cupola.

All the world was like this: facilities for thousands available to mere dozens. Cities with small-town populations; towns numbering no more citizens than a one-time village; and villages holding only three or four families. Whole streets of houses of which half a dozen were homes while the others, empty, silent and glassy-eyed, stared at the lowering sky.

There were just over one million people on this world. Once upon a time they had numbered four thousand million. The vanished numbers had long since taken to the star-trails, not like rats leaving a sinking ship but boldly, confidently, as those whose destiny has become magnified until too great for the confines of one planet.

The small remainder were to follow as soon as they were ready. And that was why the two hundred were here, waiting in the hall, fidgety, chattering, a little on edge as they listened for the fateful blare of the caller-trumpet.

"Eight-two-eight Hubert," it suddenly gave forth. "Room Six."

A blond giant came up from his seat, stalked down the aisle watched by almost two hundred pairs of eyes. Voices were temporarily silent. He went past Melisande who smiled and murmured low.

"Good luck!"

"Thanks!"

Then he was gone through the distant door. The chatterers resumed. Melisande sat herself at the end of a row, next to a thin, swarthy youth of some seven and a half centuries, little older than herself.

"I'm a minute late," she whispered. "Have they been calling long?"

"No," he assured. "That last name was the fourth." He stretched out his legs, pulled them in, stretched them out again, surveyed his fingernails, shifted in his seat, registered vague discomfort. "I wish they'd hurry up with this. The strain is rather—"

"Nine-nine-one Jose-Pietro," boomed the trumpet. "Room Twenty."

He heard it with his mouth open, his eyes startled. The way he came to his feet was slow, uncertain. He licked thin lips suddenly gone dry, cast an appealing glance at Melisande.

"That's me!"

"They must have heard you," she laughed. "Well, don't you want to go?"

"Yes, of course." He edged past her; his gaze on the door through which the blond Hubert had gone. "But when it comes to the point I sort of go weak in the knees."

She made a negligent gesture. "Nobody's going to amputate your legs. They're simply waiting to give you a document—and maybe it'll be one with a gold seal."

Throwing her a look of silent gratitude, he speeded up, exited with a mite more self-assurance.

"Seven-seven Jocelyn—Room Twelve."

And immediately after, "Two-four-oh Betsibelle— Room Nineteen."

Two girls went out, one dark and plump and smiling, one tall, slender, red-haired and serious.

Came a series of names in quick succession: Lurton, Irene, George, Teresa-Maria, Robert and Elena. Then, after a short interval, the summons for which she was waiting.

"Four-four Melisande—Room Two!"

The man in Room Two had light gray eyes, snowy hair and smooth, unlined features. He might have been middle-aged—or old, extremely old. There was no way of telling at a time when a person could retain a seamless face and snowy locks for more than a thousand years.

Waiting for her to be seated, he said: "Well, Melisande, I am happy to say you have passed."

"Thank you, my tutor."

"I felt sure you would pass. I viewed it as almost a foregone conclusion." He smiled across at her, went on, "And now you want to know where you are weak, where you are strong. Those are the essential details, aren't they?"

"Yes, my tutor." She uttered it in low tones, her hands folded demurely in her lap.

"In general knowledge you are excellent," he informed. "That is something of which to be proud—that one should hold the immense storehouse of wisdom described by the inadequate name of general knowledge. You are also most satisfactory in sociology, mass-psychology, ancient and modern philosophies and trans-cosmic ethics." He leaned forward, looking at her. "But you are rather poor in general communications."

"I am sorry, my tutor." She bit her lower lip, vexed with herself.

"You are nontelepathic and seem quite unable to develop even rudimentary receptivity. When it comes to visual signaling you are somewhat better but still not good enough. Your communication-rate is sluggish, your mistakes numerous, and you appear to be handicapped by a form of tactile uncertainty."

She was now looking at the floor, her face wearing a blush of shame. "I regret it, my tutor."

"There is nothing to regret," he contradicted sharply. "One cannot excel in everything, much as one might like to do so." He waited for her eyes to come up, then proceeded, "As for purely vocal forms of communication, you are no more than fair in the guttural languages." A pause, then: "But you are superb in the liquid ones."

"Ah!" Her features brightened.

"Your oral and written tests for liquid languages were taken in the speech-patterns of the Valreans of Sirius. Your errors were exactly none. Your vocal rate was three hundred twenty words per minute. The average for the Valreans is three hundred fourteen. That means you can speak their language a little better than they can themselves." He smiled to himself, deriving much satisfaction from the thought that his pupil could outshine the very originators of a linguistic mode. "So now, Melisande, the time has come to make serious decisions."

"I am ready, my tutor." Her gaze forward was steady, level and unswerving.

"First I must give you this." He handed her a thin scroll from which dangled a crimson cord terminating in a gold seal. "I congratulate you."

"Thank you!" Her fingers took it, held it, fondled it like something infinitely precious.

"Melisande," he asked, gently, "do you desire children?"

Her answer came evenly, undisturbed, quite without trace of embarrassment. "Not yet, my tutor."

"Then you consider yourself free to go out?" He gestured toward the window beyond which a multimillion lights gleamed and beckoned.

"Yes."

IIis face became solemn. "But you will not abandon all thoughts of children of your own? You will not plunge so deeply and become so absorbed as to be forgetful of your own shape and kind?"

"I think not," she promised.

"I am glad of that, Melisande. We are scattered afar, in little groups and numbers over an immensity of places. There is no need to increase our count within the cosmos, no need at all. But we should not reduce that count. We should maintain it. That way lies immortality as a species."

"Yes, I know. I have thought of it often." She studied her scroll without really seeing it. "I shall play my little part when the right moment comes."

"You have plenty of time, anyway. You are very young." He sighed as if he wished he could say the same of himself. Crossing the room to where a machine stood by the wall, he opened a cabinet at its side, took out a thick wad of cards. "We'll sort the applications and narrow them down to those most suitable."

He fed the cards one by one into the machine. They were no more than rectangles of thin, white plastic each bearing a reference number at the head, the rest being perforated with many circular or square-shaped holes. When the lot had been inserted he opened a cover revealing a small keyboard. On this he typed, "Nonvocals," and pulled a lever at one side.

The machine clicked, whirred, expelled cards in rapid succession. When it had finished, he glanced at its retention-counter.

"Eighty-four left."

Again resorting to the keyboard, he picked out the word, "Gutturals." The machine responded by throwing out another spray of cards. "Supersonics." More cards. "Staccatos." Out shot a little bunch. "Whistlers." No result.

"Twenty-one." He glanced at his pupil. "They are all liquid speakers now but I think it would be as well if we eliminated the slow ones, don't you?" Getting her nod, he reset the keyboard, "300-max." Several cards emerged. Extracting the remainder, he shuffled them in sensitive fingers, eyed the stars through the window. "There are eleven, Melisande. You have eleven worlds from which to choose."

Filing the first card into a different part of the machine, he set a pair of dials and pressed a stud. The apparatus emitted a faint hum while it warmed up, then a voice came from its hidden speaker.

It said: "Application Number 109,747, Valrea, a union of four planets located in—"

Abruptly it cut off as he jabbed another stud in response to a wave of Melisande's hand.

"You are not interested?"

"No, my tutor. Perhaps I ought to be because I already know their language and that would save a lot of bother. But they have some of us already, haven't they?"

"Yes. They applied for four hundred. We sent them thirty-six and, much later on, another twenty." He regarded her with almost paternal solicitude. "You would have company there, Melisande. You would have others of your own kind, few as they are."

"That may be," she admitted. "But is it fair that people like the Valreans, who have gained some of what they want, should be given still more while others who have none should continue to be denied?"

"No, it is not." He fed in a second card.

"Application 118,451," said the machine. "Brank, a single planet located in the Horse's Head Nebula, Section A71, Subsection D19. Mass 1.2. Civilization type-F. The dominant life form is a bipedal vertebrate as shown."

A screen above the apparatus glowed in full colors, depicted several gaunt, greenish-skinned creatures with long, spindly arms and legs, seven-fingered hands, hairless skulls and enormous yellow eyes.

For another two minutes the voice poured forth a flood of data concerning Brank and its emaciated inhabitants. Then it ceased and the machine went quiescent.

"Thirty years ago they asked for a hundred of us," he told Melisande. "We sent ten. They have now been allocated another six, of which you may be one if you so desire."

Seeing that she was noncommittal, he slid another card into the apparatus.

"Application 120,776. Nildeen, a planet with one large satellite, heavily populated, located in the Maelstrom, Section L7, Subsection CC3."

It went on and on. The appropriate life form displayed itself on the screen, a tentacular, eyeless type of being with esp-organs protruding from its head like an insect's antenna. The Nildeens already had had forty of Melisande's kind, still wanted more. She turned them down.

The eleventh and last card aroused her greatest interest, caused her to lean forward with ears alert and eyes alight.

"Application 141,048. Zelam, a single planet located on the fringe of the known, reference numbers and coordinates not yet filed. Recent contact. Mass I. Civilization type-J. Dominant life form is reptilian as shown."

They had a faint resemblance to erect alligators, though Melisande did not know it. All of her own planet's lizardlike species had vanished a million years ago.

There were now no local forms to which she could liken these horny-skinned, long-jawed and toothy Zelamites. By the standards of the dim past they were appallingly ugly; but by the standards of her especial planet and her especial era they were not ugly. They were merely an individualistic aspect of the same universal thing which is named Intelligence.

True, the varying forms might also vary in the accuracy with which they reflected this elusive but cosmos-wide thing, yet, taking the long view, it was nothing but a variation in time. Some had more centuries to catch up than did others. Some had come early on the scene and that was their good fortune. Others had come late and that was their hard luck. They were like differently handicapped runners in the same field, spread out, panting, some in front, some behind, but all heading the same way, all destined to pass the finishing line. The Zelamites were held-back runners.

"I will go to those," she said, making it an irrevocable decision.

Spreading the eleven cards across his desk, he surveyed them with a bothered frown. "They asked for sixty. Everyone asks for far too many, especially the newcomers. We've none to spare just yet. But we don't like to refuse anyone."

"So?"

"It has been suggested that we send them one, just one, as a beginning. It would show willingness if nothing else."

"I am one," she pointed out.

"Yes, yes, I know." He had the resigned air of a person about to be cornered without hope of escape. "We would rather that one were masculine."

"Why?"

"Dear me!" It defeated him completely. "There is no reason at all except that we would prefer it."

"Surely, my tutor, it would be a retrograde step and quite unworthy of us to insist upon something without any reason?"

"Not if it does no harm," he countered. "There is the true test—whether it does harm or good."

"Does it do the Zelamites good to refuse them a suitable volunteer?"

"We are not refusing them, Melisande. There are others besides yourself. Someone else may also have chosen Zelam. A dozen may wish to go there. At this stage, with so many applications, we just can't send all of them. Only one can go now. Others may follow later."

"Find out for me, please," she begged.

A mite unwillingly he flicked the switch on his desk and spoke into the silver instrument beside it.

"How many have selected Zelam, Reference 141,-048?"

There was quite a long wait before the answer came, "None."

Switching off, he leaned back, eyed her thoughtfully. "You will be lonely."

"All first arrivals are lonely."

"There may arise perils beyond imagining."

"Which will remain the same whether borne by one or shared by a hundred," she gave back, undismayed.

Searching around for one last item of discouragement, he told her, "The Zelamites are nocturnal. They will expect you to work at night and sleep by day."

"Those of us on Brank have been doing the same for years, and many more elsewhere. My tutor, should it be harder for me than for them?"

"No, it should not." He came across to her. "I see that you are determined in your choice. If it be your destiny, it is not for me to thwart it." Taking her hand, he raised it gently, impressed a light kiss upon her fingers in the conventional farewell. "Good luck, Melisande. I am glad to have had you as a pupil of mine."

"Thank you, my tutor." Holding her scroll tightly to her breast, she paused in the doorway as she went out, gave him a final bright-eyed smile. "And I am proud to have had you!"

Long after she had gone he sat and gazed absently at the door. They came and they went, one after another.

Each arrived as an utter stranger, departed like a child of his very own taking some of his essential essence with them.

And each one that went forever among the vast concourse of stars made his dying world a fraction smaller, barer, less possessed of life. It is not easy to remain with a long-loved sphere which is nearing its end, to watch the flame die down, watch the shadows creep and grow.

Even at the terrific velocities of this age the journey to Zelam was long and tedious, stretching through days and weeks into many months. It involved several changes, first from a huge hyperspatial mainliner to a smaller branchliner, then to a light blue sphere crewed by dumb Xanthians, then to a battered old rocketship manned by a weirdly mixed mob among whom were two bipeds of Melisande's own kind. Finally to a strange, wedge-shaped and mysteriously powered contraption which sinuous and scintillant Haldisians employed for trading around a small group of systems in one of which was the planet called Zelam.

Beyond this point was a great sprawl of darkness in which reposed a coil of brilliant mist that eventually would be reached by bigger and better ships. Another island universe. Another mighty host of living shapes and forms the highest of which would share one thing in common—and therefore prove willing to share it yet again.

But the length of the trip had been useful. With the aid of a phonetic dictionary and a rudimentary phonograph provided by Zelam, plus her own natural aptitude, she had become an accomplished speaker of the language by the time the planet rolled into view.

Lacking ladder, ramps or anything of that nature, the Haldisians got rid of her by the simple expedient of throwing her through the outer door of the air lock. A power exerted by them personally or perhaps by some unseen apparatus within the vessel—she did not know which—took hold of her, lowered her gently the forty feet to earth. Her luggage followed the same way. So did two of the crew. Another two came out but floated upward, gained the ship's flat topside, commenced opening cargo hatches.

There was a small Zelamite deputation to meet her, the news of her coming having been received a few days before. They were bigger than she had expected, for the screen on which she had first seen them had given no indication of relative size. The shortest of them towered head and shoulders above her, had sharp-toothed jaws the length of her arm and looked as if he could cut her in half with one savage snap.

The largest and oldest of the group, a heavily built and warty-faced individual, came forward to meet her as the others hastened to pick up her bags.

"You are the one named Melisande?"

"That's me," she admitted, smiling at him.

He responded with what looked remarkably like a threatening snarl. It did not mislead her in the least. Her kind had learned a thousand centuries ago that those with different facial contours and bony structure perforce must have different ranges of expressions. She knew that the alarming grimace was nothing but an answering smile.

The tone of his voice proved it as he went on, "We are pleased to have you." His orange-colored eyes with their slot-shaped pupils studied her a moment before he added in mild complaint, "We asked for a hundred and hoped to get ten, perhaps twenty."

"More will come in due course."

"It is to be hoped so." He threw a significant glance toward the ship, from which items of cargo were floating down. "The Haldisians have twenty. We are tired of hearing them boast about it. We think we are entitled to at least as many."

"They started with two of us," she pointed out. "The others came later—as yours will do. We have no choice but to deal with applications in strict rotation."

"Oh, well—" He spread the long fingers of one hand in the Zelamite equivalent of a shrug, conducted her to a six-wheeled vehicle standing nearby, superintended the loading of her luggage, then got in beside her. "I must compliment you on your fluency. It is remarkable."

"Thank you."

She concentrated on the blue-moss-coated and yellow-flowered landscape as he drove to town at a fast pace. His body exuded a faintly pungent odor which her nostrils noted but her brain ignored. That was another very ancient lesson; that different metabolisms produce different manifestations. How boring would the universe be if all its creatures were identically the same!

They drew up before a long, low stone-built edifice with high-tilted roofs and plastic windows. The place was imposing mostly because of its lengthy facade. It stretched at least half a mile, had a blue-moss carpet along its front and a railed yard at each end.

"This is your college." He pointed to the nearer end. "And there is your home." Observing her expression he added by way of explanation, "Of course, we cannot expect more than one person can do. We built apartments for ten, with space for extensions if we were lucky enough to get more of you."

"I see." Getting out, she watched her bags being taken inside. Despite centuries of training, free choice of destination and months of anticipatory journeying, some adjustment still was necessary. "And there is your home," he had said. It would take her at least a week and perhaps a month to get used to thinking of it as home. Probably even more because domestic routine would be topsy-turvy so long as she slept daytimes and worked nights.

"Before you go in," he suggested, "what about something to eat?"

"Good heavens, no!" She gave a tinkling laugh. "The Haldisians insisted on providing a farewell dinner. They didn't know when to stop. I don't feel like looking at any more food for days."

"*Armph!*" The twist on his reptilian face suggested that he'd have liked it better if the Haldisians had left well enough alone. "In that case, all I can offer you is the rest and relaxation you must need. Do you think you might be ready to start work tomorrow evening?"

"Most certainly."

"You can have longer if you wish."

"Tomorrow evening will do," she assured.

"Good—I will tell Nathame. He is our chief cultural supervisor and high in governmental affairs. He will call to see you shortly before you begin."

Giving her another wide-jawed and toothy smile, he drove away. She watched him go, then went and inspected her front door, which the luggage-bearers had left invitingly open. It was a simple vertical shutter affair wound up and down by a side handle and could be fastened from the inside only by means of a small bolt.

Beyond it lay the passage, solid, motionless, solely to be walked upon and not for automatic transport. And lights that had to be switched because they knew nothing of perpetual illumination. But it was home-to-be.

She stepped inside.

Nathame came with the twilight on the next day. A sharp-eyed, alert specimen of Zelamite life, he wore glittering insignia on his shoulder-straps, bore himself with authoritative self-assurance. For a while he chatted inconsequentially, his keen gaze never shifting from her face, then added a grumble to the effect that if one person were another world's idea of a hundred it might be better to ask for ten thousand and thus obtain the number really required.

He fell silent for a bit, occupied by his own thoughts, then said: "Before we made contact with other people we had no history but our own. Now we've had to learn the lore of a whole galaxy. It is a record voluminous enough to absorb a lifetime. Nevertheless, I have specialized in it and have learned one thing: that your own particular kind of life is supremely clever."

"Do you think so?" She watched him curiously.

"I do not *think* it. I *know* it." He warmed to his subject. "History records that between sixty and seventy life forms have disappeared from the universal scene.

Some warred together and exploded each other's worlds. Some were the victims of cosmic collisions that could be neither foreseen nor avoided. They vanished—*pouf!*—like that! The large majority died when their suns died and warmth went away from them and supernal cold took over." His orange-colored orbs still stared at her unblinking. "It proves one thing: that an entire species can be exterminated and become as though it had never been."

"Not necessarily," she contradicted, "because—"

"Ah!" He held up a hand to halt her. "Of a verity it is for *your* kind to deny the possibility. What or who can wipe out a life form scattered over a hundred million worlds? Nothing! Nobody!"

"I don't think anyone would wish to try."

"Not unless they were completely crazy," he agreed. "You have made yourselves invincible. You have preserved yourselves for eternity. I call that cleverness of the highest order." He pulled a face. "And how have you done it?"

"How do you imagine?" she invited.

"By using your great experience and immense wealth of wisdom to exploit the snobbery of lesser races."

"I don't see it that way."

Ignoring her, he went determinedly on, "Your people anticipated disaster. They foresaw that when your sun collapsed no other planet and no other system could or would accept a sudden influx of refugees numbering thousands of millions. But nobody minds a few dozen or hundreds, especially if they add to their hosts' prestige. Comes the master stroke: you persuade them to scramble for self-esteem like children clamoring for gifts. You made them *want* you."

"But surely—"

He silenced her again, clasped his hands together in a peculiarly artificial manner, minced across the room and spoke in high-pitched, long-drawn vowels, manifestly imitating a type of character with which she was not yet familiar.

"*Really,* Thasalmie, we wouldn't *dream* of sending

our children to a *state* school. We've shipped them to the central college at Hei. *Terribly* expensive, of course. They have *Terran* tutors there and it makes *such* a difference in later life when one can say that one has been educated by *Terrans*."

Relaxing into a normal pose, he said, "You see? Since the first Haldisian ships discovered us we've had visits from about twenty life forms. Every one of them took up a patronizing attitude. What, you have no Terrans? By the stars, you must be backward! Why, we have twenty on our world—or forty, or fifty as the case may be." His nostrils twitched as he emitted a loud snort. "They boast and they brag and act so superior that everyone on this world develops a severe inferiority complex and starts screaming for an army of Terrans without delay."

"Braggarts and boasters are not Terran-educated," she informed. "We don't produce that kind."

"Maybe you don't, but that's the effect of your presence among those you've not yet taught. They shine in reflected glory. So I say again that you are supremely clever, and on three counts. You are making use of the fact that the more intelligent a people the less they enjoy being thought stupid. Secondly, you have thus insured your own survival for all time. Thirdly, by being content merely to maintain your numbers and not increase them you are also maintaining the confidence of your various hosts. Nobody views with alarm an alien colony that never grows."

She smiled at him and remarked, "All along you've been inviting me to say, 'Look who's talking!' Haven't you?"

"Yes, but you were too diplomatic." Moving nearer and speaking with greater seriousness, he continued, "We asked for a hundred of your kind. Had we got them we would have asked for more. And more again. Not for prestige, but for other and better reasons."

"Such as?"

"We look far ahead. The Haldisians, who know more about it than we, say that ours is a short-term sun. That means an end similar to the end of your world. We must seek the same way out because we can conceive no other. The path your kind has made our kind can tread also. The demand for Terrans is greater than the supply—and there aren't many more of you, are there?"

"Not many," she admitted. "About a million. The old world hasn't long to go."

"Some day we shall be compelled to say that, too. It would be nice if by that time the Zelamites had become an acceptable substitute for Terrans." He made an imperative gesture. "So there is your job as far as one can take it. It's a hard job. Starting with our brightest children, you must make us clever enough to share your salvation."

"We'll do our best," she promised, deliberately using the plural.

It did not escape him. Even his face could register gratification. Saluting her, he took his departure. Re-angling her mind and directing it exclusively to the task in hand, she hurried along the main corridor, reached the room from which was coming a shrill uproar.

Silence dropped like a heavy curtain as she entered. Taking her place by the desk, she surveyed the hundred small, thin-snouted, slot-eyed faces that in turn were examining her with youthful candidness.

"We shall commence tonight with the basic subject of transcosmic ethics," she informed. Turning around, she faced the dark rectangle that had no counterpart on Terra, picked up the white stick at its base and wrote upon the blackboard in a firm, clear hand.

"Lesson One. Intelligence is like candy. It comes in an endless variety of shapes, sizes and colors, no one of which is less delectable than the others."

She glanced over her shoulder to insure that they were giving attention, found them copying it down, orange eyes intent. One had his tongue out, its purple tip laboriously following the movements of his writing instrument.

Involuntarily her gaze shifted to the transparent roof through which the galactic host looked down. Somewhere within that gleaming swarm was a little red light, weak and dimming. Somewhere near to it was another, silvery blue, shining to the very last.

The ancient fountain.

The guiding star.

Old Mother Earth.

where wandering gleaming eyes . . . her a little . . . light . . . and glittering, dumbfoundedly to it was a . . . place . . . paid to . . . ignore . . . .

I Am Nothing

DAVID KORMAN RASPED, "Send them the ultimatum."

"Yes, sir, but—"

"But what?"

"It may mean war."

"What of it?"

"Nothing, sir." The other sought a way out. "I merely thought—"

"You are not paid to think," said Korman, acidly. "You are paid only to obey orders."

"Of course, sir. Most certainly." Gathering his papers, he backed away hurriedly. "I shall have the ultimatum forwarded to Lani at once."

"You better had!" Korman stared across his ornate desk, watched the door close. Then he voiced an emphatic, "Bah!"

A lickspittle. He was surrounded by lickspittles, cravens, weaklings. On all sides were the spineless ready to jump to his command, eager to fawn upon him. They smiled at him with false smiles, hastened into pseudo-agreement with every word he uttered, gave him exaggerated respect that served to cover their inward fears.

There was a reason for all this. He, David Korman, was strong. He was strong in the myriad ways that meant full and complete strength. With his broad body, big jowls, bushy brows and hard gray eyes he looked

249

precisely what he was: a creature of measureless power, mental and physical.

It was good that he should be like this. It was a law of Nature that the weak must give way to the strong. A thoroughly sensible law. Besides, this world of Morcine needed a strong man. Morcine was one world in a cosmos full of potential competitors, all of them born of some misty, long-forgotten planet near a lost sun called Sol. Morcine's duty to itself was to grow strong at the expense of the weak. Follow the natural law.

His heavy thumb found the button on his desk, pressed it, and he said into the little silver microphone, "Send in Fleet Commander Rogers at once."

There was a knock at the door and he snapped, "Come in." Then, when Rogers had reached the desk, he informed, "We have sent the ultimatum."

"Really, sir? Do you suppose they'll accept it?"

"Doesn't matter whether they do or don't," Korman declared. "In either event we'll get our own way." His gaze upon the other became challenging. "Is the fleet disposed in readiness exactly as ordered?"

"It is, sir."

"You are certain of that? You have checked it in person?"

"Yes, sir."

"Very well. These are my orders: the fleet will observe the arrival on Lani of the courier bearing our demands. It will allow twenty-four hours for receipt of a satisfactory reply."

"And if one does not come?"

"It will attack one minute later in full strength. Its immediate task will be to capture and hold an adequate ground base. Having gained it, reinforcements will be poured in and the territorial conquest of the planet can proceed."

"I understand, sir." Rogers prepared to leave. "Is there anything more?"

"Yes," said Korman. "I have one other order. When you are about to seize this base my son's vessel must be the first to land upon it."

Rogers blinked and protested nervously, "But, sir, as

a young lieutenant he commands a small scout bearing twenty men. Surely one of our major battleships should be—"

"My son lands first!" Standing up, Korman leaned forward over his desk. His eyes were cold. "The knowledge that Reed Korman, my only child, was in the forefront of the battle will have an excellent psychological effect upon the ordinary masses here. I give it as my order."

"What if something happens?" murmured Rogers, aghast. "What if he should become a casualty, perhaps be killed?"

"That," Korman pointed out, "will enhance the effect."

"All right, sir." Rogers swallowed and hurried out, his features strained.

Had the responsibility for Reed Korman's safety been placed upon his own shoulders? Or was that character behind the desk genuine in his opportunist and dreadful fatalism? He did not know. He knew only that Korman could not be judged by ordinary standards.

Blank-faced and precise, the police escort stood around while Korman got out of the huge official car. He gave them his usual austere look-over while the chauffeur waited, his hand holding the door open. Then Korman mounted the steps to his home, heard the car door close at the sixth step. Invariably it was the sixth step, never the fifth or seventh.

Inside, the maid waited on the same corner of the carpet, her hands ready for his hat, gloves and cloak. She was stiff and starched and never looked directly at him. Not once in fourteen years had she met him eye to eye.

With a disdainful grunt he brushed past her and went into the dining room, took his seat, studied his wife across a long expanse of white cloth filled with silver and crystal.

She was tall and blond and blue-eyed and once had seemed supremely beautiful. Her willowy slenderness had made him think with pleasure of her moving in his arms with the sinuosity of a snake. Now, her slight curves had gained angularity. Her submissive eyes wore crinkles that were not the marks of laughter.

"I've had enough of Lani," he announced. "We're precipitating a showdown. An ultimatum has been sent."

"Yes, David."

That was what he had expected her to say. He could have said it for her. It was her trademark, so to speak; always had been, always would be.

Years ago, a quarter of a century back, he had said with becoming politeness, "Mary, I wish to marry you."

"Yes, David."

She had not wanted it—not in the sense that he had wanted it. Her family had pushed her into the arrangement and she had gone where shoved. Life was like that: the pushers and the pushed. Mary was of the latter class. The fact had taken the spice out of romance. The conquest had been too easy. Korman insisted on conquest but he liked it big. Not small.

Later on, when the proper time had come, he had told her, "Mary, I want a son."

She had arranged it precisely as ordered. No slipups. No presenting him with a fat and impudent daughter by way of hapless obstetrical rebellion. A son, eight pounds, afterward named Reed. He had chosen the name.

A faint scowl lay over his broad face as he informed, "Almost certainly it means war."

"Does it, David?"

It came without vibrancy or emotion. Dull-toned, her pale oval features expressionless, her eyes submissive. Now and again he wondered whether she hated him with a fierce, turbulent hatred so explosive that it had to be held in check at all costs. He could never be sure of that. Of one thing he was certain: she feared him and had from the very first.

Everyone feared him. Everyone without exception. Those who did not at first meeting soon learned to do so. He saw to that in one way or another. It was good to be feared. It was an excellent substitute for other emotions one has never had or known.

When a child he had feared his father long and ardently; also his mother. Both of them so greatly that their passing had come as a vast relief. Now it was his turn. That, too, was a natural law, fair and logical. What is gained from one generation should be passed to the next. What is denied should likewise be denied.

Justice.

"Reed's scoutship has joined the fleet in readiness for action."

"I know, David."

His eyebrows lifted. "How do you know?"

"I received a letter from him a couple of hours ago." She passed it across.

He was slow to unfold the stiff sheet of paper. He knew what the first two words would be. Getting it open, he found it upside-down, reversed it and looked.

"Dear Mother."

That was her revenge.

"Mary. I want a son."

So she had given him one—and then taken him away.

Now there were letters, perhaps two in one week or one in two months according to the ship's location. Always they were written as though addressing both, always they contained formal love to both, formal hope that both were keeping well.

But always they began, "Dear Mother."

Never, "Dear Father."

Revenge!

Zero hour came and went. Morcine was in a fever of excitement and preparation. Nobody knew what was happening far out in space, not even Korman. There was a time-lag due to sheer distance. Beamed signals from the fleet took many hours to come in.

The first word went straight to Korman's desk, where he posed ready to receive it. It said the Lanians had replied with a protest and what they called an appeal to reason. In accordance with instructions the fleet commander had rejected this as unsatisfactory. The attack was on.

"They plead for reasonableness," he growled. "That means they want us to go soft. Life isn't made for the soft." He threw a glance forward. "Is it?"

"No, sir," agreed the messenger with alacrity.

"Tell Bathurst to put the tape on the air at once."

"Yes, sir."

When the other had gone he switched his midget radio and waited. It came in ten minutes, the long, rolling, grandiloquent speech he'd recorded more than a month before. It played on two themes: righteousness and strength, especially strength.

The alleged causes of the war were elucidated in detail, grimly but without ire. That lack of indignation was a telling touch because it suggested the utter inevitability of the present situation and the fact that the powerful have too much justified self-confidence to emote.

As for the causes, he listened to them with boredom. Only the strong know there is but one cause of war. All the other multitudinous reasons recorded in the history books were not real reasons at all. They were nothing but plausible pretexts. There was but one root-cause that persisted right back to the dim days of the jungle. When two monkeys want the same banana, that is war.

Of course, the broadcasting tape wisely refrained from putting the issue so bluntly and revealingly. Weak stomachs require pap. Red meat is exclusively for the strong. So the great antenna of the world network comported themselves accordingly and catered for the general dietary need.

After the broadcast had finished on a heartening note about Morcine's overwhelming power, he leaned back in his chair and thought things over. There was no question of bombing Lani into submission from the upper reaches of its atmosphere. All its cities cowered beneath bombproof hemispherical force fields. Even if they had been wide open he would not have ordered their destruction. It is empty victory to win a few mounds of rubble.

He'd had enough of empty victories. Instinctively, his gray eyes strayed toward the bookcase on which stood the photograph he seldom noticed and then no more than absently. For years it had been there, a subconsciously-observed, taken-for-granted object like the inkpot or radiant heat panel, but less useful than either.

She wasn't like her picture now. Come to think of it, she hadn't been really like it *then*. She had given him obedience and fear before he had learned the need for these in lieu of other needs. At that time he had wanted something else that had not been forthcoming. So long as he could remember, to his very earliest years, it had never been forthcoming, not from anyone, never, never, never.

He jerked his mind back to the subject of Lani. The location of that place and the nature of its defenses determined the pattern of conquest. A ground base must be won, constantly replenished with troops, arms and all auxiliary services. From there the forces of Morcine must expand and, bit by bit, take over all unshielded territory until at last the protected cities stood alone in fateful isolation. The cities would then be permitted to sit under their shields until starved into surrender.

Acquisition of enemy territory was the essential aim. This meant that despite spacegoing vessels, force shields and all the other redoubtable gadgets of ultra-modernism, the ordinary foot soldier remained the final arbiter of victory. Machines could assault and destroy. Only men could take and hold.

Therefore this was going to be no mere five-minute war. It would run on for a few months, perhaps even a year, with spasms of old-style land-fighting as strong points were attacked and defended. There would be bombing perforce limited to road blocks, strategic junctions, enemy assembly and regrouping areas, unshielded but stubborn villages.

There would be some destruction, some casualties. But it was better that way. Real conquest comes only over real obstacles, not imaginary ones. In her hour of triumph Morcine would be feared. Korman would be feared. The feared are respected and that is proper and decent.

If one can have nothing more.

Pictorial records in full color and sound came at the end of the month. Their first showing was in the privacy of his own home to a small audience composed of himself, his wife, a group of government officials and assorted brass hats.

Unhampered by Lanian air defenses, weak from the beginning and now almost wiped out, the long black ships of Morcine dived into the constantly widening base and unloaded great quantities of supplies. Troops moved forward against tough but spasmodic opposition, a growing weight of armored and motorized equipment going with them.

The recording camera trundled across an enormous bridge with thick girders fantastically distorted and with great gaps temporarily filled in. It took them through seven battered villages which the enemy had either defended or given cause to believe they intended to defend. There were shots of crater-pocked roads, skeletal houses, a blackened barn with a swollen horse lying in a field nearby.

And an action-take of an assault on a farmhouse. A patrol, suddenly fired on, dug in and radioed back. A monster on huge, noisy tracks answered their call, rumbled laboriously to within four hundred yards of the objective, spat violently and lavishly from its front turret. A great splash of liquid fell on the farmhouse roof, burst into roaring flame. Figures ran out, seeking cover of an adjacent thicket. The sound track emitted rattling noises. The figures fell over, rolled, jerked, lay still.

The reel ended and Korman said, "I approve it for public exhibition." Getting out of his seat, he frowned around, added, "I have one criticism. My son has taken command of a company of infantry. He is doing a job, like any other man. Why wasn't he featured?"

"We would not depict him except with your approval, sir," said one.

"I not only approve—I order it. Make sure that he is

shown next time. Not predominantly. Just sufficiently to let the people see for themselves that he is there, sharing the hardships and the risks."

"Very well, sir."

They packed up and went away. He strolled restlessly on the thick carpet in front of the electric radiator.

"Do them good to know Reed is among those present," he insisted.

"Yes, David." She had taken up some knitting, her needles going *click-click*.

"He's my son."

"Yes, David."

Stopping his pacing, he chewed his bottom lip with irritation. "Can't you say anything but that?"

She raised her eyes. "Do you wish me to?"

"Do I wish!" he echoed. His fists were tight as he resumed his movements to and fro while she returned to her needles.

What did she know of wishes?

What does anyone know?

By the end of four months the territorial grip on Lani had grown to one thousand square miles while men and guns continued to pour in. Progress had been slower than expected. There had been minor blunders at high level, a few of the unforeseeable difficulties that invariably crop up when fighting at long range, and resistance had been desperate where least expected. Nevertheless, progress was being made. Though a little postdated, the inevitable remained inevitable.

Korman came home, heard the car door snap shut at the sixth step. All was as before except that now a part of the populace insisted on assembling to cheer him indoors. The maid waited, took his things. He stumped heavily to the inner room.

"Reed is being promoted to captain."

She did not answer.

Standing squarely before her, he demanded, "Well, aren't you interested?"

"Of course, David." Putting aside her book, she

folded long, thin-fingered hands, looked toward the window.

"What's the matter with you?"

"The matter?" The blond eyebrows arched as her eyes came up. "Nothing is the matter with me. Why do you ask?"

"I can tell." His tones harshened a little. "And I can guess. You don't like Reed being out there. You disapprove of me sending him away from you. You think of him as your son and not mine. You—"

She faced him calmly. "You're rather tired, David. And worried."

"I am not tired," he denied with unnecessary loudness. "Neither am I worried. It is the weak who worry."

"The weak have reason."

"I haven't."

"Then you're just plain hungry." She took a seat at the table. "Have something to eat. It will make you feel better."

Dissatisfied and disgruntled, he got through his evening meal. Mary was holding something back, he knew that with the sureness of one who had lived with her for half his lifetime. But he did not have to force it out of her by autocratic methods. When and only when he had finished eating she surrendered her secret voluntarily. The way in which she did it concealed the blow to come.

"There has been another letter from Reed."

"Yes?" He fingered a glass of wine, felt soothed by food but reluctant to show it. "I know he's happy, healthy and in one piece. If anything went wrong, I'd be the first to learn of it."

"Don't you want to see what he says?" She took it from a little walnut bureau, offered it to him.

He eyed it without reaching for it. "Oh, I suppose it's all the usual chitchat about the war."

"I think you ought to read it," she persisted.

"Do you?" Taking it from her hand, he held it unopened, surveyed her curiously. "Why should this particular missive call for my attention? Is it any different from the others? I know without looking that it is addressed to you. Not to me. To you! Never in his life has Reed written a letter specifically to me."

"He writes to both of us."

"Then why can't he start with 'Dear Father and Mother'?"

"Probably it just hasn't occurred to him that you would feel touchy about it. Besides, it's cumbersome."

"Nonsense!"

"Well, you might as well look at it as argue about it unread. You'll have to know sooner or later."

That last remark stimulated him into action. Unfolding it, he grunted as he noted the opening words, then went through ten paragraphs descriptive of war service on another planet. It was the sort of stuff every fighting man sent home. Nothing special about it. Turning the page, he perused the brief remainder. His face went taut and heightened in color.

"Better tell you I've become the willing slave of a Lanian girl. Found her in what little was left of the village of Bluelake, which had taken a pretty bad beating from our heavies. She was all alone and, as far as I could discover, seemed to be the sole survivor. Mom, she's got nobody. I'm sending her home on the hospital ship *Istar*. The captain jibbed but dared not refuse a Korman. Please meet her for me and look after her until I get back."

Flinging it onto the table, he swore lengthily and with vim, finishing, "The young imbecile."

Saying nothing, Mary sat watching him, her hands clasped together.

"The eyes of a whole world are on him," he raged. "As a public figure, as the son of his father, he is expected to be an example. And what does he do?"

She remained silent.

"Becomes the easy victim of some designing little skirt who is quick to play upon his sympathies. An enemy female!"

"She must be pretty," said Mary.

"*No* Lanians are pretty," he contradicted in what

came near to a shout. "Have you taken leave of your senses?"

"No, David, of course not."

"Then why make such pointless remarks? One idiot in the family is enough." He punched his right fist several times into the palm of his left hand. "At the very time when anti-Lanian sentiment is at its height I can well imagine the effect on public opinion if it became known that we were harboring a specially favored enemy alien, pampering some painted and powdered hussy who has dug her claws into Reed. I can see her mincing proudly around, one of the vanquished who became a victor by making use of a dope. Reed must be out of his mind."

"Reed is twenty-three," she observed.

"What of it? Are you asserting that there's a specific age at which a man has a right to make a fool of himself?"

"David, I did not say that."

"You implied it." More hand-punching. "Reed has shown an unsuspected strain of weakness. It doesn't come from me."

"No, David, it doesn't."

He stared at her, seeking what lay unspoken behind that remark. It eluded him. His mind was not her mind. He could not think in her terms. Only in his own.

"I'll bring this madness to a drastic stop. If Reed lacks strength of character, it is for me to provide it." He found the telephone, remarked as he picked it up, "There are thousands of girls on Morcine. If Reed feels that he must have romance, he can find it at home."

"He's not home," Mary mentioned. "He is far away."

"For a few months. A mere nothing." The phone whirred and he barked into it, "Has the *Istar* left Lani yet?" He held on a while, then racked the instrument and rumbled aggrievedly, "I'd have had her thrown off but it's too late. The *Istar* departed soon after the mailboat that brought his letter." He made a face and it was not pleasant. "The girl is due here tomorrow. She's got a nerve, a blatant impudence. It reveals her character in advance."

Facing the big, slow-ticking clock that stood by the wall, he gazed at it as if tomorrow were due any moment. His mind was working on the problem so suddenly dumped in his lap. After a while, he spoke again.

"That scheming baggage is not going to carve herself a comfortable niche in my home, no matter what Reed thinks of her. I will not have her, see?"

"I see, David."

"If he is weak, I am not. So when she arrives I'm going to give her the roughest hour of her life. By the time I've finished she'll be more than glad of passage back to Lani on the next ship. She'll get out in a hurry and for keeps."

Mary remained quiet.

"But I'm not going to indulge a sordid domestic fracas in public. I won't allow her even the satisfaction of that. I want you to meet her at the spaceport, phone me immediately she arrives, then bring her to my office. I'll cope with her there."

"Yes, David."

"And don't forget to call me beforehand. It will give me time to clear the place and insure some privacy."

"I will remember," she promised.

It was three-thirty in the following afternoon when the call came through. He shooed out a fleet admiral, two generals and an intelligence service director, hurried through the most urgent of his papers, cleared the desk and mentally prepared himself for the distasteful task to come.

In short time his intercom squeaked and his secretary's voice announced, "Two people to see you, sir—Mrs. Korman and Miss Tatiana Hurst."

"Show them in."

He leaned backward, face suitably severe. Tatiana, he thought. An outlandish name. It was easy to visualize the sort of hoyden who owned it: a flouncy thing, aged beyond her years and with a sharp eye to the main chance. The sort who could make easy meat of someone young, inexperienced and impressionable, like Reed. Doubtless she had supreme confidence that she could butter the old man with equal effectiveness and no trouble whatsoever. Hah, that was her mistake.

The door opened and they came in and stood before him without speaking. For half a minute he studied them while his mind did sideslips, repeatedly strove to coordinate itself, and a dozen expressions came and went in his face. Finally, he rose slowly to his feet, spoke to Mary, his tones frankly bewildered.

"Well, where is she?"

"This," informed Mary, with unconcealed and inexplicable satisfaction, "is her."

He flopped back into his chair, looked incredulously at Miss Tatiana Hurst. She had skinny legs exposed to knee height. Her clothing was much the worse for wear. Her face was a pale, hollow-cheeked oval from which a pair of enormous dark eyes gazed in a non-focusing, introspective manner as if she continually kept watch within her rather than upon things outside. One small white hand held Mary's, the other arm was around a large and brand new teddy-bear gained from a source at which he could guess. Her age was about eight. Certainly no more than eight.

It was the eyes that got him most, terribly solemn, terribly grave and unwilling to see. There was a coldness in his stomach as he observed them. She was not blind. She could look at him all right—but she looked without really perceiving. The great dark orbs could turn toward him and register the mere essential of his being while all the time they saw only the secret places within herself. It was eerie in the extreme and more than discomforting.

Watching her fascinatedly, he tried to analyze and define the peculiar quality in those optics. He had expected daring, defiance, impudence, passion, anything of which a predatory female was capable. Here, in these radically altered circumstances, one could expect childish embarrassment, self-consciousness, shyness. But she was not shy, he decided. It was something else. In the end he recognized the elusive factor as absentness. She was here yet somehow not with them. She was somewhere else, deep inside a world of her own.

Mary chipped in with a sudden "Well, David?"

He started at the sound of her voice. Some confusion still cluttered his mind because this culmination differed so greatly from his preconceptions. Mary had enjoyed half an hour in which to accommodate herself to the shock. He had not. It was still fresh and potent.

"Leave her with me for a few minutes," he suggested. "I'll call you when I've finished."

Mary went, her manner that of a woman enjoying something deep and personal. An unexpected satisfaction long overdue.

Korman said with unaccustomed mildness, "Come here, Tatiana."

She moved toward him slowly, each step deliberate and careful, touched the desk, stopped.

"Round this side, please, near to my chair."

With the same almost-robotic gait she did as instructed, her dark eyes looking expressionlessly to the front. Arriving at his chair, she waited in silence.

He drew in a deep breath. It seemed to him that her manner was born of a tiny voice insisting, "I must be obedient. I must do as I am told. I can do only what I am told to do."

So she did it as one compelled to accept those things she had no means of resisting. It was surrender to all demands in order to keep one hidden and precious place intact. There was no other way.

Rather appalled, he said, "You're able to speak, aren't you?"

She nodded, slightly and only once.

"But that isn't speech," he pointed out.

There was no desire to contradict or provide proof of ability. She accepted his statement as obvious and left it at that. Silent and immensely grave, she clung to her bear and waited for Korman's world to cease troubling her own.

"Are you glad you're here, or sorry?"

No reaction. Only inward contemplation. Absentness.

"Well, are you glad then?"

A vague half-nod.

"You are not sorry to be here?"

An even vaguer shake.

"Would you rather stay than go back?"

She looked at him, not so much to see him as to insure that he could see her.

He rang his bell, said to Mary, "Take her home."

"Home, David?"

"That's what I said." He did not like the exaggerated sweetness of her tone. It meant something, but he couldn't discern what.

The door closed behind the pair of them. His fingers tapped restlessly on the desk as he pictured those eyes. Something small and bitterly cold was in his insides.

During the next couple of weeks his mind seemed to be filled with more problems than ever before. Like most men of his caliber, he had the ability to ponder several subjects at once, but not the insight to detect when one was gaining predominance over the others.

On the first two or three of these days he ignored the pale intruder in his household. Yet he could not deny her presence. She was always there, quiet, obedient, self-effacing, hollow-cheeked and huge-eyed. Often she sat around for long periods without stirring, like a discarded doll.

When addressed by Mary or one of the maids she remained deaf to inconsequential remarks, responded to direct and imperative questions or orders. She would answer with minimum head movements or hand gestures when these sufficed, spoke monosyllabically in a thin little voice only when speech was unavoidable. During that time Korman did not speak to her at all—but he was compelled to notice her fatalistic acceptance of the fact that she was no part of his complicated life.

After lunch on the fourth day he caught her alone, bent down to her height and demanded, "Tatiana, what is the matter with you? Are you unhappy here?"

One brief shake of her head.

"Then why don't you laugh and play like other—?" He ceased abruptly as Mary entered the room.

"You two having a private gossip?" she inquired.

"As if we could," he snapped.

That same evening he saw the latest pictorial record from the fighting front. It gave him little satisfaction. Indeed, it almost irked him. The zip was missing. Much of the thrill of conquest had mysteriously evaporated from the pictures.

By the end of the fortnight he'd had more than enough of listening for a voice that seldom spoke and meeting eyes that did not see. It was like living with a ghost—and it could not go on. A man is entitled to a modicum of relaxation in his own home.

Certainly he could kick her back to Lani as he had threatened to do at the first. That, however, would be admission of defeat. Korman just could not accept defeat at anyone's hands, much less those of a brooding-child. She was not going to edge him out of his own home nor persuade him to throw her out. She was a challenge he had to overcome in a way thoroughly satisfactory to himself.

Summoning his chief scientific adviser to his office, he declaimed with irritation, "Look, I'm saddled with a maladjusted child. My son took a fancy to her and shipped her from Lani. She's getting in my hair. What can be done about it?"

"Afraid I cannot help much, sir."

"Why not?"

"I'm a physicist."

"Well, can you suggest anyone else?"

The other thought a bit, said, "There's nobody in my department, sir. But science isn't solely concerned with production of gadgets. You need a specialist in things less tangible." A pause, then, "The hospital authorities might put you on to someone suitable."

He tried the nearest hospital, got the answer, "A child psychologist is your man."

"Who's the best on this planet?"

"Dr. Jager."

"Contact him for me. I want him at my house this evening, not later than seven o'clock."

Fat, middle-aged and jovial, Jager fell easily into the role of a casual friend who had just dropped in. He chatted a lot of foolishness, included Tatiana in the conversation by throwing odd remarks at her, even held a pretended conversation with her teddy-bear. Twice in an hour she came into his world just long enough to register a fleeting smile—then swiftly she was back in her own.

At the end of this he hinted that he and Tatiana should be left by themselves. Korman went out, convinced that no progress was being or would be made. In the lounge Mary glanced up from her seat.

"Who's our visitor, David? Or is it no business of mine?"

"Some kind of mental specialist. He's examining Tatiana."

"Really?" Again the sweetness that was bitter.

"Yes," he rasped. "Really."

"I didn't think you were interested in her."

"I am not," he asserted. "But Reed is. Now and again I like to remind myself that Reed is my son."

She let the subject drop. Korman got on with some official papers until Jager had finished. Then he went back to the room, leaving Mary immersed in her book. He looked around.

"Where is she?"

"The maid took her. Said it was her bedtime."

"Oh." He found a seat, waited to hear more.

Resting against the edge of a table, Jager explained, "I've a playful little gag for dealing with children who are reluctant to talk. Nine times out of ten it works."

"What is it?"

"I persuade them to *write*. Strangely enough, they'll often do that, especially if I make a game of it. I cajole them into writing a story or essay about anything that created a great impression upon them. The results can be very revealing."

"And did you—?"

"A moment, please, Mr. Korman. Before I go further I'd like to impress upon you that children have an inherent ability many authors must envy. They can express themselves with remarkable vividness in simple language, with great economy of words. They create telling effect with what they leave out as much as by what they put in." He eyed Korman speculatively. "You know the circumstances in which your son found this child?"

"Yes, he told us in a letter."

"Well, bearing those circumstances in mind I think you'll find this something exceptional in the way of horror stories." He held out a sheet of paper. "She wrote it unaided." He reached for his hat and coat.

"You're going?" questioned Korman in surprise. "What about your diagnosis? What treatment do you suggest?"

Dr. Jager paused, hand on door. "Mr. Korman, you are an intelligent person." He indicated the sheet the other was holding. "I think that is all you require."

Then he departed. Korman eyed the sheet. It was not filled with words as he'd expected. For a story it was mighty short. He read it.

I am nothing and nobody. My house went bang. My cat was stuck to a wall. I wanted to pull it off. They wouldn't let me. They threw it away.

The cold thing in the pit of his stomach swelled up. He read it again. And again. He went to the base of the stairs and looked up toward where she was sleeping.

The enemy whom he had made nothing.

Slumber came hard that night. Usually he could compose his mind and snatch a nap any time, anywhere, at a moment's notice. Now he was strangely restless, unsettled. His brain was stimulated by he knew not what and it insisted on following tortuous paths.

The frequent waking periods were full of fantastic imaginings wherein he fumbled through a vast and cloying grayness in which was no sound, no voice, no other being. The dreams were worse, full of writhing landscapes spewing smoky columns, with things howling through the sky, with huge, toadlike monsters crawling on metal tracks, with long lines of dusty men singing an aeons-old and forgotten song.

"You've left behind a broken doll."

He awakened early with weary eyes and a tired mind. All morning at the office a multitude of trifling things conspired against him. His ability to concentrate was not up to the mark and several times he had to catch himself on minor errors just made or about to be made. Once or twice he found himself gazing meditatively forward with eyes that did not see to the front but were looking where they had never looked before.

At three in the afternoon his secretary called on the intercom, "Astroleader Warren would like to see you, sir."

"Astroleader?" he echoed, wondering whether he had heard aright. "There's no such title."

"It is a Drakan space-rank."

"Oh, yes, of course. I can tend to him now."

He waited with dull anticipation. The Drakans formed a powerful combine of ten planets at a great distance from Morcine. They were so far away that contact came seldom. A battleship of theirs had paid a courtesy call about twice in his lifetime. So this occasion was a rare one.

The visitor entered, a big-built youngster in light-green uniform. Shaking hands with genuine pleasure and great cordiality, he accepted the indicated chair.

"A surprise, eh, Mr. Korman?"

"Very."

"We came in a deuce of a hurry but the trip can't be done in a day. Distance takes time unfortunately."

"I know."

"The position is this," explained Warren. "Long while back we received a call from Lani relayed by intervening minor planets. They said they were involved in a serious dispute and feared war. They appealed to us to negotiate as disinterested neutrals."

"Ah, so that's why you've come?"

"Yes, Mr. Korman. We knew the chance was small of arriving in time. There was nothing for it but to come as fast as we could and hope for the best. The role of peacemaker appeals to those with any claim to be civilized."

"Does it?" questioned Korman, watching him.

"It does to us." Leaning forward, Warren met him eye to eye. "We've called at Lani on the way here. They still want peace. They're losing the battle. Therefore we want to know only one thing: Are we too late?"

That was the leading question: Are we too late? Yes or no? Korman stewed it without realizing that not so long ago his answer would have been prompt and automatic. Today, he thought it over.

Yes or no? Yes meant military victory, power and fear. No meant—what? Well, no meant a display of reasonableness in lieu of stubbornness. No meant a considerable change of mind. It struck him suddenly that one must possess redoubtable force of character to throw away a long-nursed viewpoint and adopt a new one. It required moral courage. The weak and the faltering could never achieve it.

"No," he replied slowly. "It is not too late."

Warren stood up, his face showing that this was not the answer he had expected. "You mean, Mr. Korman—"

"Your journey has not been in vain. You may negotiate."

"On what terms?"

"The fairest to both sides that you can contrive." He switched his microphone, spoke into it. "Tell Rogers that I order our forces to cease hostilities forthwith. Troops will guard the perimeter of the Lani ground base pending peace negotiations. Citizens of the Drakan Confederation will be permitted unobstructed passage through our lines in either direction."

"Very well, Mr. Korman."

Putting the microphone aside, he continued with Warren, "Though far off in mere miles, Lani is near to us as cosmic distances go. It would please me if the Lanians agreed to a union between our planets, with common citizenship, common development of natural resources. But I don't insist upon it. I merely express a wish—knowing that some wishes never come true."

"The notion will be given serious consideration all

the same," assured Warren. He shook hands with boy-
ish enthusiasm. "You're a big man, Mr. Korman."

"Am I?" He gave a wry smile. "I'm trying to do a bit
of growing in another direction. The original one kind
of got used up."

When the other had gone, he tossed a wad of documents into a drawer. Most of them were useless now.
Strange how he seemed to be breathing better than ever
before, his lungs drawing more fully.

In the outer office he informed, "It's early yet, but
I'm going home. Phone me there if anything urgent
comes along."

The chauffeur closed the car door at the sixth step. A
weakling, thought Korman as he went into his home. A
lamebrain lacking the strength to haul himself out of a
self-created rut. One can stay in a rut too long.

He asked the maid, "Where is my wife?"

"Slipped out ten minutes ago, sir. She said she'd be
back in half an hour."

"Did she take—"

"No, sir." The maid glanced toward the lounge.

Cautiously he entered the lounge, found the child
resting on the settee, head back, eyes closed. A radio
played softly nearby. He doubted whether she had
turned it on of her own accord or was listening to it.
More likely someone else had left it running.

Tiptoeing across the carpet, he cut off the faint music. She opened her eyes, sat upright. Going to the settee, he took the bear from her side and placed it on an
arm, positioned himself next to her.

"Tatiana," he asked with rough gentleness, "why are
you nothing?"

No answer. No change.

"Is it because you have nobody?"

Silence.

"Nobody of your own?" he persisted, feeling a queer
kind of desperation. "Not even a kitten?"

She looked down at her shoes, her big eyes partly
shielded under pale lids. There was no other reaction.

Defeat. Ah, the bitterness of defeat. It set his fingers

fumbling with each other, like those of one in great and unbearable trouble. Phrases tumbled through his mind.

"I am nothing."

"My cat . . . they threw it away."

His gaze wandered blindly over the room while his mind ran round and round her wall of silence seeking a door it could not find. Was there no way in, no way at all?

There was.

He discovered it quite unwittingly.

To himself rather than to her he murmured in a hearable undertone, "Since I was very small I have been surrounded by people. All my life there have been lots of people. But none were mine. Not one was really mine. Not one. I, too, am nothing."

She patted his hand.

The shock was immense. Startled beyond measure, he glanced down at the first touch, watched her give three or four comforting little dabs and hastily withdraw. There was heavy pulsing in his veins. Something within him rapidly became too big to contain.

Twisting sidewise, he snatched her onto his lap, put his arms around her, buried his nose in the soft part of her neck, nuzzled behind her ear, ran his big hand through her hair. And all the time he rocked to and fro with low crooning noises.

She was weeping. She hadn't been able to weep before. She was weeping, not as a woman does, softly and subdued, but like a child, with great racking sobs that she fought hard to suppress.

Her arm was around his neck, tightening, clinging and tightening more while he rocked and stroked and called her "Honey" and uttered silly sounds and wildly extravagant reassurances.

This was victory.

Not empty.

Full.

Victory over self is completely full.

Weak Spot

A GREAT FLEET of black ships sprang out of the starfield and took Demeter in thirty hours. There was little destruction and hardly any slaughter. The onset had been too sudden and well-timed, the element of surprise too great to enable the garrison to put up maximum resistance. Demeter fell in a day and a night. It was a triumph for the Barbs and a defeat for the Empire.

The Barbs ran all over the stricken planet and gloated. What they'd got consisted of one medium-sized but livable world on which were three towns, eleven villages, fifty-two mines, fourteen manufacturing plants, a sizable hydroelectric power station, one modern spaceport and seventy thousand prisoners. All in good condition and fit for further service.

Moreover they now had a space station and a potentially redoubtable military outpost thirty degrees around the rim of the Empire with respect to their own eight-planet system. Considering that the said Empire incorporated fifteen hundred solar systems with more than six thousand planets, the Barbs weren't doing so badly for little fellers.

The victors pulsed the news back home, where it caused bellicose rejoicing. Millions marched the streets forty abreast in military rhythm, carrying banners, blowing long silver horns and chanting war songs. Kalandar, their supreme overlord, posed on a balcony,

waved and smiled while an immense mob in the square
below howled its joy and shook defiant fists at the sky.
Conscious of the hugeness of the defeated foe, the
crowd delighted in the thought that the bigger they
come the harder they fall.

Kalandar did not miss that point either. True, Demeter was only one habitable world and the Empire had a
great number more. But what can be done once can be
done again—and again and again. So he grinned tooth-
ily and drew roars of applause with a bow and a salute.

The situation was one of the most commonplace in
history: battle, conquest and the drunkenness of victory. It differed from all others in a single detail of
which Kalandar and his warrior hordes remained blissfully unaware, namely, that deep in the heart of the
Empire a small group of leaders rejoiced with them.

Demeter has fallen, hurrah, hurrah!

In the big Green Room of the Palace of Administration seventeen men sat around a horseshoe table and, in
effect, composed the living mind of Empire. Beyond the
windows soared numberless towers and spires of Gilstrand, capital city of six thousand worlds.

Eldon, a white-haired, big-boned man with immense
width of shoulder, accepted a slip of paper from a soft-
footed messenger, glanced at it, said evenly to the others, "The Barbs captured Demeter this morning."

"Ho-hum!" said one.

"Nice work!" commented another in the manner of
appreciating a favor.

"We must make the most of it, of course," continued
Eldon. He turned attention to a sharp-nosed, gimlet-
eyed individual sitting on his right. "Get busy, Wanstell.
Paste it on the walls."

Wanstell nodded and went out.

The remaining sixteen resumed their original discus-
sion much as if a war and the loss of a world were just
one of those things. They talked for an hour coolly,
calmly, unhurriedly, with the air of men whose kind lost
all capacity for melodramatics twenty, fifty or a
hundred generations ago.

In this respect they differed radically from the lizard-skinned, but otherwise humanlike, Barbs who could and did froth and foam all over the place on slightest pretext. The Barbs were by nature hot-blooded fighters, turbulent, truculent, restless, impetuous and supposedly unbeatable by anything less than complete extermination. The seventeen leaders of Empire were by nature cold-blooded calculators, men who esteemed as mightier than the sword the ability to reckon two plus two.

So the ones at the horseshoe table sat undisturbed and chatted until they reached their several decisions and went their various ways. After the last had gone Eldon stood at a window and watched orange rays from the setting sun slowly piercing the purple sky.

Eventually he moved to his desk, sat down, studied a plaque fastened to the wall above. It bore words raised in gilt. He smiled only with the corners of his eyes as he read them.

"An insect may bite a lion—but the insect remains an insect and the lion remains a lion."

Wanstell, as head of the Department of Imperial Communications, officially gave the news to most of a galaxy.

"The government admits the loss of outer solar system T.K.490 containing four planets one of which, Demeter, is habitable and settled. Seventy thousand Empire citizens were on Demeter when it was seized by a task force of the Barbs today. The government is about to commence negotiations for the exchange of prisoners and in short time action will be taken to recapture Demeter. All citizens of Empire can rest assured that the situation is well in hand and there is no undue cause for alarm."

Smooth political words such as had been used back to the dawn of time, when the birthplace of Empire was a watery world called Terra. And, exactly as it had been in those far-off days, the independent news-services heated the handout and distributed it on the boil.

SWIFT BARB VICTORY screamed the radiocasts around Sirius. DEMETER LOST WHILE NAVY SLUMBERS snarled the always irritable and antigovernmental videos of the Wolf system. THE HOUR IS AT HAND editorialized the primitive but influential news sheets of the distant Rimbold group.

"For at least twenty thousand years," lectured the dignified Gilstrand *Sentinel,* "and for nobody knows how much longer the Barbarians have been an unmitigated nuisance. While they continue to exist as a unified fighting force the fringes of Empire remain unsafe. So long as once in every century they make a reckless penetration of our sphere of space there is no security anywhere. It is high time we brought accord among our conflicting interests, ceased our petty squabbling, stood firmly shoulder to shoulder and put an end to this menace once and for all."

And so on and so on. Each solar group fulminated according to the peculiar psychology of that group. Time had run on so long that while all citizens of Empire were men they were different groups with different cultures, different motivations, different modes of thought. The Empire had incubated fifteen hundred new races with fifteen hundred angles on any one problem.

The repercussions following the fall of one relatively unimportant planet jolted far across the cosmos and proved that action and reaction may be opposite but grossly unequal. The effect somewhat resembled the ripples that once spread across an oldtime world after a minor massacre by Sioux.

These things were to be expected. Indeed, experts in such matters could plan them in advance and calculate with a reasonable degree of precision the amplitude and impact of the emotional splash on some sparsely settled planet a thousand light-years away.

The Barbs worked with furious energy typical of their kind. Their ships fled back and forth pouring troops and supplies into Demeter in haste to consolidate the position before the Empire could organize its counterblow.

None doubted that ultimately such a wallop would come or that when it did it would be good and hard. They knew the Empire fully as well as it knew them. The two foes had lived in juxtaposition a long time, a very long time. They enjoyed the mutual understanding of those who coexist for millennia in a state of platonic hatred.

While the Barbs moved heaven and earth to turn Demeter into an inviolable fortress of space, certain of their vessels made fast runs to the neutral world of Kvav, where prisoners were solemnly exchanged. This was a post-victory formality unthought-of before the expanding frontiers of Empire had reached them. In olden times prisoners were enslaved, worked until they dropped and then slaughtered. The Empire had introduced the swap-system and after a period of dark suspicion the Barbs had accommodated themselves to it. Since in their own opinion one Barb was worth ten Imperials an even trade had them head of the queue at the bargain counter.

Prisoner-exchange had changed the shape of neverending war so far as the Barbs were concerned. Space battles and territorial conquests were no longer enough. Now there must be raids to obtain prisoners whenever the numbers held by both sides failed to balance. For some unaccountable reason the onus of redressing the balance fell on the Barbs more often than on the Empire. Today it was a major victory to snatch a thousand Empire citizens and thus insure the return of one thousand of their own.

A minor Barb squadron ferried between Demeter and Kvav, dumped seventy thousand of the enemy, took home the same number of Barbs, some of whom had waited four or five years for rescue. The whole procedure went like clockwork.

Nobody bollixed the arithmetic by seizing a Barb ship coming or going.

The Empire had vast fleets patrolling elsewhere.

And nobody thought it strange.

Eldon and Wanstell sat at the former's desk checking intelligence reports. Reactions of Empire news-channels were in their estimation most satisfactory. The doings of the Barbs were also pleasing. Both men were humorously conscious of their inability to solve the problem of how to give Kalandar a medal without creating ructions around fifteen hundred suns.

They and the absent ones had a task that an ordinary engineer would consider beyond credulity: they were skilled operators of a gigantic machine that functioned better for a monkey wrench thrown in the works.

Proof lay before them. On Quimper a threatening revolt of the young against the old had gone pop like a burst bubble as overenergetic ringleaders rushed into the space-navy. Twenty-four worlds planning an independent customs union had dropped the notion in favor of a common space-push.

Two hundred eighty highly individualistic frontier planets, yesterday increasingly defiant of central authority, today had taken alarm and were yelling for protection. The pacifist Rigellians were offering a contribution to defense formerly refused. The twin systems near Bootes had abandoned fatheaded ideas of civil war and decided to rival each other in smacking the Barbs. Public opinion around Arcturus had upped and voiced itself against a strong movement for secession.

A thousand items in more or less similar strain proved that in given circumstances a thrown wrench boosts efficiency by quite a percentage.

Only one thing threatened to spoil the whole business and of that they knew nothing just then. Outside, slowly mounting the stairs, was a trio bearing a metaphorical wrench far too big.

One of these three, who was a Palace of Administration official, knocked and entered, leaving the others beyond the door. He said to Eldon, "Sir, we have struck a slight complication over exchange of prisoners."

"In what way?" Eldon asked.

"Kalandar demands the return of Jazan, his youngest

son, a former pilot. We captured him two and a half
years ago, if you recall."

"I do not recall," said Eldon, frowning. "He is of no
importance to us anyway. It is a strict rule that prisoners be returned in order of capture regardless of rank or
station. I know of no reason why Jazan should not be
handed over." He cocked an eye at the other. "Is there
any reason?"

"Yes, sir."

"What is it?"

"Jazan does not wish to return—just yet."

"Does not wish to?" Eldon echoed it incredulously.
A Barb uneager to resume the fray was unique. "Why
not?"

"That, sir, might be better explained by the chaplain
if you would care to see him."

"Show him in," ordered Eldon.

The other went to the door, brought back a plump,
solemn-faced cleric. The newcomer sat in response to
Eldon's gesture, folded hands in his lap.

"Well, what do you wish to tell me?"

"As you may know, I am the chaplain of Number
Twelve camp," the newcomer explained. "It is a difficult post. It means one must try to create a little flock
out of a bunch of wolves. However, I have made an
important convert."

"Jazan?"

"Yes." He brooded a moment, looked vaguely uncomfortable. "You know the nature of the Barbs. They
are highly emotional and tend toward fanaticism. The
good Lord made them that way for reasons of His
own."

"Well?"

"Generally speaking, a converted Barb tries to be ten
times more Christian than any Christian. His make-up
being what it is, there's no holding him back. He wants
to go out and save the whole of Creation. He has the
inborn character of a missionary—and a martyr."

"What does this mean to us?"

"Everything is created for a good and wise purpose,"
asserted the chaplain. "Jazan firmly believes that he

and his kind were made to be the Empire's missionaries in the great beyond, in the vastnesses of space yet to be explored. He wishes to discuss the matter with you and refuses to go home until he has done so."

Eldon glanced toward Wanstell, found that worthy studiously examining the ceiling. He returned his attention to the chaplain.

"All right, I will see him now—alone."

Jazan proved to have the typical thinness, height and lizard skin of his kind. He also had the fiery eyes, though now they were modified by the light of inward mysticism.

He stood before Eldon, head slightly bowed, hands behind his back, and said quietly, "It is for me to lead my father into the path of truth. Also my brothers and my people. I ask you to cease all hostilities coincidental with my return."

"And if we do not?"

"I shall pray for you as for every other sinner."

"We shall stop fighting after your people have learned to be good, not before," declared Eldon, flatly. "And that's going to be a long, long time."

"They will see the light. And, seeing it, they will bear it abroad. Your ships will follow in peace the paths our feet have trod."

"We'll try it when that day comes," said Eldon. "But it isn't here yet."

The fire momentarily blazed in Jazan's eyes. A characteristic blue flush of temper swept across his face but was suppressed. For a Barb he was unusually intelligent and self-disciplined.

He said, "I am going to change my people whether you cooperate or not. The meek shall inherit while the proud shall be laid low. You should be willing to help. My kind could be most useful to you some day." His lowered head came up and he gazed straight into Eldon's eyes as he added, "Even more useful than they are now!"

"What do you mean by that?" demanded Eldon.

"As a true believer I have learned something of the

real power of the Empire. It is infinitely greater than my own people believe. It is so great that you could destroy us overnight, could have done so many centuries ago." His gaze met the other again. "Why haven't you destroyed us?"

Eldon pointed to the plaque. "You cannot diminish the lion no matter how much you bite."

"Why permit us to bite at all?"

Resting himself on the corner of the table, Eldon said:

"I'll have to use a simple analogy. You know how a steam boiler functions?"

"Yes, of course."

"In theory a weak spot in a boiler could lead to an explosion. In practice it doesn't. Like me to tell you why?"

"Go on."

"Because the intelligent human mind is anticipatory. When we construct a boiler we build in a weak spot preset to give way at a little above maximum working pressure. The accidental bang never comes because it's beaten to the draw by a predesigned fizz. The created weak spot is called a safety valve. It pipes away surplus pressure."

"I can understand that much."

"The Empire," Eldon continued, "can be likened to an enormous boiler working under a multitude of varying pressures created by competition, rivalries, conflicting interests and scores of other inevitabilities. It cannot be made bigger until we find a way of crossing the great chasms beyond our borders."

"I see."

"Meanwhile, your warlike people hang around and obligingly pipe off our surplus steam. It is very kind of you. We appreciate it. So long as you continue to play your part we're not in danger of going bang."

"Have you any objection to me giving my people these facts?"

"None at all," assured Eldon, smiling. "Most of them will not believe you and the few who do will be mightily annoyed. The latter will find themselves in a chronic jam because they cannot vent their annoyance without playing our game."

"And you refuse to call off the war?"

"We cannot end that which we did not start in the first place," said Eldon. "Look, if you care to check history, you'll find the Empire has never struck first. It has always waited to be hit before hitting back, carefully and judiciously so as not to impair your function as a necessary enemy. Aggression is your proper part. We have no desire to deprive you of it."

"That means the initiative lies with us," observed Jazan, shrewdly. "And you cannot dictate our use of it. Therefore I am going home. I am going to face you with the problem of peace."

"If your bellicose folk will let you live that long."

Jazan departed, quietly. Eldon walked twice round the room, had his usual look out the window and then returned to his desk. Fingering the intercom board, he selected a button, pressed it, spoke to the voice that answered.

"Sanders, time is getting too short for my liking. That research into the super-drive must be given top priority as from now." He paused, listened, exclaimed, "Damn the armaments campaign! I said top priority!"

The chasm was the real foe.

Allamagoosa

IT WAS A long time since the *Bustler* had been so silent. She lay in the Sirian spaceport, her tubes cold, her shell particle-scarred, her air that of a long-distance runner exhausted at the end of a marathon. There was good reason for this: she had returned from a lengthy trip by no means devoid of troubles.

Now, in port, well-deserved rest had been gained if only temporarily. Peace, sweet peace. No more bothers, no more crises, no more major upsets, no more dire predicaments such as crop up in free flight at least twice a day. Just peace.

Hah!

Captain McNaught reposed in his cabin, feet up on desk, and enjoyed the relaxation to the utmost. The engines were dead, their hellish pounding absent for the first time in months. Out there in the big city four hundred of his crew were making whoopee under a brilliant sun. This evening, when First Officer Gregory returned to take charge, he was going to go into the fragrant twilight and make the rounds of neon-lit civilization.

That was the beauty of making landfall at long last. Men could give way to themselves, blow off surplus steam, each according to his fashion. No duties, no worries, no dangers, no responsibilities in spaceport. A haven of safety and comfort for tired rovers.

Again, hah!

Burman, the chief radio officer, entered the cabin. He was one of the half-dozen remaining on duty and bore the expression of a man who can think of twenty better things to do.

"Relayed signal just come in, sir." Handing the paper across, he waited for the other to look at it and perhaps dictate a reply.

Taking the sheet, McNaught removed the feet from his desk, sat erect and read the message aloud.

Terran Headquarters to BUSTLER. Remain Siriport pending further orders. Rear Admiral Vane W. Cassidy due there seventeenth. Feldman. Navy Op. Command. Sirisec.

He looked up, all happiness gone from his leathery features. "Oh, Lord!" he groaned.

"Something wrong?" asked Burman, vaguely alarmed.

McNaught pointed at three thin books on his desk. "The middle one. Page twenty."

Leafing through it, Burman found an item that said:

Vane W. Cassidy, R-Ad. Head Inspector Ships and Stores.

Burman swallowed hard. "Does that mean—?"

"Yes, it does," said McNaught without pleasure. "Back to training-college and all its rigmarole. Paint and soap, spit and polish." He put on an officious expression, adopted a voice to match it. "Captain, you have only seven ninety-nine emergency rations. Your allocation is eight hundred. Nothing in your logbook accounts for the missing one. Where is it? What happened to it? How is it that one of the men's kits lacks an officially issued pair of suspenders? Did you report his loss?"

"Why does he pick on us?" asked Burman, appalled. "He's never chivvied us before."

"That's why," informed McNaught, scowling at the

wall. "It's our turn to be stretched across the barrel."
His gaze found the calendar. "We have three days—and
we'll need 'em! Tell Second Officer Pike to come here
at once."

Burman departed gloomily. In short time Pike entered. His face reaffirmed the old adage that bad news
travels fast.

"Make out an indent," ordered McNaught, "for one
hundred gallons of plastic paint, Navy-gray, approved
quality. Make out another for thirty gallons of interior
white enamel. Take them to spaceport stores right
away. Tell them to deliver by six this evening along
with our correct issue of brushes and sprayers. Grab up
any cleaning material that's going for free."

"The men won't like this," remarked Pike, feebly.

"They're going to love it," McNaught asserted. "A
bright and shiny ship, all spic and span, is good for
morale. It says so in that book. Get moving and put
those indents in. When you come back, find the stores
and equipment sheets and bring them here. We've got
to check stocks before Cassidy arrives. Once he's here
we'll have no chance to make up shortages or smuggle
out any extra items we happened to find in our hands."

"Very well, sir." Pike went out wearing the same expression as Burman.

Lying back in his chair McNaught muttered to himself. There was a feeling in his bones that something
was sure to cause a last-minute ruckus. A shortage of
any item would be serious enough unless covered by a
previous report. A surplus would be bad, very bad. The
former implied carelessness or misfortune. The latter
suggested barefaced theft of government property in circumstances condoned by the commander.

For instance, there was that recent case of Williams
of the heavy cruiser *Swift*. He'd heard of it over the
spacevine when out around Bootes. Williams had been
found in unwitting command of eleven reels of electric-fence wire when his official issue was ten. It had taken
a court-martial to decide that the extra reel—which had
formidable barter-value on a certain planet—had not

been stolen from space stores or, in sailor jargon, "tele-portated aboard." But Williams had been reprimanded. And that did not help promotion.

He was still rumbling discontentedly when Pike returned bearing a folder of foolscap sheets.

"Going to start right away, sir?"

"We'll have to." He heaved himself erect, mentally bidding goodbye to time off and a taste of the bright lights. "It'll take long enough to work right through from bow to tail. I'll leave the men's kit inspection to the last."

Marching out of the cabin, he set forth toward the bow, Pike following with broody reluctance.

As they passed the open main lock Peaslake observed them, bounded eagerly up the gangway and joined behind. A pukka member of the crew, he was a large dog whose ancestors had been more enthusiastic than selective. He wore with pride a big collar inscribed: *Peaslake—Property of S.S. Bustler.* His chief duties, ably performed, were to keep alien rodents off the ship and, on rare occasions, smell out dangers not visible to human eyes.

The three paraded forward, McNaught and Pike in the manner of men grimly sacrificing pleasure for the sake of duty, Peaslake with the panting willingness of one ready for any new game no matter what.

Reaching the bow-cabin, McNaught dumped himself in the pilot's seat, took the folder from the other. "You know this stuff better than me—the chart-room is where I shine. So I'll read them out while you look them over." He opened the folder, started on the first page. "K1. Beam compass, type D, one of."

"Check," said Pike.

"K2. Distance and direction indicator, electronic, type JJ, one of."

"Check."

Peaslake planted his head in McNaught's lap, blinked soulfully and whined. He was beginning to get the others' viewpoint. This tedious itemizing and checking was a hell of a game. McNaught consolingly lowered a hand and played with Peaslake's ears while he plowed his way down the list.

"K187. Foam rubber cushions, pilot and co-pilot, one pair."

"Check."

By the time First Officer Gregory appeared they had reached the tiny intercom cubby and poked around it in semi-darkness. Peaslake had long departed in disgust.

"M24. Spare minispeakers, three-inch, type T2, one set of six."

"Check."

Looking in, Gregory popped his eyes and said, "What the devil is going on?"

"Major inspection due soon." McNaught glanced at his watch. "Go see if stores has delivered a load and if not why not. Then you'd better give me a hand and let Pike take a few hours off."

"Does this mean land-leave is cancelled?"

"You bet it does—until after Hizonner had been and gone." He glanced at Pike. "When you get into the city search around and send back any of the crew you can find. No arguments or excuses. It's an order."

Pike registered unhappiness. Gregory glowered at him, went away, came back and said, "Stores will have the stuff here in twenty minutes' time." With bad grace he watched Pike depart.

"M47. Intercom cable, woven-wire protected, three drums."

"Check," said Gregory, mentally kicking himself for returning at the wrong time.

The task continued until late in the evening, was resumed early next morning. By that time three-quarters of the men were hard at work inside and outside the vessel, doing their jobs as though sentenced to them for crimes contemplated but not yet committed.

Moving around the ship's corridors and catwalks had to be done crab-fashion, with a nervous sideways edging. Once again it was being demonstrated that the Terran lifeform suffers from ye fear of wette paynt. The first smearer would have ten years willed off his unfortunate life.

It was in these conditions, in mid-afternoon of the second day, that McNaught's bones proved their feelings had been prophetic. He recited the ninth page while Jean Blanchard confirmed the presence and actual existence of all items enumerated. Two-thirds of the way down they hit the rocks, metaphorically speaking, and commenced to sink fast.

McNaught said boredly, "V1097. Drinking-bowl, enamel, one of."

"Is zis," said Blanchard, tapping it.

"V1098. Offog, one."

"Quoi?" asked Blanchard, staring.

"V1098. Offog, one," repeated McNaught. "Well, why are you looking thunderstruck? This is the ship's galley. You're the head cook. You know what's supposed to be in the galley, don't you? Where's this offog?"

"Never hear of heem," stated Blanchard, flatly.

"You must have done. It's on this equipment-sheet in plain, clear type. Offog, one, it says. It was here when we were fitted out four years ago. We checked it ourselves and signed for it."

"I signed for nossings called offog," Blanchard denied. "In zee cuisine zere is no such sing."

"Look!" McNaught scowled and showed him the sheet.

Blanchard looked and sniffed disdainfully. "I have here zee electronic oven, one of. I have jacketed boilers, graduated capacities, one set. I have bain marie pans, seex of. But no offog. Never heard of heem. I do not know of heem." He spread his hands and shrugged.

"There's got to be," McNaught insisted. "What's more, when Cassidy arrives there'll be hell to pay if there isn't."

"You find heem," Blanchard suggested.

"You got a certificate from the International Hotels School of Cookery. You got a certificate from the Cordon Bleu College of Cuisine. You got a certificate with three credits from the Space-Navy Feeding Center,"

McNaught pointed out. "All that—and you don't know what an offog is."

"Nom d'un chien!" ejaculated Blanchard, waving his arms around. "I tell you ten t'ousand time zere is no offog. Zere never was an offog. Escoffier heemself could not find zee offog of vich zere is none. Am I a magician perhaps?"

"It's part of the culinary equipment," McNaught maintained. "It must be because it's on page nine. And page nine means its proper home is in the galley, care of the head cook."

"Like hail it does," Blanchard retorted. He pointed at a metal box on the wall. "Intercom booster. Is zat mine?"

McNaught thought it over, conceded, "No, it's Burman's. His stuff rambles all over the ship."

"Zen ask heem for zis bloody offog," said Blanchard, triumphantly.

"I will. If it's not yours it must be his. Let's finish this checking first. If I'm not systematic and thorough Cassidy will jerk down my pants along with my insignia." His eyes sought the list. "V1099. Inscribed collar, leather, brass studded, dog, for the use of. No need to look for that. I saw it myself five minutes ago." He ticked the item, continued, "V1100. Sleeping basket, woven reed, one of."

"Is zis," said Blanchard, kicking it into a corner.

"V1101. Cushion, foam rubber, to fit sleeping basket, one of."

"Half of," Blanchard contradicted. "In four years he have chewed away other half."

"Maybe Cassidy will let us indent for a new one. It doesn't matter. We're okay so long as we can produce the half we've got." McNaught stood up, closed the folder. "That's the lot for here, I'll go see Burman about this missing item."

Burman switched off a UHF receiver, removed his earplugs and raised a questioning eyebrow.

"In the galley we're short an offog," explained McNaught. "Where is it?"

"Why ask me? The galley is Blanchard's bailiwick."

"Not entirely. A lot of your cables run through it. You've two terminal boxes in there, also an automatic switch and an intercom booster. Where's the offog?"

"Never heard of it," said Burman, baffled.

McNaught shouted, "Don't tell me that! I'm already fed up hearing Blanchard saying it. Four years back we had an offog. It says so here. This is our copy of what we checked and signed for. It says we signed for an offog. Therefore we must have one. It's got to be found before Cassidy gets here."

"Sorry, sir," sympathized Burman. "I can't help you."

"You can think again," advised McNaught. "Up in the bow there's a direction and distance indicator. What do *you* call it?"

"A didin," said Burman, mystified.

"And," McNaught went on, pointed at the pulse transmitter, "what do you call *that?*"

"The opper-popper."

"Baby names, see? Didin and opper-popper. Now rack your brains and remember what you called an offog four years ago."

"Nothing," asserted Burman, "has ever been called an offog to my knowledge."

"Then," demanded McNaught, "why the blue blazes did we sign for one?"

"I didn't sign for anything. You did all the signing."

"While you and others did the checking. Four years ago, presumably in the galley, I said, 'Offog, one,' and either you or Blanchard pointed to it and said, 'Check.' I took somebody's word for it. I have to take other specialists' words for it. I am an expert navigator, familiar with all the latest navigational gadgets but not with other stuff. So I'm compelled to rely on people who know what an offog is—or ought to."

Burman had a bright thought. "All kinds of oddments were dumped in the main lock, the corridors and the galley when we were fitted out. We had to sort through a deal of stuff and stash it where it properly belonged, remember? This offog-thing might be anyplace today. It isn't necessarily my responsibility or Blanchard's."

"I'll see what the other officers say," agreed McNaught, conceding the point. "Gregory, Worth, Sanderson, or one of the others may be coddling the item. Wherever it is, it's got to be found."

He went out. Burman pulled a face, inserted his earplugs, resumed fiddling with his apparatus. An hour later McNaught came back wearing a scowl.

"Positively," he announced with ire, "there is no such thing on the ship. Nobody knows of it. Nobody can so much as guess at it."

"Cross it off and report it lost," Burman suggested.

"What, when we're hard aground? You know as well as I do that loss and damage must be signaled at time of occurrence. If I tell Cassidy the offog went west in space, he'll want to know when, where, how and why it wasn't signaled. There'll be a real ruckus if the contraption happens to be valued at half a million credits. I can't dismiss it with an airy wave of the hand."

"What's the answer then?" inquired Burman, innocently ambling straight into the trap.

"There's one and only one," McNaught announced. "*You* will manufacture an offog."

"Who? *Me?*" said Burman, twitching his scalp.

"You and no other. I'm fairly sure the thing is your pigeon, anyway."

"Why?"

"Because it's typical of the baby-names used for your kind of stuff. I'll bet a month's pay that an offog is some sort of scientific allamagoosa. Something to do with fog, perhaps. Maybe a blind-approach gadget."

"The blind-approach transceiver is called 'the fumbly,' " Burman informed.

"There you are!" said McNaught as if that clinched it. "So you will make an offog. It will be completed by six tomorrow evening and ready for my inspection then. It had better be convincing, in fact pleasing."

Burman stood up, let his hands dangle, and said in hoarse tones, "How the devil can I make an offog when I don't even know what it is?"

"Neither does Cassidy know," McNaught pointed out, leering at him. "He's more of a quantity surveyor than anything else. As such he counts things, looks at things, certifies that they exist, accepts advice on whether they are functionally satisfactory or worn out. All we need do is concoct an imposing allamagoosa and tell him it's the offog."

"Holy Moses!" said Burman, fervently.

"Let us not rely on the dubious assistance of Biblical characters," McNaught reproved. "Let us use the brains that God has given us. Get a grip on your soldering-iron and make a topnotch offog by six tomorrow evening. That's an order!"

He departed, satisfied with this solution. Behind him, Burman gloomed at the wall and licked his lips once, twice.

Rear Admiral Vane W. Cassidy arrived dead on time. He was a short, paunchy character with a florid complexion and eyes like those of a long-dead fish. His gait was an important strut.

"Ah, Captain, I trust that you have everything ship-shape."

"Everything usually is," assured McNaught, glibly. "I see to that."

"Good!" approved Cassidy. "I like a commander who takes his responsibilities seriously. Much as I regret saying so, there are a few who do not." He marched through the main lock, his cod-eyes taking note of the fresh white enamel. "Where do you prefer to start, bow or tail?"

"My equipment-sheets run from bow backward. We may as well deal with them the way they're set."

"Very well." He trotted officiously toward the nose, paused on the way to pat Peaslake and examine his collar. "Well cared for, I see. Has the animal proved useful?"

"He saved five lives on Mardia by barking a warning."

"The details have been entered in your log, I suppose?"

"Yes, sir. The log is in the chart-room awaiting your inspection."

"We'll get to it in due time." Reaching the bow-cabin, Cassidy took a seat, accepted the folder from McNaught, started off at businesslike pace. "K1. Beam compass, type D, one of."

"This is it, sir," said McNaught, showing him.

"Still working properly?"

"Yes, sir."

They carried on, reached the intercom-cubby, the computer-room, a succession of other places back to the galley. Here, Blanchard posed in freshly laundered white clothes and eyed the newcomer warily.

"V.147. Electronic oven, one of."

"Is zis," said Blanchard, pointing with disdain.

"Satisfactory?" inquired Cassidy, giving him the fishy eye.

"Not beeg enough," declared Blanchard. He encompassed the entire galley with an expressive gesture. "Nossings beeg enough. Place too small. Everysings too small. I am chef de cuisine an' she is a cuisine like an attic."

"This is a warship, not a luxury liner," Cassidy snapped. He frowned at the equipment-sheet. "V.148. Timing device, electronic oven, attachment thereto, one of."

"Is zis," spat Blanchard, ready to sling it through the nearest port if Cassidy would first donate the two pins.

Working his way down the sheet, Cassidy got nearer and nearer while nervous tension built up. Then he reached the critical point and said, "V1098. Offog, one."

"*Morbleau!*" said Blanchard, shooting sparks from his eyes, "I have say before an' I say again, zere never was—"

"The offog is in the radio-room, sir," McNaught chipped in hurriedly.

"Indeed?" Cassidy took another look at the sheet. "Then why is it recorded along with galley equipment?"

"It was placed in the galley at time of fitting out, sir. It's one of those portable instruments left to us to fix up where most suitable."

"H'm! Then it should have been transferred to the radio-room list. Why didn't you transfer it?"

"I thought it better to wait for your authority to do so, sir."

The fish-eyes registered gratification. "Yes, that is quite proper of you, Captain. I will transfer it now." He crossed the item from sheet nine, initialed it, entered it on sheet sixteen, initialed that. "V1099. Inscribed collar, leather . . . oh, yes, I've seen that. The dog was wearing it."

He ticked it. An hour later he strutted into the radio-room. Burman stood up, squared his shoulders but could not keep his feet or hands from fidgeting. His eyes protruded slightly and kept straying toward McNaught in silent appeal. He was like a man wearing a porcupine in his breeches.

"V1098. Offog, one," said Cassidy in his usual tone of brooking no nonsense.

Moving with the jerkiness of a slightly uncoordinated robot, Burman pawed a small box fronted with dials, switches and colored lights. It looked like a radio ham's idea of a fruit machine. He knocked down a couple of switches. The lights came on, played around in intriguing combinations.

"This is it, sir," he informed with difficulty.

"Ah!" Cassidy left his chair and moved across for a closer look. "I don't recall having seen this item before. But there are so many different models of the same things. Is it still operating efficiently?"

"Yes, sir."

"It's one of the most useful things in the ship," contributed McNaught, for good measure.

"What does it *do?*" inquired Cassidy, inviting Burman to cast a pearl of wisdom before him.

Burman paled.

Hastily, McNaught said, "A full explanation would be rather involved and technical but, to put it as simply as possible, it enables us to strike a balance between opposing gravitational fields. Variations in lights indicate the extent and degree of imbalance at any given time."

"It's a clever idea," added Burman, made suddenly reckless by this news, "based upon Finagle's Constant."

"I see," said Cassidy, not seeing at all. He resumed his seat, ticked the offog and carried on. "Z44. Switchboard, automatic, forty-line intercom, one of."

"Here it is, sir."

Cassidy glanced at it, returned his gaze to the sheet. The others used his momentary distraction to mop perspiration from their foreheads.

Victory had been gained.

All was well.

For the third time, hah!

Rear Admiral Vane W. Cassidy departed pleased and complimentary. Within one hour the crew bolted to town. McNaught took turns with Gregory at enjoying the gay lights. For the next five days all was peace and pleasure.

On the sixth day Burman brought in a signal, dumped it upon McNaught's desk and waited for the reaction. He had an air of gratification, the pleasure of one whose virtue is about to be rewarded.

Terran Headquarters to BUSTLER. Return here immediately for overhaul and refitting. Improved power-plant to be installed. Feldman. Navy Op. Command. Sirisec.

"Back to Terra," commented McNaught, happily. "And an overhaul will mean at least one month's leave." He eyed Burman. "Tell all officers on duty to go to town at once and order the crew aboard. The men will come running when they know why."

"Yes, sir," said Burman, grinning.

Everyone was still grinning two weeks later, when the Siriport had receded far behind and Sol had grown to a vague speck in the sparkling mist of the bow starfield.

Eleven weeks still to go, but it was worth it. Back to Terra. Hurrah!

In the captain's cabin the grins abruptly vanished one evening when Burman suddenly developed the willies. He marched in, chewed his bottom lip while waiting for McNaught to finish writing in the log.

Finally, McNaught pushed the book away, glanced up, frowned. "What's the matter with you? Got a belly-ache or something?"

"No, sir. I've been thinking."

"Does it hurt that much?"

"I've been thinking," persisted Burman in funereal tones. "We're going back for overhaul. You know what that means. We'll walk off the ship and a horde of experts will walk onto it." He stared tragically at the other. "Experts, I said."

"Naturally they'll be experts," McNaught agreed. "Equipment cannot be tested and brought up to scratch by a bunch of dopes."

"It will require more than a mere expert to bring the offog up to scratch," Burman pointed out. "It'll need a genius."

McNaught rocked back, swapped expressions like changing masks. "Jumping Judas! I'd forgotten all about that thing. When we get to Terra we won't blind *those* boys with science."

"No, sir, we won't," endorsed Burman. He did not add any more but his face shouted aloud, "You got me into this. You get me out of it." He waited quite a time while McNaught did some intense thinking, then prompted, "What do you suggest, sir?"

Slowly the satisfied smile returned to McNaught's features as he answered, "Break up the contraption and feed it into the disintegrator."

"That doesn't solve the problem," said Burman. "We'll still be short an offog."

"No we won't. Because I'm going to signal its loss owing to the hazards of space service." He closed one eye in an emphatic wink. "We're in free flight right now." He reached for a message pad and scribbled on it while Burman stood by, vastly relieved.

> *BUSTLER to Terran Headquarters. Item V1098, Offog, one, came apart under gravitational stress while passing through twin-sun field Hector Major-Minor. Material used as fuel. McNaught, Commander. BUSTLER.*

Burman took it to the radio-room and beamed it Earthward. All was peace and progress for another two days. The next time he went to the captain's cabin he went running.

"General call, sir," he announced breathlessly and thrust the message into the other's hands.

> *Terran Headquarters for relay all sectors. Urgent and Important. All ships grounded forthwith. Vessels in fight under official orders will make for nearest spaceport pending further instructions. Welling. Alarm and Rescue Command. Terra.*

"Something's gone bust," commented McNaught, undisturbed. He traipsed to the chartroom, Burman following. Consulting the charts, he dialed the intercom phone, got Pike in the bow and ordered, "There's a panic. All ships grounded. We've got to make for Zaxted-port, about three days' run away. Change course at once. Starboard seventeen degrees, declination ten." Then he cut off, griped, "Bang goes that sweet month on Terra. I never did like Zaxted, either. It stinks. The crew will feel murderous about this and I don't blame them."

"What d'you think has happened, sir?" asked Burman.

"Heaven alone knows. The last general call was seven years ago, when the *Starider* exploded halfway along the Mars run. They grounded every ship in existence while they investigated the cause." He rubbed his chin, pondered, went on, "And the call before that one was when the entire crew of the *Blowgun* went nuts. Whatever it is this time, you can bet it's serious."

"It wouldn't be the start of a space war?"

"Against whom?" McNaught made a gesture of contempt. "Nobody has the ships with which to oppose us. No, it's something technical. We'll learn of it eventually. They'll tell us before we reach Zaxted or soon afterward."

They did tell him. Within six hours. Burman rushed in with face full of horror.

"What's eating you now?" demanded McNaught, staring at him.

"The offog," stuttered Burman. He made motions as though brushing off invisible spiders.

"What of it?"

"It's a typographical error. In your copy it should read 'off. dog.' "

"Off. dog?" echoed McNaught, making it sound like foul language.

"See for yourself." Dumping the signal on the desk, Burman bolted out, left the door swinging. McNaught scowled after him, picked up the message.

Terran Headquarters to BUSTLER. Your report V1098, ship's official dog Peaslake. Detail fully circumstances and manner in which animal came apart under gravitational stress. Cross-examine crew and signal all coincidental symptoms experienced by them. Urgent and Important. Welling. Alarm and Rescue Command. Terra.

In the privacy of his cabin McNaught commenced to eat his nails. Every now and again he went a little cross-eyed as he examined them for nearness to the flesh.

Into Your Tent I'll Creep

MORFAD SAT IN the midship cabin and gloomed at the wall. He was worried and couldn't conceal the fact. The present situation had the frustrating qualities of a gigantic rattrap. One could escape it only with the combined help of all the other rats.

But the others weren't likely to lift a finger either on his or their own behalf. He felt sure of that. How can you persuade people to try to escape a jam when you can't convince them that they're in it, right up to the neck?

A rat runs around a trap only because he is grimly aware of its existence. So long as he remains blissfully ignorant of it, he does nothing. On this very world a horde of intelligent aliens had done nothing about it through the whole of their history. Fifty skeptical Altairans weren't likely to step in where three thousand million Terrans had failed.

He was still sitting there when Haraka came in and informed, "We leave at sunset."

Morfad said nothing.

"I'll be sorry to go," added Haraka. He was the ship's captain, a big, burly sample of Altairan life. Rubbing flexible fingers together, he went on, "We've been lucky to discover this planet, exceedingly lucky. We've become blood brothers of a life-form fully up to our own standard of intelligence, space-traversing like ourselves, friendly and cooperative."

Morfad said nothing.

"Their reception of us has been most cordial," Haraka continued enthusiastically. "Our people will be greatly heartened when they hear our report. A great future lies before us, no doubt of that. A Terran-Altairan combine will be invincible. Between us we can explore and exploit the entire galaxy."

Morfad said nothing.

Cooling down, Haraka frowned at him. "What's the matter with you, Misery?"

"I am not overjoyed."

"I can see that much. Your face resembles a very sour *shamsid* on an aged and withered bush. And at a time of triumph, too! Are you ill?"

"No." Turning slowly, Morfad looked him straight in the eyes. "Do you believe in psionic faculties?"

Haraka reacted as if caught on one foot. "Well, I don't know. I am a captain, a trained engineer-navigator, and as such I cannot pretend to be an expert upon extraordinary abilities. You ask me something I am not qualified to answer. How about you? Do you believe in them?"

"I do—*now*."

"Now? Why now?"

"The belief has been thrust upon me." Morfad hesitated, went on with a touch of desperation. "I have discovered that I am telepathic."

Surveying him with slight incredulity, Haraka said, "You've discovered it? You mean it has come upon you recently?"

"Yes."

"Since when?"

"Since we arrived on Terra."

"I don't understand this at all," confessed Haraka, baffled. "Do you assert that some peculiarity in Terra's conditions has suddenly enabled you to read my thoughts?"

"No, I cannot read your thoughts."

"But you've just said that you have become telepathic."

"So I have. I can hear thoughts as clearly as if the words were being shouted aloud. But not your thoughts nor those of any member of our crew."

Haraka leaned forward, his features intent. "Ah, you have been hearing *Terran* thoughts, eh? And what you've heard has got you bothered? Morfad, I am your captain, your commander. It is your bounden duty to tell me of anything suspicious about these Terrans." He waited a bit, urged impatiently, "Come on, speak up!"

"I know no more about these humanoids than you do," said Morfad. "I have every reason to believe them genuinely friendly but I don't know what they think."

"But by the stars, man, you—"

"We are talking at cross-purposes," Morfad interrupted. "Whether I do or do not overhear Terran thoughts depends upon what one means by Terrans."

"Look," said Haraka, "whose thoughts *do* you hear?"

Steeling himself, Morfad said flatly, "Those of Terran dogs."

"Dogs?" Haraka lay back and stared at him. *"Dogs?* Are you serious?"

"I have never been more so. I can hear dogs and no others. Don't ask me why because I don't know. It is a freak of circumstance."

"And you have listened to their minds ever since we jumped to Earth?"

"Yes."

"What sort of things have you heard?"

"I have had pearls of alien wisdom cast before me," declared Morfad, "and the longer I look at them the more they scare hell out of me."

"Get busy frightening me with a few examples," invited Haraka, suppressing a smile.

"Quote: the supreme test of intelligence is the ability to live as one pleases without working," recited Morfad. "Quote: the art of retribution is that of concealing it beyond all suspicion. Quote: the sharpest, most subtle, most effective weapon in the cosmos is flattery."

"Huh?"

"Quote: if a thing can think it likes to think that it is God—treat it as God and it becomes your willing slave."

"Oh, no!" denied Haraka.

"Oh, *yes!*" insisted Morfad. He waved a hand toward the nearest port. "Out there are three thousand million petty gods. They are eagerly panted after, fawned upon, gazed upon with worshiping eyes. Gods are very gracious toward those who love them." He made a spitting sound that lent emphasis to what followed. "The lovers know it—and love comes cheap."

Haraka said, uneasily, "I think you're crazy."

"Quote: to rule successfully the ruled must be unconscious of it." Again the spitting sound. "Is that crazy? I don't think so. It makes sense. It works. It's working out there right now."

"But—"

"Take a look at this." He tossed a small object into Haraka's lap. "Recognize it?"

"Yes, it's what they call a cracker."

"Correct. To make it some Terrans plowed fields in all kinds of weather, rain, wind and sunshine, sowed wheat, reaped it with the aid of machinery other Terrans had sweated to build. They transported the wheat, stored it, milled it, enriched the flour by various processes, baked it, packaged it, shipped it all over the world. When humanoid Terrans want crackers they've got to put in man-hours to get them."

"So—"

"When a dog wants one he sits up, waves his forepaws and admires his god. That's all. Just that."

"But, darn it, man, dogs are relatively stupid."

"So it seems," said Morfad, dryly.

"They can't really *do* anything effective."

"That depends upon what one regards as effective."

"They haven't got hands."

"And don't need them—having brains."

"Now see here," declaimed Haraka, openly irritated, "we Altairans invented and constructed ships capable of roaming the spaces between the stars. The Terrans have done the same. Terran dogs have not done it and won't do it in the next million years. When one dog has the brains and ability to get to another planet I'll eat my cap."

"You can do that right now," Morfad suggested. "We have two dogs on board."

Haraka let go a grunt of disdain. "The Terrans have given us those as a memento."

"Sure they gave them to us—at whose behest?"

"It was wholly a spontaneous gesture."

"Was it?"

"Are you suggesting that dogs put the idea into their heads?" Haraka demanded.

"I know they did," retorted Morfad, looking grim. "And we've not been given two males or two females. Oh no, sir, not on your life. One male and one female. The givers said we could breed them. Thus in due course our own worlds can become illuminated with the undying love of man's best friend."

"Nuts!" said Haraka.

Morfad gave back, "You're obsessed with the old, out-of-date idea that conquest must be preceded by aggression. Can't you understand that a wholly alien species just naturally uses wholly alien methods? Dogs employ their own tactics, not ours. It isn't within their nature or abilities to take us over with the aid of ships, guns and a great hullabaloo. It *is* within their nature and abilities to creep in upon us, their eyes shining with hero-worship. If we don't watch out, we'll be mastered by a horde of loving creepers."

"I can invent a word for your mental condition," said Haraka. "You're suffering from caniphobia."

"With good reasons."

"Imaginary ones."

"Yesterday I looked into a dogs' beauty shop. Who was doing the bathing, scenting, powdering, primping? Other dogs? Hah! Humanoid females were busy dolling 'em up. Was *that* imaginary?"

"You can call it a Terran eccentricity. It means nothing whatever. Besides, we've quite a few funny habits of our own."

"You're dead right there," Morfad agreed. "And I know one of yours. So does the entire crew."

Haraka narrowed his eyes. "You might as well name it. I am not afraid to see myself as others see me."

"All right. You've asked for it. You think a lot of Kashim. He always has your ear. You will listen to him when you'll listen to nobody else. Everything he says makes sound sense—to you."

"So you're jealous of Kashim, eh?"

"Not in the least," assured Morfad, making a disparaging gesture. "I merely despise him for the same reason that everyone else holds him in contempt. He is a professional toady. He spends most of his time fawning upon you, flattering you, pandering to your ego. He is a natural-born creeper who gives you the Terradog treatment. You like it. You bask in it. It affects you like an irresistible drug. It works—and don't tell me that it doesn't because all of us know that it *does*."

"I am not a fool. I have Kashim sized up. He does not influence me to the extent you believe."

"Three thousand million Terrans have four hundred million dogs sized up and are equally convinced that no dog has a say in anything worth a hoot."

"I don't believe it."

"Of course you don't. I had little hope that you would. Morfad is telling you these things and Morfad is either crazy or a liar. But if Kashim were to tell you while prostrate at the foot of your throne you would swallow his story hook, line and sinker. Kashim has a Terradog mind and uses Terradog logic, see?"

"My disbelief has better basis than that."

"For instance?" Morfad invited.

"Some Terrans are telepathic. Therefore if this myth of subtle mastery by dogs were a fact, they'd know of it. Not a dog would be left alive on this world." Haraka paused, finished pointedly, "They don't know of it."

"Terran telepaths hear the minds of their own kind but not those of dogs. I hear the minds of dogs but not those of any other kind. As I said before, I don't know why this should be. I know only that it *is*."

"It seems nonsensical to me."

"It would. I suppose you can't be blamed for taking that viewpoint. My position is difficult; I'm like the only one with ears in a world that is stone-deaf."

Haraka thought it over, said after a while, "Suppose I were to accept everything you've said at face value—what do you think I should do about it?"

"Refuse to take the dogs," responded Morfad, promptly.

"That's more easily said than done. Good relations with the Terrans are vitally important. How can I reject a warm-hearted gift without offending the givers?"

"All right, don't reject it. Modify it instead. Ask for two male or two female dogs. Make it plausible by quoting an Altairan law against the importation of alien animals that are capable of natural increase."

"I can't do that. It's far too late. We've already accepted the animals and expressed our gratitude for them. Besides, their ability to breed is essential part of the gift, the basic intention of the givers. They've presented us with a new species, an entire race of dogs."

"You said it!" confirmed Morfad.

"For the same reason we can't very well prevent them from breeding when we get back home," Haraka pointed. "From now on we and the Terrans are going to do a lot of visiting. Immediately they discover that our dogs have failed to multiply they'll become generous and sentimental and dump another dozen on us. Or maybe a hundred. We'll then be worse off than we were before."

"All right, all right." Morfad shrugged with weary resignation. "If you're going to concoct a major objection to every possible solution we may as well surrender without a fight. Let's abandon ourselves to becoming yet another dog-dominated species. Requote: to rule successfully the ruled must be unconscious of it." He gave Haraka the sour eye. "If I had my way, I'd wait until we were far out in free space and then give those two dogs the hearty heave-ho out the hatch."

Haraka grinned in the manner of one about to nail down a cockeyed tale once and for all. "And if you did

that it would be proof positive beyond all argument
that you're afflicted with a delusion."

Emitting a deep sigh, Morfad asked, "Why would
it?"

"You'd be slinging out two prime members of the
master race. Some domination, eh?" Haraka grinned
again. "Listen, Morfad, according to your own story
you know something never before known or suspected
and you're the only one who does know it. That should
make you a mighty menace to the entire species of dogs.
They wouldn't let you live long enough to thwart them
or even to go round advertising the truth. You'd soon
be deader than a low-strata fossil." He walked to the
door, held it open while he made his parting shot. "You
look healthy enough to me."

Morfad shouted at the closing door, "Doesn't follow
that because I can hear their thoughts they must necessarily hear mine. I doubt that they can because it's just
a freakish—"

The door clicked shut. He scowled at it, walked
twenty times up and down the cabin, finally resumed
his chair and sat in silence while he beat his brains
around in search of a satisfactory solution.

"The sharpest, most subtle, most effective weapon in
the cosmos is flattery."

Yes, he was seeking a means of coping with four-
footed warriors incredibly skilled in the use of Creation's sharpest weapon. Professional fawners, creepers,
worshipers, man-lovers, ego-boosters, trained to near-
perfection through countless generations in an art
against which there seemed no decisive defense.

How to beat off the coming attack, contain it,
counter it?

"Yes, God!"

"Certainly, God!"

"Anything you say, God!"

How to protect oneself against this insidious technique, how to quarantine it or—

By the stars! that was it—*quarantine* them! On

Pladamine, the useless world, the planet nobody wanted. They could breed there to their limits and meanwhile dominate the herbs and bugs. And a soothing reply would be ready for any nosy Terran tourist.

"The dogs? Oh, sure, we've still got them, lots of them. They're doing fine. Got a nice world of their very own. Place called Pladamine. If you wish to go see them, it can be arranged."

A wonderful idea. It would solve the problem while creating no hard feelings among the Terrans. It would prove useful in the future and to the end of time. Once planted on Pladamine no dog could ever escape by its own efforts. Any tourists from Terra who brought dogs along could be persuaded to leave them in the canine heaven specially created by Altair. There the dogs would find themselves unable to boss anything higher than other dogs, and, if they didn't like it, they could lump it.

No use putting the scheme to Haraka, who was obviously prejudiced. He'd save it for the authorities back home. Even if they found it hard to credit his story, they'd still take the necessary action on the principle that it is better to be sure than sorry. Yes, they'd play safe and give Pladamine to the dogs.

Standing on a cabin seat, he gazed out and down through the port. A great mob of Terrans, far below, waited to witness the coming takeoff and cheer them on their way. He noticed beyond the back of the crowd a small, absurdly groomed dog dragging a Terran female at the end of a thin, light chain. Poor girl, he thought. The dog leads, she follows yet believes *she* is taking *it* some place.

Finding his color-camera, he checked its controls, walked along the corridor and into the open air lock. It would be nice to have a picture of the big send-off audience. Reaching the rim of the lock he tripped headlong over something four-legged and stubby-tailed that suddenly intruded itself between his feet. He dived outward, the camera still in his grip, and went down fast through the whistling wind while shrill feminine screams came from among the watching crowd.

Haraka said, "The funeral has delayed us two days. We'll have to make up the time as best we can." He brooded a moment, added, "I am very sorry about Morfad. He had a brilliant mind but it was breaking up toward the end. Oh well, it's a comfort that the expedition has suffered only one fatality."

"It could have been worse, sir," responded Kashim. "It could have been you. Praise the heavens that it was not."

"Yes, it could have been me." Haraka regarded him curiously. "And would it have grieved you, Kashim?"

"Very much indeed, sir. I don't think anyone aboard would feel the loss more deeply. My respect and admiration are such that—"

He ceased as something padded softly into the cabin, laid its head in Haraka's lap, gazed soulfully up at the captain. Kashim frowned with annoyance.

"Good boy!" approved Haraka, scratching the newcomer's ears.

"My respect and admiration," repeated Kashim in louder tones, "are such that—"

"Good boy!" said Haraka again. He gently pulled one ear, then the other, observed with pleasure the vibrating tail.

"As I was saying, sir, my respect—"

"Good boy!" Deaf to all else, Haraka slid a hand down from the ears and massaged under the jaw.

Kashim favored Good Boy with a glare of inutterable hatred. The dog rolled a brown eye sideways and looked at him without expression. From that moment Kashim's fate was sealed.

Study in Still Life

"WHAT BURNS ME UP," said Purcell bitterly, "is the fact that one cannot get anything merely on grounds of dire necessity."

"Yeah," said Hancock, carrying on with his writing.

"If one gets it at all," continued Purcell, warming to his subject, "it is for a reason that has nothing whatever to do with need or urgency. One gets it because and only because one has carefully filled out the correct forms in the correct way, got them signed and countersigned by the proper fatheads and submitted them through the proper channels to the proper people on Terra."

"Yeah," said Hancock, the tip of his tongue moving in sympathy with his pen.

"Yeah, yeah, yeah," echoed Purcell in somewhat higher tones. "Can't you say anything but yeah?"

Hancock sighed, ceased writing, mopped his forehead with a sweaty handkerchief. "Look, let's do what we're paid for, shall we? Griping gets us nowhere."

"Well, what are we paid for?"

"Personally, I think that pilots grounded by injuries should be found employment elsewhere. They never settle down to routine work."

"That doesn't answer my question."

"We're here upon Alipan, in the newly settled system of B417," informed Hancock ponderously, "to coordinate the inflow of essential supplies, making the best use of cargo space available. We are also here to deal with internal demands for supplies and assign priorities to them."

"Priorities my foot," said Purcell. He snatched up a form and flourished it in midair. "What sort of priority should be given to twenty-four cases of gin?"

"If you bothered to look, you'd see," Hancock gave back. "Class B import. I stamped it myself and you initialed it."

"I must have been momentarily blind. Who says gin gets priority over high-pressure oxygen flasks, for instance?"

"Letheren." Hancock frowned, fiddled with his pen. "Mind you, I don't agree with it myself. I think it's an iniquity. But Letheren is a senior official. As a pilot you may have cocked many a snoot at senior officials and got away with it. But you're not a pilot now. You're just another desk-squatter. As such you'd better learn that it isn't wise to thwart senior officials. They get moved around and up as more senior ones die of fatty degeneration. In five, ten or fifteen years' time Letheren may be my boss. By then I'll be treading on his heels. I won't want him to turn around and kick me in the teeth."

"You really think that after all that time he'd hold it against you because you refused to bring in his gin?" asked Purcell incredulously.

"No, I don't. I'm bringing it in. He'll have no reason to gripe."

"What a system!" said Purcell. He glowered through the window at the B417 sun. It's greenish hue made him feel slightly sick. "I can see now what I suspected years ago; space is slowly but surely being conquered by a few crazy coots not because of Terra but in spite of Terra. It's being done by a small bunch of hotheads who like to zoom around in rocketships. They're getting results in the face of every handicap we can place upon them."

"Having been a pilot, you're prejudiced in their favor," said Hancock defensively. "After all, somebody has to do the paperwork."

"I'd agree if the paperwork was necessary and made sense."

"If there wasn't any paperwork, we'd both be out of a job."

"You've got something there. So on this planet there are two thousands of us sitting on our fundaments busily making work for each other. In due time there'll be five thousand, then ten thousand."

"I'm looking forward to it," commented Hancock, brightening. "It'll mean promotion. And the more subordinates we have the higher our own status."

"That may be so. I won't take it with an easy conscience but I'll take it just the same. Frail human flesh, that's me." Purcell scowled at his desk, went on, "Guess I'm not yet old enough and cynical enough to accept the general waste of time and effort. There are moments when I could go off with a very large bang. This is one of them."

Hancock, who had picked up his pen, put it down again and asked resignedly, "Exactly what irks your reformist spirit right now?"

"There's a fellow here, a bugologist—"

"An entomologist," Hancock corrected.

"You will kindly allow me to choose my own words," Purcell suggested. "This bugologist wants a cobalt-60 irradiation outfit. It weighs three-eighty pounds."

"What for?"

"To clear the Great Forest area of a disease-carrying fly."

"How's he going to do that?"

"According to section D7 of his application form under the heading of REASONS, he says that treated male flies will effectively sterilize all female flies with whom they mate. Also that if he traps, irradiates and frees enough males he can wipe out the species. Also that several centuries ago Terra got rid of screwworm, tsetse and other flies by precisely the same method. He claims that he can make the whole of the Great Forest area inhabitable, exploitable and save an unknown number of lives. Therefore he asks for top priority."

"That seems reasonable," Hancock conceded.

"You would give his dingus top priority, eh?"

"Certainly. A Class A import."

"That is real nice to know," said Purcell. "I am heartened to find sweet reasonableness sitting behind a desk and wearing oilskin pants." He slung the form across to the other. "Some bead-brained four-eyes has stamped it Class L. So this bugologist won't get his fly-killer for at least another seven years."

"It wasn't me," protested Hancock, staring at it. "I remember this one now. I got it about four months ago and passed it to Rohm for his approval."

"Why?"

"Because he's in charge of forestry."

"Holy cow!" said Purcell. "What have flies got to do with forestry?"

"The Great Forest area is the responsibility of Rohm's department. Anything pertaining to it must be passed to him."

"And he's stamped it Class L. He must be off his head."

"We cannot assume inefficiency in another department," Hancock pointed out. "There may be a thousand and one things Rohm needs more urgently. Medical supplies for instance."

"Yes, to cure people of the staggers after being bitten by flies," Purcell riposted. "If space-scouts operated the way we work, they'd still be preparing photostats of their birth and marriage certificates in readiness for an attempt on the Moon." He took the form back, eyed it with distaste. "Letheren's gin aggravates me. I have always hated the stuff. It tastes the same way a dead dog smells. If he can wangle a dollop of booze, why can't we wangle a cobalt-60 irradiator?"

"You can't buck the system," declared Hancock. "Not until you're one of the top brass."

"I'm bucking it as from now," Purcell announced. He reached for a fresh form, started filling it in. "I'm making a top priority demand for a fly killer for Nemo."

"Nemo?" Hancock looked stupefied. "What's that?"

Purcell waved a careless hand toward the window. "The newly discovered planet out there."

Shoving back his chair, Hancock waddled to the window and gazed through it a long time. He couldn't see anything. After a while he came back, puffed, mopped his forehead again, reached for the intercom phone.

Purcell snapped, "Put that down!"

Letting go as if it were red-hot, Hancock complained, "If they've started operations on a new planet, Collister's department should have notified us in the proper manner. I object to this sloppy method of passing news along by word of mouth during lunch-hour gossip. Essential information should be transmitted in writing and distributed to all the individuals concerned."

"Collister's crowd know nothing about Nemo."

"Don't they? Why not?"

"I just invented it," said Purcell evenly.

"You *invented* it?"

"That's what I said." Completing the form, Purcell smacked it with a huge red stamp bearing the letters TP, then with a smaller one reading *Consign via Alipan B417*. While Hancock goggled at him he signed it, shoved it into the pneumatic tube. Within four minutes the radio-facsimile would be flashed Earthward.

Hancock said, aghast, "You must be mad."

"Crazy like a fox," admitted Purcell, undisturbed.

"They won't accept a requisition for an unregistered planet without official advice of its discovery and notification of its coordinates."

"The demand is an advice and I included the coordinates."

"They'll check on this," warned Hancock.

"With whom? The department for Nemo?"

"There isn't one," said Hancock.

"Correct. They'll have to check with Yehudi."

"They'll find out sooner or later that they've been taken. There will be trouble. I want you to know, Purcell, that I hereby disclaim all responsibility for this. Officially I know nothing whatever about it. It is solely and wholly your own pigeon."

"Don't worry. I'm willing to accept the full credit for a praiseworthy display of initiative. Anyway, by that time the bugologist will have got his equipment and all the flies will be dead."

Hancock simmered down for five minutes then took on a look of horror as a new thought struck him. "If they load three-eighty pounds of scientific hardware, it's highly likely that they won't load the gin."

"That's what I like about it."

"Letheren will run amok."

"Let him," said Purcell. "He thinks he's heap big. To me he's just a big heap."

"Purcell, I will accept no responsibility for this."

"So you said before." Then he added with some menace, "Always bear one thing in mind, Hancock—I don't look as daft as I am!"

At Terra the indent landed on Bonhoeffer's desk, he being in charge of the Incoming Mail (Pre-sorting) Department. Bonhoeffer was a real woman's man, big, handsome, muscular, stupid. He owed his eminence solely to the fact that while in ten years the incoming mail had increased by twelve per cent the number of his subordinates had gone up one hundred forty per cent. This was more or less in accordance with the rules laid down by Professor C. Northcote Parkinson.*

Bonhoeffer picked up the form with much reluctance. It was the only item on his desk. The slaves dealt with everything as a matter of daily routine and nothing was brought to his personal attention unless there was something awkward about it. This suited him topnotch; it gave him plenty of time not to think.

So he knew in advance that this particular form contained the subject of an administrative quibble and that he must demonstrate his intelligence by finding it alone and unaided. Slowly and carefully he read it from top to bottom four times. As far as he could see there was nothing wrong with it. This irritated him. It meant that he must summon the individual who had passed the in-

*Parkinson's Law, *circa* 1958.

visible buck and do him the honor of asking his opinion.

He examined the form's top left corner to see who would be thus honored. The initials scrawled thereon were F. Y. That meant the buck-passer was Feodor Yok. He might have expected it. Yok was a clever bum, an office showoff. He looked like Rasputin with a crewcut. And he wore the knowing smirk of a successful ambulance chaser. Bonhoeffer would rather drop dead than ask Yok the time of day.

That made things difficult. He studied the requisition another four times and still it looked plenty good enough to pass any determined fault-finder, even Yok. Then it occurred to him that there was an escape from this predicament. He, too, could transfer the grief, preferably to an eager beaver. It was as easy as that.

Switching his desk-box, he ordered, "Send in Quayle."

Quayle arrived with his usual promptitude. He was built along the lines of a starving jackrabbit and tried to compensate for it with a sort of military obsequiousness. He wore a dedicated look and was the sort of creep who would salute an officer over the telephone.

"Ah, Quayle," began Bonhoeffer with lordly condescension. "I have been watching your progress with some interest."

"Really, sir?" said Quayle, toothy with delight.

"Yes, indeed. I keep a careful eye on everyone, though I doubt whether they realize it. The true test of managerial competence is the ability to depute responsibility. To do that one must know and understand the men under one. Naturally some are more competent than others. You gather my meaning, Quayle?"

"Yes, sir," agreed Quayle, straining to expand his halo.

"Yok has seen fit to bring this requisition form to my attention." Bonhoeffer handed it over. "I was about to transfer it for necessary action when it occurred to me that it would be useful to know whether the question it raises is as obvious to you as it was to Yok and myself, also whether you can be as quick to determine what should be done about it."

Quayle's halo faded from sight while his face took on the look of a cornered rat. In complete silence he studied the form from end to end, reading it several times.

Finally he ventured in uncertain tones, "I can find nothing wrong with it, sir, except that it is a demand for Nemo. I don't recall seeing that planet upon the supply list."

"Very good, Quayle, very good," praised Bonhoeffer. "And what do you think should be done about it?"

"Well, sir," continued Quayle, vastly encouraged but still weak at the knees, "since the requisition emanates from Alipan, which is on the list, I'd say that it is valid so far as our department is concerned. Therefore I would pass it to the scientific division for confirmation of the reasons given and the correctness of the specification."

"Excellent, Quayle. I may as well say that you have come up to my expectations."

"Thank you, sir."

"I am a great believer in giving encouragement where it is deserved." Bonhoeffer bestowed a lopsided smile upon the other. "Since you have the form in your hands you may as well deal with it. Yok brought it in but I prefer that you handle it in person."

"Thank you, sir," repeated Quayle, the halo bursting forth in dazzling glory. He went out.

Bonhoeffer lay back and gazed with satisfaction at the empty desk.

In due course—meaning about three weeks—the scientific division swore and deposed that there really was such an article as a cobalt-60 irradiator and that it could in fact cause flies to indulge in futile woo. Quayle therefore attached this slightly obscene certificate to the requisition and passed it to the purchasing department for immediate attention.

He felt fully justified in doing this despite that the mysterious Nemo was still absent from the official supply list. After all, he had been authorized by Bonhoeffer to take the necessary action and the scientific division had duly certified that there was something with which to act. He was covered both ways, coming and going. In effect, Quayle was fireproof, a much-to-be desired state of existence.

The form and attached certificate now got dumped on Stanisland, an irascible character generally viewed as the offspring of a canine mother. Stanisland read them to the accompaniment of a series of rising grunts, found himself in the usual quandary. The purchasing department was supposed to know the prime sources of everything from peanuts to synthetic hormones. To that end it had a reference library so large that a fully equipped expedition was needed to get anywhere beyond the letter F. The library was used almost solely to demonstrate frenzied overwork whenever a high-ranking senior happened around, the safest place being atop the ladder.

It was easier to ask the right questions in the right places than to go on safari through a mile of books. Moreover Stanisland could admit ignorance of nothing in a room full of comparative halfwits. So he adopted his favorite tactic. Scowling around to make sure nobody was watching, he stuffed the papers into a pocket, got up, hoarsely muttered something about the men's room and lumbered out.

Then he trudged along three corridors, reached a bank of private phone booths, entered one, dialed the scientific division and asked for Williams. He uttered this name with poor grace because in his opinion Williams had been designed by Nature specifically to occupy a padded cell.

When the other came on, he said, "Stanisland, purchasing department, here."

"How's the bile flowing?" greeted Williams, conscious that neither was senior to the other.

Ignoring that, Stanisland went on, "You have issued certificate D2794018 against a cobalt-60 irradiator on demand by Alipan."

"I don't take your word for it," said Williams. "Give me that number again and wait while I trace the copy."

Stanisland gave it and waited. He stood there about ten minutes knowing full well that Williams was taking one minute to find the copy and allowing him the other nine in which to grow a beard. But he was impotent to do anything about it. Finally Williams came back.

"My, are you still there?" he asked in mock surprise. "Things must be pretty quiet in your department."

"If we were as bone idle as other departments, we'd have no need to consult them," shouted Stanisland. "We'd have all the time in the world to dig up information for ourselves."

"Aha!" said Williams, nastily triumphant. "You don't know where to get an irradiator, eh?"

"It isn't a question of not knowing," Stanisland retorted. "It's a question of saving time finding out. If I search under C for cobalt, it won't be there. It won't be under I for irradiator either. Nor under S for sixty. In about a week's time I'll discover that it's under H because the correct technical name for it is a hyperdiddlic honey or something like that. Things would be a lot easier if you eggheads would make up your minds to call a spade a plain, ordinary spade and stick to it for keeps."

"Shame," said Williams.

"Furthermore," continued Stanisland with satisfying malice, "every alleged up-to-date supplement to the library comes to us seven years old. Why? Because your crowd keep 'em on file and won't part until they begin to stink."

"We need them to stay up-to-date ourselves," Williams pointed out. "The scientific division cannot afford to be behind the times."

"There you are then," said Stanisland, winning his point. "I don't want to know who was making rudimentary irradiators way back when television was two-dimensional. I want to know who is making them *now*. And I don't want to put in to Abelson an official complaint about delayed data and willful obstruction."

"Are you threatening me, you baggy-eyed tub?" asked Williams.

Stanisland started shouting again. "I don't want to

touch Abelson with a ten-foot pole. You know what he's like."

"Yeah, I know, I know." Williams let go a resigned sigh. "Hold on a piece." This time he was gone twelve minutes before he returned and recited a short list of names and addresses.

Reaching his desk, Stanisland rewrote the list more clearly, attached it to the form and certificate, passed the bunch to a junior.

In tones hearable all over the office, he said, "It's a lucky thing that I had the handling of this demand. It so happens that I know all the people who make such a rare piece of apparatus. Now you get their estimates as quickly as possible and submit them to me."

Then he glared happily around at all and sundry, enjoying their dead faces and knowing that they were hating him deep in their hearts. By hokey, he'd shown them who most deserved to be jacked up a grade.

Forman Atomics quoted the lowest price and quickest delivery. A month later they got a request for copy of their authorization as an approved supplier. They mailed it pronto. Three days afterward they were required to send a sworn affidavit that their employees included not less than ten per cent of disabled spacemen. They sent it. Two intelligence agents visited their head office and satisfied themselves that the flag flying from the masthead was a genuine Terran one in substance and in fact.

Meanwhile a subordinate from the Finance (Investigation) Department made search through the files of the Companies (Registered Statistics) Department, aided by two juniors belonging to that haven of rest. Between them they made sure that not one dollar of Forman stock was held or controlled by the representative of any foreign power, either in person or by nominee. Admittedly, there was no such thing in existence as a foreign power but that was beside the point.

By now the original requisition had attached to it the following:

1. The scientific division's certificate.

2. An interdepartmental slip signed by Quayle informing Stanisland that the requisition was passed to him for attention.

3. A similar slip signed by Bonhoeffer saying that he had ordered Quayle to do the passing.

4–11. Eight quotations for an irradiator, Forman's having been stamped: "Accepted subject to process."

12. A copy of Forman's supply authorization.

13. Forman's affidavit.

14. An intelligence report to the effect that whatever was wrong with Forman's could not be proved.

15. A finance department report saying the same thing in longer words.

Item twelve represented an old and completely hopeless attempt to buck the system. In the long, long ago somebody had made the mistake of hiring a fully paid-up member of Columbia University's Institute of Synergistic Statics. Being under the delusion that a line is the shortest distance between two points, the newcomer had invented a blanket system of governmental authorizations which he fondly imagined would do away with items thirteen, fourteen and fifteen.

This dastardly attempt to abolish three departments at one fell blow had gained its just reward; a new department had been set up to deal with item twelve while the others had been retained. For creating this extra work the author of it had been hastily promoted to somewhere in the region of Bootes.

Stanisland added the sixteenth item in the shape of his own interdepartmental slip informing Taylor, the head of the purchasing department, that to the best of his knowledge and belief there were no remaining questions to be raised and that it was now for him to place the order. Taylor, who had not been born yesterday, showed what he thought of this indecent haste. Throwing away the overstrained paper-clip, he added his own slip to the wad, secured it with a wide-jawed bulldog fastener and fired it back at Stanisland.

The slip said, "You are or should be well aware that a consignment of this description may not be within the capacity of the Testing (Instruments) Department. If it is not, we shall require a certificate of efficiency from the Bureau of Standards. Take the necessary action forthwith."

This resulted in Stanisland taking a fast walk around the corridors while the surplus steam blew out of his ears. He had never liked Taylor, who obviously enjoyed his seniority and would turn anyone base over apex for the sadistic pleasure of it. Besides, in his spare time the fellow lived the full life breeding piebald mice. With his beady eyes and twitching whiskers he bore close resemblance to his beloved vermin.

When pressure had dropped to the bearable, Stanisland returned to his desk, called a junior and gave him the wad plus a slip reading, "Can you test this thing?"

Within ten days all the papers came back accompanied by the reply. "For emission only. Not for functional purpose. To test for the latter we would require an adequate supply of the proposed subjects, namely and to wit, Nemo flies. Refer to Imports (Pest Control) Department."

So he phoned through to Chase who was sunbathing by a window and brought him back to his desk and Chase said with unnecessary surliness, "Importation forbidden."

"Can you quote authority for that?" asked Stanisland.

"Certainly," snapped Chase. "See the Bacteriological Defense Act, volume three titled Alien Insects, subsection fourteen under heading of Known Or Suspected Disease Carriers, I quote—"

"You needn't bother," said Stanisland hastily. "I've got to have it in writing anyway."

"All right. Give me those reference numbers again and I'll send you a documentary ban."

"I don't see how the testing department is going to cope in these circumstances."

"That's their worry, not yours," advised Chase. "Be your age!"

In due time—meaning another three weeks—Chase's prohibition arrived properly stamped, signed and countersigned. It got added to the growing bunch. Stanisland was now faced with the very serious question of whether a mere test for emission was adequate and in accordance with the rules. To resolve it one way or the other meant reaching A Decision. And that could be done only by an official in A Position Of Responsibility.

Yeah, Taylor.

At the prospect of consulting Taylor a great sorrow came upon him. It would imply that he, Stanisland, couldn't summon up the nerve. But the alternative was far worse, namely, to exceed his authority. He blanched at the thought of it.

For two days Stanisland let the papers lie around while he tried to think up some other way out. There was no other way. If he dumped the wad on Taylor's desk during his absence and then went sick, Taylor would hold the lot pending his return. If he transferred the file to the next department, it would be bounced back with malicious glee plus a note pointing to the lack of an order. Obviously he had to see Taylor. He had nothing to fear but fear itself.

Finally he steeled himself, marched into Taylor's office, gave him the documents and pointed to the last two items.

"You will see, sir, that an adequate test cannot be performed because of an import restriction."

"Yes, my dear Stanisland," said Taylor, courteous in a thoroughly aggravating manner. "I suspected some such difficulty myself."

Stanisland said nothing.

"I am somewhat surprised that you failed to anticipate it," added Taylor pointedly.

"With all respect, sir, I have a lot of work to do and one cannot foresee everything."

"I am more impressed by efficiency than by apologies," commented Taylor in sugar-sweet tones. "And so far as I am concerned the test of efficiency is the ability to handle potentially controversial matters in such a manner that this department, when called upon to do so, can produce documentary justification for everything it has done. In other words, so long as there are no routine blunders within our own department it is not our concern what mistakes may be made in other departments. Do you understand me, my dear Stanisland?"

"Yes, sir," said Stanisland with bogus humility.

"Good!" Taylor lay back, hooked thumbs in armholes, eyed him as if he were a piebald mouse. "Now, have you brought the order in readiness for my signature?"

Stanisland went purple, swallowed hard. "No, sir."

"Why haven't you?"

"It appeared to me, sir, that it would first be necessary to obtain your ruling on whether or not a test for emission is sufficient."

"My ruling?" Taylor raised his eyebrows in mock surprise. "Have you taken leave of your senses? I do not make decisions for other departments, surely you know that?"

"Yes, sir, but—"

"Anyone with the moral fortitude to look a fact in the face," interrupted Tayor, tapping the papers with a long, thin forefinger, "can see that here we have a written statement from the appropriate department to the effect that this piece of apparatus can be tested. That is all we require. The question of how it is tested or for what it is tested does not concern us in the least. We have enough responsibilities of our own without accepting those properly belonging to other departments."

"Yes, sir," agreed Stanisland, not inclined to argue the matter.

"Already there has been far too much delay in dealing with this requisition," Taylor went on. "The demand is now almost a year old. Disgraceful!"

"I assure you, sir, that it is not my—"

"Cut out the excuses and let me see some action."

"You wish me to write out the order at once, sir?"

"No, you need not bother. Go get your order book, give it to my secretary and tell her that I wish to deal with it personally."

"Very well, sir." Stanisland departed sweating a mixture of ire and relief.

Finding the order book, he took it to the secretary. She was a frozen-faced female who never lost an opportunity to admire his ignorance. She was named Hazel, after a nut.

On the face of it something had now been accomplished. A gadget had been demanded, the demand had been checked, counterchecked and approved, estimates had been obtained and the order placed. It remained for Forman Atomics to supply the irradiator, the Testing Department to test it, the Shipping (Outward) Department to authorize dispatch to Alipan and the Loading (Space Allocation) Department to put it aboard the right ship.

True, a dozen more departments had yet to handle the growing mass of papers which by now had attained the dignity of a box-file. Between them they'd fiddle around for another two years before the wad was reluctantly consigned to the morgue of the Records (Filing) Department. But all these were strictly post-shipment departments; the days, weeks and months they spent playing with documents did not matter once the consignment was on its way. Any irate hustle-up note from the top brass in Alipan could now be answered, curtly and effective, with the bald statement that Action Had Been Taken.

Stanisland therefore composed his soul in bilious peace, satisfied that he had hurdled an awkward obstacle to the accompaniment of no more than a few raspberries from Taylor. He gained some compensation for the latter by reminding everyone in the office that he was peculiarly qualified to advise on rare apparatus without first getting himself lost in the library. Having instilled that fact in their minds he carried on with routine work and began gradually to forget the subject. But he was not left in peace for long.

In more than due time—meaning at least twice three weeks—his telephone shrilled and a voice said, "This is Keith of Inspection Department."

"Yes?" responded Stanisland warily. He had never heard of Keith, much less met him.

"There's a difficulty here," continued Keith, smacking his lips. "I have been on to Loading about it and they've referred me to Shipping who've referred me to Testing who've referred me to Purchasing. I see by the papers that the order was placed by Taylor but that you did the processing."

"What's wrong?" asked Stanisland, immediately recognizing the swift passing of an unwanted buck.

"The manifest of the *Starfire* includes a thing called a cobalt-60 irradiator for delivery to Alipan. It has been supplied by Forman Atomics against your department's order number BZ12-10127."

"What of it?"

"Testing Department has issued a guarantee that emission is satisfactory," Keith continued. "You know what that means."

Stanisland hadn't the remotest notion of what it meant but was not prepared to say so. He evaded the point by inquiring, "Well, what has it to do with this department?"

"It has got plenty to do with *some* department," Keith retorted. "They can't *all* disclaim responsibility."

Still feeling around in the dark, Stanisland said carefully, "I may have to take this to Taylor or even to Abelson. They will insist on me repeating your complaint in exact terms. Is there any reason why you can't send it round in writing?"

"Yes," said Keith. "There isn't time. The ship takes off this evening."

"All right. Exactly what do you want me to tell Taylor?"

Keith fell into the trap and informed, "This cobalt-60 contraption cannot have satisfactory emission without being radioactive. Therefore it comes under the heading of Noxious Cargo. It cannot be shipped by the *Starfire* unless we are supplied with a certificate to the effect that it is properly screened and will not contaminate adjacent cargo."

"Oh!" said Stanisland, feeling yet again that the only thing between him and the top of the ladder was the ladder.

"Such a certificate should have been supplied in the first place," added Keith, drowning his last spark of decency. "Somebody slipped up. I'm holding a wad three inches thick and everything's here but that."

Annoyed by this, Stanisland bawled, "I fail to see why the production of a non-contaminatory certificate should be considered the responsibility of this department."

"Testing Department say they offered to check for emission only and that you accepted this," Keith gave back. "The documents show that their statement is correct. I have them here before my very eyes."

"That is sheer evasion," maintained Stanisland. "It is your job to make them take back the apparatus and check it for screening."

"On the contrary," shot back Keith, "it is not, never has been and never will be my job to make good the shortcomings of other departments. The *Starfire* takes off at ten tonight. No certificate, no shipment. Sort it out for yourself." He cut off, effectively preventing further argument.

Stanisland brooded over the injustice of it before he went to see Taylor again, this time looking like hard luck on two feet. Taylor responded by meditating aloud about people who could not paint a floor without marooning themselves in one corner. Then he grabbed the phone and spent ten minutes swapping recriminations with Jurgensen of Testing Department. Jurgensen, a confirmed bachelor, flatly refused to hold the baby.

Giving the waiting Stanisland an evil stare, Taylor now tried to foist the problem onto the Scientific Division. All he got for his pains was a piece of Williams' mind, the piece with the hole in. Muttering to himself, he phoned Keith, who promptly gave him the merry ha-ha and repeated in sinister tones his remark about no certificate, no shipment.

Finally Taylor thrust the phone aside and said, "Well, my dear Stanisland, you have made a nice mess of this."

"Me?" said Stanisland, paralyzed by the perfidy of it. "Yes, you."

This was too much. Stanisland burst out, "But you approved the order and tended to it yourself."

"I did so on the assumption that all routine aspects of the matter had been seen to with the efficiency that I expect from my subordinates. Evidently my faith was misplaced."

"That is hardly fair judgment, sir, because—"

"Shut up!" Taylor ostentatiously consulted his watch. "We have seven hours before the *Starfire* leaves. Neither the Testing Department nor the Scientific Division will issue the document Keith requires. We have no authority to provide one ourselves. But one must be got from somewhere. You realize that, don't you, Stanisland?"

"Yes, sir."

"Since you are directly responsible for this grave omission it is equally your responsibility to make it good. Now go away and exercise your imagination, if you have any. Come back to me when you have incubated a useful idea."

"I cannot forge a certificate, sir," Stanisland protested.

"It has not been suggested that you should," Taylor pointed out acidly. "The solution, if there is one, must be in accordance with regulations and not open to question by higher authority. It is for you to find it. And don't be too long about it."

Returning to his desk, Stanisland flopped into his chair and chased his brains around his skull. The only result was a boost to his desperation. He gnawed his fingers, thought furiously and always arrived at the same result; nobody, *but* nobody would produce anything in writing to cover up a blunder in another department.

After some time he went for a walk to the phone booths where he could talk in private, called the scientific division and asked for Williams.

"Williams," he said oilily, "I was there when Taylor baited you an hour ago. I didn't like his attitude."

"Neither did I," said Williams.

"You have been of great help to us on many occasions," praised Stanisland with an effort. "I'd like you to know that I genuinely appreciate it even if Taylor doesn't."

"It's most kind of you to say so," informed Williams, letting go a menacing chuckle. "But you still won't cajole from this department a document we are not authorized to give."

"I am not trying to do so." Stanisland assured. "I wouldn't dream of it."

"Taylor tried. He must think we're a bunch of suckers."

"I know," said Stanisland, gratefully seizing the opportunity thus presented. "To be frank, I wondered whether you'd be willing to help me give Taylor a smack in the eye."

"How?"

"By coming up with some suggestion about how I can get over this noxious cargo business."

"And why should that have the effect of twisting Taylor's arm?"

"He thinks he's got me where he wants me. I'd like to show him he hasn't. Some of these seniors need teaching a thing or two." He paused, added craftily, "Abelson for instance."

The effect of that name in the other's ears clinched the deal and Williams said without a moment's hesitation, "All right, I'll tell you something."

"What is it?" asked Stanisland eagerly.

"No reputable outfit such as Forman's would ship a radioactive apparatus inadequately screened. Probably seventy per cent of that irradiator's weight is attributable to screening. Ask Forman's and they'll tell you—in writing."

"Williams," said Stanisland delightedly, "I'll never forget this."

"You will," contradicted Williams. "But I won't."

Stanisland now phoned Forman's and explained the position in complete detail. Their response was prompt: they would prepare a written guarantee of safety and deliver it by special messenger to Keith within two hours. Stanisland sighed with heartfelt relief. Seemed there were times when the efficiency of private industry almost approached that of bureaucracy.

Over the next few days Stanisland waited with secret pleasure for a call from Taylor. It never came. Unknown to him, Taylor had phoned Keith to find out what had happened, if anything. Taylor then realized that an interview with Stanisland would permit that worthy a moment of petty triumph. It was unthinkable that a senior should permit a subordinate to gloat. He would summon Stanisland into his presence when and only when he had some pretext for throwing him to the crocodiles. So Stanisland went on waiting, first with growing disappointment, then with dull resignation, finally with forgetfulness.

The weeks rolled on while the wad of papers crawled through various offices and gained in mass at each desk. Then one day it reached the Documents (Final Checking) Department. It now weighed five pounds and was solid with words, figures, stamps, names and signatures.

From this mountain of evidence some assiduous toiler dug out the strange word Nemo. His nose started twitching. He made a few discreet inquiries and satisfied himself that (a) someone had blundered and (b) the cretin was not located within his own office. Then he steered the wad toward the Spatial Statistics Department.

Far away on Alipan a copy of the *Starfire*'s manifest landed on Hancock's desk. He scanned it carefully. Most of the stuff had been demanded three to four years ago. But he had a very good memory and the moment his eyes found an irradiator the alarm bells rang in his brain. He was swift to give the list to Purcell.

"You'd better deal with this."

"Me? Why? You got writer's cramp or something?"

"The ship is bringing an expensive present for a planet that doesn't exist. I don't handle consignments for imaginary worlds."

"Windy, eh?" said Purcell.

"Sane," said Hancock.

Examining the manifest, Purcell grumbled, "It's taken them long enough. Nobody broke his neck to get it here. If scout-pilots moved at the same pace, Lewis and Clarke would still be pounding their dogs along the Oregon Trail."

"I am," announced Hancock, "sick and tired of the subject of scout-pilots."

"And where would you have been without them?"

"On Terra."

"Doing what?"

"Earning an honest living," said Hancock.

"Yeah—filling forms," said Purcell.

Hancock let it slide and pretended to be busy.

"Now this is where our right to determine priorities reaches its peak of usefulness," Purcell went on, flourishing the manifest as if it were the flag of freedom. "We issue an overriding priority in favor of our bugologist, his need being greater than Nemo's. The fly-killer will then be transferred to him without argument because nobody questions a proper form, properly filled, properly stamped and properly signed. Thus we shall have served humanity faithfully and well."

"You can cut out every 'we' and 'our,'" ordered Hancock. "I am having nothing to do with it." He put on another brief imitation of overwork, added as an afterthought, "I told you before, you can't buck the system."

"I have bucked it."

"Not yet," said Hancock positively.

Taking no notice, Purcell made out the priority, stamped it, signed it, studied it right way up and upsidedown, signed it again.

"I've forged your signature. Do you mind?"

"Yes," yelled Hancock.

"I am receiving you loud and clear." Purcell examined the forgery with unashamed satisfaction. "Too bad. It's done now. What's done can't be undone."

"I'd like you to know, Purcell, that in the event of that document being challenged I shall not hesitate to declare my signature false."

"Quite a good idea," enthused Purcell. "I'll swear mine is false also."

"You wouldn't dare," said Hancock, appalled.

"It'll take 'em at least ten years to figure who's the liar and even then they couldn't bet on it," continued Purcell with indecent gusto. "In the meantime I'll suggest that maybe every document of Alipan's and half of Terra's have phony signatures attributable to subordinates bypassing their seniors in order to avoid criticisms and conceal mistakes. The resulting chaos ought to create work for ten thousand checkers."

"You're off your head," declared Hancock.

"Well, you can keep me company," Purcell suggested. He exhibited the manifest at distance too far for the other to read. "I've got news for you."

"What is it?"

"No gin."

Hancock sat breathing heavily for quite a time, then said, "You're to blame for that."

"Nuts! I've no say in what Terra loads on or leaves off."

"But—"

"If you've told me once," Purcell went on remorselessly, "you've told me a hundred times that in no circumstances whatever will any department on Alipan accept responsibility for decisions made on Terra. Correct?"

"Correct," agreed Hancock as though surrendering a back tooth.

"All right. You ordered the gin and can prove it. You gave it high priority and can prove it. You're armorplated front and back. All you need to do is go see Letheren and say, 'Sorry, no gin.' When he zooms and rotates you say, 'Terra!' and spit. It's so easy a talking poodle could do it."

"I can hardly wait to watch you get rid of Nemo the same way," said Hancock, making it sound sadistic.

"Nobody has said a word about Nemo. Nobody is the least bit curious about Nemo. Finally I, James Walter Armitage Purcell, could not care less about Nemo."

"You will," Hancock promised.

In due time—which on Alipan attained the magnitude of about three months—the intercom speaker squawked on the wall and a voice harshed, "Mr. Purcell of Requisitioning (Priorities) Department will present himself at Mr. Vogel's office at eleven hours."

Hancock glanced at his desk clock, smirked and said, "You've got exactly thirty-seven minutes."

"For what?"

"To prepare for death."

"Huh?"

"Vogel is a high-ranker with ninety-two subordinates. He controls four departments comprising the Terran Co-ordination Wing."

"What of it?"

"He makes a hobby of personally handling all gripes from Terra. Anyone summoned by Vogel is a gone goose unless he happens to be holding the actual documentary proof of his innocence in his hot little hands."

"Sounds quite a nice guy," Purcell commented, unperturbed.

"Vogel," informed Hancock, "is a former advertising man who got flatfooted toting his billboard around the block. But he's a natural for routine rigmarole. He's climbed high on the shoulders of a growing army of underlings and he's still climbing." He paused, added emphatically, "I don't like him."

"So it seems," said Purcell dryly.

"A lot of people don't like him. Letheren hates the sight of him."

"That so? I don't suppose he's choked with esteem for Letheren either, eh?"

"Vogel loves nothing but power—which in this racket means seniority."

"Hm-m-m!" Purcell thought a bit, went out, came back after twenty minutes, thought some more.

"Where've you been?" asked Hancock.

"Accounts Department."

"Getting your pay while the going is good?"

"No. I have merely satisfied myself that one hundred and five equals seventeen hundred."

"It wouldn't save you even if it made sense." Hancock continued to busy himself with nothing and kept one eye on the clock. When the moment arrived he said, "On your way. I hope you suffer."

"Thanks."

Opening his desk Purcell extracted an enormous roll of paper, tucked it under one arm. He tramped out, found his way to the rendezvous, entered the office. Vogel, dark-eyed, dark-haired and swarthy, studied him without expression.

"Sit down, Purcell," He bared long, sharp teeth and somehow managed to look like Red Riding Hood's grandmother. "Terra has brought to my attention a demand originating from a planet named Nemo."

"That, sir, is—"

Vogel waved an imperious hand. "Please be silent, Purcell, until I have finished. Your own remarks can come afterward." Again the teeth. "A lot of very valuable time has been spent checking on this. I like to have all the facts before interviewing the person concerned."

"Yes, sir," said Purcell, nursing his roll of paper and looking suitably impressed.

"I have found firstly that Terra's statement is quite correct; such a demand was in fact made and you processed it. Secondly, that the subject of the demand, an irradiator, was transferred by you to an address upon this planet. Thirdly, that no planet discovered before or since the date of this demand has been officially given the name of Nemo." He put hands together in an attitude of prayer. "One can well imagine the trouble and exasperation caused on Terra. I trust, Purcell, that you have a thoroughly satisfactory explanation to offer."

"I think I have, sir," assured Purcell glibly.

"I'll be glad to hear it."

"The whole bother is due to someone on Terra jumping to the erroneous and unjustifiable conclusion that Nemo is the name of a planet when in fact it is a code word used by my department to indicate a tentative priority as distinct from a definite one."

"A tentative priority?" echoed Vogel, raising sardonic eyebrows. "What nonsense is this? Don't you realize, Purcell, that all demands must be rated strictly in order of importance or urgency and that there is no room for indecision? How can anything have a *tentative* priority?"

"I find it rather difficult to tell you, sir," said Purcell, radiating self-righteousness.

"I insist upon an explanation," Vogel gave back.

Assuming just the right touch of pain and embarrassment, Purcell informed, "Since cargo space is severely limited the problem of granting priorities is a tough one. And when a senior official practically orders my department to assign to his demand a priority higher than it deserves it follows that, if we obey, something else of similar weight or bulk must accept lower priority than it deserves. But regulations do not permit me to reduce the status of a high-priority demand. Therefore I am compelled to give it a tentative priority, meaning that it will gain its proper loading-preference providing nobody chips in to stop it."

A gleam came into Vogel's eyes. "That is what happened in this case?"

"I'm afraid so, sir."

"In other words, you claim that you are suffering unwarranted interference with the work of your department?"

"That," said Purcell with becoming reluctance, "is putting it a little stronger than I'd care to do."

"Purcell, we must get to the bottom of this and now is not the time to mince words. Exactly what were you ordered to ship at high priority?"

"Gin, sir."

"Gin?" A mixture of horror and incredulity came into Vogel's face. But it swiftly faded to be replaced by a look of suppressed triumph. *"Who* ordered you to bring in gin?"

"I'd rather not say, sir."

"Was it Letheren?"

Purcell said nothing but assumed the expression of one who sorrows for Letheren's soul.

Gratified by this, Vogel purred. He rubbed his hands

together, became positively amiable. "Well, Purcell, it appears to me that you have been guilty of no more than a small oversight. Should you find it necessary to employ code words as a matter of administrative convenience it is obvious that Terra should be notified through the proper channels. Without regular notification Terra would eventually find itself trying to cope with incomprehensible jargon. An impossible situation as doubtless you now appreciate, eh, Purcell?"

"Yes, sir," said Purcell, humble and grateful.

"But in the present circumstances it would not be wise to advise Terra of the true meaning of Nemo. To do so would be tantamount to admitting that our priority system is being messed up at anybody's whim. I hope you see my point, Purcell."

"I do, sir."

"Therefore I propose to inform Terra that the inclusion of this word was due to a departmental error born of overwork and lack of sufficient manpower." He exposed the teeth. "That will give them something to think about."

"I'm sure it will, sir."

"Purcell, I wish you to drop the use of all code words except with my knowledge and approval. Meanwhile I shall take the steps necessary to put a stop to any further interference with your department."

"Thank you, sir." Purcell stood up, fumbled with his roll of paper, looked hesitant.

"Is there something else?" asked Vogel.

"Yes, sir." Purcell registered doubt, reluctance, then then let the words come out in a rush. "I thought this might be an opportune moment to bring to your attention a new form I have devised."

"A form?"

"Yes, sir." He unrolled it, put one in Vogel's hands. The other end reached almost to the wall. "This, sir, is a master-form to be filled up with the origin, purpose, details, progress and destination of every other form that has to be filled in. It is, so to speak, a form of forms."

"Really?" said Vogel, frowning.

"By means of this," continued Purcell greasily, "it will be possible to trace every form step by step, to identify omissions or contradictions and to name the individual responsible. Should a form get lost it will be equally possible to find at what point it disappeared and who lost it." He let that sink in, added, "From what I know of interdepartmental confusions, many of which are hidden from senior officials, I estimate that this form will save about twenty thousand man-hours per annum."

"Is that so?" said Vogel, little interested.

"There is one snag," Purcell went on. "In order to save all that work it will be necessary to employ more people. Since their work would be wholly coordinatory they would come under your jurisdiction, thus adding to your responsibilities."

"Ah!" said Vogel, perking up.

"In fact we'd have to create a new department to reduce the total of work done. However, I have studied the subject most carefully and I am confident that we could cope with a minimum of thirteen men."

"Thirteen?" echoed Vogel, counting on his fingers. He sat staring at the form while into his face crept a look of ill-concealed joy. "Purcell, I believe you have something here. Yes, I really do."

"Thank you, sir. I felt sure you would appreciate the potentialities. May I leave the form for your consideration?"

"By all means, Purcell." Vogel was now well-nigh jovial. Fondly he stroked the form, his fingers caressing it. "Yes, you must certainly leave it with me." He glanced up, beaming. "If anything is done about this, Purcell, I shall need someone to take charge of this new department. Someone who knows his job and in whom I have the fullest confidence. I cannot imagine a better candidate than yourself."

"It is kind of you to say so, sir," said Purcell with grave dignity.

He took his departure but as he left he turned in the

doorway and for a moment their eyes met. A glance of mutual understanding sparked between them.

Back in his own office Purcell plonked himself in a chair and recited, "Whenever two soothsayers meet in the street they invariably smile at each other."

"What are you talking about?" demanded Hancock.

"I was quoting an ancient saying." He held up two fingers, tight together. "Vogel and I are just like that."

"You don't fool me," Hancock scoffed. "Your ears are still red."

"Vogel loves me and I love Vogel. I hit him right in his weak spot."

"He hasn't any weak spots, see?"

"All I did," said Purcell, "was point out to him that if the number of his subordinates should be increased from ninety-two to one hundred and five he'd be automatically jacked up from a Class 9 to a Class 8 official. That would gain him another seventeen hundred smackers per year plus extra privileges and, of course, a higher pension."

"Nobody has to tell Vogel that—he knows it better than anyone."

"All right. Let's say I merely reminded. In return he was good enough to remind me that a disabled hero bossing twelve underlings is far better off than one sharing an office with a surly bum."

"I neither ask nor expect the true story of your humiliation," growled Hancock. "So you don't have to cover up with a lot of crazy double-talk."

"Some day," offered Purcell, grinning, "it may dawn upon you that it is possible to buck a system, *any* system. All you need do is turn the handle the way it goes—only more so!"

"Shut up," said Hancock, "and talk when you can talk sense."